"This is Mark Holden," came the voice over the phone. His crisp voice, instead of sounding businesslike, sounded sexy. "I have a job for you."

"Yes?" Terry answered, wanting to pinch herself to see if it was a dream.

"It's a housekeeping position, and you'll be taking care of a seven-year-old girl. There's a small apartment for you and your daughter."

"I've never been a housekeeper before . . ." Her skills as a cook were adequate, but as a housekeeper, she would never do.

"Is it beneath your job experience?" Mark cut into her thoughts. "You claimed you were willing to be a home companion."

"I have no objection," Terry answered. "Who will I be working for?"

There was a pause before Terry heard Mark's voice through the phone. "You'll be working for me."

SPICE UP YOUR LIFE
WITH ARABESQUE ROMANCES

LAYLE GIUSTO
HOME FIRES

Pinnacle Books
Kensington Publishing Corp.

http://www.arabesquebooks.com

PINNACLE BOOKS are published by

Kensington Publishing Corp.
850 Third Avenue
New York, NY 10022

First Printing: February, 1996

Printed in the United States of America

10 9 8 7 6 5 4 3 2

Chapter One

Overqualified!

Good Lord, I hate that word, thirty-year-old Terry Redding thought. If I hear it one more time, I won't be responsible for my actions.

The early spring day was unseasonably warm, and at first she had been glad to step into the air-conditioned bus. Now, she was shivering in the frigid air that poured from the vents. She clasped her hands together in her lap. Her feet ached after she'd spent so many hours job hunting. She shifted her slim five-foot-four frame into a more comfortable position.

To make matters worse, she wasn't feeling too well. She had skipped breakfast that morning and then decided to forgo lunch, too. It had been a mistake. The rocking motion of the bus, compounded with the lack of food, made her feel strange and light-headed, almost as if she was coming down with something. That terrified her. She simply couldn't afford to get sick. When she stepped down from the bus, back into the too-warm sun, Terry wondered if she could manage the three-block walk to her apartment.

She glanced at the corner building that housed Holden-McNeil Home Health Care Providers, Inc. There was a sign in the window that read, "Home Health Care Aide Wanted." The sign had been there for a week and she wondered why, since jobs were pretty scarce.

Her second thought was, why not her? True, she had been trained in business and on her last job had worked herself up to office manager, a fancy title that meant she was nothing more than a "gofer." She had done everything and smiled, but maybe she could be trained as a health care aide, too. Maybe the firm was asking for a nurse's aide. She'd worked in a hospital one summer during high school as one. She stared at the sign for a few minutes.

There was no denying that she desperately needed work. She hadn't had a steady job in ten months. And yesterday she had reached the very end of her rope, but she wouldn't think of that now. It would only make her panicky. She needed a cool head.

Before opening the door and walking in, she checked her reflection in the window. She smoothed her medium-length, lightly permed hair and used a tissue to wipe the shine from her nut-brown skin, then glanced hastily at her watch. She wanted to get home before Makeda, her eight-year-old daughter, came from school.

It was a lot better inside than out on the street. For one thing, it was shaded and cooler, but not as chilly as the bus had been. The waiting room was decorated in neutral tones with swatches of brightly colored yellows, maroons, and greens in an African print. An attractive older woman with gray hair sat behind the receptionist's desk. The woman, whose desk nameplate said "Mrs. Dougan," looked up when Terry entered.

"Hello. May I help you?" the woman asked with a pleasant smile.

"I'm here about the position you have posted in your window," Terry answered, and tried to smile under her pounding headache.

"We just hired someone," the receptionist said regretfully, "and I haven't had time to remove that sign."

Terry's disappointment was monumental, and she wasn't sure why she was so upset. She was a woman who believed seriously in Murphy's Law, so she shouldn't have been surprised that the job was gone.

She felt foolish when she realized that she was on the verge of crying. Self-pity almost overwhelmed her. She shouldn't have been as upset as she was. Perhaps it was the unseasonable heat.

"Oh dear, I'm so sorry," Mrs. Dougan said, upon seeing Terry's expression. Looking concerned, the woman opened a desk drawer and took a piece of paper from it. Then she stood up and rushed around the desk.

"Listen, darling, why don't you fill out this application? I'll put it on file. Then, the next time something comes up, you'll be called first." In a more conspiratorial voice, she added, "Mr. McNeil's gone now. He's the one who does the interviewing." Then, with an audible sniff, she said, "Seems he's gone most of the time, lately."

Terry took the paper Mrs. Dougan held out to her with a "thank you."

She tried to concentrate on the talkative older woman but soon realized that the cool office hadn't totally dispelled her fuzzy feelings of being unwell.

"Now, our Mr. Holden never misses a day. And if you ask me, he's the only reason this business is booming. That man could sell freezers to the Eskimos in the dead of winter, I want to tell you." The receptionist went back behind the desk. Then, like an afterthought, she suddenly asked, "Do you have any experience as a health care aide?"

"I worked as a nurse's aide one summer when I was in high school," Terry answered.

The woman looked dubious, then glanced quickly at the closed door with the name "Mark Holden, Sales" engraved on it in gold lettering.

She threw out her hands expansively. "Fill it out anyway. Things are really bustling here. They need more and more help every week."

Terry looked at the paper for a split second, thinking how she needed a job right now. Suddenly, she had to admit why she'd had so little to eat that day: it had been an attempt to save a few dollars. That was how low her hopes had fallen.

Each week, it seemed she had to wait longer for the check from her temporary office work. Her current income, which kept her and Makeda going, couldn't cover all her expenses. What small savings she'd once had had been quickly depleted, and her payments were steadily falling behind.

Clutching the application, she sat on a comfortable chair to fill it out. It was foolish not to grab at whatever little hope was offered. It took only a few minutes, but when she stood up, she again felt light-headed. She dropped her purse, which opened, scattering its contents, and sat down heavily.

Terry heard the receptionist let out a shout. "Mr. Holden, come quick!"

However, it wasn't something Terry paid much attention to; she was more concerned with not passing out. Then, without warning, her whole day changed.

Suddenly, a huge, good-looking man was towering over her. He was about six-two and appeared to be about thirty-four. His skin looked like rich coffee sweetened with a touch of cream. He was dressed in well-fitting pants, a pale blue shirt, and a handsome silk tie. His broad shoulders filled out the shirt as if it had been made for him.

He was so well built he could have passed for a football player, or better yet, a lumberjack. Waves of barely caged energy shimmered from his gorgeous body. He looked like a man who could run the hundred-meter dash without working up a sweat.

He seemed coiled and ready to spring upon the world.

Her muddled brain had just enough time to register how attractive he was before he pounced, grabbing her head and pushing it below her knees.

While the position did clear her head, it also made her poor, acidic stomach complain. As she was struggling to disengage his hand, the receptionist took time to introduce them.

"This is Mr. Holden, darling. He'll take care of you."

The woman bent down to collect the things that had fallen out of her purse. Terry had enough presence of mind to be embarrassed.

She found herself staring at the woman's upside-down face. It was totally exasperating to have the woman behave as if it was perfectly natural for this huge, strange man to hold her.

"Call an ambulance, Dougan," the man snapped in an authoritative voice.

I must be sicker than I realized, Terry thought. Even in this position, he sounded sexy.

But hearing that she would soon have a new bill from some emergency room made Terry know that she had to do something quickly. She tried to push up against the hand that was holding her head down. Finally, she was able to say, "No!" He released his hold and she sat up. "I'm not sick. It's just that I haven't had anything to eat today."

She couldn't help fiddling with her hair; she could imagine what a mess he'd made of it. She wanted to look her best, though why for this presumptuous neanderthal-type, she wasn't sure.

"Nothing to eat?" He was taken aback. "You women. You'd starve yourself to death! When will you stop this kind of insanity?" Then he stepped back, looking exasperated. "Besides, as skinny as you are, what can you afford to lose?"

Usually, when people called her skinny, it was pure balm

for her ego. She felt that she had more padding across breast and bottom than she wanted. She would have killed to lose another five pounds.

Hearing she was too skinny from this man didn't make her feel as happy as it should have. He stepped back and she heard him grumble something about ". . . exasperating woman who pass out in my waiting room."

"She came for the job," Mrs. Dougan babbled, "so I let her fill out an application. The next thing I knew, she was like that." The finger Mrs. Dougan pointed at her seemed to Terry to be full of disappointed accusations.

The man took the application and after a careless quick perusal, said with exaggerated patience, "Dougan, this woman is overqualified." He tapped the paper. "We don't need an office manager. We need nurses and health-care aides." Each word had been carefully enunciated as he waved the application.

Poor Mrs. Dougan looked quite crushed. Terry's thoughts weren't on the receptionist, but on herself. She felt as if the top of her head had blown off in her anger. All thoughts of passing out were forgotten.

It was his calling her overqualified. She couldn't remember how many times she had heard that phrase in her months of job hunting. If someone didn't give her a job, she was going to be put out of her home because her landlady didn't consider her qualified enough to continue living there. Her anger had brought quite a bit of heated blood to her head.

She stood up and said, "Don't you dare say that. Just because I've been trained in another field doesn't mean that I don't need to work."

"What for?" he asked, his tone snide. "Obviously, you don't eat much. Look." He glanced at her application. "Look, Redding," he read her name off the paper. "Excuse me—*Ms*. Redding," he corrected, pointing a finger at her. "Just stay where you are." He left her to stalk back into his office. He moved fast, and had an indescribable manly grace.

Why am I worried about his looks? Forget his being handsome, the man is too presumptuous. She couldn't for the life of her figure out how he could be a salesman. There was no way she was waiting for him to return and start insulting her again. She was leaving.

She started collecting her belongings, including the purse that the receptionist was still holding. The problem was that when she stood up again, she was still a bit woozy. It didn't matter, she decided, and headed for the door.

Before she could get out, he was right behind her, pulling on his suit jacket and lugging a huge, jam-packed fine leather attaché case.

"Just a minute, I'll get you a cab." He spoke as if he wouldn't listen to anything she might care to say.

No way, she thought. "Thank you, but no thank you. I live in Glen Cove, and I'd rather walk. It'll help my diet," she added, which earned her another scowl.

When he called back to the receptionist, "Please, make note of this lady's name, address, and the time. I'm going to see that she gets home safely, and you're my witness."

Terry couldn't believe he'd said that. Why was he being so helpful, she wondered, and then realized he was probably trying to protect himself against any liability suit. People in the health care professions were notoriously liability conscious, she knew. They did most of their paperwork just to avoid such eventualities. Even a hint of litigation gave them apoplexy.

That thought almost made her want to argue again, but it would have taken too much energy. She was more determined than ever to escape from him. As soon as she reached the door, he had moved in front of her in a speed with which bewildered her.

"Let's go, Redding," his voice boomed much too close to her ear.

She had a sudden urge to hit him with her purse, which was heavy enough to be lethal. While the idea appealed to her, she barely had the stamina to hold on to it. And as for swinging it, that didn't seem likely.

"Maybe I'll drive. I don't think you'll make it home alone." Then he took her arm and swept her through the open doorway and out onto the street in a flash. Before she could take a breath, she had been rushed across the pavement and found herself holding on for dear life to the door frame of a gorgeous maroon Mercedes as the man tried to stuff her into the passenger seat.

"Stop!" It was the first time she'd been able to make a protest. He paused long enough to scowl down at her before he continued on with what he had been doing. Now she understood how he sold things: his self-confidence was monumental, and he seemed to move at the speed of light.

Perhaps she'd have resisted more, but when the heat of the sun struck, she knew she dared not try to walk those three blocks alone. So she took a deep breath and said, "Maybe I will accept your offer."

She tried to sound as ungracious as she could. However, considering that by the time she'd given her consent, Mark Holden had already managed to seat her in his car, she certainly didn't want him to change his mind now and dump her on the street.

"Thanks a lot, your ladyship," he muttered under his breath, as he went around to climb gracefully into the driver's seat.

Once belted in, Terry had time to think. The most disturbing thing about this fantastic jungle cat of a man had occurred when he'd taken her arm to guide her. Bolts of electricity had shot through her.

He stopped at a local fast food store on the short drive to her house. She had wanted to make him take her directly home, but he insisted. She kept quiet as he drove through. Several times she caught him looking sideways at her but didn't remark on it. In truth, the only reason she kept *catching* him looking was because she was looking at him. And she didn't want to remind him of that. She sighed. There was no denying he was a good-looking man, even if he was rather obnoxious.

At her door, of her Long Island home getting out of the car and stepping back into the sun, she felt weak again and embarrassed when he insisted that he was coming in. Before she could take a breath, they were at the entrance of her building and he was in possession of her key. The man was absolutely exhausting.

She wasn't in any shape to argue with him, but she wasn't particularly afraid, either. Then he launched into an incredibly convincing spiel of smooth fast-talk as he urged her up the steps to her apartment. She agreed to walk up only after he threatened to carry her.

"Would you stop bullying me?" she demanded.

By this time, she was standing in front of her apartment. Fortunately, his having to struggle with her dicey lock gave her a moment when her thinking could snap into gear.

Her landlady was also her neighbor and very nosy, which came in handy at moments like this. She planned to leave the door open, knowing that Mrs. Carter would be listening. Just in case, Terry decided, maybe the mighty Mr. Holden should know about Mrs. Carter, too.

"I have a very nice neighbor who listens to everything that happens in this apartment," she informed him.

"Good. I suppose I'm safe, then." He laughed, showing perfect white teeth.

It was the first time she'd seen him do anything other than scowl, and it stopped her right in her tracks. She gaped at him in fascinated wonder. Lord, the man was positively gorgeous.

With a sweep of his arm and a bow, he had her through the door and sitting in a chair. Terry looked around, glad that she had straightened up last night because the place wasn't in its usual cozy untidiness. She also held tightly onto the chair in case he got any more ideas about moving her again.

He opened a large bag of food and took a sandwich out,

which he shoved to within six inches of her face. "Eat," he commanded.

He didn't sit down, but stood over her. The thought occurred to her that he probably wished he could force her to eat.

When she looked askance at the food, he said, "I want you to eat this right now." Grudgingly she took it. Looking satisfied, he popped the lid on a cup of coffee and held it out to her.

She peeked at the sandwich and said, "This is red meat!" She tried to hand it back.

"Eat up," he said, refusing to take it.

Though she wasn't particularly fond of roast beef, she was hungry and decided to eat as he looked around her apartment.

She had to admit that she was proud of her home. She had taken a great deal of thought in decorating the apartment. It was in her own style and was cozy and comfortable. She liked to call her ideas "early grandmother."

By early grandmother, she meant the style that she'd grown to love in her grandmother's home. It was a collection of beautifully crafted nineteenth-century Victorian furniture. The pieces were dark and massive. She had inherited them from her grandmother, who in turn had received them from her own mother.

Terry loved those pieces and knew that if she'd tried to buy such things today, she wouldn't be able to afford them. They were collector's items. Some of the smaller pieces had also been inherited—things like Depression glassware, worth quite a bit in today's collectibles market.

She could see by his expression that he liked it, though the care she'd taken with decorating usually went to waste because she was inclined to be untidy.

Mark Holden was quieter now, walking more slowly, and no longer a storm that rattled her world and blew around her. But his beauty still held her, smooth as black marble.

At that moment, the sound of footsteps on the outside stairs came and both of them turned to the door. Terry knew it would be her daughter. Glancing across at him, she saw him frown. He seemed on guard.

"Why did you do this?" Terry finally asked. "You didn't have to drive me home and you most certainly didn't have to buy food."

"I'm a gentleman . . ."

"Of sorts," Terry finished.

"And you were in distress."

He probably thought he'd have to explain to her husband, his manhandling her, she thought. A small part of her wished that she did have a husband to walk through the door and bully this man, just as he had her. She put down what was left of her sandwich. Now that she had appeased her hunger, she could be more discriminating. Lord, she hated red meat.

The footsteps stopped outside the door and the lovely smiling face of Makeda peeped around the door frame, saying a cheery, bright-eyed, "Hi."

The little girl's attention was immediately arrested by the sight of a strange man, and she bounced in, saying, "My name's Makeda. Who are you?"

Terry watched her daughter come into the room, thinking, as she always did, what an incredible gift Makeda had been to her. Terry had been a plain child, until her adolescence, when she'd learned the correct use of subdued makeup and hair-styling. Then she had bloomed. Makeda, who looked like Terry's mother, had been born beautiful, yet she never seemed overly aware of it.

She was tall and slim, with lovely ebony satin skin. Her beautifully carved features were perfect. Her crinkly hair was worn in a thick ponytail which hung past her shoulders. She's going to be a heartbreaker, Terry thought.

The child was going through that stage wherein her two front teeth hadn't grown in yet. It was a fact that sometimes annoyed Makeda. Terry wanted to smile when Makeda covered her bright smile with her hand. Mark Holden seemed bursting to smile, too.

But it wasn't Makeda's beauty that caused Terry's heart to constrict with pain. It was the fact that yesterday, she had learned that Makeda had a heart murmur, one her doctor said might require cardiac surgery. It was the most frightening thing that had ever happened to Terry. Just thinking about it made her panic. But Makeda was braver than her mother. She was a positive thinker; Terry tended to be morose.

Finding a man in her home with her mother aroused Makeda's curiosity, and Terry knew she would be bombarded with questions later. Now, Terry thought, was a great moment to get Mr. Take-Charge out of her home. She stood up and extended her hand toward him.

"Well, let me show you the way out."

It sounded terribly ungracious, but he made her uncomfortable. He was too big for her small apartment. He didn't seem to be paying her any attention as he handed Makeda a sandwich. Her child looked surprised and smiled sweetly.

Terry tried again. "Don't let us keep you, Mr. . . . ."

"Mark," he said, then, smiling at Makeda, added, "and I hope *you* had breakfast and lunch today." He cast a disapproving glance at Terry.

"Oh, yes," Makeda answered. "Mommy fixed my breakfast and I ate lunch in school."

Mr. Holden, Terry noticed—refusing to call him Mark, which was far too familiar for her peace of mind—had the nerve to look mollified. He apparently thought he had the right to question how she ran her home or raised her child.

Makeda skipped across the room to hug and kiss her mother. "Any luck today, Mommy?"

"Not today," Terry responded, giving the child a hug. "Your mommy's overqualified." The remark went over Makeda's head straight to Mark Holden, who looked exasperated and shifted in his chair, crossing one foot over his knee.

"Well, don't worry. Just remember, things work out. You'll have a job just when you least think it," Makeda said.

Terry smiled, as usual, cheered by Makeda's sunny personality. She couldn't for the life of her understand where the child had acquired such a quality. Neither she nor her ex-husband, Ronald, was like this. She glanced across the room, wondering what Mr. Superiority thought of this. She was annoyed with herself to realize that she was almost embarrassed about Makeda's determined, positive attitude.

When Terry realized that Holden hadn't moved, all her annoyance was once again centered on him and on all the liberties he'd taken since she'd first set eyes on him, but she didn't want to say anything in front of Makeda. She tried never to upset her daughter.

Although the doctors claimed that they expected the very best outcome, with or without surgery, Terry still worried. Makeda was such a joy to her that Terry feared anything that might even remotely hurt her child. *My grandmother used to say that I always expected the worst to happen, and my grandmother was right.*

Makeda went into her room and Terry took the opportunity once again to encourage Holden's exit. "Thank you again, Mr. Holden. It was very nice of you to see me home."

"You're thanking me *again,* Redding?" He accepted her hand but didn't rise. "Somehow, I don't remember the first thank you."

She was stymied. His reminding her of how ungracious she had been embarrassed her, especially as she could now see that he was only trying to be nice. All she knew was that she wanted him to leave because he made her uncomfortable.

She heard Makeda giggle from inside her bedroom. Mark Holden's attention seemed totally captured by that giggle and he looked far away for a second.

But then he turned to her and his pleasant mood was strained as he said, "Is that nosy neighbor you spoke of enough to

protect that little girl with a latchkey hanging around her neck
for the whole world to see?"

That was a low blow that made Terry almost cringe. "That's
none of your business. And she knows to hide it under her
clothes when she's not at home. I have to provide for us, and
I'm doing the best I can."

He looked around again, a curious expression on his face,
and when he turned back, there was something new about his
manner. It reminded her of a man ready to sign a contract in
his business. It was a funny thought.

"You know perfectly well," he said suddenly, "despite your
display of temper, that you are overqualified as a home care
aide." She was a bit taken aback. "So why did you apply for
the job?"

"Why do you want to know? Is this an interview?"

"Maybe. You *did* apply for a job, didn't you?"

That stumped her for a second, and she decided to answer
his question just in case there was a chance of her getting
employment.

"I have a child to support and we have to live, too," she
retorted. Her voice was sharper than she'd intended it to be.
"Every place I go, people say that I'm overqualified. I could
starve in this city." That last had come out sounding more
desperate than she'd planned.

He shifted and looked pained at her remark. She hadn't meant
to say anything about starving. She preferred that he thought
she was a vain woman who was dieting rather than she was
that down and out. But suddenly it occurred to her that her
pride could be very expensive. She needed a job.

"You shouldn't take it personally," he said. "Just because an
interviewer says you're overqualified doesn't mean they want
to give you a hard time. I've personally found that if a job is
beneath a person's ability, they will soon become bored or
frustrated and quit. I need to depend upon my people."

"You could depend on me," she leaned forward with both hands on her knees.

"Many of these jobs are live-in positions with free room and board. Are you married?"

Her hopes took a nosedive. "No. But I have Makeda. I couldn't stay away from her for a whole workweek."

"Suppose you took your daughter with you?"

It took her a while to figure out how it would work. Actually, she realized it might solve one of her problems. Her rent was overdue.

"Can you cook?" He cut into her thoughts.

"Cook?" she squeaked.

Her heart fell. Cooking was definitely not one of her biggest accomplishments. Although she was not totally useless in the kitchen, she'd never been an expert, either. Her best efforts were in preparing steamed vegetable meals like those she and Makeda ate. It was healthy, but few people found such a simple menu attractive.

"My mother's the best cook in the world," Makeda interjected from the doorway, having overheard his question.

He laughed and said, "At least you have one fan," and oddly, that thought brought a fleeting look of sadness to his face.

"Well . . ." she took a deep breath, planning to explain to him how limited her cooking skills were, but he cut in before she could get the words out.

"Have you ever been bonded?"

"Yes, but . . ." she hesitated after one swift look at Makeda. Her daughter knew that she was going to mention the cooking, but at the child's pleading expression, Terry paused again.

"All our employees are thoroughly checked, as they have to work in people's homes," Mark Holden said.

Terry sat up pertly. "Are you going to hire me?"

"I'm not making any promises, but let me think on it overnight."

"Yes!" Makeda said, coming to hug Terry again. "You see? I *told* you everything was going to be all right."

"Now, I didn't say for sure; I only said maybe."

"It's going to happen, you'll see," Makeda said.

After Mark Holden left, Terry and Makeda stared at each other for a few seconds.

"I have to tell him," Terry told her daughter. How could she do any less, she thought, when she was always emphasizing the importance of honesty?

"But Mommy, you *are* a good cook. You always make food that's good for us."

"Yes, but that's only part of what's needed here. I also need to make food that's tasty and interesting."

"Maybe you won't have to cook very much," Makeda suggested hopefully.

She had a point, Terry thought. To Makeda, she said, "You're right. I'll be a home health care aide, not a cook. Maybe I'll have to be certified or something, but surely I won't have to do much cooking. And if it's just something like preparing lunch, I can do that."

"Sure you can, Mommy."

Terry hugged Makeda to her. "You're the best thing that's ever happened to me, honey."

Later, Terry made a light, quick dinner of steamed vegetables. The sandwiches that Mark Holden had bought had cut into their appetites. Makeda went to do her homework.

After Makeda went to bed, Terry pulled out her bills and went through them. Her attention span was short because she kept thinking about the possibility of Mark Holden employing her. She also thought quite a bit about the man himself, remembering the strangest things that she had observed about him.

His walk had stuck in her brain, and she could call it up in a second. He was straight as an arrow and seemed to have a magnificent command over his body. He looked like an athlete, lean and mean. Yet each motion was poetic. And that thought brought her up short. Why in the name of sanity was she mooning over the man, and why was she comparing his body to . . . poetry?

She looked down at the bills spread before her on the dining table and thought, I'd better use my fertile imagination where it's most needed—how to pay off this mountain of debt.

If only Ronald made his child support payments, I wouldn't be in this fix. She had divorced her ex-husband Ronald when Makeda was two. Her daughter barely knew her father, and that hurt Makeda, but on the other hand, it was a cloud with a silver lining. It was her lawyer who'd convinced her to seek child support from her ex. Terry had wanted nothing more than to see the last of him. She had allowed Ronald to make private arrangements, and when he'd fallen behind, she'd never taken him to court.

Terry's grandmother had warned her not to marry him, but Terry had been full of foolish dreams and hadn't listened. She had been hurt badly enough to realize that she would never become involved with a man in such a relationship again. Maybe others could do it, but not her. Never again, Terry had vowed, when she'd finally escaped.

Since the divorce, Ronald avoided seeing Makeda, and at first this was distressing, but eventually Makeda came to prefer his reticence. Ronald had never taken to fatherhood. Having a child had frightened him. Makeda sensed that he avoided her. Terry tried to explain that it was Ronald's problem, not Makeda's, but she wondered if her daughter understood this.

Ronald was not the man she'd married. Or rather, he was not the man she'd thought she was marrying. Ronald had been a smooth talker, not to mention good-looking. Well, she had soon learned that neither necessarily meant he'd be a good husband, but by then it was too late. Makeda's birth had inspired her to stick it out longer, but it hadn't worked.

In truth, even without Makeda, Terry would have worked hard to keep her marriage. Marriage had always seemed sacred to her, and she believed that people should do everything they could to keep it intact. She still had guilt about her failure.

Lately, Ronald had taken to harassing her, despite the six years since their divorce. She couldn't understand what was happening. Maybe it was because he was out of work and he might have lost some of his old self-confidence.

He called frequently and came around to beg for money. He had become another of her problems. One of many, she thought, as she put any further thoughts of her ex-husband away.

With a sigh, she left an "I'm available" message with her temp-work agency. She couldn't gamble on Holden just yet. It was terribly frustrating, because she had to work several days a week in order to make enough to live on.

Working those days meant she couldn't job hunt at the same time. If she was lucky, she'd work on the weekend and have more days free for job hunting, but that meant having to leave Makeda with a sitter. Her bills had piled up. She couldn't keep up with them because her temp jobs paid less than she'd been making at her previous job.

If Mark Holden gives me a sleep-in job, I won't be coming back here. Gazing around the apartment she had spent so much time and energy to decorate, Terry felt regretful. She would hate leaving it. Yet she knew it was a blessing in disguise. The landlady was rapidly losing patience with her delayed payments. At least the work would solve this problem.

Chapter Two

After leaving Terry Redding's apartment, Mark went to pick up his own daughter, Yvette, at her after-school program. She was sitting all alone, as she often seemed to do, on a long wooden bench. He wished she could be more sociable. She sat there, clutching her bookbag to her chest, solemnly watching the other children as they ran and played. He stood and stared for a few seconds.

Yvette was a small child, very thin, even fragile-looking. Her hair was cropped short, with a crinkly, curly texture. Her toasted-almond complexion, with a sprinkling of freckles across her nose and cheeks, sometimes appeared sallow. There was a promise of future beauty, Mark thought, if she could ever overcome her tendency toward melancholy.

Mark thought of himself as a high-energy man, and usually he moved fast through his day, accomplishing more than most men could do in twice the time. At least, that's what people told him. Yet whenever he was around his small daughter, Yvette seemed so fragile that he felt the need to contain himself and move more slowly. He feared that he would startle her.

Mark waited, wondering if she would realize that he was there. She didn't for Yvette often daydreamed. It made his chest tight. How he loved this thin, dreamy child. He wanted so much for her.

As he gazed at Yvette's saddened little face, he remembered Terry Redding's daughter, Makeda. What he wouldn't give to have his own daughter smiling and giggling so easily.

He felt responsible for Yvette. Although his ex-wife, Marlene, had said before they'd married that she wanted children, she really hadn't. When Yvette had come, Marlene had felt trapped and resentful. It was he who had taken over the responsibility for Yvette, having nannies in during the day. He had assumed Yvette would remain with him when he and Marlene divorced.

That's why he had been surprised when, during their divorce, Marlene had suddenly insisted upon being the custodial parent. It had enraged him, but the courts had ruled in her favor.

Only six months ago Marlene had become engaged to marry her live-in lover, and then she had allowed Yvette to live with him. He'd rarely seen Yvette's timid little smile in the time that she had been with him. Sometimes, he thought he could easily hate Marlene, especially when he thought of how withdrawn the child had become while living with her mother. But hate was too strong an emotion for so shallow a woman. And he knew that it wasn't abuse per se. Marlene was too self-absorbed to abuse the child. It was neglect ... emotional neglect, the child psychiatrist had called it.

Yvette was naturally sensitive and had come to consider herself as not worth much because her mother had rarely paid her any attention. He felt himself grow resentful toward his ex-wife. When they'd divorced, he had wanted shared custody of his daughter. Marlene had fought him. Had she been fighting out of any maternal need, he'd have felt better. However, he soon came to understand why Marlene had become such an interested parent. She wanted him over a barrel.

Later, when Mark stopped the car, both he and Yvette sat

staring listlessly at his huge, Tudor-style house. He gazed at it, thinking it was too large for just the two of them. It sat empty and closed up all day. Why had he bought it? This was a question he'd often asked himself. The answer was because he'd wanted a quiet, normal life with a wife and children, and a dog that brought his slippers and paper at night. It comes from watching all those old television sit-coms, he chided himself, and turned to Yvette.

"Okay, kitten, up and at 'em. Let's go in and do our homework." They had already eaten, having stopped at a local restaurant, where Yvette had barely picked at her food.

"I did my homework already, Daddy."

"You did?" He was a little disappointed but rallied, "Then maybe you can show your old dad how it's done." And he chucked her under the chin. The touch gained the reward of a wan smile. It wasn't much, but it lifted his spirits.

Later, when his small, thin daughter sat on his lap to show him her homework, it made his day, because she didn't often want to be touched. He took a chance and tickled her in the ribs and received almost a real smile this time. She quickly put a pretty hand over her mouth to hide the fact that her front teeth were missing.

He wanted to smile at this demonstration of feminine vanity, but he managed to keep a straight face. It reminded him of little Makeda Redding, who had done the same thing earlier that day.

Too quickly, Yvette became serious again. By her tentative expression, he knew she wanted to say something.

"Daddy, I like living with you," she said. Then, in a small, barely audible voice, she added, "Do you think Marlene will come and take me back?"

Over my dead body, Mark thought. But to the little girl, he said, "Well, I think she'll get lonely and want you to visit. Let's wait and see, all right?" He said this for Yvette's sake.

Personally, he suspected Marlene could easily forget Yvette's existence.

She smiled wanly and nodded her head. At bedtime, she went quietly, and he found himself remembering his own childhood, when they'd stalled by frequently asking for glasses of water, which were then followed by several trips to the bathroom. How he longed for Yvette to try such foolishness. She was much too serious for a seven-year-old. He wanted her to enjoy these years. Each minute was precious, and he wanted her to have every bit of the fun a child was entitled to.

That night he read from her favorite storybook about Br'er Anancy, the spiderman. It was a compilation of old stories from Jamaica. No one was certain where the stories of Br'er Anancy had originated, but some believed they'd been carried from West Africa.

Yvette seemed to enjoy them, but her pleasure was a contained, almost adultlike joy. When she started to doze off, he closed the book and watched her for a few moments before bending to kiss her damp forehead. She had a clean, fresh child scent.

It was satisfying, having her live with him. He knew that he'd do anything to keep Marlene from ever taking her away again. Yvette had always been a quiet child but she'd also had a delightful shy playfulness that had enchanted him when he first became aware of it. Where had that playfulness gone? Would it ever return?

He found himself saying a short prayer and felt a little foolish. But why not, he mused. *I could really appreciate a little divine intervention about now.*

It's modern marriage, he thought. Marriage had been different for him and his brothers than for his parents. One of his parents' most important goal was to raise their sons and they had sacrificed some of their own pleasures. He'd never felt that he could ever repay them for that. The same had been true of his grandparents. Many of the families then had been more committed to family and children and they sacrificed to maintain them.

Now, marriage seemed too limiting, too restricting. It had been so for Marlene. Hell, it had been hard for him, too, trying to live with Marlene.

For some weird reason, he remembered the woman who had almost fainted in his office today. Terry, nice name. Nice legs too, he thought. That brought him out of the eerie mood he was in. *Don't know why I'm sitting here, drooling over that woman's legs. Surprised I even noticed her legs, considering what a nuisance she was.*

"It's not as if I don't have plenty of work to do," he muttered, and went to find his attaché case.

He had been sitting in his home office for two hours, totally engrossed with trying to make a column of figures add up, when the telephone rang.

Mark found himself staring at the instrument as if it were a snake. A quick glance at his watch showed that it was close to eleven o'clock. It was too late for a business call. No, he thought, the snake was probably going to be on the line.

His jaw clenched. Chances were, it was James McNeil, his partner, calling. He dreaded talking with James because the man was going through a personal crisis and had become almost useless in the business. It wasn't that he couldn't sympathize with his partner, but he needed McNeil to make a decision. The business was expanding rapidly. It was a critical time, and he needed McNeil to be more committed or all the work would fall on him.

Not now, James, Mark thought. *Wait until after the Underwood takeover. Then you can spend all the time you want on your personal problems.*

And what was McNeil's problem? Women. Naturally, Mark thought, what else? Women were the bane of most men's lives. The man's marriage was falling apart. *Glad it's not me.* Marriage was a hard row to hoe when you were trying to run a business.

However, those thoughts were just delaying his answering the phone. He picked up the receiver. "Holden here."

"Mark, is that you?" a sultry female voice asked.

"What is it, Marlene?" It was his ex-wife, the other problem in his life. He wanted to growl in frustration.

"Just thought I'd call and chat with you and Yvette."

"It's after eleven. Yvette's already asleep."

"So I guess it'll have to be just you and me, darling."

"Yes?" He answered a little more sharply than he'd intended and deliberately counted to ten to slow himself down. He couldn't afford to antagonize her because he didn't want her to change her mind about Yvette living with him.

"Well, you don't have to sound so unwelcoming, Mark."

"Sorry. I'm tired."

"Should I come over? I always knew just how to relax you, darling."

You also knew how to make life a living hell, he thought. "No, that won't be necessary. Besides, I thought you were getting married." *Or at least, I certainly hoped so.*

"Well, maybe," Marlene drawled.

What the hell does that mean? he wondered. Was she going to try and take Yvette back? No way, he answered his own question.

"Are you still there?" Marlene asked, when he didn't say anything.

"Yeah. Why are you calling?"

"Oh, I guess I miss you. And I was thinking that I'd much rather be marrying you again than old Weston Barkley."

She's getting tired of Barkley already. "I doubt that, Marlene. You were married to me, and it didn't work. If you remember, *you* were the one who left."

"Oh, I didn't really mean that to be a permanent split. But you didn't seem sorry when I was gone, either." Mark felt as if he could almost hear her pout. It made him impatient.

"Anyway," she went on, "Weston can't hold a candle to you when . . ."

He cut her off sharply. "Marlene, I've got a mountain of work sitting here, so I'm going to say goodnight."

"Really, Mark, you're still the same old workaholic you were when we were married. Maybe that's why I left you."

"It doesn't matter now, does it? We'll talk at another time."

"Wait!" She rushed on. "I did have another reason for calling."

"Let's hear it."

"I need more money."

"I just sent you a check. What did you do with the money?"

"It's not enough."

"It's more than you were getting when you had Yvette. That was what you asked for."

"Are you implying that you bought my child?"

"No, I'm not." He had to swallow several times. She always got his goat whenever he had to back down. But he went along because he wanted his daughter, and Marlene could be a vengeful woman when she wanted. "I'll put a check in the mail for you," he promised, thinking it would be cheap if he could get rid of her tonight.

"Why can't I come over and collect it—personally?"

He knew she was trying to sound seductive. It annoyed the hell out of him. "No! I'll be too busy, and you'll be bored."

When she realized he was not going to allow her to come over, she became angry. It had been years since their divorce, and still Marlene refused to accept that it was over between them.

"I need the money now," she persisted.

"Okay, I'll send it by messenger tomorrow morning."

They hung up soon after that. Mark stared at the phone a moment, thinking that at one time, he'd have allowed her to come over. But that was a long time ago, and he was glad it was no longer true.

Now she bored him to tears. If he was honest, Marlene's whole appeal had been his own desire to settle down and get away from the chasing-women syndrome he'd been into for a couple of years. He'd known right from the beginning that it was a mistake. But Marlene had sworn she was pregnant. It should have been impossible, but he'd been willing to accept his responsibility.

Once they were married, he'd hoped it would work. Even after Marlene had claimed to have miscarried, he'd wanted it to work. Now, he'd come to see that he'd only been hanging onto the dream of creating a family, rather than to any love he'd ever had for Marlene.

Marlene, he knew, could always be stalled with money, but he did have a real problem. He sat for a long time in his study, wondering.

He was always pressed for time, and his partner, James McNeil, hadn't been much help recently, which meant that his workload was even heavier than it needed to be.

Mark sensed that at any moment, James would ask to be bought out. And although that would be a problem, he was hoping it would materialize, and soon. Things couldn't continue long as they were. Without James, at least he'd be able to hire someone to head the office.

Now, he was trying to do both. His own talents were better utilized out in the field, in sales. Holden-McNeil was the perfect business at the right time in history. But it needed careful tending during this critical period.

Also, there was the Underwood takeover. He had been working upon expanding the business with a buyout of another company. The owners wanted guarantees that he would not simply fire all the employees, use their accounts and equipment, and auction off everything that couldn't be converted.

Mark sincerely believed that Holden-McNeil could make this guarantee, but it meant that he couldn't expand his own company until after the buyout, when he would know where they stood and what could simply be merged, as well as what had to be eliminated.

He was trying to nurture his rapidly expanding business. The hospitals were discharging their patients early to save money. Many a patient went home and found himself weak, frightened, a burden upon his family, and unable to obtain the health care still desperately needed. Mark's business provided a real service by stepping in at this point and tiding the client over until he could take up his life once again.

Because the service was delivered right in the clients' own homes, they were able to offer it at a greatly reduced cost. Everyone won in the end—the client, the doctors, the nurses, and other helpers, not to mention the insurance companies.

The problem was that the business consumed so much of his time and he worked irregular hours. In starting a new business this was to be expected, but now that he had Yvette, he had to make some sort of arrangements for when he wasn't at home.

He needed someone reliable to care for his daughter. It couldn't be just anyone. Yvette needed more than the afterschool center. He didn't want her isolated as she was now, observing instead of participating. He wanted her to be a part of what was going on around her. She needed stimulation as well as safety.

The thought made him admit that he'd already made a decision. It had occurred the moment he'd met little Makeda. He wanted Yvette to be exposed to the other child's cheerfulness. Even as he'd sat in Terry Redding's apartment, Mark had wondered if the woman and her happy well-adjusted, outgoing child might be just the solution for his problem.

But instead of thinking about Makeda and Yvette, he suddenly had a mental image of how Terry Redding's blouse had draped across her breasts. This was getting out of hand. He hadn't realized she'd made that much of an impression on him. Why, she wasn't even his type. He shook his head.

He jumped up and started to do push-ups. Whenever he felt stressed or anxious, he did push-ups. He did them at work in his suits and at home in sweats. It was one thing Marlene found infuriating.

The push-ups didn't stop his thoughts of Terry.

He'd never really liked those serious businesswomen types. It had surprised him to see she had a child. She looked totally career oriented. But if she was a good cook, and he'd witnessed for himself that her apartment looked cozy and comfortable, she might work out to be exactly what he needed.

Before he could reach for the phone, he realized it was too late for calling.

"Tomorrow is soon enough," he said aloud.

When Terry arrived home that next evening, it was close to six o'clock. She had picked Makeda up from the landlady's apartment downstairs. Having someone near who could keep an eye on her daughter was one of the arrangements that she would miss if she moved. And it looked as if she would have to.

Originally, when she'd been working in her field, she had been doing well. She had started a savings account, stashing away a small part of her take-home pay. She'd been really proud and had had no problems paying her bills.

But when she was laid off, the temporary jobs she got paid much less. After months of budgeting and working to hold on, she continued to fall behind.

A few months ago, Mrs. Carter, Terry's landlady, a retired older woman, had suggested a reduced payment plan. She allowed Terry to pay only seventy-five percent of the rent. This was supposed to be a temporary solution.

Despite this, the rent was still higher than Terry could afford now. Although it was a godsend, Terry felt bad because she knew the woman needed the income.

Both had believed a better position was just around the corner. Times were difficult, and this particular recession had dragged on longer than they'd expected. Companies were downsizing, and many people were job-hunting. Now, months later, she was still looking for permanent work. Terry was lucky that morning because when she called the temp agency, it had work for her.

She thought of Mark Holden as she had innumerable times that day. But she rationalized that he was on her mind because he might have a position for her. She only prayed the salary would be acceptable because she really needed to settle down.

And while her brain dwelled upon these things, an unbidden image of Mark Holden floated into her mind. She couldn't help remember how flat his stomach was and how his expensive, well-cut pants had fit his tight derrière.

Why am I dwelling on thoughts of his bottom? My interest doesn't have anything to do with the way he fits into his clothes nor his flashing smile, she thought. Though she had to admit those ideas had been in her mind as much as thoughts of a job.

As soon as she walked into the apartment, Terry noticed the blinking light on her answering machine. She wanted to rush over and rerun the tape but decided to open the windows in the closed-in apartment first. Makeda dashed past to drop her books in her room.

"Listen, honey," Terry called after her daughter, "take your bath now, because it may be awhile before dinner is ready, such as it is. And don't stay in the tub too long."

"Why?" The mischievous child asked. "Because you're afraid I'll turn into a prune?"

Terry chuckled as she went to tug at the window sash. Just as she had finished opening the room to a refreshing breeze and before she could get to the phone, a knock sounded at the door. Terry peeped through the viewer before unlocking it. Mrs. Carter stood there, breathing heavily from exertion.

"I'm sorry, darling," Terry's landlady said, "but I was trying to catch you before you sat down to eat. I tried to speak to you, but you left so quickly when you picked up Makeda tonight."

Terry's spirits did a plunge downward. She'd left quickly just to avoid Mrs. Carter. She felt guilty about it, but what could she do? Terry knew the woman wanted to ask when they could resume the regular monthly rent. They had always had an amicable relationship, but if things didn't change soon, Terry would have to move into someplace she could afford. *Talk about "When it rains, it pours . . . "*

"I hate to keep asking," Mrs. Carter said, "But you know I have to explain at tax time to the IRS when I rent this apartment for less money."

"Yes," Terry said, feeling low as a flea, "I remember your saying that."

"Life is hard on everyone these days, you know," the woman said sadly.

"I'm really trying to find work, Mrs. Carter."

"I know that, dearie." She patted Terry's hand with a sympathetic shake of her head. The older woman seemed to perk up as she said, "The women at my church's ladies' auxiliary league are praying for you. One of the women, Mrs. Hawkins, had a word of knowledge about you. She says something wonderful is coming your way—eventually."

Oh, no, Terry thought. She had already heard these stories about Mrs. Carter's church, and sometimes the stories were lengthy. Terry stood there listening and nodding. Her mind was a million miles away.

" . . . Don't you think so?" Mrs. Carter said.

"Huh?" Terry's attention lurched back to the present. "Sorry, what did you say?"

"That's all right." The woman patted her arm again. "You young people have enough on your minds without listening to an old woman's ramblings." She moved slowly and heavily toward the top of the stairs.

Terry felt guilty. It seemed so thoughtless of her. Mrs. Carter had been very kind, and here she couldn't even pay attention for a few moments. She walked out onto the landing to watch the older woman go heavily down the stairs.

Mrs. Carter stopped in her slow progress to say, "Don't forget. Something wonderful. Maybe you and that nice husband will get back together."

God forbid, Terry thought. On one of Ronald's visits, he'd managed to charm the older woman and she'd been predicting a reunion for Terry and Ronald ever since. Could it get any worse? Terry thought.

It felt as if she had barely closed the door and turned away from it before someone knocked again.

"Was that Mrs. Carter?" Makeda asked, on her way to the bathroom.

"Yes, and it seems she's forgotten something." Terry turned to open the door again.

It was not Mrs. Carter but her ex-husband, Ronald Brown, standing there, and none too steadily, either. Terry could have spit. If she hadn't believed it was her landlady returning, she wouldn't have opened the door. Ronald had become a problem to her recently, even when he was sober, and if he'd had a drink, he was impossible.

"Hey, baby," he said, and tried to push himself through the door.

Terry moved faster than Ronald, probably because she was completely sober. She jammed her foot against the door to prevent its opening and wrestled the chain lock in place.

Terry glanced around to see if Makeda knew her father had come and was grateful to hear the water running in the bathroom.

"What do you want, Ronald?" she asked firmly, though she was afraid. Ronald always had that effect upon her. After all these years, she had learned to be quite assertive with the rest of the world, but not with Ronald. Old fears rose whenever he was around. The two years they'd been together had been bad, but it was the last night of their marriage that she remembered

the most. She had to forcibly push the memory away. Any
strength she might show was always purely a bluff. He terrified
her no matter how much she pretended.

"Is that any way to treat the man who still loves you and
only wants to be a friend?"

"You never loved anyone except yourself."

"Now, baby, you know that ain't true. Why don't you open
the door?"

The sound of Makeda singing in the bath floated out to them.
Terry was glad the child couldn't witness this scene. She didn't
want her daughter to see him in this condition.

"Say what you want," Terry said, wanting to get rid of him
before Makeda became aware of his presence. The child had
always been a little intimidated by her father. Ronald had been
too self-absorbed to be interested in fostering any sort of positive relationship between himself and his daughter.

"I only want to talk to you."

"I'm too busy to stand here, talking about nothing."

"I have a right to see my daughter."

This was one of Ronald's ploys. He never mentioned his
visitation rights unless it was a last resort to manipulate her.

When they were first divorced, Terry had believed he should
have visitation rights. She had tried to encourage him to see
his daughter despite her personal fear. But soon she realized
that Ronald was a disappointment to their daughter. She came
to feel that he caused Makeda more worry than good; then she
had come to dreading his visiting. In the end, she was glad that
he showed so little interest.

"When you haven't been drinking," Terry said.

"I've only had a couple of beers."

"If you don't go, I'll call the police, and where will that get us?"

Chapter Three

"No, you won't," Ronald sneered. "You're too afraid of upsetting Makeda. You're too afraid of everything else, too." He was right, she thought, but she was also afraid of him.

"If you don't tell me what you want right now, you'll be wasting your time later," she said.

"Give me ten bucks and I'll go away."

Now she was heartsick. She couldn't afford to give Ronald ten dollars. Ten dollars was coming to look like a small fortune these days. He was becoming bolder, too. Ronald had never asked for more than carfare before, a few dollars. However, he'd always been an exploiter, even to his own mother, so she shouldn't have been surprised that her unemployed ex-husband would try to get money out of her.

"Okay," she said, "take your foot out of the door."

"Don't try to get funny and lock me out," he said, before finally allowing her to ease the door closed.

She went quickly to find her purse and rummaged through the few bills there. When she opened the door again, she shoved a five-dollar bill through to him.

"Hey, this isn't ten," he protested.

"It's all I can spare."

He tried to argue further, but she closed the door as quietly as she could and put her ear against the wood to listen. She heard him move away. He stumbled before starting down the stairs. She wondered how he had gotten in. It was quite possible that Mrs. Carter had opened the door for him. The older woman knew Ronald, and he was very good at fooling people.

One look at her shaking hands and she knew she was more frightened than she wanted to admit. She was trying to get up enough courage to go downstairs and lock the front door.

Whenever she saw Ronald now, she couldn't help remembering him as he'd been in college, full of big dreams. What she hadn't realized at first was that the image he'd projected back then had been an illusion. Ronald hadn't been disciplined enough to see his dreams through. He'd flunked out of Howard and was attending a local community college when they met. He was prone to exploiting others to do things for him.

Terry had been so eager to marry and avoid the arid lives of her mother and grandmother that she'd rushed into the relationship.

"See?" Makeda's voice came from behind her. "Am I a prune yet?" She was wrapped in an oversized towel.

Makeda's coming out of the bathroom made Terry abandon the thought of going downstairs. Just in case Ronald was still there, she didn't want Makeda to see him. Terry straightened away from the door and took a deep breath.

She tried to look natural as she said on a shaky laugh, "No, more like a raisin this time."

Makeda seemed to have picked up on Terry's mood, for she looked puzzled.

"Are you all right, Mommy?"

"Of course."

"Was that someone at the door?"

"Mrs. Carter was here for a little while," Terry said, as she turned and headed toward the kitchen. "Anyway, if I don't fix something to eat, we'll drop from starvation."

She wanted to distract the child. Part of her attention was straining to hear any sounds from downstairs. She crossed her fingers in hopes that Ronald was gone.

"Maybe we'll drop from the cooking," Makeda teased.

"Disrespectful child." Terry smiled as she swatted at Makeda's bottom. "Go put on your pajamas."

"It's too early for bed," Makeda protested.

"If all your homework is finished," Makeda nodded yes, "then after dinner we can jump right into bed and watch videos for a while."

On the way to the kitchen, Terry realized that the light on the answering machine was still flashing. She went to rewind the machine. Sure enough, there was a message from Mark Holden, requesting that she call him. He'd left two numbers, one of which was probably his home number, as he'd asked her to use it if she called after six. It surprised her to think that he would go home so early, as most small business owners worked long hours.

Maybe he goes home early to his wife and family.

She hadn't had a date in several years, but she had friends who had. According to them, there were no men out there. It seemed that the men either were not interested in women, were on drugs, or were in jail. And of the few who had managed to avoid all of the above, they either were adamantly against commitment or were already married. Of course, there were a few married ones who advocated plural wives, but they only made her laugh. Mark Holden hadn't seemed like any of these.

In truth, none of this had ever worried her. She had decided after her divorce that she didn't ever want to get involved again. *Once burned, twice shy, as my grandmother used to say.*

Yet she had to admit that something inside her didn't want Mark Holden to be married. The unwelcome thought had come before she could push it away. *I must be more tired than I* thought, she told herself, and shrugged. Then, taking a deep breath, she dialed the number Mark had left. There was no answer. Terry looked at her watch, thinking it was still early, and decided to call again later.

After dinner, Makeda popped the videotape of a favorite story into the VCR.

"We have to fix your hair first."

Makeda, who already had the remote aimed at the VCR, said, "Can't that wait?"

Makeda had a head of long, thick, crinkly hair that took a long time to care for. It was a job that had to be done at night because it took too much time in the morning. It could have been permed, but Terry loved Makeda's hair the way it was. She also enjoyed the nightly ritual of combing it.

"Sure, we can wait until you're all sleepy and cranky," Terry answered.

"I promise I won't get cranky."

"You know the deal," Terry spoke firmly.

"Why can't I have short curly hair that I can wash in the shower?" her daughter asked, as she brought a large-toothed comb, hair preparation, and water.

This question was part of the ritual, too.

"Maybe because you have beautiful long, crinkly hair that needs more careful tending?"

"But I hate hair that needs careful tending."

"Sit." Terry pointed to the stool. "Someday, you're going to love this hair—probably after you've cut and permed it," Terry warned.

"Hah. No, I won't," the girl pouted.

Makeda sat between Terry's legs, and as Terry combed, they talked about the day's events.

As soon as Makeda's hair was finished, the child tumbled into Terry's bed and snuggled close.

The video was called *Zeleke's Beautiful Daughter.* It was an African movie that had been recorded from a showing on a public broadcasting station. The story was about a beautiful East African girl, and as with all fairy tales, there was, of course, a handsome prince. They had viewed the tape so many times that Makeda knew it by heart and sometimes moved her lips along with the actors.

Terry watched the gorgeous man who played the prince and suddenly thought of Mark Holden. She could just see him as a tall, powerful warrior prince. Lordy, he'd be just perfect.

"Doesn't the prince remind you of Mr. Holden?" Makeda asked, and shook her mother's arm to get her attention.

"What?" Terry answered, rattled by her daughter's remark. She felt as if the child had read her thoughts.

"Not exactly in looks," Makeda went on to explain. "Mr. Holden's really more handsome, and he looks like a real hero. Don't you think so? And if he comes to our rescue and gives you a job—then it will be like a real fairy tale."

"Well . . . " Terry wondered if she was a hypocrite for what she was about to say. "First, you can't judge people by the way they look, honey, and second, I hope you remember what I've told you about these stories."

"Oh, Mommy, I know. You told me these stories are only make-believe. I remember."

"Good."

"But Mr. Holden *does* look like a hero," Makeda said, still trying to convince her mother.

"Tomorrow, we'll watch an adventure movie," Terry said, to change the subject.

Thirty minutes later, Makeda went to get a glass of water and Terry glanced at the clock. She decided to call Mark again. She reached for the receiver and stopped. *I won't expect any miracles.* There had been many disappointments in the last few months, and for some reason, this time it seemed as if it would hurt more than before. Maybe because it would come from him?

Before Terry could pick up the phone, it rang.

"This is Mark Holden." His crisp voice, instead of sounding businesslike, sounded sexy. "I have a job for you."

"Yes?" She wanted to pinch herself to see if it was a dream.

"It's a housekeeping position, and you'll be taking care of a seven-year-old girl."

"Housekeeping?" she repeated, feeling stupid.

"There's a small apartment for you and your daughter." The salary he mentioned made her ears buzz. She asked him to repeat it. It was more than she'd made at her last job! And she wouldn't be paying room and board.

"I've never been a housekeeper before. What will my duties be?" She felt put off balance by this unexpected offer.

"Cooking and some light housecleaning, although there will be a cleaning woman two times a month. Mostly, you'll be taking care of a little girl."

"Uh, cooking?" she asked, in a strangled voice. This was going to be worse than cleaning the house! She remembered Makeda's telling him that she was a great cook yesterday, but that was a family joke—one between her daughter and her. Her cooking skills were adequate because she had to provide a good diet for Makeda. However, as a housekeeper for someone else, it would never do. Her meals were much too simple.

While married to Ronald, they'd stayed at his mother's house. That had been one of the problems during her marriage, though certainly not the worst one. Ronald's mother had resented her using the kitchen. As a child she'd also been banned from the kitchen. Her grandmother had had a small catering business, but she hadn't wanted Terry to learn to cook.

Learning to cook had had a very low priority when Terry'd found herself having to support herself and Makeda. Of course, she was sure she could work on her skills, but what about the interim period before she did learn?

"Is it beneath your job experience?" Mark cut into her thoughts, sounding a bit annoyed. "You claimed you were willing to be a home companion. That certainly at times requires you do a little housekeeping. Or is it the child that you object to?"

"I have no objection," Terry said, accepting his offer immediately.

"You'll be working for me," he explained, "and my seven-year-old daughter, Yvette."

"You?" She realized with some sadness that her earlier thoughts were correct—he was married and had children too.

"There's a small apartment for you and your daughter."

"About my cooking . . ."

"Just breakfast and dinner. Yvette eats lunch in school, and sometimes we eat out. Nothing more than what you do for yourself and Makeda."

I doubt it, Terry thought, but she didn't say any more about her cooking. I'll tell him later, she promised. She didn't understand why he had chosen her for the job. Yesterday he'd been full of disapproval when she'd admitted that she'd skipped breakfast.

"Why did you pick me?" She voiced her doubts.

There was a slight pause before he answered. "I like the way you've raised your daughter, and I think you'd be good for Yvette."

"Oh," was all she could think to say.

"How soon can you start?"

"Right away."

"You have to meet Yvette first. If you're free on Sunday, you and Makeda can come over and get to know her. Also, we can use the time for you to get organized and to have your things moved. Let's say by next week, Wednesday. Can you be ready by then?"

"No problem."

She knew by the tone of his voice that meeting Yvette would be the criterion by which he would hire her. If she didn't get along with his daughter, there would be no job. That didn't worry her, as she loved children and they usually took to her.

"You can come to the house on Sunday afternoon to meet Yvette. By then I'll have all the details for you and you can sign the contract. However, you'll get paid as of today."

"Contract? Why do we need a contract?" She was a little puzzled by this. Getting paid even before she started seemed too good to be true, too.

"It's for my daughter's sake. I don't want you to stay for a few months and then decide you're bored."

"Oh," she said, but refrained from being snide or questioning why he didn't consider her overqualified for this position. Best not to bring that up, she wisely decided. But somehow, her mouth got the better of her and she spoke before thinking. "You feel this is a job for me?"

There was another small pause before he said, "Do you think you can handle it?"

Just like him to answer my question with another question, she thought, but hastily answered, "Yes, certainly."

Her first feeling when she hung up was, strangely enough, disappointment. It took a while for her to realize that it was finding out he was married, rather than the job offering, that had been a disappointment. The idea was so preposterous, she immediately pushed it away. She wondered how they were going to live in the same house without killing each other, if the atmosphere of yesterday was any indication of how well they would get along.

Makeda came back with her hair tied up to keep it fresh while she slept.

"Good news," Terry said, and couldn't help the big smile that spread across her face.

"You're going to perm my hair?" Makeda said with a grin.

"No, troublesome child. I have a job."

"From Mr. Holden?" Makeda squealed.

"Yes!"

"Didn't I tell you? He's rescued you. It's just like a story. Now you won't be worried about money and paying the rent."

Makeda let out a loud whoop and did an Indian dance around the room.

Makeda's knowing about her worries surprised Terry. She thought that she had hidden them from her child. Obviously, that wasn't always possible.

After hanging up, Mark's only thought was, I must be crazy, bringing this woman into my home. But then he remembered how cozy her own home was; surely she must be doing something right to have raised such a sweet child.

For some reason, the image of how Terry Redding's skirt had tightened over her shapely hips when she'd bent over came into his imagination. It seemed the sight had made an indelible impression upon his memory, because it had popped up a number of times already. He was beginning to wonder about his tendency to remember how attractive she was. He sat up straight. *This is happening too often.*

He got up and paced.

It wasn't such a big deal that he'd noticed; he was a man, after all. What surprised him was the thought staying with him all this time. Well, he told himself, there will be no more of that. Living with Marlene had cured him of wanting intense relationships with women.

Now all he wanted from a woman was something quick and with no entanglements. This Redding woman seemed too serious. She was one of those who, if you touched her, would take it as a proposal. Not me, he thought. He wasn't going to put himself in the position of having more woman trouble. Look at what was happening to everyone he knew! Look at how it was messing up his partner, James McNeil!

He loved women, but he liked them glamorous, sophisticated, and knowing the score. Redding had a fast mouth and looked competent, but there was something too wide-eyed-innocent about her.

She looked the type that someone would marry. Definitely not for me. Never again, he thought, and decided he'd go for a run that night before retiring.

Two days later, on Sunday, Terry and Makeda returned from church. They barely had time to change their clothes before Mark came for them. Terry was surprised he hadn't brought his daughter.

"I thought it would be better if the first meeting was on her own home ground," he explained, then went on to add, "She's a little shy."

He was all dressed up in a suit and tie, and Terry was a bit surprised. She had assumed he'd change into something very casual, like jeans and flannel shirt, off the job. She couldn't get a handle on this man.

Mark's home was a huge, sprawling Tudor-type edifice that looked as if it should have been called "the Holden Estate" or some such grand name. It was in one of Long Island's prime areas. While her own apartment was satisfactory, it seemed strange that just a few miles away people lived in such luxury.

The house, which had a semicircular gravel driveway, was bordered on one side by a row of tall, swaying trees. There were gardens in the front that seemed to run around the sides and back.

They stepped out of the car and followed Mark, who showed Makeda a beautiful playground and a pool. The pool was covered with a tarp, but the play-gym looked ready and waiting.

Upon sight of it, Makeda's face broke out in a smile of pleasure. Turning shiny eyes on Mark, she asked excitedly, "Can I play in it?"

"Sure. Why don't you try it out while your mother and I go inside?"

Makeda didn't ask twice. She was up the slide and gracefully whizzing down it in seconds.

"This is absolutely beautiful," Terry said.

Mark looked around and she could see that he was proud of it. "Sometimes I feel like a fool for buying this property," he said with a rueful head shake.

"Oh, you shouldn't, though I can see it must have cost a fortune."

He smiled. "Not as much as you'd think. The previous owners were an elderly couple. The husband had health problems and they wanted to unload and move to Arizona. I offered them a retirement package for no money down. Before I could get the words out, they'd accepted my deal. It was pure luck; I came along at the perfect time. We all came away with a 'win-win' deal."

"You have a right to be proud. Your daughter must be in heaven, having this in her own backyard." Terry indicated the play-gym and pool.

His chest rose and fell on a silent man-sized sigh. Then he looked into her eyes, and there was pain there. "Yvette can't swim, and to be honest, she never comes out here." Mark gestured for Terry to follow him and they started toward the house. "Let's go in. We can see your daughter from there. Maybe we can entice Yvette to come out this time and play with Makeda."

They walked along a flagstone walkway and passed a small section that appeared to have been added onto the house.

"That's the apartment where you'll stay," Mark explained. However, they did not go through the back, but went around to enter through the front door.

As Terry walked into his home, she was more curious about Mark's wife and daughter then about her surroundings. But there were no wife and child waiting to look her over. Instead, she stood with her mouth agape as she looked around in amazement.

While the grounds were lovely and had captivated Makeda, it was the inside of the house that caught Terry. It was fantastic.

She immediately fell in love with the foyer and its crystal-and-gold chandelier. The furniture had the subdued patina only old, well-kept furniture had. The woods were cedar and mahogany. Some pieces were works of art.

"Many of these pieces are handmade and were imported from the Caribbean," Mark explained, when he saw how fascinated she was.

There were finely beaded tabletops scattered about. She had seen such things in stores that imported goods from Africa. The floors were an expanse of glasslike, high-gloss surface. Lovely African rugs were placed along the way. Sunlight filtered through silk drapes hanging from windows at least fifteen feet tall. There were metal African masks, items that came from the kingdoms of ancient Benin and of the Swahili people, whose language was still used for trade *even* to this day. To one side a wide staircase ran up to the second floor. An Oriental runner was molded to the marble steps. This was not a European house, but rather the best of many cultures.

It took a few minutes before she noticed what should have become apparent to her immediately. Once the beauty and sumptuousness of the furnishings were accepted, she realized how perfectly kept everything was. The light scent of lemon wax clung to the furniture. The shine reflected from everything.

Omigod, I'm in real trouble! He wants me to keep his home clean? For Pete's sake, I need whoever cleaned this to come help out at my place.

Her anxiety level shot sky-high. Can I do this? she wondered. More important, should I do it? This wasn't a case of making a simple meal or a snack. This setting went along with several courses at breakfast, lunch, and dinner. And while she was fairly okay at home for herself and Makeda, she felt really out of her depth here. Suppose they wanted gourmet meals?

"This is the blue room," Mark continued.

Blue room, she thought, looking around.

But she wanted the job, and she really needed it. Besides,

she thought, surely her managerial office skills could be used in a house. They were both jobs that needed organization and attention to detail. True, she'd never been particularly good in a house before, but she was a quick learner. *I can do it*. She accepted the challenge by squaring her shoulders.

She glanced around, noticing that the room looked unused. However, her eye spied a small table near an easy chair. There were audiocassette tapes scattered across the top. Her curiosity burned to know what type of music Mark had been listening to.

"I'd like you to meet Yvette before we do a tour," Mark said. He went to open the French windows that lined one wall. The silk drapes billowed into the room. Terry could see Makeda outside, walking around examining things.

"Mrs. Young," Mark called, and a staunch-looking middle-aged woman came into the room. He introduced them. "Mrs. Young will continue to come in regularly to do the major housework so you'll be able to concentrate on Yvette." The woman smiled cordially. Then Mark asked Mrs. Young, "Where's Yvette?"

"She's in her room, talking to her mother," the woman responded. She glanced curiously at Terry.

"Marlene is here?" Mark asked, sounding testy, and started out toward the marble stairs. Terry suspected he would give the offending person a real dressing down.

"On the phone," Mrs. Young hastily added. "She called a few minutes ago, and Yvette is taking the call in her room."

Mark frowned and turned to Terry. "We'll take that tour as soon as you've met Yvette. It may take a while for you to get used to the house."

That's an understatement, Terry thought. The place is huge. "I'll get used to it. Is Mrs. Holden here today?" she asked, surprised that his wife hadn't made her appearance. It seemed strange, as usually a housekeeper would be more of an interest to a woman than to a man. She had expected to be interviewed by his wife.

Mark's head swung around and he stared intently at her for long moments. "Mrs. Holden?" Then his mouth tightened as he went on, "Marlene and I are divorced. We've suffered the ills of modern marriage like everybody seems to be doing these days." It sounded as if he was speaking about a pet peeve, she thought. He added, "Yvette has been living with me for the last six months."

"I'm sorry."

Terry always felt sorry when marriages broke up. She was too aware of how much pain people suffered in failed relationships. Something about Mark Holden's voice made her sense that his divorce had caused him pain. He tilted his head and gave her that same intent glance again.

"Don't be sorry. When people marry for foolish reasons like love and romance, the marriage tends to fall apart and it's the children who suffer." He sounded bitter. Then he seemed to catch himself. "Well, enough of that."

She had to admit that mostly she agreed with him. Her own marriage had been built on her fantasy that she would have romance. But some inner pang hit her when he said that he had married for love and romance himself.

Still, she was glad to hear there would be no Mrs. Holden, so glad that she began to suspect her own motives. *It would be harder to fool a woman with my lack of skills.* She tried to rationalize away any other possible reason. She promised herself then that she was going to be the world's best cook and housekeeper even if it killed her.

"Does your daughter miss living with her mother?" she asked, before Yvette made an appearance.

He was glancing toward the head of the stairs, his face full of concern. Her question caught his attention and he turned to speak with her. "Not as much as we'd originally feared. Yvette has another sort of problem."

"Oh?"

"We can wait in here." He indicated the room they had just stepped out of.

Yvette's delay in coming downstairs seemed to worry him, for he kept glancing at the door. They were both facing the wall of windows. She could see that Makeda was enjoying the play area that Mark had built for Yvette.

"My daughter sees a child psychologist," Mark said. "When she first came, I felt she was too quiet and withdrawn."

"Maybe she's just lonely," Terry said.

"Could be," he acknowledged. "I'm hoping Makeda's presence will help that."

"It will," Terry said with a smile. "Makeda will be working on her right off the bat. But don't you think that a new housekeeper might be overwhelming for your daughter?"

"I thought of that, but I'm hoping it will work out." He paused before going on, "The child psychologist says that aside from low self-esteem, Yvette is fine."

"It'll work out," Terry said, and was quiet for a moment. "I know how hard it is when you're worried about a child."

"You do? Makeda seems happy enough."

"Makeda has always had a sunny nature. But" Terry said softly. "she has a heart murmur. Her doctor says if it doesn't resolve soon, she may need surgery."

"I'm sorry to hear that," he said, sounding genuine. "She's such a nice little kid."

"Yes," Terry answered. But because talking about Makeda's health always made her want to cry, she changed the subject. "Does Yvette have any hobbies or special games she likes to play?"

He appeared to have to think about that. "I don't know." He sounded slightly overwhelmed and even shamefaced. "I work long hours, you see."

She sensed that he felt as if things were out of his control and this was an unusual situation for him. It was the first indication the mighty owner of Holden and McNeil ever had any doubt, and she liked him better for it.

Some voice in her head said she'd been liking the handsome man all the time. Terry decided not to listen too closely to any voices that spoke in her head.

"Sometimes, all a shy child needs is to develop whatever his or her talents are. It can help them learn to appreciate themselves."

"Did you study child psychology?" he asked.

She looked up, thinking he was making fun of her, but on seeing his sincere expression, she realized he was quite serious. "When I was pregnant with Makeda, I read everything I could get my hands on."

He gazed through the window at Makeda, who was now squatting contentedly near the flowering hedges. Daffodils and irises sprouted new buds, and the small girl intently examined the yellow and violet blossoms.

"It was time well spent," he said.

His praise made Terry suddenly feel warm and happy.

I'll have to remember not to start blushing like a schoolgirl, she thought. It would damage her credibility as an appropriate caretaker for his child, she suspected, as she stood looking out the window with him.

Makeda seemed to sense their attention and glanced up. She stood up to skip happily through the French doors.

"Where's your little girl?" the irrepressible child asked, looking about the room.

"She's a little bashful," Mark said, "I'll go and bring her out." They watched him go up the stairs.

While they waited, Makeda began to wander around the beautiful room, peeking at things. "Please don't touch anything, Makeda," Terry warned. *That's all I need, for my daughter to break one of these priceless objects.*

Terry looked through the audiocassette tapes she had noticed earlier. They weren't music tapes but seemed all to be motivational. They were the types of tapes salespeople listened to while driving. These were speeches of Les Brown, the well-known black motivational speaker. Looking at the titles gave her a funny feeling, as if she was looking into Mark Holden's heart. It made her feel like she knew him better. When she heard him coming, she put them down and turned to face him.

Mark appeared a little uncomfortable as he walked toward her, saying, "Yvette will be down in a second."

He had seen her looking at the tapes, but he didn't say anything. He kept glancing up at the stairs.

Several minutes passed and Yvette didn't come. Mark looked increasingly more uncomfortable. He walked from the window to the door several times. She wished he'd just sit down. "Give her a little time," he said.

"It's all right," Terry answered. "She's probably caught up with talking to her mother."

"No, she's not on the phone now. She's just . . . " He stopped and shrugged, as if not knowing how to explain it.

"I'll get her," Makeda piped up. Mark glanced at the child. A worried frown played upon his broad, handsome brow. He moved his arm as if to stop her.

Finally, he said, "Upstairs. It's the last door on the right."

Makeda didn't need any more encouragement and turned to walk sedately up the stairs. Terry watched Makeda's steady tread up the stairs and her heart hurt. She remembered her daughter as a child who ran everywhere. She had to find a way to get the surgery done as soon as possible.

"Do you think it'll be all right?" he asked.

Terry felt empathy at the sight of his worried face. "Sure, it will," she answered, but she wasn't as certain as she sounded. "If they're going to live together, they have to start someplace."

Mark returned to gazing at the stairs, and neither of them spoke for some time. Terry realized this was a test. If today didn't work, she wouldn't be getting the job. Mark's daughter was terribly important to him.

Chapter Four

A moment later, Makeda was standing at the top of the staircase with a shy, obviously curious Yvette in tow. If this moment was any indication, the two girls were going to hit it off famously. This was far from the only problem Terry had anticipated, but it was a relief to see it turn out so well.

Yvette already had a tentative smile on her lips. Terry felt her heart go out to the girl immediately, and she had an urge to hug the small-boned child.

She heard Mark exhale sharply. They looked at each other and smiled in relief. As their gaze locked far longer than was necessary, Terry felt her heart skip a beat. Mark's eyes narrowed and he seemed to be considering something about her before he stopped and turned away.

After the introductions, Mark suggested the two girls go outside to the playground, and as they left, already seemingly comfortable enough to be holding hands, Yvette turned around to her father.

"Marlene called, Daddy."

Marlene, Terry remembered, was the name of his ex-wife.

It surprised Terry to hear the little girl call her mother by name. It seemed out of character for such a subdued child.

While the girls were outside playing, Mark showed her the rest of the house. It was enormous, with three floors. And there was a den for simple family entertainment. The house had been built for a big family. It seemed strange that only Mark Holden and one seven-year-old girl were in residence.

Her own living quarters would consist of three rooms, two bedrooms, and a sitting room. It was quite attractively done, considering it was the servants' quarters. But if her apartment impressed her, the kitchen blew her away. They only peeked from the doorway because Mrs. Young was in the process of cooking lunch. It was a large area with a cheerful breakfast nook off in the corner. Terry glanced around the sunny yellow-and-white-tiled room, thinking that it contained every gadget known to the western world.

Seeing this made her know without a doubt that her new employer was expecting gourmet cooking. How was she going to tell him the truth?

Mark glanced at her. She thought he looked a little sheepish when he remarked, "I bought all this some time ago. I used to like to putter around in the kitchen back then. Of course, I rarely do this anymore, what with the business taking up so much of my time."

"Really," she said, trying to appear normal. Oh, no, she thought. *If he cooks, then it's worse than I thought.*

After the tour, when the children had come in, Mark asked Mrs. Young to serve lunch. They all sat at a long table in the formal dinning room. It was a grand room with another gorgeous chandelier hanging from the fifteen-foot ceiling. It made her think of something you would see two hundred years ago.

Lunch was prepared by Mrs. Young. An intricately folded, snowy white damask napkin sat at each place setting. The first course was a salad. Soup followed, ladled from an exquisite china tureen. The food was delicious, but it was heavier than what Terry would have prepared.

Mark was seated at the head of the table with her placed at his right and both girls side by side on his left. As children are inclined to do, suddenly the two girls put their heads together and giggled. Even to Terry's ears it seemed strange, as up to that moment, the house had been quiet, even somber.

Mark's reaction, however, was the real surprise. Turning sharply at the sound of the girl's laughter, he hit his soup bowl, sloshing soup across the table linen and almost overturning the fine chinaware. His face was a study in pure male shock. Both girls paused at this and turned perplexed eyes on him.

"What's wrong, Daddy?" Yvette's little voice showed her concern.

Mark's eyes swung to look at Terry. She, too, was puzzled by his behavior. Then, with a big grin, he looked back at the children with, "Not a thing, Kitten. Your Daddy's feeling just fine." After Mrs. Young had sponged the spilled soup up, he went back to eating. The mood of the meal lightened appreciably after that.

Mark teased the girls and they giggled throughout the meal. The more they laughed, the happier he looked. When both girls covered their missing teeth to laugh, he appeared absolutely charmed. Terry felt better, too, and almost forgot that she was going to have to tell him about her cooking.

After lunch, the girls went to the den to play videogames and Mark led her into the library, which had been taken over for his home office. It was a man's room. The walls were lined with books. An Oriental rug muffled all sound, creating a quiet oasis. Two leather couches were set in a grouping at one side. A large desk, complete with desktop computer, dominated the other side. A green banker's lamp gave off a cozy glow.

Terry knew that the time had come to sign her contract. Her conscience gave her some real kicks and suddenly she was jittery.

Mark went around the desk to sit and produced a very official-looking document. Her hands shook as she held it to read. Tell him, her mind kept prompting.

He tapped a pencil on the blotter and said, "I think things went quite well today . . . don't you agree?"

A strangled-sounding "Yes" squeaked past her tight throat and she swallowed convulsively.

"Are you feeling all right?" he queried.

"Yes." Terry tried to cough away the tightness this time.

She was going to pick up the expensive gold pen that laid near the document, then she stopped, accepting that she had to be honest with this man. "Mr. Holden . . . "

"Call me Mark. This is a small household. 'Mr. Holden' sounds too formal."

At another "Yes, Mr. Holden," he looked at her as if he thought she wasn't too bright. "Mark," she corrected. She took a deep breath, then rushed on as if afraid she'd change her mind again. "I think you should know that I can't cook."

"What?" he roared. "Say this again, Redding. Am I to understand that you can't cook! How can you raise a child without cooking?"

"I cook certain foods. Like steamed vegetables and . . . "

"Rabbit food?" His eyebrows shot up.

"It's good food."

"But you swore . . . "

"Not me. It was Makeda who said that I could cook. She was making a joke. A family joke," she finished lamely.

"Are you saying that you feel no responsibility for this fraud?"

"It wasn't a fraud. I *do* feel responsible." Now, that's not what she'd meant to say. She didn't want to sound as if she'd committed a major crime. "I'm trying to explain that I'll need a little time to learn to cook the things you're used to." He didn't look impressed with this, so she went on in a more conciliatory voice, "I wanted the job so much that . . . " She trailed off.

"Yes, go on. Let's hear the rest."

"I'm a fast learner. You won't be sorry."

He stared at her a long time. "Okay," He exhaled with a loud exasperated sound. "It shouldn't be too difficult learning simple, basic meals. I'm a steak-and-potato man."

She didn't say anything, knowing that her position after her confession wasn't too good. But she couldn't help compressing her lips. Potatoes were all right, but steak—ugh—all that red meat and cholesterol. Mark Holden had noticed her displeased expression.

"You want to say something about steak and potatoes?" he prompted, looking none too pleased.

"Oh, no, of course not," she answered quickly. But mentally she promised to show him better, once she had the chance.

"For your own sake, don't turn your nose up at a little fat in the diet. You should know that young children *need* animal protein. Not to mention that a woman's body needs a higher fat content in order to function . . . er . . . in order to function." He had obviously found himself in hot water, trying to talk about a woman's body.

She didn't know what to make of this. Fortunately, he didn't expect any response as he continued on.

"The way you women are always starving yourselves . . . " Now he seemed too exasperated to go on.

Oh, glory, she thought. He wants to discuss women's health issues? Maybe I'll get sick from listening to this self-righteous nonsense.

"Sign the contract," he said in a clipped tone, and handed her the pen.

He leaned back in his chair and watched her over tented fingers. "There's going to be a dinner party in two weeks for some potential clients."

The pen fumbled in her suddenly nerveless fingers and she

straightened to her full height, squaring her shoulders. "I can't learn to cook for a fancy dinner party in two weeks!" she almost shrieked.

He stopped her outburst. "The dinner will be fully catered," adding after a heartbeat, "thank God."

If she hadn't needed the job so badly, she'd have walked out right then. However, she clenched her fists at her side. *Maybe I deserved that.*

She said, "In that case, you can be totally at ease. I've had experience planning dinner parties and such." She only hoped this recaptured some of her credibility.

His next words showed she hadn't.

"Mrs. McNeil, my partner's wife, will be handling everything. All you'll need to do is make yourself available to her."

He'd said it with such smugness that she'd suddenly had the urge to kick him in the shins. But she murmured, "As you wish."

By midweek, Terry was overseeing the movers in her old apartment. Mrs. Carter, her landlady, came to say goodbye.

The woman's eyes were watery, and Terry felt an answering moisture in her own.

Mrs. Carter hugged her and said, "I'm going to miss you, honey. You were my best tenant ever."

Then the woman dabbed a crumbled tissue to her eyes. She had been like family to Terry, who was momentarily unable to speak.

"Who knows?" Mrs. Carter went on, and she appeared suddenly to have cheered up. "This could be that 'something wonderful' that the church sisters saw for you."

Terry laughed through her tear-clouded eyes. "Well, it will certainly help me pay off some of my debts."

"Honey, you know I'm sorry about that." Mrs. Carter looked as if she was about to cry all over again.

"I didn't mean it that way," Terry reassured her. "You were more than kind," and then, because Terry felt the waterworks would start again, she tried to be more practical. "You have my address, right? Call me if you need anything. Anything at all."

Mrs. Carter's face suddenly clouded. "What about poor Ronald, your husband? Does he have your new address?"

"*Ex*-husband," Terry corrected. She snapped her bag closed. She didn't know how to explain what she had to say. "No, he doesn't," she finally admitted.

"Terry, you can't do that. I know he's been a problem at times, but he *is* Makeda's father."

"Yes, I know, and I'm going to arrange for him to visit . . . in time. But please don't give him my address."

"Oh, honey, I don't know . . . "

"Please, just give me a little time. Then I'll tell him myself."

"Well, okay," Mrs. Carter said. Terry gave the woman another big hug.

The second day after she and Makeda had moved into Mark's magnificent home, Mark took the morning off from work because he intended to take Terry to rent a car for her use. Terry was inordinately pleased, feeling like a kid with a new toy. She waited at home while he dropped the girls off at school.

She was in her room when she heard Mark walk in. She hurried into the foyer to meet him. Just as she entered, Mark seemed to be falling.

"Mr. Holden!" she shouted.

Believing he was having some sort of seizure, she ran forward to catch him. They both wound up on the floor in a tangle of arms and legs. She had meant to soften his fall, yet somehow, she wound up laying on top of him. She was certain that this was his fault, because she suspected he'd shifted their positions at the last minute in order not to fall on her. There she sat atop his washboard stomach, as close as a lover. Her breathing became positively erratic.

He lay beneath her, staring up with an exasperated expression on his face. "Would you mind telling me what your problem is?" His voice sounded peeved, and as if he was dealing with a not-too-bright child.

"*My* problem? I thought you were falling or something."

"I wasn't falling. I was doing a few push-ups."

"Push-ups?" she asked.

"Yes, I like to exercise whenever I'm delayed by tardy people," he said. "Would you mind stepping off my stomach?"

Hastily she jumped off. She couldn't figure out which insult to answer first—whether she should tell him that she wasn't attacking him, or that she wasn't tardy. Or should she say that she hadn't been stepping on his stomach? Egad! Push-ups? Did the man have sudden irresistible urges to exercise? How was she going to stand him? He'd exhaust her.

When they finally left for the car rental office, she was still fuming. While they were waiting for her car to be driven up, Mark had a distracted air. He kept whistling through his teeth and glancing at his watch. Terry watched him surreptitiously. Pleased as she was to be driving again, she found him far more interesting, aside from the fact that he was also obnoxious.

Suddenly from nowhere, an unwelcome thought came into her mind. *We're going to be a two-car "family"—house!* Terry hurriedly corrected mentally. *We're going to be a two-car house.*

The second car did come in handy. It was a forty-minute drive to Makeda's school. Since Mark's business was nearby, he drove Makeda in the morning. Now, with her own car, Terry could chauffeur Yvette. In the afternoon, she would first pick up Yvette and then drive in to collect Makeda. There was enough flexibility in all this to change according to any special plans.

Because there was so little time left in the school year, Terry planned to transfer Makeda in September, rather than disrupt her in May. Next September, if things worked out, both girls would be going to the same school. It was a highly rated private school where children learned on computers and had serious science courses from the first grade. Terry could barely believe her good luck. Of course, these plans depended upon whether she was still employed by Mark by that time.

That afternoon, after picking up the girls after school, Terry started one of her first efforts to make herself into the perfect housekeeper. They took a trip to the local public library, where she picked up an armful of cookbooks.

Once at home, she commenced to work on akee and salt fish. It was a recipe from Jamaica. Both Makeda and Yvette were fascinated with the preparations. They sat in the kitchen while she worked, poring over sumptuous color photos of delicious dishes.

"I like to cook," Yvette informed Terry, who seemed especially interested in what she was doing.

"I think I'll hire a cook when I'm a great and famous surgeon," Makeda explained to them.

Terry was feeling rather smug with her efforts, which looked pretty good. She glanced around the kitchen at the two girls and felt contented. She smiled and hugged them both.

Makeda, who was used to impulsive, affectionate gestures from her mother, gave Terry a rather distracted hug in return. Yvette at first was startled by the unexpected physical contact. But after a few moments of puzzled wonder, her face was wreathed in a bright smile and she gave Terry an enthusiastic squeeze.

Terry understood then that physical expressions of affection were unusual to the small girl. It made her wonder about Marlene.

While nothing that happened those first few days was earth-shaking, it did require Terry and Mark to coordinate their efforts.

Within days, things were working out so well that both she and Mark were congratulating themselves. And maybe that was a symptom of what nagged at her. They had begun to look more like a family rather than the employer and employee.

A family without a father, unfortunately, because once Mark saw that Terry had transportation, he became conspicuous by his absence. Mark worked late every night and came home after everyone had gone to sleep.

This was hard on Yvette, for she missed her father, and it annoyed Terry. She wasn't familiar with what Mark liked and was concerned about being left to supervise his home without consulting with him.

There was one specific problem worrying her quite a bit. It concerned his blessed dinner party. On the second day she had called Beverly McNeil. The woman had been totally indifferent to Terry's offer of help.

Terry had shrugged after hanging up, thinking she had done her part. If Beverly needed her, she could call back. Several days went by with no further contact.

On impulse, Terry decided to check into what china and silverware were available. She thought linen could be rented from the caterers. She found some lovely Limoges in cabinets in the pantry. She washed it and polished the beautiful intricate silverware that was in the sideboard. At least they'll be ready when Beverly calls, she thought.

Then the caterers called. Mark had hired them, but they had been unable to contact Mrs. McNeil. This was a puzzle to Terry. The caterers wanted information she couldn't give. The man sounded a bit testy when he asked that Mrs. McNeil call them back as soon as possible.

Terry had relayed the messages to Beverly only to get another brush-off. She had been tempted to call Mark, but he'd been very specific in telling her that she wasn't to interfere. She was quite tired of ending up looking the fool in front of him.

Now, ten days later, she still had no further information. If there's one thing I know, it's that these events can't be done overnight, she thought. What's holding that McNeil woman up? She's wasting valuable time. Just because I don't cook greasy steaks doesn't mean I'm totally inept . . .

Well, it wasn't her affair, as Mr. Mark Holden had already implied. As far as she knew, nothing had been done about this magnificent event that Mark thought was so far above her. The whole thing gave her a bad feeling.

She would certainly like to show *him* a thing or two. True, he hadn't been too impressed with her skills as a housekeeper, but she *had* planned dinner parties.

What she hadn't told Mark was that her grandmother, who'd started as a cook and domestic worker, had eventually owned a catering business. She had maintained her clients from her cooking days and by word of mouth had managed to develop a fairly successful small concern. While Terry had never been allowed in that kitchen, she certainly knew about planning such events.

Now, how would I do this? She was suddenly off on a daydream as she went through straightening the house. She remembered a local Haitian caterer in Queens, where she had once lived. I'd hire them, she thought. And I'd have them serve something delicious and ethnic. That would show Mr. Smarty Pants Holden. She grabbed a pen and pad and jotted down her ideas. Suddenly she stopped. Why am I worrying about it? Hadn't he said it'd be handled?

"Forget it, girl," she said out loud. "Didn't he insinuate that all this was totally above you?" But she couldn't. She knew, even with her meager experience, that perfect dinner parties didn't grow on trees. They took careful planning.

Later that day, she answered the phone, to find it was the caterers again.

"Mrs. McNeil, please."

"Sorry, she's not here. You can reach her at . . . "

But before she could finish, the man cut in with a voice that was frayed around the edges. Not that Terry could blame him. "She's never there, and I've called several times. We are canceling as the caterer for this dinner party. There simply is not enough time to do a satisfactory job."

Suddenly, adrenaline galvanized her. "Wait," Terry said. "Please don't do that."

"We have our reputation to consider," he said, sounding very waspish.

"Will you at least wait until I can speak with Mrs. McNeil again? I'm sure she can straighten everything out."

"I'm sorry, we cannot wait."

"Please reconsider. I'm quite certain Mrs. McNeil will call immediately . . . " she said, wondering if she was stepping too far out of line, making promises for Beverly McNeil.

" . . . Impossible . . . " the man said, just before the dial tone.

"Well, really," she said, once she couldn't be heard.

She couldn't blame the man for being peeved. He was only trying to do his job, and he'd been calling ever since she'd come to live here.

Suddenly, she had the urge to call Mark. He'd said this party was important to his business, and she couldn't help but wonder if he knew that according to the caterers, nothing had been planned yet.

Pushing that away, she dialed the McNeils'. The phone rang a long time. Frustration caused her to bang the phone down. *Why am I getting involved?* Beverly probably had the whole thing under perfect control. The woman could have simply changed caterers without notifying anyone. However, her doubts persisted. If James McNeil was unreliable —suppose his wife was no better?

She hesitated to call Mark, not wanting to get her head bitten off. She picked up the phone and then quickly hung it up again. A memory of Mark's first telling her about the party came. "Mrs. McNeil will handle everything," she mimicked his lofty manner.

Finally she gathered up the nerve to dial. *I've probably put my foot into it this time.* She had planned to leave the message with Mark's receptionist, Mrs. Dougan. But when Terry recognized the older woman's voice, she remembered the woman's efforts to be kind on the first day. Terry took the time to have a few words with her, explaining about her new position as Mark's housekeeper.

"Housekeeper?" The woman sounded terribly confused. "But I thought that you were overqualified."

"It's a little complicated," Terry said breezily, before the receptionist transferred the call to Mark's office.

He took the news about the caterer quietly, saying a simple, "Thank you."

That night Mark came home early. When he walked in, the aroma of something mouthwatering hit him right in the gut. His stomach growled with hunger. He'd been too busy to eat today.

"Daddy!" Yvette rushed to meet him with a big hug and kiss.

When he noticed Makeda standing in the background, looking left out, he offered a cheek to her also. She grinned, actually forgetting to hide the gap where her front teeth were missing.

Coming home to the kids, the smells of good food cooking, and a warm house made him feel incredibly good—as if life was worth all the effort.

"Daddy, Terry bought me some new clothes. Some real t-shirts," Yvette said excitedly.

"Me, too," Makeda added.

"Is that so?" he said, and then, sensing that Terry was there, he looked up. The sight of her rocked him.

She wore shorts and a loose shirt. Her rounded bare brown arms were folded across her breasts, and she held a large wooden spoon in one hand. She reminded him of something that he couldn't quite place. She stood in the doorway, one hip jutted higher than the other, with a provocative grace that seemed totally unconscious. His heart raced and his groin stirred.

"Dinner's almost ready," Terry said.

In his aroused state, she sounded as alluring as if she'd given some irresistibly erotic invitation.

"Okay." Was that gruff grumble his voice? He cleared his throat and said, "I'll wash up."

He didn't want to leave her, but with both girls hanging onto him, there wasn't much else he could do. They followed him into his room and bathroom while he washed his face and hands.

Despite all the delicious smells, dinner was a disaster. It smelled great, but it was a squashed mess on a plate. Terry looked at her efforts with helpless frustration. She reminded Mark of a young wife just learning to cook. That thought was like a dash of cold water in the face.

Whose young wife? he wondered. *Certainly not mine.*

Truthfully, he was glad her dinner had fallen flat, because it took his mind off her legs.

"Okay, Redding, let's call for Chinese," he said to her glum expression.

After they ate, he played Chinese checkers with the girls for a while, though his thoughts kept wandering to the kitchen and what Terry was doing.

When they finished the last game, he sent the girls to bathe and get ready for bed. He ambled into the kitchen as if drawn there by a magnet.

He didn't see her at first, but he heard her bumping around in the walk-in pantry. As he gazed around, he remembered buying all those gadgets that were visible everywhere. At the time, he had convinced himself that Marlene would find them useful. Though Terry obviously didn't have a clue as to how to use most of them, she was game. He couldn't help admiring her enthusiasm, he thought, as he flicked through a cookbook on Zaire cuisine.

When she did come out of the pantry, she jumped as if startled to find him there. "Sorry," he said, feeling big and clumsy.

"I didn't hear you."

He wanted to stare at her again and he couldn't help remembering how earlier she had looked like a contrite young housewife over the ruined dinner. The sight of her threatened to captivate him again. To break the spell, he walked around, toying with various kitchen gadgets.

"Thank you for calling me this morning. It was good thinking on your part. I really hadn't kept up with the plans and believed everything was going along fine." Suddenly, her face softened toward him. It made him want to reach out and touch her. He moved away, scared that he'd follow the impulse. "Your calling gave me an idea. Have you ever planned or given a dinner party?"

"Yes, although nothing quite so elaborate."

"Well, how about it?" he said suddenly.

She looked a bit shocked. He hadn't meant to say that, but the idea had come suddenly. Chances were, she thought she was employed by a totally irrational man.

"You were willing to sign on as a housekeeper and cook without the slightest idea of how that was done. Why chicken out now? Most of it can be left to the caterer. Have them prepare the food, set it up, and serve. You can manage that." It was more a challenge than a request, and she caught on immediately.

"Of course I can," she responded. "I can do anything I set my mind to."

"Good, it's a deal. You're in charge," he said.

She hadn't expected him to take her up on it.

"You call the caterers and make the arrangements. By the

way . . . " He paused, reluctant to go on. "You're going to have to play hostess."

"Hostess? But don't you think that's a bit inappropriate?"

"Who else can I find at this late date?"

"How should I know? What about Mrs. McNeil? If I do all the planning, all she has to do is be here."

"The McNeils are having a lot of personal problems, and I can't vouch they'll even attend. So I'm delegating you to fill in. Have someone from the caterer stay to serve and buy yourself something to wear. No one's going to know you're my house-keeper, and if they do, it's none of their business. Actually, it would look better if we didn't mention that. I've decided to take a risk and carry on with this cursed idea, which I was against from the beginning."

He knew it sounded insane, but he wanted this account. And some instinct told him that she could handle it.

The company was owned by three brothers, and one of the partners wanted his company to handle their account. The other two were holding out. Mark's partner, McNeil, had originally made the contact with the company and had previously been very good in dealing with situations such as this. Lately, McNeil was worse than useless.

"Now that it's gone this long, I don't want to cancel. There will be eight attending, and with you and me, that makes ten."

"This is so unorthodox," she complained.

"What's unorthodox about a housekeeper planning a sit-down dinner? You said you'd done it before."

"I've done similar things before."

"So?"

"All right," she agreed.

"You'll also need someone to clean and pick up afterward. Mrs. Young can help you with some of the details."

He decided to leave while he was still ahead, but before that, he pulled out his wallet and laid several hundred dollar bills on the table, saying, "Get yourself something to wear."

"You don't need to do that."

"Take it."

He left quickly after that. The desire to gape at her shorts-clad legs was undoing him. He went and put on his shorts and went running.

In her room, Terry was going through her closet. How annoying the man could be, she thought in a huff, as she jerked garments out, checked them quickly, and angrily threw them into a nearby chair. Had he forgotten that she hadn't been a housekeeper before he'd hired her?

She hesitated over one lovely black silk jumpsuit. It had spaghetti straps and a long tunic jacket. It was several years old, but the classic style made it totally current. She would wear silver earrings and maybe even have a facial. She'd show him.

When she heard the door close, she knew Mark was headed out for one of his incessant runs.

Didn't he ever slow down? Where did he get the energy?

Chapter Five

On the night of the dinner party, all Terry could do was cross her fingers. The doorbell rang. Mark took her hand as they went to greet the first guest. "Okay, Redding, give them that drop-dead smile of yours. That should put them in the mood to buy anything," Mark said.

She hadn't expected him to say anything so flattering. It warmed her so completely that she started grinning immediately at everyone.

Earlier that evening, he'd complimented her on the silk jumpsuit. "That's some outfit," he'd said with a touch of appreciation.

They opened the door to his guests. The clients were two brothers who, when Terry first met them, seemed to resemble two of the Three Stooges. They were dead ringers for Larry and Curly; only Moe was missing. The men's wives were simple, charming middle-aged women.

The family owned a large medical supply business. Mark was interested in subcontracting with this company. A third brother had not come who was preventing them from signing a contract.

When Terry caught sight of Yvette and Makeda upstairs, peeking through the banister at the guests, she smiled. "Come down, you two."

The girls didn't have to be asked twice; they rushed down the stairs, although they were already in their pajamas.

"Oh, what lovely children you have," "Curly's" wife exclaimed. It took about fifteen minutes for the girls to preen and milk all the attention they could from the visitors. Then they went off to bed reluctantly.

When the guests heard Makeda call Terry "Mother," Terry realized they'd automatically assumed she was Mark's wife. She glanced at Mark, wondering how he'd get them out of this mess. Mark didn't correct the mistake.

"Larry's" wife patted Terry's arm. "These are the best years, darling—when you and your husband are still young and the children are going through that adorable stage."

Everyone laughed, including Mark. Terry, who had been ready to make a disclaimer, shut her mouth when Mark frowned ever so slightly in her direction.

Mark spoke up, saying, "Yes, the girls are a pleasure to us. Don't you think so, dear?" he asked Terry.

Terry got the message; he didn't want her to give away that she was just the housekeeper. Going along with the charade gave her a peculiar feeling of being Cinderella for a few moments. Then she shook her head, reminding herself that it was only because Mark wanted her to play hostess to his guests. Still, it did shake her up.

She had to clear her throat before answering a squeaky, "Yes."

Aside from this, the dinner party was off to a good start— much better than she could have anticipated, Terry thought. They were a good group, truth be told. The only people out of sorts were the McNeils.

When the bell rang, Terry went to answer the door, leaving a suddenly alert Mark with the guests. James and Beverly

McNeil stood on the doorstep. They had that unmistakable air of a couple who'd just had an argument. Neither spoke a word to the other.

"Well, hello," James said, eyeing Terry in her sleek black lounging pajamas. Beverly looked her over, too, with a sharp, assessing eye.

James stood about two inches shorter than his wife. He was a little on the plump side, while Beverly was tall and tan and gorgeous. The dress she wore was slashed up almost to her hip and showed a great deal of leg whenever she moved.

Suddenly Mark was there right behind her. "Glad you could make it," Mark said, helping Terry take their wraps. "Terry, here," Mark paused pointedly, waiting for both Beverly and James to understand his words, "my wife—has been very busy with our guests."

Beverly's head turned sharply to look more carefully at Terry.

"Wife?" James's eyes widened as he mouthed the word.

"We'll discuss it later," Mark said.

Both the McNeils turned to stare at her.

"Shall we rejoin our guests?" Mark asked, and herded their little group back into the blue room.

Beverly took to hanging at Mark's side, while James sat next to Terry.

"How do you like the Two Stooges? Any minute, Moe will arrive and start knocking their heads together," he commented *sotto voce* about the guests.

"Shush," Terry hissed at James, surprised he could be so rude—and voice the thought.

It was annoying and unkind. He was at best careless. Terry thought it strange for a businessman to be so flippant that he chanced alienating a potential customer.

James continued, "But seriously, now, wouldn't it be something if brother number three does actually look like Moe?" At that she politely excused herself and went to talk with one of the wives.

Beverly sauntered over. "My, you seem right at home here, and everything looks so cozy. Are you sure you've only just met Mark? You do know that Mark is still very much in love with Marlene, I hope? It would be such a shame for anyone to get involved with him now when he's—what do they call it— on the rebound. If Marlene was willing, Mark would take her back in a snap."

"I'm afraid you're getting the wrong impression here," Terry said, feeling uncomfortable with the woman's manner. "The guests mistook us for a married couple, and Mark doesn't want to explain right now. There's nothing between us."

"Really? Oh, I know you're supposedly just the housekeeper and that you're only filling in for tonight, but I have a funny feeling about this whole thing. There's more here than meets the eye."

After dinner, Mark came and leaned over her. "I'm going to be in the library with the men. Serve our coffee in there."

"Okay," she said, surprised that Mark would participate in such a sexist arrangement but kept her thoughts to herself.

She went to the kitchen to get the Jamaican Blue Mountain coffee herself. It was a special treat that she had found in a shop that catered to Jamaicans living in New York. Terry carried the ornate silver coffeepot and tray into the library.

The men stood up when she entered and were so kind that she felt quite pleased. Mark gave her a look that said he appreciated her efforts.

However, when she poured the man's drinks, Mark said, "No espresso?"

She smiled at him, saying "This is better—I promise."

The men's defection left the women together in the green room for their coffee. When the other wives went to freshen up, Beverly came and sat next to Terry. "I hope you're not upset with what I said. But I do think you should know that you're not Mark's type."

"Mark and I have a strictly business relationship, so I couldn't care less whether I'm his type or not." Although she knew she was being snippy with Mark's guest, there was no way she wanted to listen to anything else Beverly had to say.

Later, after they said their last goodbyes to the guests, "Curly" said to Mark, "Next time, we'll have my older brother. Once he sees what you can do for us, we'll have all the loose ends tied up."

"I'm confident we'll be able to convince him," Mark assured the brothers.

When everyone was gone, Mark walking behind Terry went back into the blue room. There she commenced to collect glasses, which she took to the kitchen. Mark carried a few and followed on her heels.

"Let's leave this for the caterer," he said.

The caterer, who had stayed behind to clean up, took over.

"Pour some more of that excellent coffee and we'll take it in the library," Mark said. They sat on a leather couch, sipping quietly for a moment. Mark appeared to be in an expansive mood. "Things turned out remarkably well."

She smiled at him, saying, "Yes, they did, didn't they?" She felt satisfied with the results and was glad he was pleased, too.

"Tonight's success is due solely to your efforts. You did a fine job stepping in at the last minute."

"Thank you," she said. The praise felt like balm to her.

"I'm sorry about their assuming that you and I were . . . well . . . "

"It's okay," she said. "I'm sure you'll straighten things out. How do you think—the McNeils feel?"

"Hey, they're the ones responsible. If Beverly had done what she'd promised . . . well, what can I expect? She's just like her sister, Marlene."

"You mean Yvette's mother? Beverly never told me they were sisters." Somehow, talking about this dampened Terry's pleasure in her success.

"Yes," he said. Then went on in a different tone, "Sorry

Beverly stuck you with all the work. Both of them—James and Beverly—have other things on their mind, as I'm sure you've noticed. It's distracting both of them."

"Yes, I understand." She knew the couple were having marital problems from talking to Mrs. Dougan.

"I suppose until they . . . um . . . get things settled, they'll both be up in the air." Mark's language was evasive.

Terry suspected that any settling between Beverly and James could easily mean a divorce. That was the impression she'd gotten from the rather glamorous couple. To her, they'd seemed to be on opposite sides of the globe, barely glancing at each other.

"Modern marriages are at an all-time low," Mark said. "People are too self-absorbed to commit to such a contract."

"Contract?"

"That's what marriage is, a contract. Instead, what happens is two people with the hots for each other marry for love. It's a ridiculous situation. At best, it lasts a few years. When it's over, their children are left to live in limbo."

She remembered Beverly saying that he still loved Marlene. She also remembered that she'd heard him say something similar before. The topic was obviously a sore one for Mark. *It's a sore one for me, too.*

Usually, she would have agreed with everything he'd said. However, tonight, she felt sad to hear this. Thoughts of her own marriage flickered into her mind. It had been pure hell. Yet she really wanted to believe that two people could maintain a loving union. Maybe it wasn't for her personally, but she didn't want to believe the whole concept was hopeless.

"I guess you're right," she said, with little enthusiasm.

"You'd better believe I'm right. But if you think marriages can be bad, think of how bad a nasty divorce can be. You're divorced, aren't you?" Mark suddenly asked.

"Yes. But my divorce was amicable," she rushed to say, not wanting to talk any further on that.

"You have no idea how lucky you are," he said.

That was the end of their talk. The caterer soon left, and they said goodnight to each other, going into their own rooms.

Once she was in bed, she lay awake a while, thinking over their conversation. Terry worried, wondering if Mark would regret having said so much to her. Mark had been rather open when they'd sat in the library. She hoped he wouldn't come to regret it.

A few days later, Mrs. Carter, her former landlady, called. "I'm sorry to call so early, but I wanted to catch you before you left the house. Listen, darling, your husband was here last evening, looking for you and Makeda."

"My ex-husband," Terry corrected, knowing it was a waste. Mrs. Carter had unfailingly shown herself to be totally unfamiliar with the concept of divorce.

"Yes, yes, of course," the woman said, and continued, "Well, I did just as you said, I didn't give him your current address, but he looked so hurt and disappointed. I thought he was going to cry about not seeing Makeda."

Yeah, sure, I'll bet. Ronald crying for anyone except himself. Terry was so peeved she could barely restrain herself. It was just like Ronald to play upon the woman's feelings. He was the perfect con artist. If they paid him for his baloney, he'd be a rich man today. But even that really wasn't true, for he'd never be able to keep it up. He was simply too unreliable and undisciplined to do something like even be consistent as a con man.

"Thank you, Mrs. Carter, for not telling him," Terry said. "It's really important to me, and I'll arrange for Ronald to have visitation rights as soon as I can."

Mrs. Carter sniffed in the background as if she didn't believe a word of it. "Well, I only hope you know what you're doing. You modern women don't seem to have a clue to what it takes to keep a man. I lived with my husband for forty years, and when he died the light went out of my life."

It was another of Mrs. Carter's favorite stories, and Terry tried to be attentive, but her thoughts were on Ronald. *All I need is for him to show up here and make a nuisance of himself.* She knew she was going to have to contact her ex—but please, she prayed, not now.

After she hung up, she wrapped her arms around herself. She was angry with Mrs. Carter, but knew that was unfair. What can I say? she thought. Ronald fooled me, too, in the beginning. Memories of the last argument she'd had with Ronald swept through her and she began to shiver in dread. She was glad it was all over, but that didn't stop her from feeling she had failed.

Mark Holden had been right, she thought: marriage *could* be a living hell.

When Mark walked into the kitchen, he saw Terry hang up the telephone. She stretched across the countertop to reach the phone base and he became acutely aware of how sexy such a simple move could be. I've been celibate too long, he thought, with a shake of his head.

He thought she had caught him gaping until he saw that she was more distracted than usual. She hadn't noticed him. His "good morning" caught her unaware, and it seemed she had to come a long way to respond.

The children came in then and swirled around him to sit at the table. They said "Good morning" and went back to chattering as they starting eating.

He picked up his breakfast and said to Terry, "Come into the library. I want to have a few words with you."

Once behind his desk, he motioned her to pull up a chair. He took a few bites of his breakfast and launched into a speech.

"I think everything's working out fine. Yvette has perked up already within what's really only been a few weeks. I guess it's what she needed all along, a feeling of family." Terry had been holding a cup of coffee when he'd said this and he noticed her hand shook momentarily. He realized she had been affected by his using the word "family." "I mean, having more people around gives off a more family-like atmosphere."

"Yes," she agreed, her voice rather low.

He decided to move on. "I think our doing things together is a good idea, things like our shared meal times. It would have been much too artificial to do otherwise. Don't you agree?"

"Yes," she said. He wondered what was going on.

"Also, if it's all right with you, I'd like to order bunk beds for them. That way, they can sleep together, just as if they were sisters. Yvette's room is big enough. They can indulge in all those foolish nights that children seem to love. I want Yvette to have as natural a childhood as possible—considering."

She agreed, but she looked uncomfortable, as if something was bothering her, he thought.

"Plus, we need to finalize some of the particulars for you. We never decided which days you want off. You haven't had a day off since you've been here."

"No." Her voice was almost a whisper, and he had to lean forward to hear her.

"You'll have Sundays off, of course, but I want you to decide what other day would be acceptable. Also, I'll need you to be flexible, as there may be times when I'll have to ask you to change."

"Of course. Umm," she started, but seemed reluctant to speak. "I'd like to have a day off today, if it's all right."

"Of course," he said, but the suddenness of her request threw him off. He sat back. "Going anyplace special?" The question came out before he'd realized it.

"No," was all she said. His antennae went up. Her evasiveness annoyed the hell out of him, though he couldn't for the life of him understand why.

"Well, take the time. I'll pick up the girls, and if I can't stay in tonight, I'll ask Mrs. Young to come over and watch them. She's usually willing."

"I'll pay for Makeda."

"Don't be silly. If I have to pay for Yvette, it won't break the bank to add Makeda."

At first he thought she was going to balk; instead she only took a deep breath. It was the deep breath that did him in. It made her breasts push against her shirt, and his gaze went immediately to them. Of course, that was the moment she chose to look up at him. This time, he thought she caught him.

He quickly glanced away and said, "When do you eat breakfast? You never sit with us in the morning. I hope you're not still starving yourself. Yvette needs a stable environment, not some woman who's going to pass out and scare her out of five years' growth."

He knew he sounded testy and that he'd spoken to keep her from questioning why he was staring at her body. Yet she did get his goat at times. *Why am I worrying about my housekeeper's eating habits?*

Terry squirmed, looking visibly peeved. "I'm in excellent health. You needn't worry about that." She sounded standoffish and self-contained. It only annoyed him more.

"God only knows how you've managed to stay alive when you can't cook."

"I can cook."

"Rabbit food? I don't think much of that."

"Healthy food."

"All right, let's not get on that again." It bewildered him how quickly they'd come so close to arguing. Also, if he was honest, it was his own fault, too. He took a different approach. "Actually, it's Yvette who's my prime concern. Is there anything else you can think of, now that you've had time to observe her?"

Another deep breath, but this time he kept his eyes steadily on her face, with no quick peeks at her heaving breasts. From the glint in her eyes, he suspected she was ready to say what had been bothering her.

"Yes. You've been late coming home almost every day that I've been here. Yvette's got to be very lonely. She's only recently been moved from her mother's house to yours."

"That's what I've hired you to do—keep her from being lonely." He was trying to remain reasonable against what he could see was a hot issue for her. Terry only looked more exasperated.

"You can't expect her to be totally satisfied with seeing only Makeda and myself, much as we've been getting along well. She needs continuity. She needs to see you. Do you think a housekeeper can take the place of her parents?"

Now she was getting to him. He felt attacked. He was doing as well as he could at what was a bad time for him. She made him feel unappreciated, too. He launched into her.

"Do you have any idea how difficult it is to nurture a small business? It's like having a newborn baby! You have to walk the floors at night with it."

She leaned away from his vehemence. Guilt hit him for taking his frustrations out on her. All she'd done was make an observation about his daughter. Heck, all she'd done was act on Yvette's behalf, and he'd reacted as if it was Terry's fault he was under so much stress. She took a while to respond to his statements.

"Well, maybe your business is the newborn, but Yvette shouldn't be neglected just because she's the eldest child." Her remark hit home; he felt like a fool. "If you don't have anything else, I'll check to see if the children are ready for school," Terry said.

He watched her leave. He glanced down at his food and realized that he'd lost his appetite. *Holden, you're a fool. Why are you taking your guilt as well as your sudden lustful thoughts out on that woman?* He knew he'd been out of line. What she'd said was true.

On the way out of the house, he paused. Terry was standing at the door, and Makeda ran up to her to bestow a quick hug and kiss. Then he watched in shock as Yvette ran up to Terry and did the same thing. He'd never seen the child voluntarily offer to touch anyone.

Before Terry could follow them through the door, he stopped her.

"Look," he said, and his tongue seemed to cleave to the roof of his mouth. "I'm sorry about jumping on you this morning. Sometimes I sound more waspish than I mean to." The admission near killed him, but he went on, "You're right. I'll try to get home earlier."

She smiled and nodded, saying only, "Okay." His gut clenched at that smile.

As if that wasn't enough, he added, after clearing his throat, "Feel free to point out anything else you may notice." She smiled again.

On the way to the office, he listened to Makeda's chatter. She was a bright child, full of adventure. He found it hard to believe that this animated child might need heart surgery. He shook his head.

Before he dropped off Makeda, he remembered Terry's request for taking today off. "I see your Mommy's taking some time off."

"Mm-mmm," Makeda murmured, looking through the window.

"Guess she's got plans, right?"

Another "Mm-mmm" from Makeda.

Naturally, he thought, she's stopped chattering just when I want to talk. Kids. It made him smile because he knew he was enjoying every moment of this patriarchal role.

However, he was dying to ask about Terry's plans for today.

Stop picking that child for information, Holden, his good angel said. He sighed and let it go.

After he dropped Makeda off at school, he thought what a nitwit Terry must have thought him when she'd turned around so quickly and he'd been caught staring at her body.

Feel free to talk up whenever you're of a mind, indeed. Feel free to come and sit on my lap, too, I guess is the next thing I'll be babbling. Good God, man, you'd better be careful. You're setting yourself up for trouble. It's a good thing she can't hear me thinking.

But the more he thought about what she'd said regarding Yvette, the more right she seemed. He'd been thinking the same thing lately. He missed the child, but how in God's name was he going to juggle to get home earlier with McNeil not carrying his weight?

Once Terry had delivered Yvette to school, she came back to the house. Remembering Mark's talking about her not eating made her fix a light breakfast. He was right, although she didn't want to admit it. The crazy racing around, finding things for everyone at the same time, took all her attention in the morning. Even Mark had begun to call her for lost items. Eating breakfast in the midst of it was impossible.

She wasn't complaining because she didn't mind it. Actually, she sort of liked it. Usually she would wait until after delivering Yvette to her class before eating.

Now, at nine-thirty in the morning, she sat in the breakfast nook with the newspaper spread out in front of her as she finished her coffee. She felt more like a housewife than a housekeeper. She knew it was because Mark had given her full sway in the house. He never vetoed any of her decisions. He had been patient with her learning to cook, except for the rabbit-food remark.

Fortunately, with Mrs. Young still coming, the cleaning

hadn't been as much of a problem as she'd feared. Also, she had noticed that Mark was sometimes picking up himself. There were mornings when she had awakened, planning to do something that had somehow already been magically corrected. It was as if elves straightened up during the night.

The only thing that made her wonder was the feeling that they were turning into a family rather than remaining employer and employee. She had to keep in mind that the contract was for only a year. The family thing was only an illusion.

An ad caught her attention: *Do you want to walk unafraid through life*? Stupid question, she thought. Of course she wanted to walk unafraid. She read the ad beneath that headline. It was an advertisement for women's self-defense classes. She sat a long time staring at it before getting up and cleaning off the table.

She put everything away, then went to see what her chores for the day were. She had been making list after list the first week she'd come, using the same system here she'd used in her job as office manager. She was getting better at making everything work. Besides, the chores took only a short time. There were days when she felt incredibly lazy and guilty.

Although Mark had said she could take the day off, she couldn't think of a thing to do and was playing with the thought of going along as if it were a regular workday. Then, thinking better of it, she decided to do something just for herself. The last ten months had been difficult ones. She hadn't had time for more than the most rudimentary personal care.

"Why should I go on like a little slavey? Today is just for me."

She put on her Aretha Franklin albums and slathered her face with cold cream. As the music played, she shampooed and set her hair, did her nails, and ran a bubble bath. After she got out of the tub, she did a pedicure, applying bright red polish to her toenails.

In the end, she sat wrapped in a towel under her old, noisy

hairdryer, singing, *"You make me feel like a natural woman . . . "* at the top of her voice when she thought she heard the phone.

Coming out from under the dryer, she nearly knocked it over and almost fell reaching for the phone.

She picked it up. "Hello," she said breathlessly, but couldn't hear a thing over the dryer. "Just a minute!" she yelled into the receiver, and put it down to go turn off the machine.

"Who is this?" a haughty female voice demanded.

Terry suddenly felt herself chilled with only the towel for covering. Some instinct made her keep her voice neutral as she answered, "This is Ms. Redding. May I help you?"

"This is Mrs. Marlene Holden. Mr. Holden's wife."

"Yes, Mrs. Holden," Terry said, trying not to show her surprise. Why, she wondered, was Mark Holden's divorced wife still calling herself "Mrs."?

"You must be the new housekeeper Beverly mentioned."

"Yes."

"Well, answering the phone certainly isn't one of your talents, is it?"

"I'm sorry about that," Terry said. *Instead of staying home, I should have gone to a movie, or something,* she thought.

"Yvette tells me she's helping to cook," the woman said.

"It's just a little activity that the girls like," Terry said a bit lamely. She understood immediately that Yvette was proud of her efforts and wanted her mother to be proud, too.

"Beverly says you played hostess at Mark's last dinner party?"

"Yes" Terry said cautiously.

"Maybe you should remember that I'm still the mistress of that house. It was me who decided upon this trial separation. I need more personal space while I pursue my creative interests."

Sure, I'll bet, Terry thought.

"Mark still loves me as much as he ever did and he's always asking for me to come back," Marlene said.

Now, what does she expect me to say to that, Terry wondered, but said, "Yes, Mrs. Holden."

"I'm telling you this for your own sake. It's never good when servants aren't properly supervised, and I'd hate to see you develop any bad habits while I'm out of the house . . . "

Enough of this, Terry thought, and cut into whatever Marlene would say next. "I'm sure you're right, Mrs. Holden. But Mr. Holden's not in at the moment. Would you like me to take a message?" She was very surprised at how neutral she sounded under the woman's abrasive attitude.

For answer, all she got was the sound of a phone slammed onto the receiver and a dial tone.

"Do go to hell, Mrs. Marlene Holden." Suddenly, Terry had developed a headache.

She thought of what the woman had said. She also remembered the expression she'd caught on Mark's face earlier that morning and realized that the good mood she had been in all day was due to her imagining that Mark's look was an indication of male interest.

Nothing like a man's wife to bring you down to earth.

No more daydreaming about that man. He's not the least bit interested in me. Besides, why should *I* care if he is? I've had men look more interested than that and it never bothered me before. What's different this time? I'm just grateful Mark gave me a job. I've confused my gratitude with my libido! Just like me to make such a mistake. What would I know about libido?

Some perversity made her march to Yvette's room, where she had glanced a photograph of the child's mother. She picked up the framed picture.

Egad! Terry thought. The woman was absolutely gorgeous. There was an obvious resemblance between Beverly and her sister, except Marlene made Beverly look like the ugly duckling in the family. Terry put the picture back carefully and left the girl's room.

Suddenly, on the way down the regal staircase, Terry decided it was pure foolishness to be stuck in the house on her day off. She went in search of the newspaper she had been reading earlier that morning. She had to dig it out of the garbage where she'd thrown it. She smoothed it out to find that ad again.

Yes, she thought, I certainly do want to walk through life unafraid. Of course, the very idea of her doing anything like martial arts was a joke, but, and she thought of Mark and his incessant push-ups, maybe she needed the exercise. It would be nice to have more confidence in her body, too. Before she could change her mind, Terry dialed the number and found there was a class starting that very evening.

Now that she'd made the decision, she felt good about herself again. It was a case of doing something she should have done years ago. She was also pleased to have someplace to go on her day off.

When it came time for her to get dressed, Terry suddenly wanted to look good. I need something for my ego; I'm starting on a new regime. No more being a pushover. A woman who's not a pushover is a woman of power.

That made her smile. She looked in the mirror and flexed a bicep like she'd seen body builders do.

There wasn't much to be impressed with, she realized, but that was all right. Just as her grandmother used to say, "The longest journey begins with a single step." She pulled out a pair of shorts and a t-shirt and packed them in a small totebag. Terry decided on a sleeveless yellow t-shirt over a gauzy print wrap skirt, which would sometimes show a little leg. Finally, she added a pair of sandals to show off her new pedicure.

When Mark walked in, he had the girls in tow. Terry was just getting ready to leave, and she looked breathtaking. The girls ran to her.

"You look super," his daughter said, and he wanted to second that.

"Mommy, you look so pretty," Makeda said.

"Thank you," Terry said, blushing prettily and smiling that delightful smile.

It was hard to say what made her look good. She wasn't dressed the way Marlene or Beverly would have dressed—in some sophisticated haute couture outfit. No, she looked quite simple and natural.

His gaze traveled downward. She had red polish on her toenails. He didn't know what to say. It seemed as if he'd discovered a secret about her.

"Well, are we going to eat?" He had spoken as if expecting her to stay home and cook.

That's when he realized that although it had been him who'd agreed that she should get out of the house, now he didn't want her to go. Not with red toenails.

Aside from the occasional quick glimpse of a slim, shapely leg, she looked quite modest. But all of a sudden his stomach clenched with annoyance. He knew he didn't want her to appear on the street looking like she did. After all, the world was full of crazy people who might not be able to resist a woman with red toenails—like me, he thought.

"Go to that burger joint that you love," she said, and sauntered, hip swaying, back into her room.

"Huh?" He caught on belatedly that she was answering his earlier question. He also knew that she was trying to be snide because she hated it when they ate fast food.

"There's food dished out on the counter. Just put it in the microwave," Terry said.

Mark was no more pleased that she'd prepared food than he'd been before. He followed her voice to her door.

"You know, as a woman, you've got to be very careful, driving alone on these roads." She was looking in the mirror, applying lipstick. The skirt pulled snugly over her hips.

He moved away from the door, and, being very careful not

to look in again, said, "You know, last year there was a man who attacked several women to take their shoes."

"Their shoes?" She looked around, frowning.

"Of course, there are rapists and murderers, too," he said, annoyed because she wasn't taking his warnings seriously enough to suit him.

She seemed to be ignoring him totally as she gave a tug on her skirt.

"Umm, have you decided where you're going?" He felt a complete fool for still trying to find what she was going to do tonight. He knew it was none of his affair. When she glanced disinterestedly at him, he said, "Just in case we need to get in touch with you." *Holden, you're a cad. Are you trying to frighten this woman?* Not that she looked the least bit frightened.

She smiled sweetly at him and said, "I'll only be a few hours." She picked up the totebag.

Suddenly he got unwelcome thoughts of her going to meet some man, and carrying female things like a sexy nightgown. He started beating around the bush, trying to find something to stall her leaving. When all else failed, he said, "I'll carry that," indicating the totebag.

"No, thanks, I can handle it." Terry sailed through the door without a backward glance.

He was miffed when she finally left, leaving him to run everything for the evening. Mark took one look at the food Terry had prepared and sniffed.

"Okay, girls!" He clapped his hands and rubbed his palms together. "What do you say? Shall we have hamburgers?"

"Hamburgers, yeah!" They shouted in unison, and rushed to get sweaters.

Later, sitting in a local fast-food restaurant, Mark watched the girls dig into their hamburgers as if they hadn't had a meal in days.

Humph, it serves Terry right, he thought. She goes out gallivanting, leaving them with me. She knows I'll give them red meat. Next time, she'll think twice before deserting us to go prancing around. Besides, it's dangerous out there.

For some reason, he couldn't eat his food. It sat on the table congealing. He wondered if guilt had made his appetite suddenly disappear.

Later, at home, Mark got serious about his duties as a sitter and became involved with homework. He enjoyed it, much to his surprise.

At bedtime, Yvette came and said, "Goodnight, Daddy." She put her little arms around his neck and kissed him.

"Goodnight, kitten," he said, charmed.

Yvette looked pointedly at Makeda and said, "Now, you. It's easy just do this," and she leaned over to hug and kiss him again.

First Makeda giggled, using a small hand to cover the space where her two front teeth should have been. She then gave him a quick peck. The girls were so adorable that he wanted to laugh.

"We're going to have a problem finding husbands for you two," he said, aiming to sound very serious.

"Why?" they said in unison.

"Because any young men marrying you two will have to be rich."

"They will?" Makeda asked with head tilted.

"Sure. They're going to have to buy teeth for both of you."

"Oh, Daddy."

"Oh, Mark."

They launched themselves at his legs and he went down on the floor as they attacked him for the remark.

After they put him through the obstacle of their multiple glasses of water, followed by an equal number of trips to the bathroom, they settled down in the bunk beds he had bought. When he tucked them in, he thought that Terry had been right. He did need to be home more.

But when he went back into his office, his mood changed and he got very little work done because he kept getting up to look through the windows.

He paced around, knowing that he needed to go for a run, but not wanting to leave the house until she was back. It's not that I'm jealous, he rationalized. It's just that I'm worried about her safety, this being a new neighborhood for her and all. Then his conscious stepped in and said, *Holden, who are you kidding? This is one of the better neighborhoods in New York. You're wondering where she's gone and what she's doing. But more important than all of that, you're wondering who is she doing it with.*

Chapter Six

Terry had been working all day, trying to get the batter to look right. She glanced over at the leftover ingredients, wondering if she had enough to make another attempt.

She'd come in earlier with Yvette following her into the kitchen, where she checked the food again. It was a real mess and it had curdled. Yvette stared into the pot with a funny little noncommittal expression that made Terry want to laugh.

"There's a fungus among us," Terry muttered.

Before she could say more, the phone rang. She picked it up to find Dr. Silvester, Makeda's cardiologist, on the line. Hearing his voice made her heart skip a beat.

"Terry? It's Dr. Silvester. I have good news."

"Yes?" Terry said. Her hands were suddenly icy cold. She trembled, her usual reaction to any calls from the man. She was always ready for the worst. It took a little while for the words "good news" to register.

"I just got Makeda's latest test results, and things are really looking good. Her cardiac condition has improved. Thought you'd want to hear it as soon as I got the information."

"Yes," she said, and breathed a sigh of relief. "Thank you for calling." When she hung up, she felt like a million dollars. She turned around and hugged Yvette.

The child smiled a little tentatively. Terry's gesture had been spontaneous, catching Yvette unprepared. The child still seemed to have some discomfort with people touching her. Then Yvette pointed to the bread that could be seen through the glass door of the oven.

"You're making sweet potato muffins."

Terry was surprised with the girl's knowledge. "How did you know?"

"From Ella," the child answered with a big smile, when she realized that Terry was really impressed. "That's Uncle Barkley's housekeeper. I used to sit in the kitchen and watch her when my mother wasn't there."

Terry suddenly had an image of a lonely little girl who felt welcome only in the kitchen, with the cook. She shook her head, realizing that it was only her own imagination and could be far from the truth.

"Well," Terry said to change the subject. "A good-looking woman who can cook, too."

"I'm not really good-looking," Yvette said very simply. "Marlene is good-looking. I wish I looked like Marlene."

"Marlene?" Terry repeated. It always surprised her to hear the small girl call her mother by her first name. "You never call her Mother or Mommy?"

"Oh, no. Marlene says she's too young to be called Mother." It had been spoken matter-of-factly, as if it was something that had been decided a long time ago. It brought back old memories for Terry. She remembered her own childhood and knew what it was for a child to have a beautiful mother.

Terry put her arm around Yvette's thin shoulders and said, "You're a pretty girl, Yvette, and you're going to be a beautiful woman." Then, feeling inspired, she took down one of the copper pots hanging on a hook over the stove and held it in front of the girl, saying, "See, you're a lovely little girl."

Yvette glanced at the shinning copper reflection of herself, then smiled sweetly up at Terry. Leaning closer to Terry, Yvette looked again.

"You really think so?" the child asked.

"Absolutely! You're very pretty—just the way God wanted you to look."

Yvette's solemn, uncertain expression smoothed out to one of stunned wonder as she once again suspiciously gazed at her reflection in the copper pot.

Terry remembered that her own grandmother had said those very words to her whenever she herself had complained as a child about not being as beautiful as her mother. The budding joy on Yvette's face was worth as much to Terry now as her own joy had been to her at the same age.

Just at that moment, Mark's voice boomed from the door, "Okay, let's shape up. The conquering hero and heroine are here. Where's the food?"

Yvette shot a look at Terry, who in turn shot a skeptical glance at the curdling sauce. "Aw . . . well . . ." Terry started when Yvette piped up.

"It'll be ready in a few minutes, Daddy. Why don't you and Makeda wash up and settle by the table?"

Terry saw that Mark was fighting to hold back a grin at the grown-up way Yvette was instructing him.

Makeda looked curiously from her mother to Yvette. Then, with her inherent intuition, she took hold of Mark's hand and said, "Good idea. Let's clean up." She pulled him from the room.

Terry shook her head, then glanced at Yvette, who was busy mixing ingredients in the very pot she had been studying her reflection in.

"Yvette, what are you doing?"

"Mixing another pot of sweet potato muffins," she said, as if she'd been cooking all her life.

"Do you know what you're doing?" Terry watched in fascinated wonder. *Lord, if this child can do this, why can't I?*

"It's not so hard; Ella showed me."

Terry poked a spoon at the crumbly mess in the other pot. "What do you think went wrong?"

Yvette wrinkled her nose at the pot. "Maybe it cooked too long?"

The two carefully followed the recipe and within ten minutes they had produced a perfect pan of batter that went into the oven.

"That looks mighty good," Mark said later, as he eyed the heaping platter of muffins appreciatively. "I hope it tastes as good as it looks."

"I'm sure it will, especially since Yvette put a lot of loving effort into making it," Terry said.

Yvette looked pleased that Terry had revealed the information. "Terry let me help," Yvette said. "I hope you like it."

"I'm going to love it, Kitten." Then he looked at Makeda and rubbed his hands together. "You ready to dig in?"

"Yeah."

"Terry," Yvette said, "how did your self-defense class go?"

Terry could see Mark's interest perk up. "Self-defense class?" he asked.

She hadn't wanted him to know that her nights out were spent in a class. She enjoyed his being mystified. Oh, well, she thought, and said, "Yes, it's sort of a martial arts class."

"Martial arts?" he spluttered. "For you?" He could barely contain his laughter.

"What's wrong with martial arts, Daddy?" Yvette queried.

"Not a thing, Kitten. It's good for women to have a nice little hobby." He patted Yvette's cheek. His tone was so condescending that Terry wanted to kick him under the table.

However, despite this little incident, dinner went well until the telephone rang and Terry had to excuse herself to answer it. When she heard Mrs. Carter, her ex-landlady, Terry had a sudden premonition. She glanced toward the dinning room, glad that she couldn't be overheard.

"I guess you should know," Mrs. Carter said, "your husband was around again today. He was so full of remorse that it near broke my heart. He broke down and cried when he talked about Makeda."

Crocodile tears, Terry was tempted to say. "Mrs. Carter, I do intend to speak with him as soon as I can."

"He even told me that he still loves you, Terry. And that life without his family didn't seem worth living. I was so afraid for his soul that I gave him your address."

"Oh, no," Terry gasped involuntarily.

Mrs. Carter sounded a bit snippy when she said, "Well, he is the child's father, after all. He said that he had visitation rights mandated by the courts."

Terry was upset enough to want to cry now herself. She didn't even want to think what this could mean.

"Terry?" Mrs. Carter said, when she didn't answer.

"Yes."

"I hope I didn't do anything really bad." Now the woman sounded worried and contrite at the same time.

"It's all right," Terry said, letting the woman off the hook. Mrs. Carter had been so kind to her for so very long. The older woman had a soft heart, and who better than Ronald knew how to take advantage of people by playing upon their sympathies? While Ronald never had any sympathy for anyone but himself . . .

"He seemed so hurt and disappointed. I couldn't help myself."

"I understand." Terry tried to reassure the older woman.

When Terry hung up, the phone fumbled out of her grasp and she looked at her hands to find them moist and slippery with perspiration. Her heart was pounding, too.

She stared out the window, expecting to find Ronald there. He was getting worse. For several years she had not heard from him, and now, he was contacting her all the time.

She rubbed her hands on her jeans, took a deep breath, and went back to the dining room table. Mark glanced up at her when she entered and his face changed immediately from laughing at something one of the girls had said to intense regard.

The last thing she needed was for Mark to get wind of her problems so she tried to smile and look as if she hadn't a care in the world. Unfortunately, he didn't look convinced.

As dinner went on, Yvette and Mark seemed to be doing most of the talking. Yet despite this, Mark also seemed totally aware of everything that went on around him. Terry glanced at Makeda, wondering about the girl's sudden silence, and caught a sad, wistful expression on her daughter's face.

Terry wondered if Makeda ever compared Mark with her own father. Terry's heart squeezed tight and she hated Ronald at that moment. She ached for her child's loss of never having had a caring father as Yvette had. She smiled across at Makeda and the child brightened immediately. Terry had to force her bad feelings away as Mark passed a platter to her. It did no good to wish for what couldn't be, she knew.

Mark had been watching when Terry came back from the telephone and didn't miss how upset she was. Seeing her in that state angered him. He'd been on the verge of demanding she tell him about the call when he'd forced himself to remember that he had no rights over this woman. He'd never thought of himself as a possessive man, but obviously, when a woman lived in his home, he felt territorial about her. At least, he hoped that was all it was.

He wondered if it was a man and had she seen him the other night when she went out.

"Daddy," Yvette touched his shirt, "my science teacher, Mr. Fonda, is getting married."

"Foolish man," Mark said before thinking. "So, do we have homework? As soon as dinner's finished, we'll get with it." He pretended it was a chore, but everyone knew how much he enjoyed doing this with the girls. Certainly they did as they giggled and went for their books.

Since he'd started coming home early, he'd found himself eagerly anticipating this little ritual of assisting the children. To be home meant he had to bring a huge briefcase of work. Also, he had to make many of his calls from the house. Still, so far, the business wasn't suffering because of it. He only wished he could say the same thing about his best friend and partner, James McNeil. But he didn't want to think of that right now. He wanted to enjoy the moment.

That was another new plus about spending more time at home—the quality of his life. He didn't have more hours in his day and was still as harassed as ever, but he'd gained the ability to live in and even enjoy the moments as they came. He had long periods of being caught up in the joy and fun of the present. It was like a gift. Naturally, Redding picked that moment to intrude upon his pleasure.

"You shouldn't turn Yvette against marriage," Terry said from across the room.

The remark sounded like a reprimand. Mark gazed back and was immediately taken with how charming she looked.

"What are you talking about?"

"Don't you want Yvette to have a happy marriage?"

It took him aback. "Any little twerp coming around to mess with my daughter had better be very careful. I'll break his kneecaps."

"Don't you want her to have children? Don't you ever think that you might some day have grandchildren?"

He was startled. Yvette, a woman? he thought. That seemed impossible. True, he liked to tease her about having to marry a rich man who would buy her some teeth, but that didn't mean he really thought she would ever grow up. "I never thought of that," he admitted. "Maybe when I'm an old man."

"How old would you want to be before she gets married?"

"You know. Like when I'm eighty or something. Then I'll be too old to beat her suitors up." He smiled impishly.

"Let me see." She paused to look up as she counted. "If you're eighty, that would make Yvette—fifty-something?"

"For Pete's sake! Do you have to take everything literally?" The woman was always telling him how to be a father. What a nuisance she could be.

"I'm only saying that you don't want to turn her against marriage with your—um—ideas."

"What's wrong with my ideas about marriage? I'm perfectly right, and all you have to do is look around you at all the messy lives to see what I mean. And if you turn on the television, the images of marriages will make you want to upchuck . . ."

At that moment, the girls returned and the conversation dropped, but he did look at Yvette thinking that Terry was right. His daughter wouldn't always be his little girl. Someday she would be a woman.

They paired off as had already become their regular way of handling the children's homework. Makeda was a math whiz and she joined him while Yvette instinctively went to Terry, who knew how to be more patient. His old den took on a cozy warmth. His chest felt tight.

He glanced across the room and deliberately avoided the sight of Terry's legs where they were curled under her. Her skirt rode up. Instead, he allowed himself only to look at the relaxed Yvette. His daughter had actually put on a pound or two on Terry's rather suspicious food.

"Mark?" Makeda's little impatient-sounding voice brought his attention back to her efforts.

"I was paying attention all the time," he said, and smiled as he pulled one of her long, thick braids.

But he found himself looking up again, and this time, his gaze went right to Terry's exposed knees. Sure enough, his pants felt as if they were going to burst.

Some time later, Makeda had finished her homework and Mark knew that he hadn't been as much help as usual because he'd been totally distracted with Terry in the room. One time she'd caught him staring at her and he'd thanked God that his complexion was too dark to reveal the blush. She'd only smiled companionably at him and in her innocence had had no idea that she was sharing that cozy moment with a sex fiend.

Terry simply looked relaxed and happy. Suddenly, it hit him that she was a beautiful woman, that all she needed was to relax and be happy and she would become the truly beautiful woman she was obviously meant to be. But she then suddenly looked uncomfortable with the eye contact and glanced away. He only hoped that she wasn't psychic, because he'd hate to have her read him right at that moment.

When everyone was finished, Mark stayed in his chair until he could get up without telegraphing to everyone what had been on his mind. The really worrisome thing was not that he found Terry Redding attractive; any man would go that far. No, the truly scary thing was that he realized that he was buying into this whole package.

He was enjoying the home cooking, though eating one of Terry's meals was quite an adventure, not to mention the less-than-spotless house. He didn't mind picking up a little, as long as he could have the package, the kids, the shared laughter, the watching the children, as well as admiring Terry's feminine charms. He wanted it all. He'd been dreaming about being a patriarch and having a son.

I must be crazy. Here I am, still daydreaming about the happy family out of the old TV sitcoms. Am I going to get suckered into that crap again? No! The only thing missing is a dog named Fido to bring my slippers and pipe. Well, maybe not the pipe; but the son would sure be nice.

Well, he thought, what's wrong with that? Most men want to settle down at some point in their lives. So, maybe I've finally reached that point at thirty-four. Isn't that why I bought this huge, impractical house? But suddenly, from nowhere, came a really scary thought: for all of that he'd need a wife. How the hell can I have a family without a wife? It was enough to stop those cozy thoughts dead in their tracks.

He glanced at the clock, and realizing that it was still early, he got the idea of calling one of his old girlfriends. Who knew— maybe he could convince one of them to go out for a drink or something. That "something" was really the watchword, he knew. *Well, it's better than sitting here, making mind pictures of Terry, who probably never even had such a thought.*

He walked right past his office, never giving the briefcase a second glance. There was no way he could concentrate with his hormones raging this way. He went into his bedroom, where he picked up his address book and flicked through it. He'd never been good at this dating bit and knew that with the long time that he'd been inactive, he would more likely get turned down. He called an old friend, thinking that she was more aware of the score than most. She never wanted more than he was willing to give.

He was surprised when Nora agreed to have a drink with him and they made plans to meet at one of the local watering holes. Mark was in and out of the shower in minutes, and now something funny occurred. He had been so eager, yet perversely, he now found he didn't want to leave the house. He felt as if by going outside, he was leaving all the warmth and happiness.

But he needed to get out before he started wanting Fido to bring his slippers again. Even the thought that such an idea could have occurred to him was more than he wanted to admit. Mark hurriedly finished dressing and was rushing out when he stopped to tell Terry where he was going.

The three of them were watching television in the den, and once again, he felt drawn to join them. But in the mood he was in, he suspected he'd better keep moving before he made a move on Terry Redding. When she stopped trying to punch his lights out, she'd probably call the police, and truthfully, he wouldn't be able to blame her.

"Eh, Terry, I'm going out for a couple of hours."

He couldn't bring himself to face her. He kept his glance on the girls. He felt that she would know why he was leaving and he wanted her to say something to stop him. But what that could be, he hadn't a clue.

Terry glanced up to find Mark had totally changed his clothes and looked as if he were going to a wedding. From out of the blue, she was really angry. *I sit around here all day, taking care of his child and cooking and cleaning while he goes out as soon as he can. I can smell the damned aftershave from here. He's all dressed up to go out tomcatting, as my grand-mother used to say.*

Even to her, that train of thought was insane. So what if she cooked, cleaned, and babysat? Wasn't that what he paid her for? she reminded herself. But it did little to cool her rising temper.

"Okay," Terry said, and surprised herself by how cool she sounded. Then, to make the act more natural, she forced herself to look at the television, despite the reality of not being able to see anything but red. For some reason, he paused there in the doorway. She wanted to yell and ask him why he didn't leave already. It was a miracle, she thought, that she was able to appear so calm when she was this mad. Am I jealous, she wondered, and then pushed the thought away.

There was no way she was jealous, she decided. She knew the heartache of getting emotionally involved with a man. She had seen her mother turn into a bitter, dispirited woman when she was so young. She had heard many times the lessons that her grandmother taught. And then, despite all that, she had deluded herself and married Ronald. With all those learning experiences, there was no way she was ever going to forget them. No more men for her. She had withdrawn from the fray. If Mark Holden wanted to go tomcatting, let him have a ball.

Finally he left, closing the door quietly behind him. Terry heard his car start and move off. She could barely wait for the end of the show to put the girls to bed. For some weird reason, she felt weepy. I'm tired, she explained to herself. Fortunately, the girls were rather subdued and went to bed without their usual fuss.

"Do you think Daddy will be back?" Yvette said, in a soft little voice.

It made Terry's heart constrict. But in a way, it was actually a good sign. At least the child was becoming comfortable with her feelings. "Of course he will, honey. Your daddy's not going to leave you," she said to reassure the child. When Yvette gave a tired smile and closed her eyes, Terry wished it was as easy to reassure herself.

It simply wasn't working, Mark decided, though he had been the one to call. Nora had agreed, he realized, because she was already planning to go out and didn't want to arrive at the pub without a date. Once they were there, all her girlfriends, those with men and those without, gave him the once-over. The whole thing seemed too predatory and reminded him that this was the reason it was often easy to get a date with these women on such short notice.

One of Nora's friends, a woman who had seemed especially close to Nora, pushed a piece of paper into his hand. When he opened it, he found her address written there.

The guys were even worse, and it gave him a glimpse of how he must have appeared when he was playing this same scene. Their whole demeanor said they intended to go to bed with someone and didn't seem too particular about which of the women it would be.

Yet what had he expected? It was the question he'd asked himself several times that night. For Nora did invite him home after a few drinks and he'd demurred, saying something about having to get up for work the next morning. I must be nuts, he kept thinking, but he'd refused.

He didn't feel too pleased with himself as he entered his house. He stood there in the foyer listening, but the lights were out and from the silence he knew that everyone had already retired. He peeked in on the girls and chanced a light kiss on Yvette's brow. Both children were breathing deeply with their own little-girl dreams. He regretted having gone out earlier, wondering what he'd missed.

At Terry's door, he'd wanted to go in but knew it was an insane gesture. Was was he going to kiss her brow as he had Yvette's? Not likely, he knew. Instead, he listened, wondering if he'd hear her breathing. But this was crazy, he warned himself, and left to enter his own room.

Terry had lain awake for several hours after Mark had left and for some reason, she thought about Ronald. She remembered how full of ideas she'd been when Ronald had proposed. She had wanted to believe that despite all she'd seen to the contrary, she could make a happy marriage with Ronald. He'd been full of promises, too. She'd even helped him finish school. But Ronald had only used her. She still believed in love and marriage. She still considered it a sacred trust but had long ago decided it was not for her.

A few hours later, Terry heard Mark come in. Despite her anger, she had waited for him. She kept imagining how he could go off the road and into a ditch. But such thoughts only made her temper worse. Once again, she was tempted to go out and confront him, only she couldn't think of any reason for why she was so angry. Instead, now that he was home, at least she could stop worrying and turn over and go to sleep.

She heard him when he came and stopped outside her door. She held her breath, wondering why he waited there so long. The temptation to get up and see what he wanted was quickly quashed. Some instinct made her wait too long, and soon he was gone.

She sighed heavily and turned over to sleep. That's when she realized that she wasn't really angry anymore. He's a grown man, she thought, and he has every right to go out whenever he wants.

What's wrong with me, she wondered, just before sleep claimed her.

Chapter Seven

Mark was late that morning and Terry was already in the kitchen. She heard him go outside for his jogging. Even that annoyed her this morning. How could any one man have that much energy? she wondered. When he came back, he went to his room to shower and dress.

She had been debating with herself all morning. Her reaction to Mark's going out last night worried her. She was aware of how grateful she felt toward him as her new employer. Because of the steady employment and the excellent salary, she had made a great deal of progress in paying off her bills. Plus, she was still able to put away a little for necessities when Makeda went into the hospital. It was expected that she would be grateful to him for this.

However, what she'd felt last night was not gratitude. She'd been enraged.

I am not jealous. I've never been jealous in my life—not even of Ronald. So why, she wondered, had Mark Holden's going out upset her so much?

The girls had already eaten when he came into the kitchen

with a paper under his arm. He was fully dressed with tie in place. She was carrying the girls' dishes to the sink and they almost collided. They moved gingerly away from each other and then circled to stay out of each other's way.

She couldn't for the life of her understand why she was so angry with him. He had every right in the world to go out anytime he wanted, she told herself. *And I shouldn't care.* So why, she wondered, did she want to throw things? At the very least, she wanted to cry.

" 'Morning," he mumbled, not meeting her eyes.

" 'Morning," she said back. He looks guilty as hell, she thought. *Anyone could see what he'd been up to last night.*

She put the dishes into the sink and they made a loud clattering sound. Mark never seemed to notice, for he had the paper up in front of his face. Her anger increased by leaps and bounds and she wanted him to know exactly what she thought of him.

She set the bowl of cereal down in front of him with another bang. This noise was not as satisfyingly loud as the dishes had been. He looked around the paper and scowled when he saw the cooked oatmeal. He had the nerve to glance up at her with an annoyed expression. It only made her foul mood worse.

"Why can't we have bacon for breakfast?" he asked.

"We had it yesterday."

"I like bacon." He sounded particularly sarcastic, as if he were talking to a moron and the effort exhausted him. She wished she could dump the cereal into his lap. "Is there any reason that we can't have it two days in a row?"

"No, of course not." She went and opened the fridge with such force that it swung back, hitting the edge of a table. "Not if you want your arteries strangulated," she muttered.

"Did you say something?"

"Me? Of course not."

Out of the fridge came the box of eggs and a package of bacon. She slammed the bacon on the wooden cutting board and reached for a frying pan. She made certain to create a clamorous rattling of cookware before she was satisfied.

At first, she thought Mark hadn't noticed the noise as he didn't move from behind his paper. The *Wall Street Journal,* naturally, she thought. Then he put the paper down and very carefully folded it into quarters.

"Never mind," he said, standing up and leaving his cereal untouched. He tucked the paper under his arm and stalked out, saying, "It's too late."

Somehow he managed to sound like the perfect wounded victim. She didn't turn as he left the kitchen. Staring down at the pan still in her hand, she wondered what he would say if she ran after him, threatening to bang him with it. Then tears stung the backs of her eyes and she had the most ridiculous urge to cry.

I don't care if he goes out every night. It doesn't mean a thing to me.

Later, on their way out the door to their respective cars, they once again almost collided. Both muttered hasty apologies without making eye contact.

"By the way," Mark said, still not quite looking at her, "I'll pick both girls up this afternoon, as I have to leave early anyway."

"All right," she answered sullenly.

Makeda had already shot past them to get in Mark's car. Yvette was following behind Terry. Mark moved down the walkway, and despite her foul mood, she stared at him, mesmerized by his long, loose stride. *That man has the sexiest walk I've ever seen,* she thought.

Yvette touched her hand. "We're going to be late, Terry."

Terry realized that she had stopped in the doorway to watch Mark. Acute embarrassment hit her. She didn't want Yvette to see her gaping like a schoolgirl with her first crush.

"Oh," Terry gasped, and started rummaging in her purse. "I was wondering if I forgot the house key."

Yvette stared after her father's back before turning with a quizzical expression to Terry. "Do you like my Daddy, Terry?"

It took Terry aback. She was quite shocked at the child's prescience. "Well, of course, I do, honey. Your Daddy's a fine and admirable man."

"No, I mean . . ." Yvette's voice trailed off and she seemed to think about what she wanted to say for a while. Finally, she finished by saying, "Never mind, it's not important."

Any other time, Terry knew she would have encouraged Yvette to share the thought—but not today. She was afraid of what the little girl would say. They went down to the car and on to the school.

After dropping Yvette off, Terry stopped off at the store to pick up the supplies she would be needing for the day's menu.

She also did something she hadn't done in over a year— look at clothes. She stopped at an upscale department store in one of the nearby malls. Just being inside the store was a treat. An expensive perfume permeated the air. Temptingly displayed colognes, make-ups, and lotions were stationed right near the doorway.

Terry walked around, looking at everything. However, she did not buy anything at that moment. My money situation may be better, but it's not that much better, she reminded herself.

After looking her fill, she took the escalator to an upper floor. She didn't hesitate because she knew exactly what she was going to buy—a new pair of sandals. Something super-sexy, with leather thongs. Just for wearing in the house, she thought. It might be a bit too much to wear in the street. She told herself this had nothing to do with Mark. *I am not trying to compete with his women, either.* She wasn't too sure about that last thought.

As she paid for the sandals, she glanced at her watch. Terry rushed home after that. She had a lot of things to do.

Today was going to be the day she would become serious

about all her plans. Excitement coursed through her and she felt the adrenaline pumping.

First, she dusted, going quickly from one room to the next. Recently, she'd had the distinct impression that Mark was sneaking around, straightening the house behind her. It had to be the most insane idea she'd ever had, but there it was. She was determined to make everything gleam.

In Mark's rooms, after dusting and running the vacuum cleaner, she quickly cleaned the bathroom. She went to remove the dirty clothing.

A woman's perfume assailed her nose when she opened the hamper in his bathroom. "Humph!" She slammed down the top and crossed her arms over her breasts. A sudden rampaging fury almost overcame her. She relieved herself by angrily snatching up his clothes. She held the things gingerly away from her as she walked quickly to the washroom. There she dumped his things unceremoniously into the washing machine. She remembered his going out the night before.

"Deserting poor Yvette," she said aloud. Well, it was true—Yvette didn't seem overly damaged by his night out—but it was the principle that counted. *I couldn't care less what he does. Wouldn't you think he'd have outgrown the need to run out in the night, looking for women? And there's no way I'm going to believe that's not what happened.*

When the house was finished, she did her defense workout. She had one class a week and was faithful about exercising on the days she was free. It was quite satisfying to imagine that it was Mark she was kicking and punching.

"Imagine how he spoke to me this morning," she said, with a vicious side kick. "And *he* had the nerve to be in a bad mood" was done with a one-two punch, arms held straight and strong. "As if he hadn't been out all night, doing only God knows what" was accompanied by a chop to the Adam's apple.

After exercising, she showered and put on a pair of shorts that were particularly flattering and her new thong sandals. A glance in the mirror and she set her hair, feeling foolish for the gesture.

When all this was finished, she took out a videotape she had recorded from a cooking show. She unhooked one of the VCRs from the den and lugged it into the kitchen. Unfortunately, it seemed to take hours to hook the thing up so that it would play, and she kept glancing at the clock, fearful that she wouldn't be finished before picking up Yvette.

The recipe was for Zairan spinach in tomato sauce, and they would have Jamaican Blue Mountain coffee after dinner. That stopped her for a moment. After-dinner coffee with just her and Mark? Maybe that wasn't such a great idea. But despite her doubts, suddenly, her imagination just carried her away and she was staring off into space. Crazy romantic images of herself and Mark Holden plagued her.

"Are you crazy, girl?" she muttered, and shook her head. "You need to find something to do with yourself."

"Yoohoo!" a woman's voice sounded outside the back door. Terry opened to find the next-door neighbor, an older woman with fully made-up face and a silk scarf over her hair. The woman wore bright hot-pink eyeglasses with rhinestones and peered at Terry over the tops. "Darling, I'm Mrs. Merkle. Can you help me? I've run out of sugar." She held out an empty cup.

"Oh, certainly." Terry opened the door, beckoning the woman to come inside. She took the cup and filled it.

When she turned around, she found the woman nosily peeking around.

"I've been meaning to come over ever since you came, but I thought I'd let you settle in first." With this, Mrs. Merkle plopped down into a chair.

"Please come anytime. I'd enjoy the company," Terry said. "Would you like some coffee?" Terry poured two cups at the woman's okay.

"This is good," the woman said after her first sip. "As I was saying to Mr. Merkle, it's about time Mark got someone in this big house. He's been alone too long. You know, his wife walked out on him right after he bought this house."

"Oh?" Terry said, knowing that she was deliberately encouraging the woman to gossip about Mark.

"I felt so sorry for the poor man. He looked so lost. But now, with you here, I guess that will all change." She eyed Terry over her hot-pink eyeglasses.

"I'm not Mark's . . . um . . . I mean, I'm just the housekeeper."

"Sure, darling, I know that. Isn't it just like that old book? You know, Jane Eyre and that Rochester man?" Terry started sputtering when she swallowed the coffee too fast. Mrs. Merkle jumped up spryly and ran around the chair to pound Terry vigorously on the back. "You want me to do the Heimlich maneuver?" Mrs. Merkle asked, still banging away.

"No!" Terry managed to say, as she tried to dodge the woman's powerful thumping.

Mrs. Merkle's rescue efforts didn't interfere with her chatter. She was still pounding away when she asked, "Ain't that Mark a handsome devil, though? I wouldn't mind being his housekeeper, myself. Every morning, I watch them gorgeous legs when he takes his run. I just love them shorts he wears."

"Please, no more," Terry managed to gasp, when she finally escaped the woman's pounding her on the back. Terry stood up and took several deep breaths as she twisted her body, testing if the woman had broken any bones.

"My, you're looking pretty today," Mrs. Merkle said, eyeing Terry's legs in the shorts and thong sandals. "Funny, though, you're not like the other women he's brought home."

"Other women?" Terry couldn't help asking, while she got into a contortionist position, trying to rub her own back.

"Yeah. They never stayed overnight, though. They were all so sophisticated looking. But I guess I should have expected him to pick one like you. You look like the marrying type."

Terry bumped into the table, almost upsetting both coffee

cups. "I really must get back to work," she said, trying to encourage the talkative elderly woman to leave.

"Don't you worry, darling. After Yvette came, he didn't bring them other women home anymore, and now that you're here . . ."

"Really, Mrs. Merkle, my employer's personal life has nothing to do with me," Terry said. It took several moments before Terry was able to get the woman out.

As Mrs. Merkle was leaving, she turned and said, "Oh, by the way . . . I wanted to warn you, there's been a strange man wandering around lately. Be careful. I've already told the security people."

Once Mrs. Merkle had gone, Terry leaned on the door and took a deep breath. "Whew. I'll bet she didn't need any sugar, either." She peeked through the curtains, watching the woman enter her house. "Just wanted to rake me over the coals." When Terry returned to the cooking, she couldn't help wondering about those "other women."

Mark had driven to Makeda's school and turned off the ignition to wait for the child's dismissal. He took the time to examine something that had been troubling him since last night. All day, he had been keeping his troubled thoughts at bay. Now that he was alone in the car, his mind wandered back to his latest dilemma, Terry Redding. He wondered what to do. He knew now that she was definitely trouble. *Should I let her go?*

He was not the least bit interested in letting his hormones get him into another bad deal. He thought about all her virtues and wondered if maybe he was wrong about her not being his type. No matter. Having an attractive woman living in his house was clearly disruptive.

He couldn't just fire her. She was good for Yvette and he couldn't let her down with Makeda needing the health insurance. "It's more icy showers, Holden, my man," he said, just as he spotted Makeda walking toward him.

As soon as he and the girl entered the house, Makeda went up the stairs and he could hear the girls greeting each other. He'd decided to come home early because he'd finished all his calls early. He'd been so jumpy and frustrated at the office that he figured he'd get more done at home.

The aroma of food cooking hung in the air, drawing him toward the kitchen. He loosened his tie as he went to tell Terry that he was home.

He had just walked through the doorway when he saw her. She was bent over in what should have been an awkward position, but on her, it looked incredibly graceful and sexy. She was searching in the cabinet under the sink.

Water was running in the sink, and obviously she hadn't heard him come in. The kitchen showed signs of her having been very busy, probably working all afternoon on one of her gourmet concoctions. She persisted in these efforts no matter how many times he suggested she stick to more simple fare.

She was wearing shorts again and a pair of sandals with cords that wound up her shapely slim legs. The sight of her shapely body made his groin ache. He had a sudden, powerful urge to touch her and almost reached out when he came to his senses and caught himself. He began to back out of the kitchen.

Terry picked just that moment to turn around and looked near ready to jump out of her shoes at finding him there. The rubber kitchen gloves she held fell to the floor as she covered her breast with one hand. "Oh! I wasn't expecting you home so early," she said, clearly flustered at finding him there.

"Sorry I startled you," he said, feeling like a fool. He prayed his jacket hid his arousal.

She made useless feminine gestures at her hair, which appeared to be rolled onto something underneath a colorful scarf. He could see that his catching her without her hair combed embarrassed her. It was incredibly endearing and he wanted to smile but didn't.

"I was looking for gloves so I could rinse the dishes," she explained unnecessarily.

Then she tilted her head and looked at him as if puzzled. He feared she had sensed how jumpy he was. And his continuing to stand there was making it worse. Now it was his turn to feel embarrassed. This is going to take a really cold shower, after at least a five-mile run, he thought.

"I . . . ah . . . came in to tell you I was home, but when I saw you were busy, I thought I'd leave it until later."

"It's all right. I shouldn't be bending over, anyway. Bad for your back."

"Uh, yeah," he could barely take his eyes off her.

Suddenly they both realized that the gloves were still on the floor and almost touched as they bent to retrieve them. It seemed unusually quiet as they both sat on their heels gazing at each other. He handed her the gloves. When they stood up, she toyed with the gloves, finding a hole in one finger. She turned to do the dishes without them.

He saw her lovely hands were newly manicured and spoke before he thought of how foolish he would sound. "I'll do them," he offered, indicating the dishes.

"What?" she seemed shocked at the idea. "Oh, no." She shook her head. "I'll do them."

"It doesn't matter if I get dishpan hands," he said. "Only a beau . . ." He stopped and then rushed on, "Only women worry about things like that."

He was coming unglued, he thought. He had started to call her a beautiful woman. What would she have thought if he hadn't stopped himself? But she *is* lovely, he thought. The longer she was there, the prettier she appeared to him. He wondered if it was his imagination. It's probably because she's more relaxed now, he thought. Some of her worries have been taken care of.

He remembered her saying that Makeda's recent test results were better than anyone had expected. Also, with the new income, some of her worries about money had eased. She had more time to care for herself. He was proud that he could do this for her.

Suddenly, he didn't want to leave. The run and shower could wait, he decided. He took off the lightweight jacket, throwing it over a chair in the breakfast nook. He busied himself by looking in the fridge. He poured some juice and sat down.

He wanted to stay in the kitchen, where the aroma of food cooking made his mouth water, but he knew that he wasn't only hungry for the food. Terry Redding had the power to create an even more powerful hunger.

Besides, with Terry, you couldn't always depend on the food. She was determined to make gourmet meals, and sometimes they might smell great but be inedible. He couldn't have cared less. However, he had to admit that lately, her cooking was definitely getting better.

He sat so he could watch her without being too obvious. Though he was terribly distracted by the shorts, he couldn't help notice that this time she had painted her toenails in a multicolored pattern. He was dying to take a good look but didn't want her to know how fascinated he was with everything about her.

He had been tense about the business when he'd come in and now he was still tense, but it had nothing to do with the business anymore. Just seeing her made him forget everything else.

"How are things going at the office?" she asked.

He shrugged. "About as well as I can expect."

"Beverly calls now and then. When James doesn't come home on time. She seems to feel there's another woman."

"Who knows? But I wouldn't take her word for it. Women always blame other women."

"And they're often right," she responded.

Mark finished off the juice and went for another. "Maybe." He shrugged again.

He has to be tired, Terry thought, after one quick glance his way. Mark kept a killing pace. Yet it never seemed to bother him. Her heart went out to him, and suddenly, she wanted to take him by the hand and lead him to a comfortable chair. The unbidden thought had come from nowhere. *And then, I'd sit on his lap and we'd have mad, passionate sex.*

It made her smile, but she forced herself from even thinking about such a thing. She'd been having increasingly more fantasies about the man and it was insane to encourage such thought.

She settled for a simple, "Things work out," and turned back to the dishes.

Mark had noticed her quick glance at him and sat to watch her again, thoroughly enjoying the view. She seemed totally unaware of how beautiful she was. Her movements were no-nonsense and without artifice, something he thought rare in many other women. Suddenly, he had a fantastic idea. Was she doing all of this beauty ritual just for herself—or maybe for him? The idea was incredibly arousing.

The erotic images were so disturbing that they drove him to stand up and pace. When he realized this wasn't helping, he abruptly walked out of the kitchen. He saw her startled, confused face before he left, but didn't stop.

He went into his bathroom and took a cold shower. Later, he sat in the library and started going through some papers. Unfortunately, he couldn't concentrate any better here than he had at the office. He heard her banging pots around in the kitchen. God, the woman managed to make more noise than any two other people.

Annoyed, Mark stormed into the kitchen to see what the problem was. When he got there, Terry turned and glared at him. That irresistible urge to touch her returned, and he found himself slowly moving closer. He had no idea what he would do, once he was near enough to touch her. His mind started sending alarm signals. It was as if someone was saying, "Don't do it, Holden." But he kept advancing toward her. Her eyes had grown large and luminous, and her lips opened a tiny bit.

He had reached out to her, his hand landing upon her shoulder. He ached to hold her.

"Hello, anybody home?" It was a man's voice from outside.

Terry jumped away and from the expression on her face, he understood that she knew who the caller was. He also saw that she was quite frightened. Sight of her fear made his hackles rise. Adrenaline pumped, and he was instantly ready to fight.

He turned to confront their visitor.

Terry, however, moved away from him as if she had been caught doing something wrong. It brought him back to reality with a bang. He sensed that much of her fear was that she didn't want this man, whoever he was, to see them together. It had all happened within a split second and his stomach clenched with jealousy.

This is crazy, Mark thought, forcing himself to unclench his fists. *I have no claim on this woman.* He moved away and they both watched the door as footsteps foretold that someone was walking up the short flight of steps outside the back door.

It seemed to take forever for the thin, haunted-looking man to come into view through the screen door.

Despite his efforts to calm his temper, Mark was still a bubbling caldron of anger. He felt territorial and was still spoiling for a fight.

One look at Terry's face and he knew he had been right. She recognized the man. After one quick, guilty glance at him, she went to open the door.

The man glanced sneakily at Mark and said, "Hello. I knocked at the front, but when no one answered, I thought I'd try the back."

"Is that what you thought?" Mark worked to sound noncommittal, but he couldn't keep all the anger out of his voice. He also couldn't seem to help taking an instant dislike to the man, but he was determined to act cool and civilized.

"Hello, Ronald," Terry said, and she seemed more composed now.

Terry glanced at Mark with a strange unreadable expression. The man, Ronald, glanced at him, too. Mark had the urge to take this Ronald by the seat of his pants and hoist him out the door.

Mark at the very least wanted to remain in the kitchen and scope out the man, who he didn't trust. Instead, he took a deep breath. *Holden, leave these people alone—before you land in jail.* Listening to his good sense talking, Mark picked up his jacket, saying, "Call me when dinner is ready." He had to force himself to leave while the man remained in his kitchen with Terry. It wasn't easy.

"What do you want?" Terry demanded of Ronald, once Mark had gone. She spoke in a hasty whisper. She stared nervously at the door Mark had just disappeared through. She had been petrified that Mark wouldn't leave, and the last thing she wanted was for him to talk to Ronald.

"Can't a man visit his wife and daughter?" Ronald glanced smugly at the empty door where Mark had exited.

"I'm not your wife. We've been divorced for six years."

"Whatever you say, baby."

Rage streaked through Terry, leaving her shaky. Much of it she turned on herself, and she fought to hold her tongue. She knew she couldn't antagonize Ronald. There was no telling what he'd do in retaliation. She wasn't so much afraid of what he'd do right now, since Ronald was in truth a coward; he wouldn't do his dirty work in front of a witness. His whole behavior in front of Mark was pure bluff. She knew Ronald would never want to get on the bad side of someone like Mark. She felt so frustrated, she wanted to scream.

Ronald moved outside the kitchen once and glanced around to see if Mark was there before going to check the green room.

"Don't go in there," she said, trying to bar his way.

He pushed her aside, but not with any force. She didn't want to make a scene because she didn't want to alert Mark. She would have died with shame if Mark had witnessed the scene between her and Ronald. She felt as if Mark would find her contemptuous if he knew the truth. Terry couldn't bear for Mark to lose respect for her. People were usually critical of women like her. There would be little sympathy for her. Besides, the last thing she needed was for Mark to pity her.

Ronald walked around the room, observing things there. She was stiff with tension and laced her fingers together. Within seconds, they felt locked in that position. Ronald stood in front of an original painting which hung on one wall. Several moments passed before his attention moved on. He hefted an antique piece of crystal as if gauging its weight. She took it out of his hand.

"Don't touch that," she snapped. The fact that she was whispering made her lack authority. Ronald paid her no attention. He was probably only too aware that she didn't want Mark to come.

She didn't like the strange expression on his face as he walked around looking. He appeared to be both admiring and predatory.

"What's this guy do?" he asked, sounding speculative.

"Why?" she demanded.

"I could always ask him," Ronald said. "He and I could have a really nice conversation. Don't you think?"

"He owns a business," she said. She didn't believe for a moment that Ronald wanted to talk to Mark but she wouldn't take any chances. All she wanted was for him to leave.

"Humm. Very interesting," Ronald replied.

He didn't stay long after that. Not once had he repeated his earlier remark about wanting to see Makeda although, once at least, he must have heard the girls playing upstairs. She didn't remind him.

Ronald looked around hastily and then said in a low voice, "Let me have a few bucks."

"Why are you always asking me for money lately?"

"You know—times are hard."

"They're just as hard for me. I have to take care of Makeda, too."

"Why not ask your boyfriend?"

"He's not my boyfriend. He's my employer."

"Yeah, sure. Just like a woman, you always land in clover."

"I'm not going to argue with you over this. And please don't come here anymore. This is my job, and I can't entertain visitors." She'd said it to discourage his coming back.

"I got rights. I'm Makeda's father."

"You only remember that when it's something you want. You can see her today, but we'll have to make other arrangements next time."

Suddenly, Ronald glanced upward at the sound of the girls playing upstairs, and he seemed more jumpy.

"Not today," he said. "We'll arrange something another time." He appeared anxious to leave.

The visit had apparently been prompted primarily by his curiosity. Before leaving, Ronald managed to bully her out of a few dollars.

Soon after Ronald departed, she heard Mark bang out the door in his running clothes. He was off down the street with no further ado.

She had forgotten about the dinner while Ronald was there. She rushed in to check upon it. After having planned and worked so hard, now it was overcooked. She was furious and threw the whole thing into the trash. Lord, how she wished she could toss Ronald into the garbage, too. And that's when she remembered the peculiar scene just before Ronald came.

She had been standing in the kitchen and Mark had touched her. This was something that had never happened before. It had been a riveting moment. She had thought he was going to kiss her. She had been prepared, eager for him to do so.

Now she wasn't so sure. She had been fantasizing so much about the man that she probably imagined the whole thing. How would she ever know?

If Ronald hadn't shown up when he had, it was quite likely she'd have thrown herself into Mark's arms. Wouldn't that have been a mess? Here I am, after all this time of believing I would never look at another man, and what do I discover? *That I have a sex drive.* I am not going to allow myself to fantasize about him anymore. It's too dangerous. Under no circumstances will I allow myself to fall for him. I would be the one hurt in the end.

Still, why *had* he put his hand on her shoulder?

As Mark was running down the street, his mind was busy with some very disturbing thoughts. Somehow, despite all his best efforts, he had been unable to wash his hands of the man who had come to visit Terry—her Ronald. He had waited until Ronald had left.

Once the man was gone, Mark had allowed himself to escape quickly. Now, some minutes later, he was still trying to make sense of the whole incident. Usually, running would clear his mind of problems, but somehow, today it hadn't worked.

There had been a sleazy quality about Ronald that Mark knew he wouldn't have liked even under better circumstances. Mark couldn't understand what Terry saw in the man. Then he stopped that path of thought as he was judging only by his own hunches. There might be nothing wrong with the man. My jealousy may be clouding my reasoning.

On the other hand, I should get down on my knees and thank him. Mark was only too aware that had they not been interrupted, they might have moved into some very troubled waters.

It just goes to show—never let your guard down around a woman, he thought. *What am I going to do?* It had come too close. *How can I be sure it won't happen again, and this time, with no Ronald to save us?*

Chapter Eight

A week later, Mark had barely seen Terry since Ronald had walked in on him only seconds away from kissing his housekeeper. Mark was trying to stay away from her in keeping with his recent decision to squelch any blossoming attraction to the woman. He'd learned in the meantime that Ronald was Terry's ex-husband.

That night, during the first homework session in a week, the girls had decided to change their usual system. This time, Makeda sat with Terry, while Yvette went to Mark, as if each wanted attention from her own parent for a change.

For Mark, these hours were still a period when his eyes would keep straying to Terry. Lately, she'd taken to sitting with her back toward him. Unfortunately, it didn't help. Now that he couldn't look at her legs, he'd discovered her derrierè. It was round and shapely, and sometimes he found himself staring. Tonight he was definitely having one of those moments.

"I need to study my spelling words, Daddy. Will you listen to me?"

"You bet, gorgeous," he answered, and felt his heart warm with the big smile that spread across her face.

He was happy to see how well she did. She'd always been an excellent student, but now she seemed to fly. Most of the spelling words came from a story about ancient Egypt, which was their current topic in class. Afterward, Yvette seemed to want to spend time with him, and indeed, he was terribly reluctant to release her. In the past, she would never have sought him out this way, and it was a rare treat, each moment of closeness.

"Daddy, do you like Terry?" Yvette asked.

"Huh?" he said, feeling incredibly stupid. He glanced hastily across the room at Terry, who looked as embarrassed as he felt.

"I said," Yvette went on, as if he hadn't heard her.

"Uh, yes, of course, I do. Terry is a fine woman," he said in a strangled-sounding voice to keep Yvette from repeating the question. Makeda glanced up at him and then a strange look passed between the girls.

"I see you're learning about ancient Egypt," he said, trying desperately to change the subject. "I loved learning about it when I was younger."

He was glad when his small child let him off the hook by saying, "Did they have ancient Egypt in the old days, Daddy?"

The tension in the room was dissipated quickly when he and Terry laughed. Terry turned to look at him and their gazes locked across the room. As the light touched her, it made her slightly mussed hair appear red. Her eyes seemed to be lit from within and appeared like precious stones—garnets, he thought. Her innocent looking t-shirt pulled across her breasts, outlining them. His mouth went dry and all thought of laughter fled.

Clearly, she saw something in his face if her suddenly strained expression was anything to go by. Probably his lust, he surmised, as she hastily turned back to what she had been doing. He ached with the loss that the broken contact caused.

When he turned back to Yvette, he didn't know what to say, but the child didn't seem to have noticed his momentary lapse and continued in her little-girl chatter. Also, considering her earlier question, he was once again in the debt of his small daughter.

"Then we went to the museum and saw how they lived. All their things had holes, Daddy. Were they poor?"

"No, honey," he answered, dragging his attention away from Terry. "But they lived a long time ago, and all the things that we have of theirs are old."

"Terry's going to take us again. She said we need to learn about the grand history of Africa." The last few words were obviously parroted.

He glanced across at Terry, but she didn't look back at him. Now he was ashamed, wondering if she had read his thoughts. Thoughts aren't illegal, he reminded himself—are they? *Keep it up, Holden and you'll soon know.*

"Why don't you come, too, Mark?" Makeda, who had been listening from across the room, asked.

"Huh?" his thoughts jerked back to the present.

"Please come, Daddy." Yvette begged. "Don't you think my daddy should come too, Terry?"

"Yes, you should come." Terry looked up at Mark but turned away shyly after a few seconds.

"I'd be honored to accompany three such lovely ladies."

This little sally brought giggles from the girls, but Terry only started collecting Makeda's homework and packing things up.

He wished she would prepare a cup of Blue Mountain coffee or make tea in the silver server as she sometimes did. He didn't have his hopes up. The way she had responded when Ronald was there made him wonder if she'd be uncomfortable having coffee with him. She might feel it was too intimate.

Terry and the girls were almost already out of the house that next Saturday. It was a delightful day, slightly cooler than it had been during the week. It was the day they had planned going into Manhattan to the Metropolitan Museum of Art. Just as they were almost out the door, the phone rang. Mark went to answer. Terry had been tempted to suggest that he not pick it up.

After hanging up, Mark gazed at each of them, saying, "I'm sorry, I'll have to cancel. That was the Three Brothers company. They want to meet me at the office this morning."

"No," both girls said together.

"Daddy, you never go with us," Yvette pouted.

Mark looked guiltily from one to the other. "Honey, I have to make this presentation. You remember the two men who came to the dinner party? Well, they've convinced their brother to talk with me, and after all this effort, I'd hate to lose the account."

"Daddy, tell them you have an appointment with us!"

Mark smiled at the girl. Though Terry smiled with him, she hated to admit it, but she was as disappointed as the children. She knew the problem. The client was a large company owned by three brothers. While Mark had wooed the first two brothers, the third partner hadn't been convinced. He was satisfied with their old vendor, though its services were inferior to those of Mark's company. He didn't know Mark or Holden-McNeil.

"You can't phone and reschedule? I'll do it," Terry offered, as she reached for the phone.

Though Mark seemed gratified at her offer, he glanced at his watch, saying, "It's too late." He stopped with a finger curled under his chin and thought for a few seconds. "We'll all go to the office and you three can wait while I give the presentation."

"Yeah," the girls hooted. They had been too keyed up to acquiesce and lose the anticipated trip.

"Okay, get your coloring books and take something to read," Terry told the girls.

"Aw, we don't need that," Makeda said.

"It will keep you quiet while Mark has his meeting."

"Don't worry about it, the office is soundproof," Mark said.

The children were so pleased that Mark had freed them of having to take books that they rushed to go out with Mark. Terry waited until they were gone and picked the books herself. She knew a few things that Mark didn't—like how short their concentration span could be.

The girls sang their triumph at saving the day in the back of the car. When Mark unlocked the office and they stepped in, the place was like an oven.

"Let me turn on the air-conditioning," Mark said, as he fiddled with the buttons. He turned, but nothing happened. The office remained as hot and uncomfortable as ever.

"Damn nuisance," Mark muttered.

"What did you say, Mark?" Makeda queried.

"Shush," Mark answered. "You two wait with Terry."

"Why not take the clients out to lunch? The girls and I can wait right here for you," Terry suggested.

"Naw. Why should you wait in the heat while they're being wined and dined in a fancy restaurant?"

"But you said yourself that it's an important account, and we'll be fine," Terry insisted.

"Forget that. I'll have them so mesmerized they won't even notice it's hot." He clapped his hands and rubbed his palms together as if unable to wait to make the deal. "You lovely ladies are going to have the opportunity of a lifetime—the chance to see a real salesman at work." The girls giggled and Terry had to smile also, feeling indulgent toward his good humor. Most men would have been grumbling. "But you have to promise to be very quiet out here while I talk to these clients, because we'll have to keep the door open."

"We will," the girls chorused with more giggles. Mark looked at them and wiggled his eyebrows. Their glee increased.

Terry, who was more inclined to question such easy promises from irrepressible little girls, pulled out the books. She decided that if they became too noisy, she would simply take them outside for a little walk.

"Oh, no," they groaned when they saw the books. Mark made a face, and shrugged.

Mark walked toward the office and looked back at Terry. Then, with a wink and a grin, he said, "Just usher them in when they arrive."

Terry's pulse did a sudden leap at his grin. How could a man be sexy when he's clowning, she wondered, before pulling her thoughts back where they belonged. Returning her attention to the girls, she settled them in the waiting room with their books, then walked around to familiarize herself with the place, peeking through files and other items.

She was rather surprised when the girls really did keep quiet for long moments, and when the clients arrived, Terry put on her best receptionist manner and showed them into Mark's office.

There was one amusing incident that could have caused problems. Terry had always been aware that two of the brothers resembled characters from the Three Stooges. But seeing the third brother almost made her laugh. So it was no surprise when both Makeda and Yvette looked ready to burst at first sight of the brothers. They watched the three men with mouths hanging open.

Makeda turned on a dime. "Mommy," she started, and stopped when Terry gave her a squelching look.

When Yvette said, "They look just like . . . " It was Makeda who turned back and gave the girl's hand a squeeze.

Terry breathed a sigh of relief and beamed maternal approval upon both girls.

The four men were in Mark's office for what seemed a long time. They could hear every word outside in the waiting area. When the girls became restless, Terry put a finger over her lips and gestured toward Mark's door. They both looked guilty, but Terry didn't have much hope for any prolonged periods of

silence. They were whispering and seemed only moments away
from an attack of girlish giggles.

At their next infraction, she gave them the look that she had
learned from her grandmother. It was a difficult look to manage
and required that she raise only one eyebrow. Unfortunately,
while her grandmother knew how to squelch her youthful foolishness, her own look was just as likely to bring out more
girlish giggles as anything.

She took out the coloring books, just in case her highly
practiced eyebrow didn't work. At most, she figured it would
be a few more moments before she would have to take them
outside.

She could hear Mark and the men talking and thought how
masterful he sounded. Her attention became riveted when he
really got into gear. The coloring books seemed to be working
as both girls had become completely quiet.

Suddenly, Terry heard Mark say, "So, gentlemen, do we have
a deal?"

When the customers exited Mark's office, Terry heard one
of the brothers say, "I told you he's a real hot dog. I knew that
you just had to hear him explain how everything will work."

"Okay, okay. So for once you were right," the third brother
said reluctantly.

A few minutes later, Mark came out and Yvette jumped up
to hug him. "Daddy, we heard you, and you were wonderful!"

"Oh, yeah?" he said, casting a grinning look at Terry and
Makeda. Terry's heart constricted and she felt foolish, for she
thought he was wonderful, too, and she was just as excited as
the children were. She hurriedly fixed her face so that he
wouldn't notice how much she admired him. "Well, your wonderful Daddy just closed a million-dollar deal!"

He picked up both girls and swung them around, causing
whoops and hysterical laughter from the duo.

When he had put them down, he stalked toward Terry, sweep-
ing her up and swinging her around in his exuberance, too. Her

head spun and she felt weightless. Her heart pounded like a tom-tom. When he put her down, they stared at each other for one long, charged moment. She was definitely rattled by the contact and she suspected he was, too. Terry straightened her clothes, pulling them down, while Mark made a little self-conscious cough before turning to the girls.

"Hum," Mark said, collecting himself. "So, what are we waiting for? On to ancient Africa."

"Ancient Africa!" his youthful admirers mimicked.

Because Mark wanted to avoid the mind boggling city traffic, they took the Long Island Railroad into midtown. The Metropolitan Museum of Art was a huge limestone building on Fifth Avenue at Eighty-second street, bordering on Central Park.

They easily found the extensive Egyptian exhibit on the first floor. Despite all of them having seen it before, they were still awed by its grandeur. The girls listened with fascination when first Terry, then Mark, revealed what they knew about Egypt's early culture.

Mark was thoroughly enjoying himself when he lapsed into his speech. "It was the true inspiration of the Western culture that we live in. Their culture inspired Greece, which in turn inspired Rome. No one quite understands how they built the pyramids. Today, many people believe there was secret wisdom from the very architecture." Here he turned to Makeda and added, "Your name came from very near this country. Did you know that?"

"Mommy told me it came from the Queen of Sheba," Makeda said.

"Your Mommy was right. The queen of Sheba was an Ethiopian. Her people called her Makeda. Maybe someday we can read her story. Ethiopia, or Kush, as it was known in those days, began in the same times. Unlike Egypt, Ethiopia remained an empire until only a few decades ago. The two lands fought many wars, but when the Egyptians were having a great deal of trouble, they called upon the Kushite throne to rule and settle their internal disputes, or so some believe."

It was a marvelous day, and by the time they got home, the girls were pleasantly fatigued and went to bed without their usual delaying actions. Terry brought coffee into the den, where she and Mark could have a last cup. She walked in to find him flicking the remote to run a film on Africa.

She set the tray on the coffee table and he turned off the film to join her on the couch. The only light was a table lamp that gave out a subdued illumination.

"Thanks for inviting me," he said. "I had a great time. African history was my minor."

"Really? I didn't know that."

"At one time, I considered teaching."

"You would have been good," she said, shaking her head. "What made you go into business?"

"Money. Is that too crass to admit?" he asked, and laid back to cross an ankle over one knee.

"What do you think?"

"Just like a woman to answer a question with another question. I had a family to support and I couldn't afford the luxury of taking anything less than the best." He paused before going on. "My ex-wife didn't particularly like my going out into my own. But I wasn't the type to be a yes man."

"It must have been a difficult decision."

"Yes, it was. I regretted not being able to have been a better husband to her," he said. He shifted restlessly. "Tell me about yourself," he said in an abrupt change. It took her by surprise.

"Well . . . I'm a New Yorker, born and raised here."

"Ah, rare creature," he remarked.

She smiled momentarily, but the next thought wrenched her heart. "My mother died when I was twelve, and my grandmother raised me."

"I'm sorry," he said, and looked intently her way. "Was your mother ill?"

Terry looked away from him at the floor. "My mother was a fragile woman." She knew her answer was evasive.

"Do you resemble her?"

"Me? Oh, no," she denied hastily. "She was beautiful. Makeda looks like her."

He didn't answer for a few moments. "It's hard to lose a parent, no matter what the age."

"Yes," she agreed, "but my grandmother was a fantastic woman."

"So, it's your grandmother who's responsible for the marvelous creature that you've become."

His statement was so out of character that it stopped her. "I guess you can say that," she answered carefully, wondering where this was taking them. "We were both plain, simple women."

"You may not look like your mother, but you certainly are not plain. Indeed, you're quite lovely." Mark sat up to lean toward her. His low, sexy voice sent shivers through her.

Somehow, the atmosphere in the room had changed drastically within the last few minutes. They seemed to have moved to a different place completely. She stood up suddenly.

"I think I'll go to bed now," she babbled, and stumbled out of the den. When she would have closed the door to her living quarters, she found Mark standing, arms akimbo, on the outside. Her stomach clenched at the realization that he'd followed her. She could still have closed the door but her fingers seemed nerveless and she stepped back, leaving it open. There was no doubt that by not shutting him out, she had invited him to do more than just enter her room.

Mark followed her, stepping inside the door and waiting as if giving her time to make him leave if she wanted. Terry glanced quickly at her bed, which loomed like a beckoning focal point. She felt helpless to stop what she knew would come next.

He moved closer and placed both hands on her shoulders.

His face drew close to hers and he said, "You are beautiful inside, too, where it's important."

Inside her the question burned, *Why don't I make him go?* She shrugged away that thought and pulled away from his touch. She walked to the mirror, where she picked up a brush to pull it through her hair.

"That's what my grandmother used to say." She spoke as if it were quite natural for him to come into her room and even to touch her as he had. "No teenage girl is satisfied with being beautiful inside. They want to be beautiful where the world can see."

Before she could say anything more, Mark drew her around and kissed her, and suddenly, whatever she was going to say flew from her mind. She turned back to the mirror.

"Do you think the world can't see when a woman shines like the sun? Inside beauty is forever. It won't wrinkle. But that's not your only beauty; you are beautiful in your charm, and you are beautiful where the world can see, too." His voice had softened, and now he was standing quite close, watching her through the mirror. She felt his body heat flow to her.

Suddenly, she almost stopped breathing as she lowered her gaze from his in the mirror. He took the brush from her hand and gently pulled it through her hair. His brushing her hair suddenly seemed the most intimate act that had ever occurred to her. For some insane reason, she wanted to cry. Her nerves felt raw, as if she was on the brink of some inevitable precipice, as if she would never survive this moment. His fingers threaded through her hair to softly touch her scalp, and she closed her eyes and swayed toward him.

He touched her face and her eyes flew to his in the mirror. He stared into her eyes for long, still moments, then, taking her chin, he turned her face to look at her profile.

"Do you remember one day when I came home and you were in the kitchen, talking to Yvette? You were telling her that she was beautiful. That she looked exactly the way God meant for her to look. Have you never realized this is true of you, too?"

She wondered what he was trying to say. "But Yvette really *is* beautiful," she insisted.

"And so are you." His hands framed her face. "Look at this," he said. Her gaze went to his hands. "A perfect curve, like none other in the world. An original." He moved his fingers to her ears and ran them down to meet at her chin, whispering several times as he did this, "A perfect curve."

Then put his thumbs behind her ears, making them stand out. "Like tiny shells."

His hand traveled over her throat and across her shoulders. "Exquisitely made," he murmured, and bent his head to rest his lips on one side of her neck.

His fingers went to the buttons at her blouse. Suddenly, all her attention focused there as he slowly freed one button after the other. Completing his task, he opened her blouse, exposing the simple white cotton bra beneath, and she wished that it was lace or silk or anything but white cotton.

She watched as if hypnotized as he removed the blouse and unhooked the bra, freeing her breasts. Instantly her nipples hardened and she wanted him to touch her there. He gazed into her eyes before he lowered his eyes to look at her breasts. His eyes gleamed like fired coals. She felt captured.

"How lovely you are," he said, and his breath caused wisps of hair to flutter around her ears. A thrill went up her spine.

She waited expectantly for him to touch her nipples, and when he did, the apex at her thighs became tortured and hungry.

His hands left her breasts to move over her abdomen and unhook the button of her shorts, slowly pulling the zipper down. The shorts slipped over her hips, leaving her in white cotton panties. The panties quickly followed and she stepped out of both garments.

She heard him catch his breath as he turned her to face him. Their mouths molded together. She sighed and her eyes drifted close. His rough chair hairs tortured her nipples and made them harden. She twisted to rub them further against him, and the friction made streaks of pure, moist pleasure pulsate between her legs.

When he began the inevitable caress over her stomach in the journey to the apex of her thighs, her stomach clenched. Leisurely, he inched his hand down to the crinkling, curling hair there. She felt the urge to speak, to tell him the flood of thoughts and images that were in her mind. How incredibly good she felt! It had *never* been like this for her—ever before. How much she had been wanting him to touch her. But her tongue cleaved to the roof of her mouth. She couldn't talk because her breathing was so shallow that she needed her energy to draw oxygen. Instead of saying the words, she rose up and kissed him hungrily.

When Mark lifted her off the floor, her head spun. He lowered her gently and her heated flesh touched the cool sheets of her bed. She was moist and ready. The intensity of her need shocked her. She had never felt this way in her life.

She watched him strip his clothing away and the sight of his sex made her pause. He was powerfully made. He moved toward her, but she was suddenly frightened of releasing herself into his hands. Mark seemed to sense her withdrawal.

"Stay with me." His voice was a hoarse whisper.

His hand went to the apex of her thighs, where he had started the surge of incredible fire before, and once again he began to stoke that same wanton desire back to life. At the same time he kissed her with mind-drugging kisses. The heat within her surged up quicker and wilder than before. She burned like a cauldron of red-hot lava.

Suddenly, he moved between her legs and she arched up to him, demanding that final merging of bodies. Though she was slick and wet, he had grown so big that he had to enter by degrees.

She wept at his strength and wrapped herself around him.

There was a transient period of stillness as they both gasped at that first incredible feeling of union. When he moved within her, she quickly caught his rhythm and then quickened it. She was so aroused that she couldn't wait.

She started to slide once again into that unknown experience. Her heart raced and seemed to be beating some sort of tandem rhythm until she realized that she was feeling both their hearts, as if somehow they had joined and were pumping their life's blood through two bodies.

"Don't stop," she pleaded, and felt tears flow from her eyes.

He drove steadily and surely, his hands holding her tightly to him. She looked up at him wide-eyed with shock from the experience. This was more than she had ever expected. Now there was no fear—only incredible sensation. There was no way she could have slipped away this time. Her body took over as she arched up to him.

He moved in that age-old rhythm of life, sliding forward and withdrawing, advancing and retreating. She moaned in her throat as the sensations began to stretch her above all thought. Her hands sought an anchor and she held onto his powerful arms, which supported him as he plunged into her over and over. They moved from his shoulders to his derrière in an effort to clutch him closer to her.

Abandonment drove her past all barriers. She muttered wanton things to him, words she had never said before.

"Oh, yes," he answered in husky, eager whispers, "fly for me."

His words drove her mad and she spiraled totally out of control. Her body seemed on the verge of shattering. She felt strained so far that she knew she would never be the same, and then she didn't care; for she climaxed and had suddenly spun out of the universe. She heard Mark cry out and knew that he had traveled through the stars with her.

When it was over, he rolled over onto his back, bringing her to rest on his shoulder. Then he pulled the covers over them.

The sweetness of that moment almost made her cry. She floated off to sleep in the arms of her lover.

Mark had gone to his room earlier that morning, leaving her asleep. But first he'd lain there, watching her deep, regular breathing. He couldn't for the life of him remember why he'd ever thought she wasn't his type.

Then he'd slipped quietly from her bed and kissed her lightly on her lips. She smiled and sighed before turning over to snuggle under the covers. She settled down again and hitched her bottom up in the air like a small child.

The intimacy of the scene made his groin tighten. He had to stop himself from climbing back under the covers and starting the whole thing all over again. But he restrained himself, instead searching in the dark for his clothes, which had been thrown everywhere in his eagerness last night. He left, closing the door quietly. He stood listening for any sound of the girls before he tiptoed into his room.

All they needed was for the girls to find him in Terry's bed in the morning. That would require a lot of explaining.

Inside his room, Mark dumped his clothing onto the first available chair. As he passed his mirror, he stopped, remembering how it had all begun last night. There was nothing he wanted more than to return to her.

Once in bed, he realized how great he felt.

Terry awoke that morning as if from a gauzy dream of sexual satiation and instinctively reached across the bed to feel for Mark only to find him gone. That woke her up completely. She bolted up, glancing quickly to the pillow beside her. It still had the indentation of his head.

She remembered that it wasn't a dream. She had actually made love last night with the gorgeous Mark Holden. Sighing, she lay back down. She felt sensual and delightful. She missed Mark but knew he couldn't sleep in her bed, due to the girls' habit of sometimes coming to wake her in the morning.

She stayed in bed for a few languid, delicious moments, stretching and looking at her arms, smiling her own secret little smiles. The bed felt like a haven away from the world, and she wanted to stay there forever, feeling this delicious, sexy feeling. She turned upon her stomach and hugged the pillow where Mark's head had rested and drew in a deep breath, reveling in his scent. Curling delightfully around the pillow, she thought about what he'd said to her and his calling her beautiful. She even stared at her toenails and remembered him kissing them once in the heat of his passion.

After long, languid moments, she swung her legs over the edge of the bed to sit up and gave herself over to more slow stretching. She had a few telltale sore spots, but otherwise, she felt glorious. She felt beautiful and desirable, a feeling that she'd never had before and was reluctant to release. Terry drew up her knees to her chin and hugged them.

When she got up, she was humming to herself and danced across the rug and all the way into the shower. She sang aloud as the water coursed over her body. When she stepped out of the shower, she drew on her terry robe. She happened to glance at the bathroom mirror. Slowly she moved closer, as if hypnotized by what she would find there. The glass was steamy and she wiped it clean with her towel.

She studied at her face and lips, leaning close to the mirror. He had said that she was beautiful. It had seemed that he was right last night when she'd been near blind with wanting him.

Yvette knocked and called through the door, "Terry, are you up?" effectively breaking the contemplative moment.

"Oh, yes, I'm up and feeling fine," Terry sang to the small girl, as she continued to gaze into the mirror.

"Am I beautiful?" she whispered to her reflection, and cocked her head first to the right and then to the left. "Am I—" and she paused to look at her slight cleavage, visible through the neckline of her robe. "Am I exquisite?" she slipped the robe off her shoulders, exposing her breasts. Her nipples hardened from both the cool air and from the trend of her thoughts. When she cupped her breasts, a fine streak of desire ran through her to her core.

Then she caught sight of the small marks on her body, several narrow streaks that were tattooed over her almost flat stomach.

"Yeah, sure, I'm a real Ms. America," she snapped to her mirrored reflection. She opened the robe further to examine her naked body more carefully. She turned to the side, looking at the angle of her breasts, remembering that they used to be uptilted—but no longer. They weren't bad, but they certainly weren't as fabulous as he'd had her believing last night.

She remembered what she had looked like before she was pregnant. Then she had been fairly all right—certainly not exquisite, but okay. Now, she had soft spots where once she had been tight, taut, and concave.

She began to chill, standing there on the tile floor after the warm shower. Sudden realization dawned on her.

Omigod, I've slept with my employer! Had she totally lost her marbles?

"How could you forget that the man's a salesman?" she accused her face in the mirror. "Just be glad he didn't sell you a bridge while he was at it! You'd have *bought* it, too. What a pushover you are for a few soft, lying words. Haven't you learned anything after that disastrous marriage?" *How am I ever going to face him again?*

She entered her bedroom in a totally different mood. She grabbed up all the clothes she had let him remove last night and with a shudder jammed them into the hamper. Then she hurriedly straightened up before going to dress.

She picked up a clean pair of shorts and decided against them. Instead, she found the plainest, baggiest pair of jeans and an old shirt. By the time she went into the kitchen, she was singing Aretha Franklin's "Respect" and she'd worked herself up into a serious case of the snits. She had managed to convince herself that she had been misused by Mark Holden and started banging pots and pans.

She was so busy thinking evil thoughts about her employer that she burned the toast and had a few moments of wanting to cry, remembering how happy she had been last night and this morning. She scraped the toast with a vengeance.

Chapter Nine

Mark had awakened in an incredibly mellow mood. He had slept in the nude. Instead of his usual quick charge out of bed and out to run, today he slowly rolled out and stood to stretch. He had a sense of well-being and felt on top of the world.

He did a few warm-up exercises and decided that would be enough. "No running today, Holden."

He showered and shaved. Steam rose in the shower cubicle as the water poured down his body. Today there was no need for icy water. He was the epitome of calm.

And as he pulled the razor over his beard, he said to his reflection, "Oh, you sly old dog, you."

Then he turned sideways and puffed up his chest and pulled in his stomach before flexing his biceps.

He started to get dressed but then had an idea. He had received a paisley silk robe last Christmas that he had never worn. He took it out of the closet and slipped it on. It had a clingy fit that he'd avoided before, but today, well, why not? This, too, he checked in the mirror and pronounced it "Good."

He splashed on some aftershave, carefully combed his hair,

and found his slippers. He stood for long moments in the tall mirror, trying to get just the right pose. All the time he was doing this, he was aware of being totally relaxed and at ease with the world.

"Cured all your problems, Holden, old boy," he said aloud.

He was whistling and danced a slow little two-step as he headed out. But at the door, he stopped and assumed a more dignified demeanor. He leisurely took the stairs down to the kitchen before he stopped, remembering to pick up the paper.

He opened the door and, looking around, saw none of his neighbors were out. Usually by this time he'd have been dressed, but this morning, wearing his clinging silk robe, he wasn't as sure as he could have been. Taking a chance, Mark stepped out onto the front steps and spied the newspapers on the lawn. With another quick glance he sprinted to pick up the paper, all the time careful to hold the silk robe closed with one hand.

He had captured the papers and was almost to the steps when he heard a voice. "Good morning, Mr. Holden." It was Mrs. Merkle. "You're getting started a bit late today, aren't you? Not going to work?"

Where did she come from? Clutching both the paper and his robe, Mark turned gingerly. Reaching for as much dignity as he could manage, he bowed politely in her direction. He eyed his door ruefully. It seemed miles away.

"Eh, yes, I am. And how are you today, Mrs. Merkle?"

"Just fine, though not as fine as you are, I think." She peered over eyeglasses that were a painful neon green. The woman's gaze traveled over his bare legs, which stuck out under the clinging fabric.

"Heh, heh." He tried to force the laugh out as he backed toward the door and possible escape.

Mrs. Merkle leaned over the fence, saying, "Hasn't it been lovely weather, compared with last year? Feels warm enough to take a dip in the pool—don't you think so?"

He was still trying to duck away as he backed up the stairs. However, he didn't want to appear as if he was uncomfortable in his robe out on the lawn first thing in the morning. What the hell was she doing out here, anyway, he thought. "Sure do," he said. He smiled and nodded in what he hoped was a reserved yet amiable manner.

"Is that what you're dressed for? A dip in the pool? I didn't know your pool was filled."

Mark smiled broadly and started counting to ten. "Heh, heh," he said. "Well, be seeing you." Finally inside, he closed the door.

When he turned around, there was Terry, frowning at his bare legs. "I thought someone was at the door," she said.

Her gaze rose to his. Her face was closed in and expressionless. Before he could say anything, she swirled around and stalked to the kitchen. He heard her mutter as she left, "How was I to know it was you, exposing yourself to the neighbors?"

Donning the robe was beginning to look like a mistake. He folded both the *Wall Street Journal* and *Barron's* to stick them under his arm and walked manfully into the kitchen behind her, hoping to have a little chat.

As soon as he was in the kitchen, he realized their chat would have to wait. Yvette and Makeda were in their seats, and they looked at him when he entered, then their gaze swung to Terry. In the end they looked at each other; no amused bouts of giggling this morning. Though Mark thought it a bit unusual, he didn't dwell on it. He was more interested in seeing how Terry had fared since last night.

One glance at Terry's back and his mind played a scene that had happened last night. This morning, she was wearing a pair of baggy jeans and shapeless t-shirt. He wanted to wriggle his eyebrows and grin at her. But when she turned, he realized that she was glaring for some reason, which bewildered the hell out of him.

He expected her to be discreet in front of the girls, but he had also expected her to be full of girlish smiles this morning. Quite obviously she was not. He glanced at the girls for a cue, but they were avoiding his eyes. This was not good, he thought.

Terry poured cereal into three bowls and set up filled juice glasses. The cereal looked like hard crinkly brown wooden twigs. Then she slammed a dish down in front of him, causing him to look down at it. Two slices of scorched discolored bread stared up at him. The bread was surrounded by charcoal specks. It was obvious that she had burned the toast and then scraped it. It wasn't terribly appetizing. Both girls had delicious smooth golden-brown toast.

Terry stood over him as if waiting for his response. He glanced up, thinking to see her usual concerned young wifelike face; instead, she stared back impassively, as if daring him to complain. He glanced back at the sad-looking toast for long moments. He was more than a little bemused. He gazed at the girls and caught a quick look pass between them.

"What, no snide remarks about breakfast this morning?" Terry cast a jaundiced gaze over the trio.

The three of them looked at Terry and then hastily began eating. No one made a peep, though she stood pointedly for a few seconds, waiting. Turning on her heel, Terry flounced back to the stove. The girls glanced at Mark as if seeking an answer, but he shrugged.

Mark took a sip and grimaced. It was tart grapefruit juice. "Tastes like battery acid," he said before he thought, and slapped the glass down.

Yvette, emboldened by Mark's remark, said to Makeda, "I hate grapefruit juice with bran cereal."

Her voice was louder than his had been. Both he and Makeda shushed her up. He glanced at Terry and knew that she had heard. Her face looked serious and her mouth tightened.

That was when Mark decided it was time to take charge. Whatever had her so up in arms, he thought, had nothing to do with the girls. He wondered briefly whether it could be postcoital depression. He got up and went to the fridge. His doing that seemed to set her off.

Terry had been holding a huge knife, actually more a cleaver, in her hand, and suddenly, without warning, she jumped in front of the fridge, preventing him from opening it.

"Whoa!" he let out, putting his hands up in surrender, and quickly took a step back.

Whatever was wrong was serious. He had seen her peeved a number of times and she'd never tried to hide her bouts of temper. But he had never seen her this put-out.

She stood there, her arms folded across her breasts, with the cleaver in one hand resting against her shoulder.

She was magnificent. She looked like a vexed ancient Egyptian queen, holding the symbols of the throne. The only thing missing was the double crown. He watched transfixed.

"What do you want?" she demanded imperiously, when he stood there gaping.

He had to swallow before he could get it out. "I was going to add a little orange juice to the girls' glasses," he explained, as he warily eyed the knife and her posture.

"I'll get it," she said.

He backed away slowly, saying, "Okay, okay."

She glared at him as she opened the fridge and took out two oranges. Suddenly her face seemed to light up. It was almost comical and reminded him of a comic strip when a lightbulb went on over a character's head.

He didn't return to his seat at the table but watched to see what she would do next. She turned deliberately toward him. Then she put the cleaver on the cutting board and took up an orange in each hand. Something alerted him that she wanted whatever would happen next to be just between the two of them. He watched closely.

She glanced at the girls and his eyes followed hers. He noticed that the girls were involved with eating and having a whispered conversation. They weren't paying the adults any attention at that moment.

Terry smiled nastily at him, held up an orange in each hand, then rolled them around tenderly for a few seconds. What was she trying to convey? he wondered. There was something about the puckered, roughened texture of the orange that teased his mind.

He almost gasped in shock as he suddenly realized what she was trying to say. *She was using the oranges to remind him of a part of his own anatomy!* Hastily he glanced at the girls again, who were still eating innocently and not interested in what was happening between their parents.

With fascinated horror, Mark watched Terry's every nuance as she turned and slammed the oranges down onto the cutting board. He couldn't help wincing visibly, almost as if he felt the pain himself. Taking up the cleaver, she held it over the oranges. As she began to sing "You're No Good," by Aretha Franklin, she whipped the cleaver through the middle of the first orange, neatly slicing it in two. Mark's eyes bugged. He couldn't help sympathize with the defenseless orange. "Heart-breaker," she sang on, cleaving another neat slice through the orange, leaving it in quarters. *"You're a liar,"* Wham! The second orange was halved. *"And you're a thief,"* she trilled, as she halved and then quartered the second orange.

By now the girls, clearly puzzled by Terry's behavior, were watching, too. Placing the two quartered oranges on plates, Terry set them in front of the girls.

Tossing an oblique glare toward Mark which was hidden from the girls, she went to the fridge and took out two more oranges. This time, when she turned to him, she held the next pair caressingly. Mark couldn't take his eyes off the fruit.

"Your turn," she said, in a syrupy-sweet voice.

"No!" His voice came out strangled. He went to the table, sat down, and picked up his juice. With no further ado, he drained the juice in one swallow. "Grapefruit juice is fine, thank you."

The girls glanced curiously at him, then at Terry, but were obviously puzzled by what was going on.

The next time Terry came to the table ostentatiously to pour him another cup of coffee, Mark pulled the silk robe tighter about his body and squeezed his knees together under the table. No sense tempting her unnecessarily, he thought.

When they were finished eating, both girls left, going to their room, but before leaving, Makeda asked, "Mommy, are you feeling all right?"

"Yes," Terry said, and shot a quick glare in Mark's direction. She added softly, "That is, aside from a few aches and pains." Mark had had a cup of coffee up to his face and started sputtering and coughing. He had to use his napkin.

She sent the girls to get their bookbags and other school items. Mark waited impatiently till they were out of hearing.

He jumped out of his chair. "What the hell's wrong with you?" he demanded, feeling just about fed up with her crazy antics.

"What an unconscionable thing to do to me."

"Huh?" He leaned away from her fury.

"I'm talking about your sexual harassment," she hissed, too quietly for the girls to hear. "You attacked me!"

"Sexual harassment? Attacked? Now, just a minute." He advanced.

"Don't you come near me, you monster!"

When he could close his mouth, he tried to make her lower her voice. "Shush," he said, placing a finger to his lips and glancing around. Then, in exasperation, he reminded her, "You loved it! All those sighs and girlish squeals and . . . "

"That's because you seduced me, and I hate you for it. And don't you *dare* mention that."

"Seduced?"

"Yes! Cold-blooded seduction. You knew I was a lonely

woman since being divorced and you took advantage of me. If you dare lay a hand on me again, I'm calling the police."

"Police?"

"Stop repeating everything I say." She put both hands on her hips. He couldn't take his eyes off her. Now she looked like a warrior queen. "And if you think I'm going to take care of your sexual needs, forget it! I was hired to take care of Yvette and keep house, and that's all I'm going to do. Besides, I quit!" She seemed as surprised as he was when she heard the words come out of her mouth.

Suddenly he knew that he couldn't let her go. "You can't quit. You signed a contract."

"You voided that contract last night when you took advantage of me."

"Remember, you never screamed. You sighed, you gurgled, you even squealed with pleasure . . . "

"Pleasure?" Now she was echoing him.

"Yes, pleasure. But never a scream or a voiced protest. I didn't have to take advantage of you. You jumped all over me." When she would have spoken, he stopped her by holding up his hands. "Okay, maybe what happened last night was bad judgment."

"Bad judgment?" She looked ready to explode.

"Let's just forget that it ever happened. I have no intention of ever touching you again." Then he took a deep breath, and after first making certain that his silk paisley robe was closed, he straightened to his full height. His height usually served him well. "So you don't have to break your contract and wind up in court, facing charges that I will bring against you for breach of contract." He said it with as much authority as he could manage, considering that he was still hanging onto that stupid robe.

Mark marched into his room and got dressed. He was having a serious attack of the snits now himself. The silk paisley robe wound up crumpled on the floor. He was so angry that he put both legs into one side of his briefs and then had to do some fancy footwork to keep from falling on his face.

All the time he muttered to himself. "I can't believe it! Imagine her saying that to me! I attacked her? After she made mincemeat of my back with those sexy painted nails? Sexual harassment? And then she had the *nerve* to threaten to quit. Hell, I should have fired her. Then I wouldn't have to listen to that big-mouthed woman ever again."

He stopped and felt dazed for a few seconds. *Why didn't I let her quit?* He was puzzled now by his wanting her to stay. "I must be crazy keeping her here. She'll probably sue and take me to the cleaners."

But for some reason, he knew he wanted her to stay. He quickly dispatched those thoughts and continued to feed his anger.

"You seduced me. You took advantage of me." He mimicked Terry in the mirror with a squeaky voice and a limp wrist. *"She's* taking self-defense. *I* should be taking it."

How could such a beautiful woman be so evil in the morning? he wondered. That stopped him for he remembered how beautiful she truly was.

"Talk about postcoital depression! That woman takes the cake."

Then he recalled how she looked standing in front of the fridge with her arms crossed over her breasts. She had been fantastic. He had to shake his head. Any minute he had been expecting the palace guard to arrive and chop off his head. What about how she'd lovingly caressed those oranges?

It wasn't my head she'd wanted chopped off. She'd wanted to castrate me! He left that thought alone.

"Mark?" Makeda's voice called from outside the door, breaking into his thoughts. "Should I wait outside for you?"

"I'll be right out," he answered, and he sounded quite dignified, he thought, considering how he felt.

He quit mugging in the mirror and finished tying his tie,

pulling it too tight with an angry jerk. He had to loosen it and when it didn't set straight, he pulled it off with a jerk and jammed it in his pocket.

When he stepped outside, it was to find both Makeda and Yvette waiting for him. They were standing together as if ready for battle.

"What's wrong with Mommy?" Makeda asked.

"She's a little under the weather," Mark answered. "She'll be all right later. Women's problems."

"Daddy, what are women's problems?" Yvette queried with a frown.

Mark wondered why he hadn't quit when he was ahead. "What I meant was that we were discussing tonight's menu." A knowing look passed between the two girls.

"Are menus women's problems?" Yvette persisted.

Mark cleared his throat. "You know how excited she gets about cooking dinner," he said, nodding his head. It was an old salesman maneuver to nod as you spoke to a potential customer. The trick was to get the customer to nod also. Once this happened, you were a short way from making the sale, because by nodding, the customer was tacitly agreeing with you.

It wasn't working with Makeda and Yvette. They didn't look the least bit convinced. They also didn't seem impressed with his rather lame explanation. He thought with a sigh how none of his great sales spiels ever worked on the three females who lived in his home.

Holden, old boy, this is not going to work.

A week later, Mark was lying abed with both hands behind his head. He'd been awakened by one of the most powerfully erotic dreams that he'd ever had in his life. Of course it had to be Redding he'd been lusting after. Good thing she couldn't

read his mind—though there were times when he wondered if
she couldn't maybe just a little.

He hadn't seen much of Terry since that morning with the
oranges. He'd been working late every night—deliberately, too.
Since that time he had tried to think out why he had made a
move on her. While it was true that he had been hot for her,
usually, a woman with an ex-husband hanging around would
have turned him off. This hadn't happened with Terry.

And why that episode with those oranges hadn't made him
see the light he still couldn't figure out. She had looked very
fierce and very serious, too. Somehow, with the distance of a
week, he found the whole thing almost funny.

My hormones are turning my brain to mush.

Even now, his imagination brought images of her feminine
curves. When he realized where his thoughts were going, he
hastily jumped out of bed and pulled on his running shorts and
shoes. After some minutes of warm-up exercises, Mark was
out the door. Since he was early this morning, he would do
more mileage. Then he'd come back and take a cool shower
. . . anything to stop his lusting after Terry Redding. She'd
threatened to sue him for sexual harassment. If she knew where
his thoughts were right now, she'd probably want him locked
up in a dungeon with the key thrown away.

Heck, I'm like a teenage boy all over again.

Once on the road, he started slower than usual; he'd cheated
on warm-up time. He loved this hour of the day. The world
seemed quiet and unclogged. He felt clear and free of the
usual mental garbage that often cluttered his life. As his body
automatically made all the correct moves and turns to maintain
his daily regime, his mind was free to travel its own byways
and pathways.

Why, he wondered for the millionth time since that morning,
hadn't he simply let her leave when she'd wanted?

Because he appreciated what she had done for Yvette? Yes.
Having the two little girls underfoot, getting into mischief, gave

Get 4 *FREE* Arabesque
Contemporary Romances
Delivered to Your
Doorstep and Join the
Only New Book Club
That Delivers These
Bestselling African American
Romances Directly to You
Each Month!

No Obligation!

WE HAVE 4 FREE BOOKS FOR YOU!

FREE BOOK CERTIFICATE

Yes! Please send me 4 *Arabesque* Contemporary Romances without cost or obligation, billing me just $1 to help cover postage and handling. I understand that each month, I will be able to preview 4 brand-new *Arabesque* Contemporary Romances FREE for 10 days. Then, if I decide to keep them, I will pay the money-saving preferred subscriber's price of just $16.00 for all 4...that's a savings of almost $4 off the publisher's price with a $1.50 charge for shipping and handling. I may return any shipment within 10 days and owe nothing, and I may cancel this subscription at any time. My 4 FREE books will be mine to keep in any case.

Name _____

Address _____ Apt. _____

City _____ State _____ Zip _____

Telephone ( ) _____

Signature _____ AP0798
(If under 18, parent or guardian must sign.)

Terms and prices subject to change. Orders subject to acceptance by Zebra Home Subscription Service, Inc. .
Zebra Home Subscription Service, Inc. reserves the right to reject or cancel any subscription.

him a feeling of having a family. Watching Terry cope only increased that feeling.

He loved her anxious face whenever they sat down to eat. She would hover until they told her the food was good. And, too, it pleased him to have her live in his house. It gave him the opportunity to see her bloom and become increasingly more lovely. Why not admit the real truth? That he wanted to hold her and make love to her again.

Mark was appalled when he realized where his thoughts had led him. *I've got to stop this before it gets me into trouble. I have no intentions of ever becoming involved with a woman again.* He was getting soft. No wonder she had been furious with him, and she was right, too.

Suddenly, he remembered some of the old stories that people used to tell about early marriages. Days when men went out to earn the bacon, and woman created homes where they could live and raise families in peace and harmony. Okay, so most of it wasn't real; at least they dreamed. Now, even the dreams were gone. The single-parent family had become the norm. Leaving the most precious element of your life, your children, in the hands of strangers while you went to work and earned a living was the acceptable way of raising children. And if that wasn't bad enough, think of how many children were actually born to single parents who were actually children themselves!

He missed the innocence of his own childhood. His parents had been a young black couple of their time, seriously involved in Gary, Indiana's, civil rights movement back in the sixties. They were a strong family unit.

How did they do it? he wondered. For that matter, how did any family do it? In ancient times, they had different rules. A young man was not allowed to wander around, grabbing at women. *If I'd lived back then, my family would have simply said, "Here you go, Holden, old boy—a wife for you." And I'd have checked out her teeth, just to see if they were good,*

*and scoped her curves on the sly. Then I'd have paid my money,
taken my wife, and probably lived happily ever after.*

*Yeah, sure. Given my luck with women, not likely. I'd proba-
bly have gotten someone like the Empress Terry, the pure one.
Then she would have hauled me before the judge because I
ogled her toes or something.*

Better leave that alone, he thought, especially as there were
times when he was inclined to ogle her toes. Instead, he did
the rest of the run. Upon his return, Mark, as was his wont,
walked through the garden. Skirting the empty pool reminded
him that it needed to be filled. He stood at poolside, looking
around at the grounds. He'd have loved to pull off his sticky
shirt and jumped into the cool waters. Instead he simply pulled
off the shirt.

By the time he walked through the back door, the house was
stirring. A familiar tingling of his spine alerted him that Terry
was in the kitchen. The savory aroma of the beef bacon he
favored and which she disapproved of was in the air. That
seemed to say that she was ready to forgive him for what she
had called a cold-blooded seduction.

He mumbled "Good morning" as he went to get a glass of
orange juice. He didn't look at her. Any sensible man would
have kept walking.

Surprisingly enough, she didn't start banging pots and singing
her Aretha Franklin songs. It seemed her mood had improved
over the last few days.

He could hear that the girls were up. Their laughter and
calling to each other sounded so normal, considering the total
silence in the kitchen. It amazed him that two such little females
could cause so much noise, but it pleased him, too.

Mark knew that Terry was watching him surreptitiously. The
skin of his back seemed to feel her eyes. Probably wants to
stick the bread knife between my shoulder blades, he thought.

"Breakfast will be ready in a few minutes," Terry said to his
back. Her voice sounded normal, totally without the anger of

the past few days. It made him turn suddenly, and he caught her staring at his body.

It seemed long moments before her gaze rose to link with his. He felt himself tighten. She looked as if she hadn't long tumbled from bed. Her hair was pinned up hastily, and strands were already fuzzing around her face. The seemingly unconscious dishabille went with her sultry relaxed face. Her full, curved lips were slightly parted.

He saw something inviting in her face. In that split second all the efforts of the prolonged run became a waste of time. He wanted her.

He wanted to touch her, to feel her, to explore her. His need was more powerful than he'd ever felt for another woman. What made the whole thing worse was that he could see that she wanted him, too. He remembered her passion that night.

Suddenly he knew that he should get out of there, but he couldn't seem to move. Without taking his eyes off her, he fumbled blindly to put the orange juice glass into the sink. It landed with a sharp crash. The sound seemed to wake both of them. He picked up the fallen glass to set it right while she turned back to the bacon. Both realized at the same time that the bacon had begun to burn, and she, in a sudden near-panic, began to scoop slices out of the pan.

He watched her do this if it were the most important thing in the world. More than anything, he wanted to stay there close to her, but he forced himself to go to his own room. There, without another word, Mark walked into the bathroom, straight into the shower stall. He didn't bother removing his running shorts but simply turned on the shocking icy cold water to sluice over his body.

When he finally came out, he started dressing as his mind worked overtime, trying to figure out what he should do.

He stood in front of the mirror, tying his tie, when suddenly he said, "This ain't going to work, Holden. You're a glutton for punishment. You're going to kill yourself under those showers. The temptation is too powerful. You're going to have to let her go, and that's all there is to it."

* * *

In the kitchen, Terry was back to banging pots again. Actually, she wasn't really banging anything, but her heart wanted to do just that.

Girl, what is wrong with you? she whispered to herself. *Just because you've discovered that you have a sex drive is no reason to start swooning over the sight of his washboard stomach. That's what you get for staring at him through the window. And don't kid yourself that he feels even remotely the same way about you that you feel about him.*

He's used to having women fall all over him. Look at how quickly he found himself a date the other night! If that don't tell you what's up, than nothing will. Sure, he'll take you to bed. Why not? He's a businessman. If he can get quick sex fixes from his housekeeper, it'll save him time and money. There'd be no need for him to go out and wine and dine some other woman. That's got nothing to do with true love, it's simple logistics.

True love? Where had that idea come from?

Before she could elaborate further upon this, Mark and the girls came into the breakfast nook and she went to get the food upon the table.

Terry noticed that Mark seemed to be watching her with new speculation in his eyes as if he was seeing her in a new way. *He'd better not try anything.*

"Gee, Terry," Yvette piped up. "I love bacon and eggs."

"Yeah, Mommy," Makeda added, "It sure beats bran and grapefruit juice."

Without thinking, Terry's gaze shot to Mark, who suddenly looked down at his plate. It made her think of banging pots again. *I swear I'll never peep at him through the window again,* she promised. *And if I can't keep my word, I'll resign. I don't*

*care what Mark Holden says, there must be a way that I can
get out of this.* Then she looked over at Makeda.

No, she wouldn't quit, she realized, not without a fight. This
was the best thing that could have happened to Makeda. Last
week when she took Makeda to the doctor, he had been very
pleased with the child's progress. He had actually put off the
surgery for a while, saying that the longer they waited, the
better. Then another totally new thought occurred to her.

Why had she assumed that Mark's glance meant he wanted
more sex in his home and coming from his housekeeper, at
that? Think of how messy that would be. He'd said it was bad
judgment. Suppose he changed his mind and fired her? She
glanced up and found Mark looking at her again. His head was
tilted slightly and his eyes were narrowed with assessment.
There was none of his usual good humor. He looked resigned.
It scared her.

Memories of how she'd chopped up those oranges rushed
into her mind. She had threatened to castrate her employer!
Why hadn't that thought occurred to her before? For that matter,
why hadn't he said anything about it?

He is going to fire me.

The thought stayed with her most of the morning. She
couldn't even distract herself by cleaning because Mrs. Young
was there doing that already today.

Terry rattled around the house before coming out to talk with
the older woman. Poor woman couldn't find much to do, and
once or twice, she looked suspiciously at Terry. Terry was a
bit jumpy, still thinking of how Mark had watched her that
morning. She regretted threatening to quit, worrying that it
would give Mark ideas.

With the noise and their trying to talk over the vacuum,
neither of them heard the phone at first.

When Terry heard the ringing, she said, "I'll take it in the
kitchen," leaving the green room where they had been talking.

She went to the wall phone.

Mark's voice came through. "What took you so long?" He sounded very annoyed.

"The vacuum cleaner was running," she answered.

Her heart started hammering and her palms began to sweat. It wasn't unusual for him to call her in the middle of the day, but after having worked herself up this morning, she was nervous. She felt foolish as she crossed her fingers and closed her eyes but she couldn't stop herself.

She waited for him to fire her.

Chapter Ten

Mark closed the door of his office after warning the staff not to disturb him for the next hour. He sat pondering his dilemma long and hard. He hated to think of firing Terry Redding because she had moved out of her apartment and had Makeda to support. *I'll give her some sort of severance pay.* He'd simply pay her for the remainder of her contract and that would give her time before she had to find other employment. He would also allow her to stay until she found another apartment. Heck, that was more than generous.

He sure as hell couldn't continue as he was. He couldn't keep his mind off her. Any day he expected to walk in front of a truck while his attention was focused on the erotic imaginings that increasingly held his thoughts.

No procrastinating, he'd tell her right away. Then he'd find someone else . . . someone who wouldn't keep him in a white heat all the time.

Somehow, despite all his good thinking, Mark still didn't want Terry to leave. He wanted to keep her, but there was no way, he reminded himself. Then he remembered the thoughts he'd been having that morning while running. There *was* a way. She would be perfect, and it wouldn't be just for sex, either. It would also be a barrier against Marlene.

Terry didn't want to lose the job because it was a true godsend. But while she thought all this, Mark just ran on. Some of it she missed.

"Well, never mind about that," Mark said breezily. He was talking fast and smooth. She'd better concentrate, she warned herself—if she wanted to keep her job. "Here's why I called. We can be of help to each other even more than just your getting room and board and me having a housekeeper and sitter. Both of us have problems that would be aided easily if we were married."

Taking the telephone away from her ear, Terry stared at it as if it were alive. Surely he hadn't said what she'd thought he'd said. Right? "Would . . . would you repeat that, please?" she stuttered.

He did, very slowly.

"Marriage?" she yelped, sure that she had misunderstood something as he was talking incredibly fast and smooth.

"Right!" he went on. "It's not that we're not dealing with our own individual situations pretty well, but this is the perfect answer. I'll explain later, after the girls are in bed."

"But . . . but . . . but . . . " She was flabbergasted. She had thought he was going to fire her! Where had this come from? She felt disoriented, as if she'd wakened up one morning and found herself on the planet Mars.

"It's a perfect solution, right?" he said. She thought he sounded smug.

"Um-um," she murmured.

"Don't you worry, I'll have all the particulars figured out and explain them tonight," he said, as if the whole conversation made perfect sense.

"Well . . . " Terry was annoyed that she didn't seem able to get anything out that made any sense, either.

Mark went on as if there was perfect understanding between them. "Don't cook tonight; I'll bring in some takeout. How about Moo-goo-gai-pan for you?"

"Moo-goo-gai-pan?" she repeated, feeling increasingly more out of it. She looked at the phone again before shaking her head in bewilderment. Mark's voice was still running on when she put it back to her ear.

" . . . We can get this whole thing accomplished so quickly that we'd be ready for anything Marlene could pull."

"Marlene?" Terry mimicked, and felt stupid.

"Listen, are you all right? Can you hear me? Maybe this is a bad connection."

"Connection?" She felt as if the world had spun away, leaving her behind.

"We'll iron out all the wrinkles later. See you then." With that, he hung up.

If she wasn't feeling as if she'd just fallen through some sort of Alice-in-Wonderland rabbithole, she'd have sworn that he sounded really pleased with himself when he hung up.

Terry gingerly held the phone a distance from herself. She went back into the blue room and found the cleaning woman dusting and polishing all the things that she had been dusting and polishing since the woman's last visit. Suddenly, she was totally unable to cope. She went to her room, where she sat on the bed for a few seconds before lying down.

"I couldn't have heard him right," she said to the ceiling. "It was probably the vacuum cleaner," she explained to the walls. "Obviously, my ears were temporarily not functioning. There's no way that man proposed to me. I must be losing my mind. I've had the hots for that man ever since I first laid eyes on him. That night, I was all over him—like fuzz on a peach. Now sexual frustration has caused my brain to soften. Why would Mark Holden propose to me? I'm not even his type. Maybe someone's playing a joke on me."

Later that evening, Terry was sitting on the couch in the den, still in a daze. She hadn't been of any use since his call that morning. Just barely had she managed to push herself out of bed when she'd heard the girls come home. Mark had picked them up and dropped them at the door. Fortunately the cleaning lady had done everything, so she needn't worry over the usual small details of their day-to-day living.

When Mark came in with the Chinese food, he took one look at her and decided that they should eat in the den with the television on. The girls were delighted as this was a rare treat. Usually they sat together at the dining room table and discussed their day.

Sitting with their trays in front of the television, Terry didn't need to make conversation. It was a godsend. Her appetite was gone, and after a couple of mouthfuls, she gave up the effort and put the fork down.

After they finished eating, Mark and the girls cleaned up. Terry didn't dare get up to help because she wasn't sure that her legs would carry her.

She never got off the couch. Then Mark took over the job of checking both girls' homework instead of the usual system. He even got them into bed and did it a lot faster than she was able to do, she had to admit. The girls were so used to having Mark do this on the evenings when he came early that only once or twice did they glance at her.

Once the children were settled down, Mark came to talk. Finally, she thought, I'll hear exactly what he meant by our getting married. But instead of talking, he set an easel that he'd taken from his office in front of the television. Leaning against the easel was a large white posterboard.

Once again, he left the room, returning quickly with a bottle of chilled champagne and two flutes. She stared as if boggled.

He handed her a glass. If she was dazed before, she was really puzzled now.

"Champagne?" She stared at the glass in her hand as if it had two heads.

"And why not?" he asked.

After opening the bottle with a pop, he filled their glasses. He picked his glass up to salute her. At his urging, she took a sip.

Moving to the easel, Mark set the posterboard on it. He turned the large white poster and Terry realized that there was a picture of an African marriage ceremony pasted to it.

She blinked several times, thinking that the one sip of champagne must have gone straight to her head. She couldn't believe it. For this, she climbed off the couch to move closer. The little drink, plus the fact that she hadn't eaten all day, made her feel slightly fuzzy.

Up close, she peered at the picture. Sure enough, Mark had glued magazine photos of an African archeological dig to the posterboard. It brought back the same feeling of never-never-land that she'd had earlier that morning on the phone with him.

Mark stepped in front of the board and eagerly rubbed his hands together. "Did you know that marriage was invented by men?"

"I thought you were against marriage," Terry responded in bewilderment.

That question seemed unwelcome as he took her arm and gently—maybe even too gently, as if she were an invalid—led her to sit back on the couch. Then he set her glass on the end table and plumped up a pillow to put behind her back. She flopped into the pillows, grateful not to be standing anymore. She eyed her glass once, but decided not to have any more. *This is bad enough without my getting tipsy.*

"Modern marriage, which is based upon an idea that was invented during the last few centuries, is the culprit," Mark explained, when he was back at his little display board. "Not the original concept of marriage, which I realize now was a sensible deal that solved problems." Terry put her head in her hands.

"I'm not talking about modern marriage," he paused for a heartbeat, "which is based on sexual attraction, but of marriage in its purest form—more or less, a mutually beneficial deal."

Surely she wasn't hearing him right. She shook her head in an effort to clear her ears. She was getting a headache from trying to keep up with him. He was definitely rushing along on the express track, while she couldn't seem to get started.

"So what do you have to say?"

"Say?" she parroted, feeling incredibly stupid and slow.

"Yes or no, Redding?" he boomed.

"Are you asking me to marry you?" Her voice came out both breathy and squeaky at the same time.

"You've got it," he said, with a smug grin on his face.

All of a sudden, she thought she understood. "Is this about my saying that I'd sue you?"

But the look of disgusted exasperation that spread across his face was quick and spontaneous, leading her to see that she still didn't understand.

"Surely not for sex?"

"Not for sex, either. Though if you'd own up to the fact that you enjoyed every moment of our night together, you'd have to admit that we're not a bad match on that front."

Heat rose to her face and she quickly lowered her eyes. Of course, she had enjoyed every moment of that night but she wasn't going to admit that. Then she looked up at him again and was annoyed by the confidence she saw in his expression.

Despite that, Terry realized, for some strange reason, she did want to say a resounding yes. But something held her back. Something kept her from throwing herself at his head. Some small last hold-out of good sense, she suspected.

"If it's not for sex, then you tell me exactly why you want to marry me."

"This will be a mutually beneficial deal for both of us. Besides, I'll have a good situation to petition the courts for shared custody for Yvette."

"Why just shared custody? Why not full custody?" It was something she'd wanted to know as long as she'd been at his house.

"I'm not trying to cut Marlene out of Yvette's life. Marlene is her mother. I'd prefer to be the caretaker parent with Marlene having visitation rights, but that's something I'd rather work out between Marlene and me."

"Let me think about your idea for a while," she finally got out in a small voice.

"Think about it?" He was clearly surprised by her answer and regarded her thoughtfully for a moment.

She was a little annoyed that he had expected her to jump at this crazy offer but didn't say this.

"Marriage is a big step," she defended, "—any kind of marriage. It shouldn't be done hastily."

"You're right," he agreed.

"A few months . . . " Terry said.

"A few days . . . " Mark said.

They had spoken together.

Mark said, "Hey, I'm not talking about a long engagement here. Months is too long. We need to act fast. How about two weeks?"

"No, that's too short," she protested.

"Okay, take six weeks," Mark said, sounding as if she had forced him into a hard bargain.

"Only six weeks? We barely know each other . . . "

"Terry, things can't go on like they have, six weeks."

"Well . . . " she hesitated, hunching her shoulders. She wasn't sure of what she wanted to say. "Okay," she said tentatively.

"Then it's a deal!" Mark said quickly, looking pleased with himself.

She was caught off balance. Had she agreed? she wondered.

She wasn't sure that she hadn't just been maneuvered by one of his slick sales spiels. But despite knowing that it was an insane proposition, she wanted to agree, so she let it go.

"So how's about a little Blue Mountain coffee to celebrate?" Mark suggested.

His sudden change of subject only made her head ache worse. "Celebrate? I didn't agree yet, what are we celebrating?" She stood up from the couch and walked on wobbly legs to the kitchen.

"The possibility of a merger."

"Merger?" It wasn't quite what she thought that a marriage was but she didn't want to discuss it with him anymore. She needed to be alone to think. "I'll make coffee for you, but if you don't mind, I'll pass. I have a headache and I'm going to bed so that I can think on your prop . . . " She paused and then said, "Your idea. I need to think on your idea."

"Don't worry about the coffee," he said, appearing rather gentle, considering his usual abrupt approach. "You go to bed." Just as she was exiting the living room, Mark said, "Let me ask you—what would it take for me to convince you?"

It sounded like another of his salesman questions, but still she stopped and thought. She wasn't sure herself what the problem was.

"I can't help believing that even though things are bad today, marriage still should be based upon love."

Mark went into another convincing spiel regarding all the problems of romantic love and of basing marriage upon something so fragile.

"Do you think our ancestors in Africa allowed such a fragile concept to rule their lives? You thought you were in love with your first husband, right? And how did that work out?"

That was a low blow. Her marriage with Ronald had been a terrible mistake, and while in the beginning she had truly believed she was in love with him, she had known that he wasn't in love with her. This wasn't something that she particuarly wanted to admit to Mark, however. Somehow it made her appear to be "damaged goods."

"Even if you're right about romantic love, and I didn't say that you were—we don't even know anything about each other," she replied.

"We'll learn."

"After we're married?"

"What do you want to know?" Mark asked. Then he counted off on his fingers, "I'm healthy. I don't drink or do drugs. I don't have a criminal record. I'm good to my parents . . . "

"I didn't even know you had parents or brothers or sisters or anyone."

"Two parents and two brothers, all living in Gary, Indiana."

She was curious about his feelings toward Marlene.

"Were you terribly in love with Marlene? Why did you break up?"

Mark took a deep breath and said, "We'll take time and court a little."

He hadn't answered her question, and she sensed that he deliberately avoided it. *Mrs. Merkle is right. He must have been head over heels in love if it still hurt to talk about it.*

In her room, Terry ran warm water in the tub and poured in foaming bath crystals. She stood staring into the steam that rose. She thought of what Mark had said.

Why, she wondered, did she want to take him up on his offer, when she knew how bad a loveless marriage could be? Why was she considering giving up the promise that she had made to herself for Mark Holden?

It had been impossible to stop Mark, once he'd got wound up. And also, what he had said had sounded so plausible, and truth be told, mutually beneficial, just as he'd explained. Not to mention the bonus of enjoying good sex. Despite all this, Terry had dire reservations, and her mind pinwheeled with her thoughts.

I'm the third generation of failed relationships. That wasn't

a thought she liked to dwell on. Her feelings about intense
relationships with men, including marriage, were incredibly
muddled and fuzzy. She had watched her mother die in bitter-
ness when her father abandoned them. She had listened to her
grandmother talk about her own disappointments. Both of them
had lived lives full of pain and frustration in their relationships
It seemed to run in her family. Having grown up in an all-
female home had made Terry insecure and awkward with men

And now, Mark's proposal, if you could call it that, was
making her pause. Why hadn't she told him no?

She sighed, removed her robe, and stepped into the warm
water. There, she sank down till the water came up to her chin.

Lack of love hadn't been the worst thing about my marriage
to Ronald. It might have been the beginning of our troubles,
but it was certainly not the worst. No, that was a whole other
problem.

My heart knew I shouldn't have married him. The whole
mess was my own fault. I had been so happy when handsome,
sought-after Ronald Brown noticed me that I was willing to
do anything to keep him. It wasn't Ronald who swept me off
my feet; my own fantasies did it . . . fantasies of love and
marriage and all that it implied.

All the signs that Ronald was a shallow exploiter were there,
if she had chosen to notice them. Her grandmother's well-
meant warnings only made her angry. She told herself that her
grandmother didn't want her to be happy. It had always been
one of the more painful things of her life, remembering how
she'd hurt her grandmother over Ronald.

Instead of following her instincts, she had let her desperation
convince her to marry. Afterward, she had to admit the truth.
Ronald had been spoiled rotten by his mother. When his mother
had refused to allow him to get over on her anymore, he'd
found Terry to play that role for a few more years. Now, Ronald
had to face the music.

Terry knew that she had been an easy victim for her ex-husband. It came from her childhood. It was with Makeda's birth that she had begun to rethink her life. She had wanted to be a good mother for her own daughter, and it made her question the past. It had also brought her to terms with it. Now, she knew that she hadn't been responsible for her mother's early death. And she had come to accept that though she was no beauty, she was all right. That knowledge had freed her somewhat.

Now, here she was, considering taking another chance on another man. One she knew didn't love her. The best they had was passion. And while that was more than she'd had with Ronald, it wasn't enough to build a marriage on.

The next morning, Mark sat at his desk. He had just opened a brochure that had come in the mail that promised him a trip to Paradise. He'd known what it was before opening the envelope, and usually he'd have simply tossed it into the wastebasket. Instead, he opened it and it set him to staring out the window, which bordered on a back alleyway.

The weather had grown milder. He felt like a kid with spring fever.

The pool people had come and made it ready. He kept thinking of Terry's saying, earlier that morning, that she was going to teach Yvette to swim and spend most of the day around the pool with the girls. It had started his mind clicking away, wondering what type of bathing suit she would wear.

It was like a film running inside his brain. First she had on a sexy black maillot that clung to her breasts and derrière in wet madness. From there the pictures showed her in a skimpy red bikini and on to all colors of the rainbow. Each time the color changed, the suit shrank and he saw more and more of her.

Actually, it was a good thing he wasn't there to see it in

person. If just his imagination could do this, the reality would probably have him walking off the side of the world.

"Mark . . . " It was James McNeil, and the interruption had effectively distracted him. "Say, are you all right?" James asked, upon catching a glance of Mark's distracted expression.

After James was gone, Mark realized there was another reason for his distraction. He felt like a kid who was not let out of school. The truth of it was that he felt left out. And it wasn't just with Yvette. No, it was with Terry. And maybe he needed a vacation, he thought. But he wondered if that was just an excuse. He glanced at a billboard across the street that had been holding his attention for the past few months. It showed sailboats at the World Cup race.

He stood up and went into the receptionist area.

"Dougan," he spoke to the attractive gray-haired woman who sat there. "Where's that vacation spot you take your grandchildren every summer?"

"Sebago," the older woman answered with a smile.

"I'd like that number, if you have it handy."

"As a matter of fact, it's right here in my address book," she said, and rummaged through her purse. "Here." She pulled out the book and copied the number on a piece of notepaper.

Mark took the paper. "I was thinking of driving the kids up for a weekend."

"Oh, it's wonderful for the whole family," Mrs. Dougan assured him.

When Mark turned to leave, he found James standing there, watching him. James followed him back to his office.

"By kids, you mean, both Yvette and your housekeeper's daughter?" James asked.

"You got something you want to say, James?" Mark felt testy.

"And if you take her child, obviously you're taking your housekeeper, too."

"That's not your business. Besides, it's not what you think." Mark bristled.

"Hey, man. What am I thinking?"

"It's just a trip."

"Sure it is. It also sounds like me when I first got involved with Beverly."

"Look," Mark started, and then realized with some trepidation that James wasn't far off the mark. He had been thinking of Terry's going more than he'd been thinking of the girls. "Forget it." He turned away to enter his office.

"Listen, I want to tell you that I think it's a good idea. You need to get on with your life. It's time for you to get involved with someone."

Mark turned back. James's face was strangely sympathetic.

With a shock, Mark realized that he was on the verge of telling James that he had just proposed to Terry. He barely managed to stop himself. *Am I planning to announce it to the world?* When a men did that, wasn't it a sign of making a real commitment? *Am I kidding myself by saying it's only temporary?*

"She beats Marlene by a landslide. She beats both those sisters," James said.

"Is it hopeless between you and Beverly?" Mark asked. He didn't want to think about what his almost admitting his plans to James might have meant.

"It's beginning to look that way."

When Mark left James, he went straight to the phone on his desk and dialed the number Mrs. Dougan had given him. Some small thought made him wonder if he wasn't being presumptuous making plans for Terry's weekend. But the sly idea occurred that if he made it appear spontaneous, Terry would be more likely to accept.

School was finally out, and on that last day, both girls tore through the house, whooping and hollering like wild creatures. Terry suddenly had a presentiment that she had better find plenty of things to do during the summer or this noise could be a portent of the days to come. Truly, she had already registered them in a local day camp that provided tutoring in academic subjects as well as a wealth of other activities. The girls would have the opportunity to swim as well as learn horseback riding and sailing. That wouldn't start for several weeks, and in the meantime, it was she who would have to entertain the two active girls.

The girls had spent the late afternoon helping Terry with the food preparation. Their meals had become progressively more appealing in the last few weeks. Yvette had been an excellent source of information and help. All those hours spent with the cook at the home of Marlene's boyfriend had not been wasted. The child had, unknowingly, picked up an incredible amount of knowledge. Makeda had been a real trouper, also.

For the past week, they had been eating al fresco, on the screened patio, so they could enjoy the beautifully landscaped gardens and pool. Most of the food was salads and fruits with a portion of chicken or fish.

As the hour neared for Mark to come home, the children watched for his car. Terry again felt more like his wife than his housekeeper.

She set the covered salad dishes on the side table that she used for the buffet. The girls helped by setting the table. They placed colorful placemats on the round dinner table.

From out of the blue, an unfamiliar idea snuck into Terry's head. It was so insidious that it took a few moments before she noticed it. She suddenly realized that she was happy. It doesn't take much to make me happy, she thought, just a safe home, children to guide—and a man to love.

Love? Where did that idea come from?

This thought was interrupted when both girls ran to Mark as soon as he entered the house and barely gave him time to close the door before they were hanging on him. He dropped his briefcase and grabbed both of them around their waists. He then walked into the living room, a child anchored under each arm.

Terry always followed the girls when they ran to greet him, and sometimes, she wondered if she wanted to jump on him, too. No, forget that, she mentally admonished; the reason you follow is because their enthusiasm is contagious. Mark always noticed and seemed pleased to see her. He always had a special smile just for her, and somehow, as foolish as it made her feel, it made her day brighter.

"Are there any really good girls living here?" Mark asked with a twinkle in his eye.

"Don't forget, good little girls have to grow up and be strong women," Terry said,

"Uh-oh," Mark responded, "am I in the den of those mighty female warriors from mythical times? Did you know many believe there were Amazons in Africa?" He set the girls on their feet.

"Like me," Makeda piped up. "I'm a mighty female warrior." She flexed her thin arms and searched diligently for her bicep.

Yvette, not to be outdone, frowned at Makeda and said to Mark, "Daddy, I'm a mighty female warrior, too—right?"

"Sure you are, honey," and he cradled both girls' heads and brought them close as he hunkered down to be on their level. "With the two of you to protect me, I'm as safe as a babe in its mother's arms."

Safety, Terry thought—that's what he provides. *One* of the things, she corrected.

Both girls rushed to hug him and Mark fell back, winding up with the three of them on the floor. The two girls sat on top.

"Are you two sure you want to kill your poor old Daddy before you hear about the surprise I bought?"

"Surprise?" the girls echoed in unison, as they jumped up and down on him.

Terry wondered that no one but herself had noticed Mark had said "Daddy" to both girls.

Chapter Eleven

Mark's calling himself "Daddy" made Terry wonder, as she had many times before, what effect Mark had upon her child. Did Makeda miss Ronald or wish he could be here instead of Mark? Or was the child coming to believe that Mark had taken Ronald's place? It made her chest feel tight.

Terry knew that she would have to talk with Makeda because she didn't want her daughter to be disappointed. True, Mark had asked her to marry him, but this did not make him Makeda's father. If she did agree, it was only a business deal; Mark himself had used that phrase. She couldn't afford for Makeda to get the wrong idea.

This time with Mark wouldn't last forever. Admitting this started a prickling feeling behind her eyes.

The children scrambled off Mark and tried to help him up. He pretended to be injured while the girls tugged at his arms. Terry smilingly watched their antics.

"Tell us the surprise," they insisted.

"After dinner," Mark said, "After you've convinced me that you're both the good girls for whom this surprise was meant."

He glanced at Terry to see if she'd say anything, but she was still feeling spooked from her new thoughts.

"We don't want to wait," Makeda said.

"Tell us right now, Daddy," Yvette insisted.

It was a pleasure to see Yvette, who had been so withdrawn and shy before, now willing to stand up and be heard at the drop of a hat. Both Mark and Terry gazed at the child and then quite naturally gazed at each other. It seemed as if both adults had the same thoughts at that moment. It also broke the trend of Terry's musings.

The girls hadn't convinced Mark to reveal his surprise throughout the hour before dinner that they'd spent splashing in the pool. Yvette demonstrated the new strokes Terry had taught her earlier that day, while Makeda, who had been swimming several years, showed what she could do, too.

Terry didn't change into her bathing suit out of some peculiar shyness with Mark. However, she wouldn't have admitted this for anything and simply demurred, despite all the persuading that Mark and the girls did.

"My Mommy looks great in a bathing suit," Makeda told Mark.

"That's right, Daddy," Yvette agreed. "She looks just like a model."

"I'm going to *be* a model," Makeda piped up. "And a surgeon."

"So how would you two lovely mermaids like to swim in a real mountain lake?" That caught their attention. "I've arranged for us to go camping this weekend."

"Camping?" Terry echoed his words dumbly. "But we don't have any equipment."

"We don't need any. I've rented a cabin in the Ramapo Mountains, right inside Harriman State Park. We won't even need a tent. Anything else we can find right here in our own kitchen. There are bathrooms with toilets and propane for cooking. It's not what my brothers and I used to call camping but it's a great way for the girls to get their first taste of life in the open. It's far from being really wild."

"What about snakes and bears and things like that?" Terry asked. Mark glanced hastily at the girls' faces. It made her realize that she shouldn't have said it in front of them. Mark gave her a mock scowl and she shrugged her apology.

She felt uncomfortable about going. Living in Mark's house was bad enough. But at least the house was big, and they could find space to avoid being close when needed, but a little cabin didn't sound as if it would protect her from her feelings at all.

"I'm not afraid of snakes and bears," the irrepressible Makeda tried to convine Mark, but she didn't sound too sure.

"Bears and snakes?" Yvette queried in a small, slightly quavery voice.

"Don't you worry," Mark said, to repair the damage Terry had done, "there hasn't been a bear or a snake sighted up there for a long time. A long, long time," he reiterated.

That seemed to reassure the girls. And they soon went to eat. After dinner, they played a little longer around the pool and Terry busied herself cleaning up the dinner dishes. She was scraping the plates when Mark came to help.

"How long has it really been?" Terry asked Mark suddenly, and when he looked puzzled, she said, "Those bears and snakes. How long since any have been spotted?"

"Not since last fall," he said confidently.

"Bears hibernate in the winter; of course, you wouldn't see any when it was still cold."

"I know," he said, "but don't worry, it's safe. We won't be isolated. The rangers have a cabin right on the grounds. I tell you, it's okay. Trust me."

But it wasn't him she didn't trust; it was herself. "Don't forget, *you're* the one who complained that I don't spend enough time with Yvette and too much with the business. We'll be able to sail on the lake and go for long, leisurely walks. And if you like, we can arrange for a full week by August."

He helped stack the dishwasher as she was finishing up. "By the way," he added, "Mrs. Merkle tells me there's been a prowler in the area."

"Yes, she told me, too."

"I'm going to have a word with security. They're being paid to police the area."

"I've talked to the girls about it."

"Good."

It had been a hectic week as they'd tried to get ready for the trip. Terry couldn't help feeling that it was a crazy idea. And she was nuts to let Mark talk her into it. But of course, she had to go on this trip with them. Mark wouldn't feel comfortable taking both girls unless she accompanied them.

Now that the girls were out of school, and before day camp began, they had a small pocket of time. The girls had also been a surprising help. They went with Terry to do most of the shopping, and it had been fun.

Crazy or not, she admired him for doing it. Although it was a weekend, it meant that he took time away from the business. If anything showed how committed he was as a father, this did. Terry knew only too well that it was a major production. Of course, he would have his cellular phone and a beeper for both the answering machines at the business as well as at the house. Still, she knew it was a problem for him not to be there right on site. Fortunately, although it seemed many miles away, the little cabin in the mountains was only a fifty-mile drive. If something did come up, he could be back in less than an hour.

It had been left to her to plan and pack. She had never gone camping in her life and didn't have a clue as to how to go about it. Mark had left a list of things to get, and she had taken a book out of the local library. There she had found several other books on topics like animal spoors and how to identify trees and wild flowers. She brought all of them home, figuring that it would be fun for the girls and that they could go on nature hikes.

Clothing was a problem. They had to wear good footwear and clothes that were lightweight but still offered protection against the insects. The state Parks Department fortunately were very good about protecting with nontoxic sprays and in keeping an eye out for any problems. While one had to be more careful today than in the past, Mark, as well as the state authorities she had called, assured her that it was a safe summer trip.

Two days before the jaunt, Terry was in the kitchen, packing some of the things they'd need in the cabin. She glanced at the foodstuffs and thought, finally, they'll have all the hamburgers and frankfurters they can possibly want.

She was waiting for Mark and the girls to return from their final shopping trip. Mark had done a great deal of the shopping on his own, for which she was grateful. He had listed a lot of things she might easily have forgotten, such as a can opener, condiments, matches, and charcoal lighter.

When she heard them come through the front door, she rushed to see what they'd bought. Mark dropped a load of packages on the floor of the foyer and went back for more. They seemed to have bought tons of camping equipment, including, of all things, safari suits and water canteens.

The girls were wearing pith helmets.

"Look, Terry," Yvette said. Both girls swirled around to show off their new headgear.

They tore through the packages to pull things out.

Makeda pushed a safari suit into Terry's hands. "This one is for you, Mommy," she said, and returned quickly to the other purchases.

Mark came in and bumped another armload of packages onto the rug. It took several trips for him to transport all the stuff from the car.

When he came in for the last time and shut the door, Terry

said, "I thought we were going on a short trip to Upstate New York. This looks like we're going to Africa's Serengetti Plains."

Now he started transferring all the purchases into the den from the foyer. Everyone grabbed a bag and followed him.

"Redding," he said, as he carried the bulk of the load, "you've gotta think ahead about things like this. We *are* going on an African Safari—someday. So we've got to practice. Right, girls?" He turned to the children on this last, and they rewarded him with loud cheers.

"Right!" they yelled in unison.

"Well, I'll just wait, if all you great black hunters don't mind," Terry responded. "Besides, I've got to finish dinner."

The girls were enchanted with their outfits and nothing could deter them from putting them on immediately. It took very little to convince Mark to wear his, too. It was Terry who begged off. As they ran to their rooms to change, she went to check on the food.

All three of them had to show off their outfits for Terry. She laughed at their antics. Mark was no better than a big kid.

Nothing would do but that they finished going through the bags once they were all costumed in their safari suits.

"We've got sleeping bags." Makeda held one up.

"We'll be in the mountains and the temperature drops at night," Mark said.

Makeda brought one of the bags to her mother, saying anxiously, "I picked yours. Do you like it?"

"Looks great to me." Terry held it up. Then she noticed that there was none for Mark. "Where's yours?" she asked him

"Daddy's going to use 'trusty old faithful.' " Yvette spoke for her father. It was obviously something she'd heard Mark say.

"That's right," Mark backed her up. "My sleeping bag has been with me on many an adventurous trip into the wilds of Gary, Indiana, when I went camping with my brothers."

"You mean, when you were a Boy Scout, Daddy?"

"Let's not get too literal," Mark said. Placing his hand atop Yvette's helmet, he gently shook the small girl's head. "You're telling all Daddy's secrets." Here, he cast a rueful look at Terry. Then he went on, "Never pays to abandon an old friend when you go on campaign into the jungle."

Makeda, who hadn't been paying much attention to this part of the conversation, had a brainstorm. "Let's fill our canteens with juice."

"No juice," Terry vetoed the idea. "You'll spoil your appetites." Then, when they all looked crushed and she felt like a real spoilsport, she added, "We'll fill them with water, okay?"

The girls ran into the kitchen to fill their canteens and she noticed that Mark gave them his canteen, too, though she could see that he tried to keep her from seeing it. It made her smile.

Sometimes, he was so full of fun that it surprised her, for at other times, he was the strict no-nonsense businessman and father. She envied him his ability to relax whenever he wanted. He wasn't like Ronald, who never seemed able to be serious, but then, never seemed to have Mark's ability for wholesome fun, either.

It certainly wasn't like her, either. She had never had the opportunity to be so fun-loving as a child growing up. Most of the energy in her grandmother's house had gone into pleasing her mother. It was strange, but Terry suddenly wondered if it had been her mother who had been the child in their home.

While the girls were gone, Mark started to roll up the sleeping bags to store them away until the trip. The girls came back during this.

"Daddy, you said that we were going into the attic to find your sleeping bag."

"We can have a hunt," Makeda, ever the fun-loving creature, said.

"Great idea," Mark agreed. "We'll climb into the attic and rescue 'Trusty Old Faithful.' It will be practice for when we go up Mount Kilimanjaro." He started marching upstairs.

"On to Kilimanjaro!" Makeda took off after him.

"Kilimanjaro," Yvette, who was becoming a real little-sister, me-too type, repeated.

Terry glanced at them, but for once, she didn't want to miss the fun. So she rushed into the kitchen and turned down the stove before drifting behind the others. Part of her felt a bit foolish, but she was also enjoying herself.

They went up two flights of stairs to the third floor, where Mark pulled a chain that was set into the ceiling, and down came a set of stairs. He led the way, still marching up the stairs into the rather closed-in attic.

It was lit by a single light hanging from the ceiling. The air was a bit stale as the area had been closed up for some time, but there was less dust than Terry had expected. Obviously, the cleaning lady was up there fairly regularly.

"Onward, troops," Mark commanded, waving a letter opener shaped like a knife that he had picked up in his travels up the stairs.

"Wait! Time for water," Yvette insisted, and they all laughed.

Yvette, who had been so withdrawn that first day, was fast learning to join the fun and make herself heard. Both Mark and Makeda opened their canteens and took a swig. Terry, who had refused to join in the costuming, now wished that she had at least brought her canteen. She looked around at the things carefully stored in packages and wondered what treasures of memories were there.

"Now," Mark said, as he capped his canteen and brushed his mouth as if he'd just quenched a very dry thirst. "It's time to save "Trusty Old Faithful."

She had to chuckle. He made the simplest acts an adventure. Why can't he be my husband? she thought suddenly. Why don't I simply say yes to him? Then I could live here with him forever. No, that's just the point; I can't live here forever. That's not what Mark offered. He doesn't want a wife. He's said that often enough. What he wants is a mutually beneficial relationship that will enable him to obtain shared custody of his child.

Mark found where his old camping stuff was and they all rummaged around in the boxes until they found his old bedroll.

"Aha!" He stood up, suddenly holding the bedding aloft.

It did almost feel as if they'd made a great discovery. At least, with Mark's obvious pleasure, it was as if they had found buried treasure. They all tromped downstairs where Mark opened the bedroll, showing great homage in the family room.

It was a real letdown.

The sleeping bag was clean, but it was also faded in a sorry state of disrepair. Terry was sure that Mark would toss it out.

"Ugh, Daddy," Yvette said, her face screwed up in disgust. "It's so old and ugly!"

"Looks don't count. Are you going to throw your Daddy out when he gets old and wrinkled?"

Yvette gave him a hug and said, "Oh, no, Daddy. I'd never throw *you* out." But she still looked askance at the bag.

"Bugs will climb in," observed the often practical Makeda.

"Nonsense," Mark said. "With the netting, I'll be perfectly safe. No bug would *dare* climb in this honorable old bag. Anyway, this is a real man's sleeping bag."

The girls didn't look too convinced.

"What do you think, Mommy?" Makeda suddenly asked Terry.

Terry didn't want to say anything, as she had noticed Mark's chagrin. However, she had been caught off balance. Mark took one look at her face and took a protective stance in front of the bag. He stood guard against the three females of his household.

"I'll never discard it!" he exclaimed. "This is a warriors' tool, a worthy friend that's sacred after having been with me through many campaigns. This would be like shooting a trusty, old warhorse."

Suddenly, Makeda's face lit up. "I know what we can do. We can give it a warriors' burial!"

That caught Yvette's imagination. "That's right, Daddy! We could bury it just like on the *Cosby Show.*"

"Yeah. When they flushed Rudy's dead goldfish down the toilet," Makeda said.

"Flush my sleeping bag down the toilet?" Mark sounded appalled.

"No. We could bury it outside, on the grounds," Makeda said.

"Bury my sleeping bag!"

Terry wanted very badly to laugh, but one look at Mark's face and she held it in. Mark looked at her for the final decision and she showed him her most serious face. Then she shrugged to let him see that his *was* the final decision. But suddenly she wanted to join the fun.

"Not bury it," Terry said, joining in. "Since it's been such a fond companion on so many nature trips, we could just return it to nature. It's made of all natural fabrics, so it would be sort of a return to its source."

Finally, with much regret, Mark gave in. "Okay," he said, "but I get to pick the spot, and it has to be picturesque."

"You got it," Terry said. "However, why don't we eat first?"

"Oh no." Mark nixed the idea immediately. "We have to do it now, while my heart's willing. I'll go outside and meditate on the perfect site."

Makeda, Yvette, and Terry watched Mark walk around outside as if in great thought. Finally, he returned.

"I've got it. We'll bury it in that copse over there." He pointed toward the edge of his lawn where trees sat near the property line. "First, though, we have to find something to bury it *in.*"

That took Mark and the girls off on another hunt to find an acceptable receptacle to serve as a coffin. Yvette was sent to pick flowers from Mark's treasured garden.

With a sigh, Terry went to check on her dinner. *There's no telling when Mark is going to release us to eat tonight.*

He took a long time to choose a bag, rejecting several of the girl's finds. The honor of covering the ragged old bedroll in the end went to a colorful plastic shopping bag. Then he was particularly careful that it should be wrapped in a certain way. He taped it so that it would be both water- and airtight. She couldn't figure why this was so important.

"But if you put it in like that, it won't be biodegradable," Terry couldn't help but point out.

When he gave her a pained look, she decided to go along with his decision.

When everything was fixed according to Mark's tastes, they had an almost solemn procession, using Makeda's Walkman and a tape of an old Chambers Brothers music to march by. Mark had gone ahead to dig the grave. They all stood around the hole, waiting for him to relinquish the bedroll. Mark reluctantly placed it into the hole and covered it with a shovel full of dirt.

Then, with a wink, Mark looked up and said, "I just want you ladies to know that I am not a fickle man. When I fall in love—it's forever."

Somehow, for her, his statement put a pall upon what had been a rather fun hour. It made her think of Marlene and of all the people who had said that Mark still loved her. Here he was agreeing, in a way, with all of those people.

The next night, he came in with a new sleeping bag. Mark had also made arrangements to take a small sailboat up on a trailer. The girls were besides themselves with excitement. Terry had to admit that she was equally as excited. She had never been sailing.

Her grandmother had been reluctant to trust her going to a sleepaway camp. She was a pretty skilled swimmer, having learned at a local YWCA during her childhood. However, she

had grown up in a household where neither mother nor grandmother was the camping type, so she had never had the opportunity to learn these skills. Terry was ambivalent about them even
now. While she wanted Makeda to have these opportunities
and found the ideas exciting, she wasn't too sure how she would
feel when she was actually there.

Finally, by Friday night, everything was packed and the girls
were geared up as if they were truly going on safari. They had
insisted upon wearing boots and having netting attached to their
helmets.

Most of this was Makeda's idea. She rarely allowed an opportunity for a little drama to pass by without trying for it. Yvette,
who was inclined to be more serious, always wanted to go
along. The girls were becoming more and more like real sisters
every day. Sometimes, Terry wondered if it was such a good
idea.

Saturday morning, all the equipment had been lugged out
into the yard before Mark went to pick up the boat with its
trailer. He had planned to rent a station wagon. He wore well-
cut khaki pants with a plaid cotton shirt—just like a lumberjack,
Terry thought, as she watched him get into his car.

When he returned with a four-seater boat, the girls nearly
swooned with joy. Terry walked around the craft and looked
at it a bit more suspiciously.

"But neither of them can swim that well," she insisted to
Mark, where they couldn't hear.

"Don't worry," he said, "They'll wear these." He held up
child-sized orange lifejackets. "They don't have to be great
swimmers with these. Also, the lake isn't that big, and it's well
patrolled. As long as they follow basic safety rules, which I
am going to teach them, they'll be fine."

She believed him. Mark wasn't a man who'd take chances
with their lives. It made her feel incredibly protected to realize

that she didn't have to be the one in control, that here was a
man who'd take care of them.

The relief this brought made her uncomfortable. She couldn't
afford to be lax. Mark wasn't a permanent fixture in her life.
Not even if she accepted his proposal could she expect that.
People who thought themselves madly in love divorced and
parted. There was certainly no guarantees with this idea of
Mark's.

For Mark, this was just a deal, a mutually beneficial relationship that would last as long as he needed to get shared custody
of Yvette. And for her, it would mean that Makeda would have
the best medical care money could buy. She threw off these
thoughts when they got into the station wagon.

The drive north on the scenic Palisades Highway was magnificent. Instead of the fifty-minute drive Mark had promised,
the trip took close to three hours. They stopped often to investi-
gate interesting sights that caught their eye. Once they made a
videotape of a hawk one of the girls sighted overhead. It was
a creature of rare beauty as it soared on random air drafts,
gliding in lazy circles.

It was a glorious early summer day when the world seemed
to have much promise. The trees were in full foliage. They saw
other cars with families going on day trips. The cars had various
paraphernalia attached to them, including rowboats, canoes,
and sailboats, not to mention bicycles and trailers.

Terry broke out the picnic basket and they ate sandwiches
and juice. True, it wasn't all she'd have insisted upon had they
been at home, but it was fun. Maybe we deserve a little variety
sometimes, she thought.

Once they stopped at a scenic overlook and got out to take
a closer look. It was glorious. They were above the Hudson
River, and Terry had a moment of feeling how it must have
looked when only the Indians had lived there. Soon they could
see the Ramapo Mountains in the distance, towering over them
like hazy purple shadows. When they began to drive up the

mountain road, their sense of urgency and excitement rose, too. The final lap of their journey was along the Seven Lake Drive. Mark deliberately took them along winding highways, up into the tree-shaded mountain roadways.

They stopped once again, this time to see a lake that was nestled in a forest of tall pines. While Terry became fascinated with the fish that came so close to the shore, the girls ran a few feet away to toss stones into the water. Mark came up beside her.

"Not sorry you came?" he asked.

"Oh, it's beautiful," she sighed.

"The lake where we'll be staying is called Sebago. It's an Indian name that means 'Big Water.' "

"Wherever did you hear about it?"

"Oh, I have my sources. You should trust me. I know what I'm saying." He looked at her for a few moments and went on in a different voice, "You should trust me about the marriage idea, too."

"Did you bring me up here to talk about that? I thought you were giving me six weeks to make a decision."

"There you go, thinking the worst of me again," he said, smiling. "Of course, you have all the time you need to think about it."

"But this trip is supposed to soften me up a little?"

"Nonsense. What makes you think that?"

"Because you're a salesman, that's why."

"It's terrible, the way the world maligns salesmen," he said, but he didn't seem serious. "Have you really been pressured to buy things you didn't want?"

"Sometimes, I regret buying things," she admitted.

"When it doesn't live up to your expectations, probably. I don't blame you, either. I make it my business never to inflate the worth of anything I sell."

She believed him, she realized. Mark was a man of integrity. He stood there with the sun shining down on his shirt, patterned by the shadows of leaves overhead. The air seemed alive and the sound of the girls chatting a few feet away made the world seem a perfect place for them to be.

She felt no fear of Makeda's pending surgery because in a world such as today all things worked out for the best. She didn't fear Ronald or wonder about Marlene or anything. With Mark here and the girls nearby, she felt in total harmony with all of life.

Yes, she was glad she'd agreed to come.

When they reached the campgrounds, Terry fell immediately in love with the beautiful sight surrounded by many tall trees.

Finally, they drove along a winding private road to the cabins, which were more rustic than she'd expected from Mark's description. Maybe to him the area was very tame, but for her and the girls, it was a pleasing blend of just enough creature comforts with a bit of the adventurous outdoors.

They all got out to unpack, but almost immediately, several little girls came and quickly made friends with Yvette and Makeda. Within minutes, the girls were all begging to be freed from the odious task of unpacking. They wanted to run away and play with their new friends. Terry was a little reluctant, but not Mark.

"Sure, go ahead," he said. He grinned at Terry and shrugged when he realized from her face that she thought the girls should help them settle in. "We have only two days; they might as well enjoy themselves."

The two unpacked in record time. She watched the car pull out when Mark drove off to take the boat down to the water. Terry looked around the area, checking the outdoor cooking facilities. The sight of the open pit under the trees, picturesque as it was, didn't fill her with much joy, nor did the grill outside the cabin. While she already loved being here, Terry wasn't too sure that she was going to like camp cooking. Her skill with the culinary arts had improved, but she still wasn't that confident.

She had already seen the inside facilities and knew they were a big improvement over the outside. There was a four-burner propane stove, which would serve almost as well as what they had at home. She had read in one of her books that cooking in the higher altitude would take a little longer but didn't expect that to be much of a problem.

She was glancing inside the cabin when Mark rushed in and took her hand to lead her outside.

"No cooking now. Besides, I'm the expert in this environment, so I'll do the cooking. Come on, we're going down to the lake. But first," he looked at the jeans she was wearing, "You'd better put on your bathing suit." His manner was off-handed.

"What for? I'm not going into the lake."

"Someone will have to rescue the girls if they start to drown," he said, in a totally expressionless voice.

"What?" She exclaimed with hands on hips. "What about the lifeguard? What about *you?*"

"Lifeguard?" Mark said, sounding as if he was totally bewildered by her meaning. Then he went on, "Oh, lifeguard. You mean that skinny adolescent kid that was totally immersed in talking with a few teenaged beauties? I wouldn't expect too much from him, if I were you. You know how these rustic places are. It's every man, woman, and child for himself. And don't forget the camera," he added. Mark walked away shaking his head as if he had just revealed a tragic truth of modern life. Then, on an afterthought, he turned around. "As for me, I thought you understood that I'll have to remain in the boat at all times." He let it stop there, not explaining what he meant.

"You brought us here where there's no lifeguard? And you can't swim?" her voice was beginning to sound shrill.

Mark shrugged his shoulders and sighed heavily and looked at the ground for a few seconds before he continued into the cabin and went into his room.

He's got to be kidding, she thought. But just in case, she

decided to don her bathing suit. She followed him into the cabin and went into her room to change.

Hearing him moving around made Terry suddenly realize how intimate the next few days were going to be. The walls were of thin plywood. She could actually hear his zipper. Egad! she thought, and hurriedly stripped. She was in her bathing suit and out of the cabin with a cover-up in a rush.

When Mark walked leisurely down the cabin stairs, he had a smug smirk on his face, and she wondered if he guessed at why she had run out of the cabin.

He glanced at her cover-up and frowned. "What are you hiding? You have a perfectly good body."

"What? Only perfectly good? Not exquisite?" She deliberately made her voice drip sarcasm.

Chapter Twelve

"Okay, okay," Mark said. "Forget I said anything. Anyway, aren't we supposed to be operating under a flag of truce?"

"You're the one who brought it up."

"Is that why you never wear your bathing suit? Just because of that one night? I'm not going to attack you!"

"You certainly are not," she mumbled. When he rolled his eyes heavenward, she let it go. As they walked on the pathway toward the lake, Terry looked around for the girls among the children playing nearby.

"Did you see where the girls went?" she asked, when she couldn't find them.

"Yes, and believe me, it'll be a miracle if we see any more of them before Sunday night. Don't worry, the grounds are closed in. They're with a group of kids over at the recreational hall, playing ping-pong. There are counselors everywhere, and the kids are perfectly safe. Now what we need is a little adult recreation."

He was right. Terry saw the girls in the rec hall on the way to the lake. She walked down with Mark and they stopped to look into a huge structure built with large stones. The tall ceiling was finished off with crisscrossed logs. Inside the rec hall were two rooms with sturdy furniture built of heavy logs and upholstered in red. Both large rooms had stone fireplaces.

Everywhere they went, smiling people of all races stopped to introduce themselves. Terry realized that the people had automatically mistaken Mark and her for a couple. It gave her a strange feeling, making her both jumpy and pleased. Mark didn't seem to mind.

If only real marriage was like this, she thought, with mutual respect and long days of walking through the forest in companionable silence. Hers hadn't been.

She had never gone anyplace with Ronald in the two years they were together. Mark was only her employer for two months, and already she had done more family activities with him than she had done with her husband in the whole time they had been married.

They finally made their way down to the lake and she saw the boat was ready to go. There were other crafts already on the water, crafts of many different makes. There were a number of sailboats, with beautiful sails of all colors, as well as the traditional white ones. There were canoes and a catamaran, as well as the simple rowboat. The sight of the boats on the lake took her breath away. It was so beautiful.

Of course, it only took one look at the lifeguards to know that Mark had played a trick about her having to be prepared to rescue the girls in case of a mishap. The lifeguards were all very serious about their jobs.

They walked over to the dock where Mark had chained their boat to an area where rowboats were also chained. Its sail was red, black, and white.

"This keeps the kids from going on illegal jaunts," he explained, indicating the lock and chain. And sure enough, they were followed by some kids. There were a number of boats both on the lake and chained to the docks. She learned the children were always looking for rides. The boat owners had to be careful. Joyriding on the waters could be dangerous for unseasoned sailors. Mark told the girls he'd take them out later.

From where she stood on the dock, it seemed a long way down to the boat. She would have loved to cancel the trip, but Mark seemed determined.

"Okay, I'll get in and help you," Mark said.

"Maybe we should do this tomorrow?"

"Don't turn chicken on me, Redding. Aren't you the woman who attacked me with a meat cleaver?"

"I don't know what you're talking about."

"Suppose Makeda finds out that you've reneged? What will she think?"

"She doesn't have to know."

"Sure, she will. I'll tell her."

By this time, he was in the boat with his arms up to help her.

"Oh, for Pete's sake," she said, and moved cautiously into his arms and into the boat.

Once she was in the boat, she was breathing rapidly. And she couldn't figure out whether it was from being in Mark's arms, or from fear.

Out on the water, Terry lay back on some of the extra lifejackets. Sailing was so peaceful. A gentle breeze kept them skimming effortlessly across the water. The sky overhead was incredibly blue and dotted with fluffy white floating clouds. A hawk swept by and she followed its progress with her eyes. Off to one side there was a lone geese swimming casually. It seemed strange, as she'd always thought that geese moved in flocks.

But it wasn't the geese nor the hawk that captured her imagination, it was Mark Holden.

Terry couldn't take her eyes off him. He was so obviously in control of the fast-moving craft. He expertly manned the tiller with one hand while the other hand held the rope that controlled the sails. He was breathtakingly handsome as he looked upward to a small red ribbon tied at the top of the mast. The ribbon spiraled in the breeze, showing the wind's direction. He also kept a watch on the water.

She thought of the many ancient African sailors—the Swahili, who built sturdy structures in South Africa and sailed across the Pacific to trade with China and other Far Eastern countries at a time when they were the lords of the sea. She remembered artifacts from Central America that had been created by the Toltec people of ancient African seamen who had visited Central and South America long before others had come.

They had been out for some time when the breeze died down. Mark was more relaxed now. There was something so reassuring about him, so marvelously competent. She sensed at that moment Mark could ask anything of her.

If he was to suddenly suggest that they sail away to the middle of the ocean, the only thing she would say would be, "Let me get the girls first."

Mark saw the smile still on her lips and his face softened. Then he looked down at her breasts where they rose and fell with every breath she took. When she saw his pupils expand, she caught her breath.

After a few seconds, Mark gazed around them. They had moved far away from the beach and the other boats. Without the breeze, they were becalmed. Mark tied the tiller in such a manner that he didn't have to sit there and tend it. The boat started slowly to drift around in a wide, lazy circle.

He came to lie next to her. He was on his side facing her. He stared for long moments into her eyes. When he reached slowly with one hand to touch her face, she shuddered—with desire or fear, she didn't know.

"Don't worry," he said in a gentling voice. "I'm just going to touch you. I'm not going to attack you."

He leaned over and kissed her gently on the lips. Without thinking, she put her arms around his neck and drew him closer to deepen the contact. She heard him groan deep in his chest. But he stopped kissing her after a few moments and rolled over to lie on his side with his head propped upon his hand, still facing her.

"You see? A purely platonic kiss. Not that I could do more, here in the middle of the lake with the whole resort watching."

She hadn't been worried; she'd wanted him to touch her; actually, she'd been longing for him to make love to her. She had been fantasizing that they would sail to faraway lands.

"Can they see us?" she asked, wondering if he could hear the disappointment in her voice. She hid her face by putting her arm across it. She wondered what he thought about her quick response to his platonic kiss.

Her asking if people could see them had made him smile gently. With a chuckle, he continued to caress her face, brushing a loose strand of hair from her forehead. "Not from the beach, but any boat that comes close enough . . . " He shrugged.

I'd better get out of here before I make a fool of myself. "Maybe we should check on the girls," she suggested.

They returned to the dock, later taking the girls and a few of their friends out for a ride on the water. One of the children dropped a barrette into the water.

"Oh, no," the child said, looking wistfully at her barrette as they moved further and further away from it.

"Here, hold this, " Mark said, putting Terry's hand on the tiller.

She knew he was up to something and tried to pull away. "No, I don't want to," she said.

It was too late as Mark dived into the water and swam like a dolphin to get the barrette. *So much for my having to rescue the girls,* she fumed. It was all a ruse to get her into a bathing suit. But she really didn't mind. She was having such a wonderful time that she had lost all her shyness.

Terry noticed that Makeda seemed slightly subdued, but she didn't think much of it.

They remained on the lake as the sun moved closer to the horizon, changing the sky into fiery slashes of red and orange across the horizon. It was breathtaking. The day had been a lazy delightful time away from all their cares. All the worries of Marlene or Ronald or the business seemed light years away.

She had no fears—not even of falling in love with this man and of having him find out that she was not the woman she pretended. She felt free of fear. Could anything go wrong in a world that gave her a day such as this?

They took a whole roll of pictures. When time came to leave the beach, after the girls had their fill of splashing in the lake, they collected their belongings while Mark secured the boat and picked up the small oars he kept in the craft.

They ambled up the path from the beach toward the cabin, making slow progress. Makeda came to walk beside Terry. Yvette ran ahead to be with her father. Makeda glanced at Terry with a puzzled frown.

"Did you have a good time, honey?" Terry asked, putting an arm around the child's shoulder and drawing her near.

"Yes," Makeda said, her face breaking into a smile. "It was wonderful." Terry chuckled, but she realized that the girl still wanted to say something. She squeezed her daughter's shoulder to encourage her. Makeda glanced around before speaking in a low voice that only Terry could hear. "Mommy, were you kissing Mark out on the lake? That's what some of the kids said."

"Makeda, that's not a question that you should ask grown-ups." Terry couldn't have told when she had felt guiltier at having to be evasive with her child.

"Okay, now it's Daddy's turn to show you how to cook," Mark said, starting to put charcoal into the grill.

"I don't think that's such a good idea now. They may not stay awake long enough."

Mark glanced at the girls. "Okay, how about something at one of the local diners?"

"Good enough."

They showered and dressed, then Mark drove to a nearby town. The girls ordered burgers but nearly fell asleep before they'd finished them. Mark had to carry both of them back to the car.

After the children were in bed, Mark started a pit fire to keep the insects away. He and Terry were both too wide awake to go to bed. While Mark rummaged inside the cabin, Terry sat outside, staring into the flames. She dreaded the moment when she'd have to go to her room. *I'll be awake all night, listening to every sound he makes and fighting my desire to go to his bed.*

"Look what I've got," Mark said. "Marshmallows."

He stood in the doorway with the light silhouetting him. She could see every beautiful muscle, and her stomach clenched with desire. She managed a controlled smile, or at least, she hoped it was controlled. Luckily, he closed the door and came downstairs. Soon he had them hunting up long twigs to use for toasting.

Terry held a marshmallow over the fire before popping it into her mouth. A delightful sugary smell permeated the air. It was delicious, toasted on the outside and gooey on the inside. Mark sat next to her and they idly shared the day's events. She was grateful that he didn't mention their kiss on the lake.

Other campfires lit the dark all around them, and sounds of contented talk and laughter wafted on the air as other families communed by their own fires.

Her next words came unbidden. "Your ex-wife is a very beautiful woman. She looks like Beverly, only more beautiful, if that's possible." He turned to her with a frown. "I saw a picture of her when I unpacked Yvette's luggage earlier," Terry said, to explain how she knew.

"Yes, I guess she is. Being beautiful isn't enough to make a marriage work, though." There was a long pause. "I guess you should know something about my first marriage."

She had been picking for information but was ashamed at how quickly he had seen through her.

"I married Marlene right out of school and we came to New York when I got a very fancy job offer. Unfortunately, I hated the job. I'm not the type to work for someone else. I hate decisions by committees. I took the position on the advice of a man I respected, Marlene's father. I soon quit to start Holden-McNeil. It meant working long hours, even longer than I do now. Marlene was left on her own too much and she became bored. Also, she didn't want children. I was the one who convinced her to have a baby. When Yvette came, Marlene felt trapped. It wasn't fair to her."

"Did you feel that you had to hold her hand?" It wasn't a benign question and she suspected Mark recognized that.

"You have to understand, Marlene isn't a person who can entertain herself for any length of time. She had been pampered and catered to in her father's house. It wasn't fair for me to take her away from that if I couldn't supply those needs."

Terry didn't say anything more after that. She was a bit annoyed with him. She resented that he was so easy on Marlene. It sounded as if he was still in love with the woman. *Why would he want to marry me when he still feels so strongly for his ex-wife?* It wasn't a question she wanted to ask, but it burned her still.

"How often does your husband . . . what's his name?"

"Ronald," she supplied. Mention of Ronald put a pall on the evening. While she had wanted to hear about Marlene, she didn't want to talk about Ronald.

"Ronald," Mark repeated, "how often does he come to see Makeda?"

"Whenever he can," she answered, knowing that she was misleading him. Then, because she really didn't want to tell him about the chaos of her own marriage, she said, "Let's walk on the beach before going to bed."

Mark smothered the fire with dirt. When it was out, they

walked the path to the lake. There was very little illumination along the way and the beach had even less light. They could barely see the geese come flying in across the water.

He put an arm around her shoulders and a powerful physical hunger soared from out of nowhere. Just the simple touch made desire ignite within her. She wanted to move into his arms and repeat the night they had made love. Instead, she shrugged his arm away.

She couldn't forget the way he'd spoken of Marlene. No matter how much she wanted him, she would never allow a man to use her to satisfy his desire for another woman. It was too degrading. Yet she couldn't deny that her body made no qualms about wanting Mark under any circumstances.

"Please don't do that," she said.

"Why not? You wanted it when we were on the lake."

"I don't think you understand how important sex is to me."

"You think it isn't important to me?" He sounded angry.

"It's not the same for a man. I need to be in love for sex to be enjoyable."

"If you weren't enjoying it the other night, I'd like to see you when you are. Just for the record—if you were 'in love' with your Ronald—you've got lousy taste in men."

That was the end of what had been an exceptionally beautiful day. They silently started back to the cabin.

Terry looked in on the girls to find them serenely sleeping. It was good to see that someone was peaceful that night. She heard Mark bang out of the cabin and start for the path. He was going to run.

Her mind was in a turmoil and sleep seemed far away. She thought of Mark's saying that she had lousy taste in men and knew he was right. Only he didn't know *how* right.

Was he jealous, as she had been? The idea was preposterous and she dropped it quickly. But when another idea came—one which should have also been preposterous—she had to accept it.

She realized somewhere during the time she had come to work at Mark's home she had fallen in love with him. It was a frightening discovery, one which upset her more than she cared to admit. Her new self-knowledge had been strengthened by the other campers' assuming that she and Mark were a couple. She also knew it was not an emotion which she could afford to indulge. *Why in all that's sane would I love a man whose energy levels are so different from mine?* It wasn't a question she expected anyone to answer.

She lay awake for a long time, and though she heard it rain briefly, she didn't hear Mark return.

That next morning, she awoke disoriented. Then she heard Mark come in. *Surely he hadn't been running all night.* One bleary glance at the clock and she knew it was time to get up. However, before she did, he was out the door again.

Soon the girls were awake, too, and she fed them breakfast. When some time had passed without Mark's return, she took the girls for a walk on the beach.

They passed a young man who was bailing water from the rowboats while an older man sat quietly in his lounge chair. The sand was cool and still a little wet from last night's rain. It had little pits like holes from where the rain drops had pelted it. She saw animal spoor there also.

The morning of walking along the same place as where she had argued with Mark the night before brought back all the longings of loving Mark with a rush. The girls dashed off to examine something in the sand, leaving her to her thoughts. When they arrived back at the cabin, Mark was there, but all their earlier feelings of comradeship were gone.

Later, she realized that he hadn't slept much the night before and that was the reason he was out again that next morning. She also discovered that he'd done his push-ups, run a couple of miles, and played several games of tennis. All she could do was shake her head.

The rest of Sunday proved to be a quieter day, without yesterday's ecstatic highs and awful lows. By sunset, Terry's mood was anticlimatic as they packed to leave. They were taking back much of the food because by eating out, they had done very little cooking. Mark had been right, she hadn't touched the stove since they'd come; and strangely enough, she missed it. It would have been challenging and it certainly would have kept her mind off Mark.

All day the girls had been begging to stay. When it came time to go, their begging became worse. Most of the families were there for two weeks. The girls and their newfound friends made vows of lifelong friendships and promises to call and write and visit.

People said, "Next time, come for a couple of weeks."

Next time, Terry thought. Did people get a next time in paradise?

The situation with James McNeil came to a head a week after they returned from Sebago. Mark started working late again. It was lucky that they had gotten away when they had. Now it seemed Mark never had any free time.

Terry rarely saw him, and when she did, he seemed to have forgotten his proposing to her. The lazy sails on beautiful Lake Sebago were like some crazy illusion in her imagination. The Underwood takeover occupied Mark's thoughts now. Though Terry knew how foolish it was, she couldn't help feeling piqued that she had lost so much of his attention.

Yvette, who was just learning to relax, missed her father on the nights he worked late. Even Makeda was particularly disappointed when they saw so little of him. Terry knew she had grown so much in love with him that when she didn't see him it was like she'd lost her best friend. It hurt especially that

the last important conversation she'd had with him had ended
with his cruel remarks about Ronald.

A week later, on a Monday evening, Terry was sitting in
front of the television in the family room to watch an old movie.
The girls had long gone to bed after giving up on waiting for
Mark.

Even she was having problems staying awake late enough
to see him. And as for the hurried breakfast time, they didn't
get to talk much then, either. She missed him horribly. The day
never seemed complete unless she had had a few words with
him.

She had curled up, hugging a throw pillow, and fallen asleep
when a sound woke her. Mark was standing in the doorway,
watching her. She quickly sat and tried to straighten her hair
and clothes. She felt exposed, as if he could see into her dreams.
And because her dreams were frequently erotic and about him,
she certainly didn't want Mark Holden seeing them.

Considering that he always seemed to be bursting with
energy, tonight Mark looked subdued.

"Girls asleep already?" he asked, as he put his attaché case
down and loosened his tie. She clicked the remote at the television and slid her feet into sandals.

"They tried to wait up, but their eyes started closing about
two hours ago," she said.

He frowned, clearly disappointed. She knew how much he
enjoyed those last few hours at night, even though they could
be quite exasperating, with all the delays the girls pulled against
going to bed. She enjoyed those moments, too. It was a curious
time. No matter how annoying the children had been during
the day, there was something about seeing them bathed, powdered and in their pajamas that made them appear angelic.

Of course, that was a joke. No two little girls who found so
much to get into would ever be angelic.

Mark's gaze slowly traveled up and down her frame. Some
message suddenly ignited behind his eyes. She responded

immediately with an arousing sexual awareness as her body started a slow boil. But an alarm bell went off in her head and she knew that she had to do something immediately or they would repeat that one night of lovemaking.

Her heart felt tight. She wished for the millionth time that she had the courage to take a chance and say yes to his proposal. Who knew what could happen? Maybe she could make him love her.

At least if they were married, she could say yes to lovemaking. But she knew that no matter how wonderful it was to go to bed with Mark, it would never be enough.

"I'll fix you something to eat," she said quickly, wanting to escape these thoughts. She had already turned away from him when he spoke.

"Terry . . . " he said. She stopped in her tracks with her back turned to him and waited. Her heart began to hammer. A curious tingling went up her spine. She wanted him to call her back more than anything right at that moment. She heard him take a deep breath before saying, "Never mind."

She continued into the kitchen, carrying a feeling of intense disappointment. There she dished up a plate for him and put it into the microwave. Mark followed her into the kitchen and sat at the breakfast nook. He removed his tie and the jacket of his lightweight business suit. The pale blue shirt fit across his broad shoulders and chest with perfection.

When the microwave pinged, she set the plate in front of him and poured a cup of coffee.

"Have some with me," he said, indicating the coffee. She poured one for herself and sat across from him.

Mark ate quietly. Though he was subdued, his appetite was fine. She had cooked his favorite, steak and potatoes. Terry knew that he needed it to fuel his energetic physical pace. She watched him as she sipped her coffee. One broad, well-shaped hand lay flat on the table as he steadily forked up his food.

She stared at his hand. It evoked memories of the world-shaking sensations that his caressing her had brought. It never took much to bring the night that they'd made love to mind.

A sudden urge to touch him almost overwhelmed her. She set the cup down with a clatter of crockery and clasped her hands to keep from reaching across the table.

"Anything new today?" she blurted out, more to distract her thoughts than anything else.

"Yeah. James didn't show up all day."

"Oh no," she said, commiserating with him.

No wonder he didn't look his usual self, she thought. She was disgusted with herself that she had been lusting after him while his mind had been on something totally different.

"Beverly says he hasn't come home all weekend and he hasn't called, either," Mark went on.

"Do you think something's happened to him?" Terry felt alarmed.

"No, I don't. I'm inclined to believe that he's just hanging out somewhere."

"What's Beverly saying?"

"She thinks he's with one of his women. I've been calling around, but no luck. The office is buzzing. This could make us look bad to some of our accounts, especially the Underwood people. They think we're a stable company, and here I've gone and lost my partner. Not that he's been much help lately . . . "

"That's not your fault. You didn't lose him. James is a grown man," Terry said angrily, and then felt embarrassed at how partisan she sounded. He smiled at her. It was the first smile in almost two weeks.

"Thanks for the vote of confidence."

"What are you going to do?" she asked.

"Carry on as best I can." The hand she had been staring at balled into a dangerous-looking fist. He looked furious. He dropped his fork into the plate and pushed it away.

She couldn't blame him for being angry.

One of the problems with James and Beverly McNeil was

that James had begun to play around with other women. There didn't seem to be a single rival for his affections, but a never-ending parade. Terry suspected that he was tired of being tied down to the business and wanting out of his marriage.

"Beverly says that she's through." Mark leaned back against the chair. "Hell, I keep telling him to just make a decision about the business. I hate to be pressuring him, but this is not the time for him to be indecisive. With this new takeover deal, we need to be working as a team. If he would only just sell out to me, then I could reorganize and we could both get on with our lives. This way, my hands are tied."

Chapter Thirteen

Wednesday evening, the girls were watching an African history video and Terry was stacking the dishwasher when the phone rang. She took it right there, using the kitchen wall phone. It was Beverly McNeil, trying to contact Mark.

"Mark's not here, but he should be in soon," Terry told her.

"I guess you know that James hasn't been home since Friday night," Beverly said.

"Yes," Terry admitted. "I'm sure he's all right," she said, trying to be reassuring.

"That bastard. You think I'm worried about him?" Beverly said. Yet despite her apparent hardness, Terry sensed there was a great deal of pain there. "Do you know what he had the nerve to tell me?"

Terry closed her eyes, wishing she could refuse to listen and just hang up. She didn't want to hear about another failed relationship . It depressed her.

Terry knew Beverly McNeil probably needed to express her feelings, but she wished that the woman had picked someone else. However, there was no escape. Aside from being rude, there was no way to stop the angry words that came out of Beverly's mouth.

"He said that he wanted to find himself." Beverly's harsh laugh grated on her ears. "Ain't that something? He should look under a few rocks. That's where he belongs—under a rock."

"Maybe you need to be patient a little longer," Terry said. Then, before she could stop, she added, "I hate to see a marriage break up." She could hear the emotion in her voice.

Beverly let out an exasperated, "You are so naive. Marriages break up all the time. A divorce seems more natural than a wedding nowadays. What a pushover for a sob story you are."

"No, I'm not," Terry defended herself. She felt foolish and old-fashioned with the cool, sophisticated Beverly.

"I'm not wasting another minute on James." Beverly was back on her personal anger. "He's a loser. James is no Mark." Terry heard the woman gasp over the line.

Terry realized that in the last few seconds they had both revealed more than they'd intended. She wanted to stop any further revelations. They didn't have the type of woman-to-woman relationship that flourished under self-exposure. Terry hoped their lapse wouldn't backfire. But before she could think much more on this, Beverly spoke again.

"I always thought Marlene was a fool to leave Mark. He gave her everything and she was too stupid to see what a good thing she had. James was never like that. It was always Mark who carried the business. James only held on to Mark's coattails. Lucky for me, we don't have any children."

"Beverly, you shouldn't be talking now. You're just worried. You need to hold off on all this until you're feeling better."

"No, I know what I'm saying. It's been coming for a long time. I knew James was running after other women. Don't you be the fool Marlene was."

"What do you mean?" Terry felt a little giddy with Beverly's sudden change of subject.

"I know Mark asked you to marry him."

"What?"

"James told me. He heard Mark talking to you on the phone. James said it was a strange proposal."

"Well . . . " Terry stammered but Beverly cut her off.

"Funny thing is, I wouldn't have thought you were his type."

"It's not what you think . . . " Terry was still trying to get a word in.

"Hey, I don't care if you marry him. Marlene's my sister, but sometimes I don't have any sympathy for her. Mark was too good for her. He really tried to make her happy. Everyone could see how much he loved her. It was Marlene who broke them up. She left him for Weston Barkley. Mark was furious when he found out how long she'd been cheating on him."

"Umm, Beverly . . . " Terry started again. She had to stop this conversation. It was more painful than she wanted to admit.

"I guess you already figured out that I used to have a crush on Mark, but there wasn't anything to it. I married James because I thought he was like Mark. What a joke. But Mark never paid any attention to me."

Terry was both glad and relieved when Beverly wound down and sounded ready to end the conversation. She didn't feel close enough to Beverly to have heard her be this vulnerable, and heaven knew she didn't want to talk about her own problems with Beverly. But it was the last thing that the other woman said that stayed in Terry's memory.

"Marlene was a totally selfish woman to deprive Yvette of Mark, but you can bet she's sorry now," Beverly said, just before hanging up.

Marlene was sorry she had left Mark? Those words made Terry's stomach lurch in anguish. She had never considered the possibility that Mark and Marlene might have a reconciliation. She had assumed Marlene's plans were to marry another man, this Weston Barkley. Her head began to ache at this news.

Suppose Marlene wanted Mark back? Everyone believed he

still loved his ex-wife. Would he take Marlene back if she was willing? *What a dumb question. Who knows better than I how much he'd do to keep his child?* Hadn't he been willing to marry her? Of course he'd take Marlene back.

Suddenly, Terry remembered the incident with the sleeping bag. It had been amusing then. Mark's attachment to his old sleeping bag had made them all laugh. But he had actually dug it up to take to Sebago. There was an important message here, one she would do well to remember, she thought.

Mark had said he was not a man to fall easily out of love. It had scared her then because she'd wondered how he felt about Marlene, but it had been a fleeting thought. Everyone said the same thing—that Mark had been very much in love with his wife. If Marlene regretted their divorce, what would stop them from getting together again?

What had made her feel that she could ever have a place in his heart? Terry was too dispirited to wait up for Mark that night. She left his dinner sitting in front of the microwave with instructions. Then she turned in soon after the girls had settled down.

Unfortunately, she was still awake and knew when Mark came home. She also heard him come to her door and wait long moments before leaving. She never heard the microwave and knew he didn't eat.

She was a long time tossing and turning that night. Her mind was on this new problem at Holden-McNeil. Ever since Terry had taken the job, she had heard about the legendary irresponsible McNeil. Mark had taken to talking quite a bit to her, and between him and Mrs. Dougan, Mark's receptionist, there was little Terry didn't know about the situation.

Terry often found herself thinking of how she would handle things if she were there. She knew that Mark could hire a manager to do James's job, but it would take time and supervision before you could trust a new employee in such a capacity.

Time was something that Mark, with the business growing so rapidly, had little of.

It was about an hour before dawn when she finally fell asleep exhausted.

By that next Friday, Mark was in an incredibly foul mood because James McNeil had made no effort to contact anyone. James's papers were in a mess, and Mark was having difficulty doing follow-up work, especially on the Underwood takeover deal. His temper was short about this, as it was still in a chancy situation after months of work. Terry learned the Underwood Corporation was a family-owned and family-run concern. The owners had promised their employees not to sell to any company that would turn them out of their jobs. It was a difficult promise to make in the current financial climate. Even multinational corporations were downsizing.

Holden-McNeil had an opportunity to obtain the company, which was doing quite well if it could prove itself stable, without laying off large numbers of workers.

But any changes in Holden-McNeil might indicate problems of instability. And with James's recent problems, he had not kept up the necessary paperwork.

Terry kept abreast of the whole story through Mrs. Dougan, who loved to chat. She could see that the unflappable Mark was concerned, and that caused her to be in a nervous state herself. It wasn't that Mark looked very worried, but just the loss of his usual exuberance alarmed her. She felt that things had to have deteriorated to make him look even slightly concerned.

It was eight o'clock Friday night and Mark hadn't come in yet. The girls had eaten and were playing videogames in the den. Terry had been trying to read—without much success— while sitting in the blue room.

After that one night when she had gone to sleep, she was back to waiting for Mark's arrival, no matter how late it was, though he had told her she didn't need to. Every few minutes, she'd glance at the antique clock in the corner.

She heard a car drive up and jumped up to look through the windows. The car didn't sound like Mark's. However, before she could see who it was, Terry heard the girls running to open the door, yelling, "We'll get it!"

Terry hastened to stop them. Mark had warned them against this and usually they were quite obedient to him. It had been a few days since he had come home before they were asleep. Tonight, their excitement and expectations of seeing Mark made them forget the rule against their opening the door.

"Don't you two dare touch that door!" Terry yelled at them. Then, trying to show a calmer demeanor, she added, "I'll answer it."

She walked past them as they glanced at each other and made faces. Her stern warning didn't keep them from falling in to follow behind her, however.

Terry looked through the peephole and was truly shocked to find James McNeil lounging there. He was slightly disheveled and mildly intoxicated. She let him in.

"Ladies," he said, and bowed unsteadily.

"Uncle James," Yvette said, and before Terry could stop the child, she rushed to hug him.

Yvette soon backed away when she got a whiff of James's alcohol breath.

"Come in, James," Terry said, as she guided Yvette away from the man. "Mark has been trying to contact you."

"I'll bet he has," James said with a silly smirk.

Terry didn't answer that but turned to the children. "You two go back into the den."

Then she guided James into the blue room and led him to a chair.

"You will be glad to hear that I'm finally going to give Mark what he wants," James said, as soon as he was seated.

Terry sat across from him and answered with a noncommittal, "Really?"

"Yes. I'm sick of the whole thing. The money is nice, but I

figure with my share I can invest in the stock market and make money without all the hassle of owning a business."

Terry hoped for his sake he'd be more vigilant in the stock market than he'd been with Holden-McNeil. It was easy to lose your shirt on Wall Street.

"You understand what I'm saying?" James asked.

"No, I don't but if it's what you really want, James, then what can I say?"

"I can't see myself trying to live with Beverly and working my butt off at this business. You don't know that woman. She's a real bitch. Just like that damn Marlene was."

There was nothing Terry wished to say to this. Suddenly, James jumped up and went to the liquor cabinet. She followed him. She touched the decanter he had taken from the cabinet, saying, "You wait here, I'll get you some coffee."

"Coffee?" He turned up his nose.

"I heard you drive up. You know this town is hard on drunk drivers." She gently pried the bottle from his hands. He let it go reluctantly.

"Well, okay, but I'm coming with you," he insisted.

She'd have preferred that he sit down and wait. There was little she could do to stop him from accompanying her to the kitchen. She glanced at her watch and said a silent prayer that Mark wouldn't be long coming.

As they walked toward the kitchen, James indulged in a sneaky amorous hug. Terry stopped to dislodge his arm.

"Don't do that," she said in a calm, authoritative voice.

He stepped back. "You know what's wrong with you? You're too businesslike. *Loosen up.*"

"You can either keep your hands to yourself and have your coffee, or you can leave. Mark doesn't pay me to accept advances from his friends."

"He pays you for *his* advances, though—*right?*"

She wanted to smack him. She put both hands on her hips and stood confronting him. "What did you say?"'

"Never mind. You're right—I'm out of line," he conceded. He moved ahead of her to enter the kitchen.

Terry gave a sigh of relief and followed behind him. She had to lead him to sit at the breakfast nook. Then she went to pour a cup of the coffee that she had made for Mark.

"I hope Mark knows what a doll you are. Not bad-looking, either." James reached to pat her. She glanced at his outstretched hand for several seconds, then put his cup into his grasping fingers.

"Here," she said coolly. He got the message and moved farther back into the booth.

"Of course, you're not his type, but maybe he needs to change his luck, anyway."

Lord, am I getting sick of people telling me that I'm not Mark's type. Isn't it enough that I know he doesn't love me? Do I have to be reminded of how little possibility there is of his ever really caring about me? She glanced at her watch again.

"You know, I was surprised when Mark said he wanted to marry you. Of course, I had already heard him propose."

"Beverly told me."

Terry thought back to what Mark had said to her that day on the phone. None of it had been very flattering to her. Mark had made it quite plain that it was just a business deal. Then James's continued rambling broke into her thoughts.

"And he was right," James said. "That Mark's a genius. I wish I'd married someone like you—a simple woman who'd be only too glad to get a husband to make any trouble."

That hurt more than she could ever have explained. Memories of her mother flashed into her mind. Sometimes she forgot. She worked hard to make the most of her looks. Usually, she felt satisfied with the results, too. Yet sometimes all it took was a few cruel words from a man like James McNeil to undo her efforts.

"His proposing to you was a real surprise," he muttered.

"So I gathered," she said, and was proud at how neutral she sounded.

"I guess you know he still loves Marlene?" It was a rhetorical question, for he didn't seem interested in her answer. He stared off into space and sighed heavily. "Same as I still love Beverly . . . " Terry glanced at her watch again. "You know how we met those two sisters?"

That got her attention. "No," she answered.

"See, Mark and I both went to the Harvard School of Business. My daddy got the money for me, but Mark received a scholarship. I mean, a real scholarship, not a grant. Mark's family could have paid, too, but with him being so smart, he could go on his own merits.

"The women who hung around that place, looking for the black MBAs, could have launched more ships than any Helen of Troy. We were considered catches.

"Then, one day, one of the biggest black businessmen in Boston invited us to dinner. He was an extremely successful man, and both of us, Mark and me, looked up to him. It was an honor to be a guest in his home. When we arrived, there, waiting for us, were two of the most gorgeous women I'd ever seen. Their father had chosen us. It was like something out of a book.

"For me it was love at first sight. But Mark had doubts. He played a little hard-to-get with Marlene. He originally wanted to teach. The MBA was a second choice. Marlene's father convinced us that business was the way to go. What he meant by "business" was a high-level job in one of the big corporations. We all came to New York for jobs like that. Those first couple of years were great. We lived it up.

"Then Mark started champing at the bit. He wanted a child. Seems Marlene had said yes before the wedding but changed her mind afterward. He wanted his own business, while Marlene liked being a corporate wife. He wanted to employ other blacks, while this wasn't a priority for her.

"Next thing I knew, Mark quit and started his own business. It was Beverly who convinced me to quit, too. She thinks Mark can do anything. That's why I joined him at Holden-McNeil.

"Then Marlene had Yvette and I thought that would satisfy Mark for a while. But when Marlene walked out, things got sort of messed up again. They almost came real close to having a nasty court battle over that little girl. Mark backed out because he didn't want to drag Yvette through that.

"Marlene never paid much attention to that little girl. You could have knocked me over with a feather when Marlene upped and said she wanted Yvette. I guess you never know," James said, as his chin sank upon his chest.

"No, you never know," Terry agreed in a soft voice as James dozed off. She wondered if Marlene kept Yvette in order to have a hold over Mark.

James began to breathe noisily and slouched down into the upholstered booth.

It was two hours before Mark came home. By that time, James had slept off some of the effects of the alcohol.

Mark sat across from James, and Terry set coffee in front of the two men. James wrapped his fingers around his cup and glanced sheepishly at Mark.

"I guess you're pissed off that I didn't come in last week," James said.

Mark, who didn't look his usual buoyant self, took his time to reply. Terry thought it unfair that Mark, who had spent the day doing the jobs of both partners, now had to deal with James's personal problems.

"James, you need to make up your mind." Mark's manner was quietly intent.

"I have," James said, staring down at his cup. Then his eyes rose to meet Mark's and he said, "I want you to buy me out."

Mark sat up. "Are you sure? You've been drinking. Sleep here tonight and we'll talk about it in the morning, when you're feeling better."

Terry put fresh linen on the bed in the guest room. And James was soon out like a light.

She waited for Mark in the kitchen. "Do you think he means it this time?" she said, as soon as Mark walked in.

"I sure as hell hope so," Mark answered. "Money's going to be a problem, though. Payday for the Underwood merger is galloping down on me, and my having to buy James out is going to give me a cash crunch. But it's the best of a bad situation." He picked up his discarded briefcase and would have left had she not stopped him.

"If James leaves now, you'll have more than just money problems," Terry said. "You're going to find yourself with new troubles."

Mark turned back, saying, "Like what?"

"You'll need to hire someone to do the things James did."

Mark set the briefcase back on the table, rubbed his eyes, and stretched both arms overhead. "The Underwood merger will bring new personnel. A lot of the paperwork will be combined. I can't extend staff now."

"It will be months before you can utilize the Underwood staff. What are you going to do in the meantime?"

"Make do with temps—what else?" He turned his head as if working a kink out of his neck. He looked irritated, as if he didn't want to hear the questions she was throwing at him. But he didn't stop her and he stayed, waiting for whatever else she would say.

"Don't forget," she said, "I'm an office manager. I could come in and help. For this no one can say that I'm overqualified."

Mark suddenly looked more alert. He also looked angry. "No way. I hired you to take care of Yvette and manage my home. With you in the office, who'd be here with the girls?"

"I could come while the girls are in day camp and return in the evening and pick them up."

"Are you kidding? You'd be exhausted. That's like holding

down two jobs. And besides, it's too unsure for the children. Suppose you ran into heavy traffic? What would they do, wait and be prone to any lowlife on the street? Or do you suggest they wear latchkeys?"

"It wouldn't have to be permanent. You need someone to manage things there, and that's what I'm trained to do."

"Forget it," he said without hesitation. "Are you getting bored with this already?"

"No," she denied. In truth, she enjoyed being Mark's housekeeper more than she'd ever expected. She actually had an affinity for the job. Of course, it helped that she also loved her boss, she knew. Face it, she thought, what you enjoy is living in Mark's house and being around him.

"The least I could do is to interview applicants. You put an ad in the papers, have Mrs. Dougan make the appointments, and I could do the interviewing."

"Have you ever done that before?"

"Yes. And I have a good idea of what you'll be needing."

"Listen, I can always get someone for the business. Hell, I can even subcontract, if necessary. That's a lot easier than finding someone who I can trust with my daughter."

"But I'd still be here for Yvette and Makeda. We could think of something. We've been through some pretty difficult things. We could handle this."

"Please don't use my own sales spiel on me." He picked up his briefcase. Before leaving the kitchen, he said, "I'd rather you focused on that which you contracted for." He was abrupt, almost insulting, but she decided not to take offense. She knew it was a hard place for him and that he was probably just blowing off steam.

There wasn't anything more said about this. Mark went to his room and shut the door with a sharp thud. Moments later, he banged out the door in his jogging outfit.

* * *

That next morning the two men were in Mark's office for several hours, and when they came out, she knew from their satisfied expressions that the deal was settled. Later, Mark told her that he was now sole owner of the business.

For the next week Mark came home later, leaving the house earlier. Yet he was still faithful to his running schedule. That was something he never neglected. Terry could only shake her head.

The girls were fully involved in the day camp, but they missed Mark during the evenings. She missed him also. She had come to feel at ease in his presence and to depend on his being there.

One morning, after dropping the girls off, she found herself driving east on the Southern State Highway. She went into the Jamaica area, knowing that subconsciously she had intended stopping at Mark's office.

What she couldn't figure out was why she had come, since Mark had adamantly vetoed her working at the business. He was her employer, after all, and he did have the right to say who would work and in what capacity. So why was she here?

The name on the door still read Holden-McNeil Home Health Care Providers, Incorporated. Mark hadn't had time to change it. She stood in front of the door for a few moments and took a deep breath, then reached and turned the doorknob.

The first thing Terry saw upon stepping through the door was Mark's receptionist, Mrs. Dougan. The older woman looked flustered and overwhelmed. Her usually beautifully arranged silver-white hair had multiple stray hairs springing out at different angles. She was trying to talk on two telephones at the same time and a third line was ringing off the hook.

The door to the inner offices kept opening while various overworked people ran back and forth to ask the poor woman questions. Terry could see that Mrs. Dougan was totally out of her depth. Tempers seemed seconds from going incendiary.

There was a new face there, too, a young man close to her

age who looked as harried as the receptionist. However, Terry soon noticed that he was handling his frustrations better than most of Mark's other employees.

"Where is Mr. Holden?" Terry asked the older woman, almost having to shout to get her attention.

"What?" Mrs. Dougan turned suddenly and her glasses slipped off one ear and hung askew across her face. The sight was almost comical, but Terry knew that if she cracked a smile, the poor woman would probably break out in tears. "He's out working on the Underwood merger," Mrs. Dougan finally collected her wits enough to answer.

Terry looked around at the chaos and shook her head. Then, without thinking what she was doing, she picked up a ringing phone and said, "This is Holden-McNeil Home Health Care Providers. May I help you?"

Chapter Fourteen

There wasn't much Terry could do except take messages and promise to get back, but at least it freed Mrs. Dougan to answer questions from the other departments. She was also another body to do the scutwork. This kind of chaos Terry understood. In no time she was back in her old element. Mrs. Dougan never questioned Terry's presence at the office. The receptionist accepted her suddenly showing up as if Mark had approved it.

Later, the young man who Terry had noticed before introduced himself, and though he was obviously as harried as anybody, he took the time to give her an appreciative male lookover.

"Hi, I'm Ned," he said. "Are you a new temp?"

Mark had been using temps in order not to create any new permanent positions until he was sure of the staff that would come with the Underwood Corporation. It made for real problems in the interim.

"I may be," she answered, aiming to be noncommittal.

"I'm a temp, too," he said, and bowed flirtatiously. "Welcome to the mine pits."

"You don't like it here?" Terry asked.

"It's okay. It's a challenge. I'd rather be here where the action is than in some impersonal mailroom in the city."

Terry nodded in understanding and asked, "How long have you been here?"

"Six months. It's like trying to work with a couple while they're getting divorced."

His choice of words threw her off. *Why is the whole world talking about either marriage or divorce?* Still, she had to admit it was a good analogy. "A divorce?" she asked.

"Yeah. They have certain irreconcilable differences and they're breaking up. Everything's disorganized."

"You're very observant."

"Have to be. They threw me in here and I was stuck with assisting the partner who's jumping ship."

"You mean, Mr. McNeil?"

"Yeah. How did you know his name?"

"It's on the door," she said, thinking quickly. She wasn't willing to explain who she was just yet. Then she had a thought and asked, "Do you know much about what McNeil was doing?"

"Some," he said, "more than anybody else knows. I'm the only one who ever worked with him." There was an element of his showing off here. That didn't bother Terry, though it did give her an idea.

Several hours later, Mark returned, and even he didn't have his usual totally well-put-together appearance. His attaché case was bulging. He couldn't zipper the lovely leather case. His tie was loosened. A beeper and his cellular phone were vying for space in the briefcase. Tucked under his arm were several file folders full of papers. He closed the door with his shoulder because both arms were full.

He stopped short right inside the door when he caught sight of Terry sitting alone behind the front receptionist desk. She had sent Mrs. Dougan out for a late lunchbreak as the woman was too frazzled to be of much help in the state she was in.

"What are you doing here?" Mark demanded.

"Helping out. And I'm going to stay until it's time to pick up the girls at camp. Do you have a problem with that?" she countered.

His eyebrows shot together, but just as he was going to say something, telephones started ringing off the hook again. Terry grabbed one, asking the caller to hold, and picked up the next call within seconds.

As Terry spoke on the phones and jotted down the messages, Mark stood there watching her. A tingle of awareness went up her spine.

When he left for his office, she followed his progress with her eyes. His door closed with a sharp thud. Her employer was not pleased, and she dreaded the confrontation that was to come.

Later, when it was time for her to leave, she went to his office and tapped on the door.

"Enter," he answered.

She opened the door and stepped inside, still holding the knob. Mark's sexy eyes rose to take her in and she shivered with need. Terry wondered how the women at Holden-McNeil ever got any work done. She pulled herself together.

"I'm going to pick up the girls now." She tried to sound normal.

Terry didn't want to provoke him, but she wasn't going to let him keep her from coming back tomorrow. She had no intention of letting him get away with that. Let him fire her if he didn't like it. True, he was her employer, but at the very least, they were friends. Surely the fact that he had once considered marrying her made them that much.

Mark had been going over some figures when Terry knocked. He looked up and found her delightfully rounded body accented against the stark white of the door. It took his breath away. His mind toyed with images of her lying beneath him and of his sinking himself deep within her. When she said that she was leaving, he'd wanted to get up and follow. It was a good thing that he didn't, because his immediate response to her would have been visible for the world to see.

It had taken a lot of nerve for her to disregard his order not to come to the office. He also had to admit that he needed the help.

She looked right at home. He realized she had the competent businesswoman look that he remembered from the first day. As his housekeeper, she often looked like a worried young housewife, concerned only with whether the dinner was burned. He liked both images. As she was leaving, he dreamily eyed the soft feminine curves of derrière and legs. It was this—the fact that she would be a distraction to him—that was part of the reason why he didn't want her here. But if he was honest, that wasn't the main reason.

Mark knew that although he did appreciate both her business-women persona and that of the young housewife, he preferred the latter. He enjoyed having her in his home. He wanted to take care of her. He wanted to take the stresses from her life and see her bloom. Most of it came down to a very simple reality. He wanted to believe that she painted her toenails just for him.

"Holden, you've got to be the world's biggest fool," he muttered to himself. He threw down the pencil he'd been holding and banged down the button on the intercom.

"Dougan, come in here." His voice came out louder and more abrupt than he had intended.

When the older woman knocked and entered, she looked a little timid, as if she thought he was going to chew her out for something.

"Yes, Mr. Holden?" she answered.

He took a deep breath and calmed himself. There was no reason to take out his frustration with that exasperating Terry

Redding on his receptionist. He made an effort to soften his voice.

"Dougan, can you tell me how Redding got involved with answering the telephones? And why did you leave your post with her covering for you?"

Mrs. Dougan looked horrified. "Why, Mr. Holden, sir, she just stepped through the door, took one look around, and picked up a phone." The woman shrugged helplessly. "I just assumed you sent her to help. She was as cool as a cucumber." Mrs. Dougan shook her head. Her face was a study in comic bewilderment.

Mark picked up his pencil again and tapped it on the papers in front of him.

"Did I do something wrong?" she asked, bringing his thoughts back to her. The woman was wringing her hands, and it made him feel guilty for speaking sharply.

"We'll talk about it tomorrow." Before dismissing her, he added, "Next time, ask me. It's not a good idea to assume something like this."

She agreed quickly and was out of the office before he could say more.

"Cool as a cucumber," the woman had said. What he didn't seem able to get out of his mind was that he had once seen Terry warm and abandoned. He knew that under her cool exterior lived a hot, passionate woman. And the knowing drove him crazy.

When Terry arrived on the second day, Mark simply took her into the office and called the entire staff together.

"I want to introduce Terry Redding, who will be acting office manager for the next few months. Please give her all the assistance you can. I know it's a difficult time, but I'm sure that if we all work together, we'll pull through."

Terry didn't miss the "acting" bit, but she never blinked. In truth, this was a gamble for Mark. She appreciated his faith that she wouldn't make a bad situation worse. His willingness to believe in her sent a sensation of happiness flowing through her. She knew only too well that with things as they were, she was in a position to do a lot of harm. He was being more agreeable than she'd expected.

There were a lot of errors she could make. She could alienate his staff; morale was already low. The workers could resent an outsider like her coming in over them and giving orders, but she had a lot of confidence in herself. She had been in tough situations before, and she was good with people. She knew how to bring out their good points and build on them.

She looked around and smiled, saying hello to the group who stood in front of her. She vowed to prove to Mark that he wasn't making a mistake.

Terry's first feeling was that there was no way a group this small could handle the volume of Holden-McNeil's business. The new accounts Mark was bringing in would soon reach a critical point where his staff couldn't do the work.

Although she had known that James McNeil was falling off these last months because Mrs. Dougan had told her, she was still surprised that he hadn't considered hiring more people. He had probably been so distracted that he'd allowed things to disintegrate even further than she'd originally thought. It was a bad omen. She dreaded what she would find in James's files.

Already she was planning what she'd do. Somehow, she'd have to convince Mark's workers to cooperate with her to satisfy Mark's clients in filling a great deal of new orders. They would probably be needing more nursing care personnel, too.

Late in the afternoon on her second day in the office, Terry picked up the telephone and recognized the woman who asked for Mark. It was Beverly McNeil.

"Who is this?" Beverly asked, rather suspiciously, Terry thought.

"Terry Redding. How are you, Beverly?" Terry squirmed, wishing she could avoid talking to the beautiful woman. Leaning against the desk, Terry wound the curling telephone cord tightly around her finger. She was thinking that Beverly already believed she and Mark were lovers; finding her there at the office would only add fuel to the fire.

"My, my," Beverly said cattily. "You certainly do know how to make hay while the sun shines. My poor sister has her work cut out for her, doesn't she?"

"What do you mean by that?" Terry challenged.

No one had even thought about Marlene in the past few days, except perhaps Yvette. What with all the problems with the business, the last thing Terry wanted to hear was that Marlene might soon pop up.

"It's not easy for Marlene to compete with you in residence, is it? Now you've moved into the office, too."

"Beverly, I don't think that's any of your business."

"Maybe not," Beverly said slyly, "but I'm sort of surprised anyway."

"Surprised?"

"Yes. It doesn't seem in keeping with your . . . high principles to be standing between Mark and Marlene's reconciliation."

Reconciliation? What is she talking about?

Terry wanted more than anything to say something really cutting but knew it would be a waste of time. She had to bite her tongue to overcome the powerful urge, deciding it was best to ignore Beverly's manipulations.

"I'll tell Mark you called," Terry said, and put the telephone down.

Terry was more than glad to be rid of the annoying woman, but the conversation made her uncomfortable. However, once she thought on it, she decided to dismiss Beverly's talk. By now, Terry knew what a troublemaker Beverly was. The woman was always stirring up something. If there was any talk about Mark going back with Marlene, she'd have heard. What witches those sisters were. Only a short time ago, Beverly was calling Marlene a fool. Now it was "my poor sister."

"I refuse to allow them to make me miserable. They've had their chances," Terry mumbled to herself. *I'm entitled to some happiness, too.*

Although Mark hadn't mentioned any more about his proposal since their return from Sebago, her thoughts had been constantly on his offer. She had promised herself that she'd accept if he should ever ask again. Unfortunately, it looked as if he'd forgotten all about that, she thought, and sighed.

I'm not going to think about Beverly or Marlene, she mused. What can they do? *And to think that I was feeling bad for Beverly when James left. She's probably just as guilty as he was . . .*

Terry spent the first few days familiarizing herself with the office. Ned proved to be an invaluable resource. Mrs. Dougan was a big help as well. Terry rushed around, trying to be effective as she opened drawers and cabinets and flipped through files. She needed to learn quickly where things were and what existing systems the staff was familiar with.

She kept a pen and pad ready to make lists of as many things as she could—from where the electrical outlets were, to placing a name to each of the office staff.

When she moved into James's office, the mess she found was indeed worse than she'd feared. She spent most of her working time straightening James's filing system. She rarely got out of the office to have lunch and had taken to bringing a brown bag. This particular practice really annoyed Mark, as he accused her of eating while on the run. He should talk, she fumed. She had taken to preparing her brown bag lunches and hiding them in her carryall.

One day, when she was about to take a long, leisurely break

and have a snack, she noticed a popular women's magazine sticking out of Mrs. Dougan's drawer.

"Can I borrow this?" Terry asked the older woman, who nodded.

Pleased, she asked Ned and Mrs. Dougan not to disturb her as she entered her office. Then, curling up on James's leather sofa, she took a bite of her sandwich and picked up the magazine. It was pure heaven. She glanced through the gorgeous clothing ads, her mouth almost watering. Then, suddenly, she turned a page and the headline of an article jumped out at her. It was one of those how-to-get-your-man articles that this kind of magazine always offered. Usually for her, this would have been a joke.

She hadn't dated in years and hadn't cared, either. Ronald had been such a negative experience that she simply hadn't been interested in any man, until Mark Holden.

Danger! Do You Have Different Energy Levels? was the blazing headline of one article. The first page showed two photos with a man in one and a woman in the other. While the man was climbing a mountain, the woman sprawled in a lounge chair, looking exhausted. A chill ran up Terry's spine.

Her gaze was riveted to the photo. She came to herself with a little shake of her head, glancing around guiltily. She absently put down the sandwich she was holding as she continued to read. It was almost as if someone had been watching her and Mark Holden.

The article summed up by saying that people of diverging energy levels were prone to problems. It left her feeling depressed and frustrated.

Since she'd come to the office, she'd found herself admiring and loving Mark more every day, though she had to admit it was easier to deal with him when she didn't have the claustrophobic feeling that he was running circles around her. She could even see how much he needed someone just like her—maybe even *her?*

She already knew she loved the handsome, competent man. She observed him the few times she got the chance.

One thing bothered her, though: as the housekeeper, she had been judging him by his schedule at home. Between his morning jogging and his night jogging, he seemed the most energetic man that she had ever known. Now, working with him as well, she realized that his schedule was worse than she could ever have imagined. Mark ran an absolutely killing day. It seemed impossible for any man to do as many things as he did. And she'd have bet money that there were more episodes of push-ups. By now, she had come to sympathize with him, and she understood what fueled all of it. It was his way of working off excess energy. It was worse whenever he was under stress. True, it kept him lean and fit, but his excessive exercising had begun to worry her for real.

She tried to remember times when she had seen him slow down and relax. At first she couldn't think of one instance, and then she remembered the night they'd made love. That next morning he had been calm and relaxed. This made her remember he'd been slow and smooth that night, too. It was she who had run out of steam. That thought made her squirm, and she didn't dwell on it.

Later, Mark rushed in to pick up some papers.

"Okay, Redding, what's up?" he asked, banging into her office. She nearly jumped out of her skin.

He expected a fast update on anything that had happened while he was out. It was the same thing that he said to her every day, but for some reason, today, it especially irritated her.

"Don't you ever stop and smell the roses?" she snapped, as she tossed the magazine aside and sat up.

His eyebrows shot up and he stalked off, muttering something about an "evil woman."

Terry lost all interest in eating and went back to working on the files. Ned had proved to be very handy with James's papers.

At first, she had expected problems from Ned. She had dizzily jumped from assistant to receptionist to acting manager. Ned proved flexible enough to accept without question the changes in her status. He seemed glad she was there. So, in time, did most of Mark's staff. Terry soon guessed that they were glad to see some order come into the place and to have someone take responsibility for organizing and giving directions.

Terry relied increasingly upon Ned's help. He was bright and willing. It was pretty obvious that among all the mismanagement James had been guilty of, he had seriously underutilized the staff. Ned was a perfect example of this. Already he was informed of much of what went on simply by having had to assist James.

He should have been hired as a permanent employee and given more responsibility. She sensed Ned felt a little neglected regarding his position. However, it wasn't Terry's intention to soothe feelings that James had hurt. She wanted to run Mark's staff more efficiently, and in doing this, she kept Ned at her side because his knowledge was invaluable.

Finding and organizing the customer files was their top priority. It proved to be a harrowing experience. Many of the later files were incomplete, as James had his own way of filing. In the end, he had taken to throwing various badly labeled and fragmented documents into miscellaneous files. It was a situation that required that they meticulously go through every piece of paper.

They were sitting on the floor with files scattered around them. Though difficult work, it was more easily done on the floor, but that created a false sense of intimacy.

Ned smiled pleasantly at her from where he sat. She sensed an element of simple male appreciation in his smile. It touched her, but it also made her remember how totally focused on Mark she had become these last few months. She smiled back but was careful to keep it light.

"So," he said, "where did the boss find you?"

"I've known Mark for quite a while," Terry answered, and realized belatedly that her words could be misconstrued. She had wanted to reassure him, but it came out as if she was an intimate friend of Mark's.

"Oh, excuse me," he said.

She didn't bother to correct his erroneous impression. He seemed to withdraw. Maybe it's better this way, she thought.

A few hours later, she heard someone whisper as she passed, "She's the boss's girlfriend."

Mrs. Dougan looked a little puzzled when she first heard this rumor but soon seemed quite well adjusted to this information. The older woman then began to pick Terry for information.

"You know, I always knew that Mr. Holden would see through that ex-wife of his sooner or later. You're more his type, if you ask me."

It made Terry want to hug the older woman. Finally, someone who didn't think she would be a total mismatch for Mark. Yet Terry knew she couldn't allow Mrs. Dougan to believe there was anything between her and Mark.

"Mark Holden is my employer, and that's all."

Poor Mrs. Dougan looked more puzzled than ever.

That afternoon, Mark picked up both girls and left them with her in the office. The girls immediately captured everyone's hearts, and Terry had to be careful that the staff didn't fill them with cookies and other sweets. Makeda and Yvette were more like sisters than friends, and this convinced everyone that Terry was more than just the new acting office manager. She realized if she said she was Mark's housekeeper, it would only further cloud the issue. People would be even more puzzled at the unorthodox situation of the boss's housekeeper now working in his office, too. Terry didn't understand it that much herself.

Mark didn't help the matter when he balked at her working at the office. True, he never said anything where the others could hear. He had a way of harping on the subject when they were out of the office.

Of course, the situation at Mark's office wasn't all resolved yet, but things had begun to lighten up. For one thing, morale had improved. Things were running better and were more organized. It had begun to look as if they could get the job done. This, she knew, was in part her doing.

Somehow it worked but to say it was a strange situation was putting it mildly. Her new job was exhilarating at first. As days went by, however, she missed those times in the house, housekeeping and cooking meals.

On days when she had other errands, they both drove their own cars and they shared the responsibility of picking up and dropping off the girls. The strange thing was that the longer it went on, the more they were bound into the family mode. She was covering so many areas in Mark's life that people simply took it for granted that they were also lovers. She knew this fueled her fantasies. It also made her feel more and more that marrying Mark Holden was inevitable. They *seemed* married already.

As for the sex, it was becoming more difficult for her to deny herself this, but some small doubt kept her saying no. Fortunately, with the two of them working at a breakneck pace, she was often too tired even to think about sex.

Her new income boggled her mind. She was literally working two very well-paid jobs. She had never made that much money in her life. And because she spent so little, her bank balance was growing again. Mark covered most of her expenses, like her room and board, as well as her transportation costs. It seemed almost indecent, how little she spent. She would have enjoyed shopping and buying herself something really nice, except there was no time for such a luxury.

That night, they stopped to have dinner in a nearby town. They chose an Italian eatery. For some reason, Mark was quite grumpy and voiced dissatisfaction with everything on the menu.

"What do you want?" he asked Terry and the girls.

Terry quickly chose vegetable lasagna. The girls ordered

chicken dishes. Mark, however, read aloud every entree several times. Each time he sounded more unhappy. Even after he'd ordered for them, he was still fidgeting with the menu and complaining that there was nothing he wanted to eat.

Lately, all he did was complain about food, no matter what it was. He had regressed back to the bad-tempered man he'd been when she was first learning to cook. He tossed the menu down on the table and, looking miserable, watched them eat. He reminded her of a spoiled brat. Even the girls behaved better.

Terry was getting impatient. His complaining was giving her indigestion. She put her fork down. "You were the one who suggested Italian," she reminded him. "We could have gone to that Chinese place you like."

"Who said I liked Chinese?"

"You used to love it."

"No, I didn't. Why don't we ever have akee and salt fish anymore?"

"You hated that." She was really exasperated now.

"I did not. It's just that we never had steak and potatoes."

"Your cleaning lady leaves steaks and potatoes every time she comes, which is twice a week now. You should be happy."

He sighed like a neglected child. He also managed to look sorrowful and mistreated. How a man who stood over six feet could do this, Terry had never figured out.

Determinedly, she picked up her fork and began eating once again. From the corner of her eye, she saw him gaze around the table into their plates as they ate.

Makeda was the first to give in. "You can have some of mine, Mark." She pushed her plate toward him. She had to coax him to eat.

Finally, he allowed Makeda to convince him. "Thank you, darling," he said to the child. After casting a smug look at Terry, he stuck a fork into Makeda's food.

"Have some of mine, too." Yvette passed her food along and he ate some from her plate also.

Terry was positively disgusted with Mark's antics. When she happened to glance up and saw him soulfully eying her food, she pulled her lasagna out of his reach and continued eating as if she hadn't noticed. He scowled at her smug expression.

Mark still hadn't eaten when dessert came. And he refused to order any dessert for himself.

"Well, I still want akee and salt fish," he said. The girls looked terribly sympathetic.

She dropped her fork into the plate with a clang. He'd carried on long enough. "It would have taken me hours to cook. We wouldn't have eaten until midnight."

"Not if you were home doing what you contracted to do, instead of trying to kill yourself at the office."

"I'm not killing myself, and I'm staying until everything's straightened out. You needn't start that again."

"You're only staying so you can sashay around that Ned." His accusing glare and remark made her mouth drop open.

"Are you jealous?" she asked.

"Of course not! Why should I be jealous?"

One of the girls made a slight movement and both Terry's and Mark's attention turned to the children. She had forgotten about them. She glanced back at Mark, who looked sheepish and had picked up the menu again. They both knew they had been on the verge of an argument.

Mark banged around the house, still in foul humor, long after they were home. The intriguing possibility that he might be jealous softened Terry up. Of course, she wound up fixing him a sandwich, though she had sworn to ignore him. *Just goes to show,* she sighed, *I'll do anything for love.*

Chapter Fifteen

Mark was gone before she woke in the morning, which annoyed Terry. She had wanted to discuss an idea that would save time and money in training new home health care aides, and she wondered if he was still smarting about Ned. Later, at the office, she spent the morning watching the door, waiting for him to appear so that she could give him the daily update.

Last night, when they'd almost had a fight in the restaurant, she'd decided to wait until tempers had cooled to discuss her new idea. Now she could barely contain her excitement.

She was still working on James's files when her thoughts turned to how things had changed in the past few weeks. In one way, she knew how unreal her life was. She never forgot for a minute that he'd proposed and that the time for her decision was running out. On the other hand, it was almost as if they were married already.

The files she was poring over were more of James's mess. They were more new accounts that hadn't been filed correctly. She stopped working on them and stared unseeing through the window at the street.

There was also the fact that he hadn't said another word about his proposal since their return from Sebago. Terry wondered if he had forgotten, or if his offer was no longer in effect. There were other times when she wondered if she had imagined the whole thing.

They had been working together as if they'd never considered getting married. Well, in a way, they hadn't. There had been no mention of love—maybe admiration and respect, but certainly not love. Mark had never promised that. She, however, loved him despite his exasperating ways.

She couldn't have cared less that he thought he was Mr. Perfect, able to leap tall buildings in a single bound, or that he often gave her a headache when he acted like a whirlwind and ran circles around her.

She had even forgiven him for casually thinking she would play house with him and be at his beck and call just because he wanted to take her to bed. And even there, she knew if he started with those salesman's ways, she'd probably fall into bed on her back.

All of this she was willing to overlook. None of it had any effect on her loving him. Her thoughts were disrupted when Mark arrived, rushing, as usual.

He stalked by her office door, calling out loudly, "Redding, come in here."

Expecting Terry to follow him, Mark didn't wait, but continued on to his office. However, he didn't realize that she was almost under his feet, and when he stepped back, he almost sent her flying. In his frustration, he peppered the air with a few choice words as he grabbed her before she fell. He had to let her go quickly, for just touching her sent his hormones racing.

"Would you be careful, for Pete's sake?" he barked.

He immediately regretted yelling. Somehow, she always

appeared more frail to him than she actually was. Also, how the hell was he supposed to concentrate if just a simple touch gave him an erection?

"Sorry," she said, as if his yelling meant nothing. She bustled around him to put a sheath of papers on his desk. When she turned back with a self-satisfied smug expression, he almost got nailed. He'd been watching her curvy derrière.

He even felt guilty because she'd apologized for something that had been his fault. He should have been looking where he was going. But worse, Mark found himself gazing at her mouth. She had an engaging habit of running her tongue over them every so often that never failed to enchant him.

He glanced away and moved around the desk. She was chatting away about something as he tried to control his urge to kiss her. He sometimes felt almost furtive in his efforts to watch her and not be seen. He only hoped none of the staff noticed how often his gaze strayed her way.

"Earth to Superman," Terry said, standing arms akimbo and glaring at him.

He hadn't heard what had preceded that statement. She'd caught him off balance. "Huh?" Mark said, sounding more inelegant than he would have preferred. *Holden, you've got to stop this. There may be a law against your thoughts.*

"You didn't hear a word I said. You never listen to me." She was spoiling for a fight.

"That's not true," he denied hastily.

"Then tell me what I said."

He shifted from one foot to the other and didn't want to meet her eyes. "I was working out how we could train more nurse's aides to fill the new slots."

"But that's what I was trying to show you."

She folded her arms across her breasts in what he liked to call her Egyptian queen position and started tapping one foot. The tapping sound made him long to glance down at her legs.

It took Herculean strength to suppress that desire and present a businesslike facade.

He fully appreciated how much good she had done in organizing the office, but he didn't expect her to make big decisions. However, he decided to keep the peace by listening to her.

"Okay, Redding. What were you trying to say?"

With a spark of excitement in her eyes, she grabbed a sheet of paper off his desk and waved it under his nose. "I know how you can save time and money training new aides. You could subcontract one of the local hospitals to do it. I'll bet they'd jump at the opportunity."

Her idea had merit, he thought, but he wasn't ready to give in too fast. "What about our own instructors? I'm not paying them to sit on their bottoms."

"They could do the final orientations."

"Yes, but . . . "

"They'd also be free to proctor the medication exams for more nurses."

"Yes, but . . . "

"No more 'buts,' Mark. You know I'm right."

Actually, he thought, she might have something. "Let me think about it."

"Don't think too long. You need to start working on one of those sticky contracts that you love so much. We need to hire now, before we're unable to cover all the slots. Make it a short-time contract, and then, if you want to reconsider, you can."

"You're right," he finally said. "By the way, what's with this Superman bit?"

Terry suddenly shifted and cleared her throat. "Ah, nothing. Just a joke."

He wondered momentarily what she'd been up to. But mostly, he thought of how she had walked into both his house and his office and kept them running smoothly. He could never thank her enough for what she had done for Yvette. His daughter had gone from a wan shadow of a child to a giggling, mischievous angel.

She did more than he'd ever expect and did it well. With James's neglect, Mark knew the staff had grown lax in the last few months. Terry had stepped in and provided both organization and encouragement.

Mark also knew it was Terry who called reluctant nurses and aides out of their beds to assign them to cases. She had no qualms about being a charming bully to suppliers who weren't prompt in getting their orders out, and last but certainly not least, remained quietly insistent to those hospitals whose checks didn't get into the mail on time.

He sure didn't have time to do this. Sometimes, he couldn't help compare Terry with Marlene. Marlene had hated the mom-and-pop aspect of his business that Terry seemed to enjoy. Terry was his greatest asset with the Underwood people, who were giving him real problems.

"Okay, I'll check your proposal, and if you're right, we'll start making inquiries with the local hospitals."

He started pacing and rubbed at the tension at the back of his neck. He knew she watched him closely. "What's wrong?" she demanded.

"How do you know there's something wrong?"

"I can tell."

"You read minds, Redding?" She went back to tapping that foot again. "Don't you have anything to do—like maybe go home and cook?" Even that didn't faze her, and her presence was too disturbing. He needed to get her out of his office if he was going to get any work done today. He was having trouble keeping his mind on business with Terry in the office. *I'll go broke if I don't stop this.* "Would you get out of here?" he finally said.

She sat down, threw her shoulders back, and waited. He managed not to watch her breasts when she took a deep breath.

"What's happening with Underwood?" she finally said.

"Who said it was Underwood?" It amazed him how well she read him. It also felt good to know he had someone with whom he could discuss the problem. "Underwood's questioning whether we can absorb a second company. And our cash flow problem is worse than we'd anticipated."

"Is it all due to buying James out?" she asked.

"Accounting seems to think so. I don't know, but I thought we were in better shape than this. If I have to borrow operating expenses, it will make us look bad. Underwood would surely back out. Bookkeeping is coming to make a complete report in thirty minutes."

Terry stayed after the accounting department left. Sure enough, their report showed an appalling lack of cash. Mark started pacing as soon as the door closed behind the others.

"There's got to be something missing here," he said, and placed the report on his desk.

As he was wont to do, he then proceeded to fall down and do push-ups. Terry watched, feeling antsy. Finally, he stopped exercising and stood up. He picked up the accounting report again and handed it to her. "See what you think."

"Mark, I've looked at this a dozen times. I'm no good in this area," she said, looking askance at the reports in her hand.

"Just check it out. How the hell can I operate without capital?" he demanded of the air.

She glanced down the columns, expecting to draw a complete blank, which she did until she was looking at the names of the companies that had made recent payments. There was something peculiar, something missing.

Suddenly it hit her. None of the recently acquired accounts, those files which had been misfiled, were on the list. It made her wonder if James had ever forwarded the information to the accounting department.

When she explained it to Mark, he had the bookkeepers do

a check. In the final analysis, the reason their coffers were low was because a number of new customers had never received bills and therefore hadn't paid.

"But what can we do now?" she asked. "It will take months to collect."

"That's okay," Mark responded, "We can use short money in the meantime. Now, we have accounts to justify it. And," he slapped his hands and rubbed his palms together, "we're going after Underwood."

She gave him a smug smile. "Maybe I can't cook so hot, but I know how to run an office."

"You're not that bad a cook, either," he said.

Her eyebrows shot upward. It wasn't much of a compliment, but she was as pleased as if she'd won an award. "What? I'm not overqualified now?"

He stared at her, looking pensive, but never answered.

The next day, they attended a conference at the Underwood Corporation. After several hours, they still hadn't come to an agreement. Finally, Mark stood up, leaned over, and placed both hands palms down on the board table. His manner was so masterful that all eyes were upon him.

"Gentleman," his voice was deceptively soft. "It's been a long, hard haul. And I, for one, feel enough time has passed for us to have made a decision by now.

"You're not going to find another company to do as much as I am able and willing to do. We all know . . . " he paused for dramatic effect, " . . . *most* of the buyout companies are going to take you over and immediately look for loopholes in the contract. Your long-term employees are going to be out of jobs within the year.

"Downsizing, gentlemen, is the name of the game. I am willing to honor my promise. As you can see, we're in a good fiscal position. We're the company of the times. We want to expand, not downsize." This was followed by a long pause as he looked from face to face of the men sitting at the table. The pause lasted so long that they began to squirm.

"There are other companies just as sound as yours," Mark said, and it was like he'd dropped a wrench into the machinery, for all the squirming came to a stop. "It's time, gentlemen, for Underwood to put up or shut up."

Mark straightened up to his full height. "If there is no signed contract on my fax machine when I arrive at nine o'clock tomorrow morning, the deal is off." He zipped his attaché case and nodded at Terry as if to say, "Okay, Redding, let's go."

Standing, Terry gathered her briefcase and papers. She prudently did not cut off the tape recorder immediately, hoping there was a chance they would make a decision before the meeting ended. When no further words were said, she unobtrusively tucked the tape recorder into her case. With a proud smile, she said goodbye to the men sitting around the conference table and followed Mark out of the office. For a few moments, she felt as if Mark was her man. She walked out of there with her head up and a purely female sway to her hips. She felt savage in her pride of this man. She ached to belong to him.

"Well, that's that," Mark said later that night, as he closed the file on an account they'd been working on.

It was nine o'clock and they were sitting in his office after tying up loose ends. The girls had fallen asleep on the long couch in Terry's office. They had been exceptionally good, considering they'd been cooped up at the office since leaving the day camp. All the staff had long since gone home.

"Yes," she answered absently, and glanced at the fax machine. His gaze followed hers.

"How about some coffee?" he suggested. "I still have to go over some contracts, but we'll be leaving pretty soon."

They both stood up and stretched. Terry went to pour the

coffee while Mark took the time to do push-ups. She shook her head. Just watching him made her jumpy and exhausted. He glanced at his watch for the millionth time in the last thirty minutes.

"You gave them until nine tomorrow." She understood what he was feeling, for she couldn't help looking at the fax machine every few minutes.

"I know," he said.

With most of the offices darkened and only one overhead fluorescent light in Mark's office, they seemed to be all alone on an island.

She hated to admit it, but the longer they waited, the less it seemed possible that the buyout would go through. She was tense with fists balled up as she mentally willed the phone to ring. Once, while waiting for Mark to finish, she had dozed off on his couch for a few minutes and dreamed that Underwood was now a part of Holden-McNeil. Waking to find Mark still poring over a sheaf of papers, Terry realized that nothing had actually happened—that it was only a dream. She was disappointed.

Mark saw she was awake and said, "So the empress has returned to the land of the living."

"Empress?"

He looked slightly sheepish and began to pack up the papers. "Just a little sally. Heh, heh." The laughter sounded forced and he appeared embarrassed, as if he'd been caught out in something.

"Mark," she said, "Suppose Underwood doesn't sell? What will you do?"

"First, I'll be ticked off because of the time spent, but then I'll call up the second company on my list and make them an offer."

"Second company?"

"Sure. There's more than one pebble on my beach. I wasn't lying to Underwood. They need me more than I do them." The man was amazing, she thought. "I've got other companies I've been looking at," he added.

"More takeovers?"

He nodded and looked around at the office. "But I won't be this close to them. The business is getting too big for that. They'll have managers."

Suddenly, the fax machine came on, and sure enough, it was the signed contract. She was afraid to touch the paper as it slowly came into view like magic. Mark waited for the machine to stop before tearing off the paper to read.

After he had gone over a number of pages, he looked up at her with a serious expression, then his face broke into a huge grin. "We did it!"

Jumping up, Terry pumped her arms in a victory symbol, saying, "Yeah! Yeah! Yeah!"

Mark grabbed her and spun her around and around. Suddenly he slowed in whirling her and they gazed at each other.

"I couldn't have done it without you," he said hoarsely, gently standing her on her feet.

"Oh, no," she said, her voice a near-whisper. "You were fantastic in that boardroom."

"Fantastic, huh?" He smiled with pleasure. "I made the sales pitch—I know that. But it's like I told you before. I have to believe in my product before I can sell it to anyone else. You pulled this place together and made me see we could do it. You made me believe in this product and that's why I could sell it to Underwood. With James, I had questions. You answered them all."

His face slowly came closer and his lips gently touched hers. She opened her mouth, inviting him to take more.

Sounds of someone stirring came from her office and they broke apart reluctantly. One of the girls had awakened. Mark slowly stepped away.

A sleepy Makeda came to stand in the doorway. "What's all the noise about?" she said, rubbing her eyes and yawning.

"Your mother and I have just closed the deal of the century." Makeda smiled fuzzily. "Go wake up Yvette, sleepyhead. We're going home."

When Makeda left, Mark glanced at Terry and said, "We deserve a celebration."

"You're right. Tomorrow's Friday. Let's all go out to dinner," she suggested.

"By all, you're including Makeda and Yvette?"

"Yes," she said, bemused by the question.

"Do you remember what tomorrow is?"

"No," she answered.

"Your six weeks are over."

"Oh." She felt breathless. They hadn't spoken of his proposal in so many weeks that she'd stopped counting. Suddenly, her stomach lurched. She was a bundle of nerves.

Mark's statement had caught her unprepared. All the problems with the meetings and the last-minute worries with Underwood had driven the thought from her head. Also, she had believed he'd forgotten.

"This should be a dinner for just the two of us," he explained softly. Her heart started pounding away, thudding against her chest like a tom-tom. "I figured we could go into Manhattan and see that remake of *Timbuktu,* then have dinner at that new restaurant, Ethiopia West. How's that sound?"

"Can we get tickets?"

"I'm a man of many talents," he said, and held up two theater tickets.

"Wonderful." She had to clear her throat when her voice croaked.

She felt a little foolish and wondered if he knew how happy she was that he still wanted to marry her. She wondered if the offer would stand if he knew how much she loved him. Mark wanted a marriage without all the entanglements of love, and here she was, croaking like a frog because he showed her a theater ticket. Would she ever learn?

Later, after a quick shower, she stood in front of the mirror over the sink and wiped the cloudy surface. One glance at her hair showed it seriously needed a touch-up. "Ouch!" she said to her reflection.

She looked a mess. While she had been only the housekeeper, she'd always been able to fix herself up. Now that she was doing double duty at Mark's office, she hadn't had the time. Her nails needed manicuring, and a glance down at her toes showed that a pedicure would be a good idea, too.

The only thing she hadn't neglected was her women's defense class. She flexed a bicep and had to admit she was looking better. The new musculature, slight as it was, was gratifying. *I may not win any contest, but that's more muscle than I ever expected to have in my life.* "I just ain't exquisite yet." She sighed.

She went into the bedroom, and once under the lightweight covers, allowed herself to relive that fleeting moment in the office when Mark had kissed her.

She sat up and hugged her knees. Her heart felt light and carefree. *No matter what happens, I'm going to say yes.*

She wanted Mark to be her husband. She wanted him more than she had ever wanted anything in her life. And she didn't want to wait. She would marry him if she had to walk across hot coals.

She was going to grab her happiness.

Terry thought briefly of Ronald and the problems that she'd had while married to him but quickly pushed that away. Just as she had learned to ignore Beverly, who still called occasionally to cry on her shoulder, she could ignore the past, too. Ronald was the past.

Wanting to look good for Mark on their date, she decided that she wouldn't go into the office that next day. Now that the Underwood buyout was resolved, and with the office running fairly smoothly, she wouldn't be missed that much. Besides, Ned could handle most of the work.

Mark was always complaining that she was working too hard, anyway. Though anyone who worked as much as he did certainly shouldn't talk.

That next morning, Terry woke feeling beautiful, languid, and lazy. It took a few moments before she remembered what had prompted such feelings. Mark had mentioned his proposal.

Memories of their clinch flooded her mind and she lay there wishing that he was lying beside her. She gazed at the second pillow and tried to picture his head lying there. She often tried to imagine what it would feel like to fall asleep with him. He had gotten up and left the night they'd made love.

She rolled over, hating to relinquish the erotic sensations that lingered. She did get up, however. After showering, she slipped into a pair of jeans and went into the kitchen. She fixed the type of breakfast that Mark liked and set it up on the warmer, atop the sideboard, in steaming glass-topped dishes.

"Hey, hey," Mark said with a big grin when he saw his breakfast. "Good living has returned to the Holden household."

The girls made oohs and aahs, too. Everyone served himself, and for once, Terry joined them. Mark looked especially pleased at this. They stared at each other for several seconds.

"I thought I'd take a day off. There are some things I want to do."

"Okay," he said with a sexy grin. It made her heart swell.

"Mommy, don't forget—we're going to help you get dressed up for tonight," Makeda said.

"Of course." Terry ruffled both girls' hair. "I wouldn't dream of doing it without your expert advice."

Mark had told the girls about the "date" during the drive home. The children had been full of girlish excitement at the idea.

After breakfast, they all left at the same time that morning, each taking a car. Both children piled in with her. She was buckling her seatbelt when Mark came to lean through the window.

"You'll be home alone today, so be careful. Don't open the door unless you know who it is. Mrs. Merkle, next door, still swears there's a strange man lurking about."

"I will." Terry didn't feel too concerned by the news as she turned the ignition. The community's private security force had been especially vigilant ever since their neighbor had complained about seeing a prowler. Besides, it was common knowledge that Mrs. Merkle saw the boogeyman everywhere.

Terry and the girls waved goodbye as they drove off.

When she dropped the children at camp, she spent a few moments watching them rush into the horse stalls to help feed the animals. The girls had become quite good with them in the few weeks they'd been at camp. She spoke with their instructor for a few seconds because she hadn't seen much of the woman since she'd begun going to the office.

Leaving the camp, she drove slowly, savoring the lovely day. There was a coolness in the morning air that would burn off by midday. She took a deep breath of the fresh air, thinking how glorious it was to be alone for a few hours.

It reminded her of those days when she had been strictly the housekeeper. With the cleaning lady coming twice a week, there had been very little to do during the day, especially with the girls in school. She'd spent a great deal of time poring over cookbooks and thinking up gourmet food to fix. She knew they had enjoyed it. Now she couldn't do these things any longer, and she missed it. But she also felt that Mark's business was more important at the moment. Though to listen to him complain about how neglected he was, you wouldn't have guessed this to be true.

The rest of the time, she had spent reading enriching books— the kind she hadn't had time to read before. Her only excuse was that it actually made her a better companion for the children. And this was actually what Mark swore he wanted for his daughter. There were many days when she had felt more like a pampered young wife than a housekeeper.

Although she wasn't going in to work, she had planned a very busy day. She stopped at the beauty parlor to get an appointment to have her hair touched up. Fortunately, the beautician was able to squeeze her in. The beautician convinced her to have the whole works, including spa bath and massage, promising they would have her out in time to pick up the girls.

She sat in a huge, gloriously bubbling tub. Someone handed her a biting-cold glass of mineral water. There was a paper-thin wedge of lemon floating in the drink. From there she went on a table and had a thorough body massage with a fragrant lotion.

After the massage, she glanced at her watch and decided to have Mark pick up the girls. She didn't want them to have to wait for her. The masseuse brought a telephone, reluctantly, saying that this was a time when she should shut out everything else and think only of being beautiful.

Mark was in the office. "Where are you?" he asked.

"At the beauty salon."

"Are they going to paint your toenails?"

His seductive voice sent chills up her spine. She didn't answer, but giggled as badly as the girls. Anyone can tell what's on my mind, she thought. He chuckled deep in his throat.

"It's taking longer than I expected," she said. "Would you mind picking up the girls?"

"No problem."

"You can leave them with Mrs. Merkle. I won't be too long."

"Don't worry about it," he insisted. "Just take your time."

She thought he seemed reluctant to hang up and so she stayed on, waiting for him to say something. When he didn't, she asked "How are things there?"—wanting to hear more of his sexy voice.

They spoke for a few minutes about the office, but Terry was only too aware of wanting to say something else, something more personal. Strangely enough, she sensed that he might feel the same way. She only hoped he hadn't changed his mind about their date.

Once their conversation was concluded, Terry lay down to take her rest. She dozed off immediately.

Later, when she saw the astronomical bill, she refused even to blink, knowing the time spent had been worth every penny. She walked out feeling truly beautiful and ready to say yes to Mark's proposal, even if it was only a business offer. She felt like a woman who could teach him to love her.

Chapter Sixteen

Mark hung up after talking to Terry, then sat quietly at his desk for several moments. He'd wanted to say something more personal to her, but it seemed too soon. He didn't want to scare her away.

"I'll tell her later," he said aloud.

Suddenly he envisioned her making herself beautiful just for him. He had to shake himself to give that image up. But thinking of her preparing herself for their night suddenly made him want to do something for her. He called the barber and made an appointment.

He had been planning tonight for quite a while and was eager for it to come. Before she had called, he had been going over in his mind what he would say tonight, trying to think of things that would convince her to say yes. Sounding too much like a salesman had blown it for him last time—or at least, so he believed. He didn't want to make the same mistake again.

Flowers! He snapped his fingers and picked up the phone to call a local florist. He ordered long-stemmed roses for the woman he wanted to make the queen of his home.

* * *

Terry stopped at the supermarket to pick up some fresh vegetables. She considered a light menu for the girls and the sitter as she walked through the aisles of the well-stocked store. A quick glance at her watch told her that she had spent most of the day at the beauty parlor. Although Mark would pick them up, she didn't want the children to stay with Mrs. Merkle too long. Best to get them settled down early; then she wouldn't worry about leaving them later.

She stopped before bins of luscious-looking fruits. Suddenly, she imagined Mark and her feeding each other peeled grapes in front of a fire.

Fire? In July? "Girl, get real," she muttered aloud.

A woman standing nearby was startled by her speaking, and she smiled at the woman before moving away. *Daydreaming about that man is making me soft in the head.* But she had to admit she had never felt better, nor looked better, either.

She spent the drive back to the house enjoying the scenery she had come to love. It was too glorious for air-conditioning but she didn't want to roll the windows down. There was no way she was going to mess up her hair after spending the whole day getting it done.

Her spirits were high as she went up the semicircular drive and parked on the gravel. She hummed a little tune as she removed the bags of groceries and wondered if the cleaning lady was still there.

When no one answered her ringing, she had to take the time and find the keys—which, of course, were at the bottom of her purse. She wanted to smile at the small annoyance. It was so tiny, considering the problems that she used to have.

Just as she pushed the door open, she heard a man snarl over her shoulder, "What the hell took you so long?"

Terry's head snapped around and her jaw dropped. "Ronald! What are you doing here?"

She went stark still. All she could think of was how she had become much too complacent in recent weeks. Her gaze darted to the street and she began praying that he would be gone before Mark came with the girls. She would die if any of them saw her in this position.

Before she could do anything, he had shoved her through the doorway, pushing in behind her. The groceries tumbled out of her arms as she went stumbling into the house. She barely managed not to fall.

"I was just about ready to leave," Ronald said. "I've been waiting here for you since you left this morning."

He smelled of alcohol again. Lately, it seemed that whenever she saw him, he had been drinking.

"What do you want?" she said, annoyed that her voice sounded weak. Apparently that fact escaped Ronald as he went on with his tirade.

"I saw you come out with your new big-deal man, so I had to wait. You're so high and mighty now that I have to wait on you like I was some sort of jerk." Terry shivered in cold dread at his menacing manner. "You think because you've got a new boyfriend it makes you anything better than you were to begin with? Well, it don't. Wait until he finds out what a wimp you really are."

"Wha . . . what do you want?" she said again, trying to regain her composure.

Ronald's gaze darted around as if he expected someone to pounce on him. Terry realized that he was frightened, too, and sensed it was Mark he feared.

"Here you are, living like a queen while I have nothing," he said, and malice seemed to waft from his rumpled clothes.

"Then get a job." Her skin was crawling. She kept glancing toward the windows and her ears were straining for any sound of Mark's car.

"Why should I, when my wife can afford to help me out?"

"We're divorced, Ronald."

"That don't mean you can't help me. I'm the father of your child. You owe me something."

"I don't owe you anything."

"Give me a couple of bucks and I'll leave. Maybe then your new man won't learn how worthless you really are."

Terry picked up her purse from where it had dropped and quickly grabbed a handful of bills. It was more than she wanted to give him, but she was desperate for him to leave. She shoved the money at him and opened the door behind him. Ronald stumbled before he caught his balance and tried to saunter out. It was a wasted effort as she saw him look around furtively before going down the driveway and turning toward the bus stop on the corner.

She glanced up and down the street for Mark's car, but it was nowhere in sight. When she shut the door, she sagged heavily against it and gave a sigh of relief. Her skin was clammy and her hands were shaking.

The groceries were all over the floor. As she bent down to pick everything up, Terry was furious with herself. She was upset that she had been so frightened of Ronald. It was as if she'd never taken the self-defense classes, so helpless had she felt. True, she had spoken up to him, but inside she was quaking. She knew only too well what Ronald was capable of.

She was also angry that she hadn't been able to hold out longer before giving in. But she had been petrified that Mark would show up with Makeda and Yvette. It would have been unbearable for them to see how frightened and inadequate she truly was. She would have done anything to keep them from seeing her humiliated by Ronald.

And in the end, she knew that she had given him too much money. It would only encourage him to come back again, looking for more next time.

It was only a matter of minutes before she heard Mark's car drive up and the girls enter the house. When Mark didn't come in, she was disappointed. Obviously, he'd gone back to the office, but she wished he'd come in first. She wanted to see him and experience the sense of safety she always felt in his presence. She wanted to feel protected, even if it was only for a few foolish moments.

Before she could shut the door after the girls, a delivery truck drove up. Mark had sent her flowers. She closed the door and buried her face in the twelve long-stemmed velvety red roses. Her heart felt as if it would break. She tried to hold them back, but suddenly big tears slid down her face to land on the petals. Her tears looked like dewdrops on the fragrant blossoms.

"Who are the flowers from?" Makeda asked from behind her.

Terry quickly dashed the tears away and turned to show the children, who stood there full of curiosity. Somehow, she managed to put her own problems away for the girls. She observed Yvette, wondering if the child would be upset at her father sending her flowers. Terry also knew she would have to be careful Yvette didn't feel left out or worried about her father getting married. However, both girls wanted only to admire the flowers.

In a few minutes they had hastily donned their bathing suits and were in the pool. Terry went outside to sit in a lounger and keep an eye on them. She put on sunglasses and sat in the shade. Fortunately, both girls had become quite competent in the water.

Old memories surfaced. Terry thought of how Ronald had been spoiled rotten by his mother. But when his mother refused to believe any more of his lies, he'd found Terry. Their life had been full of his bluffing and lying during the two years they'd been married. Now that Ronald had to face the music, he seemed to be seeking the things from the past where he had been the winner. It was a strange thought, but she felt it was true. However, the insight did her no good. She simply wanted to see the end of him.

"Are you all right, Terry?" Yvette asked.

Terry opened her eyes to look at the small girl who stood by her lounge, wrapped in a towel. The child was shivering. Makeda came up out of the water like a young otter and rushed to join them. Terry realized from Yvette's concerned expression that she had been inattentive and had alarmed her young charge.

"I'm okay, honey," Terry tried to reassure her, "just a little headachy, I guess."

"Maybe you shouldn't lie in the heat anymore," Makeda suggested, sounding terribly grown up.

"Yes, I think you're right. I'll go lie on the couch for a while. Will you two mind coming in now?"

"We don't mind and we'll be so quiet you'll forget we're here," sunny Makeda said.

"Don't forget, we're going to help you get dressed," Yvette piped up.

Terry wanted to groan, for she had forgotten. She wondered if she would be able to go through with her promise now. But she knew that she couldn't disappoint the children. They both grinned up at her.

She smiled at them, thinking what a joy it was to care for them. Then she went into the den, and after removing her shoes and putting an ice pack on her forehead, she lay down. She would have preferred going to her room and closing the door, but she didn't want to leave the children to their own devices. The girls went to their room and she could hear them play as they changed into dry clothes.

"Don't leave those wet bathing suits in the middle of the floor," she called out to them.

"Okay," they both called back with giggles.

It made her smile, but it couldn't take her mind off the thoughts that had been going on for the past few hours.

She hadn't been able to do a thing after the confrontation with Ronald. The food she had bought to cook went into the fridge and she decided to have something delivered.

Every unexpected sound had her jumping. She kept expecting

Ronald to materialize out of the air like a malignant genie. Even with the pleasant sound of the girls playing in their room, the house was eerily tense.

Strangely enough, later, after Mark had come home, the tension seemed worse. He was quiet and seemed distracted. On a better day, Terry knew she would have been quick to question him as to what new aggravation had come up at the office. But not that evening. She was too self-absorbed to focus on anything beside her own pain.

Terry went about arranging for the date, though in the state she was in, all she wanted was to cancel. The only reason she didn't was because it would have been too difficult to explain. Besides, she refused to allow Ronald's coming to spoil Mark's celebration. Mark didn't deserve that. Her ex-husband wasn't Mark's problem; he was hers.

Somehow, she did manage to have the girls share the experience of her getting ready. Mark had spent most of the evening in his room.

While Terry dressed, the girls made up their faces, too, and stumbled around in her high-heeled shoes. It should have been a wonderful experience, one they would all remember for years to come. Instead, Terry was a wreck and her headache had turned into a continuous dull throb.

"I can't wait until I'm big enough to have dates," Yvette said. She applied lipstick and stood back to admire her handiwork.

"I don't mind going out on dates as long as I don't have to kiss any boys," Makeda explained matter-of-factly.

"Kiss boys? Is that what you have to do?" Yvette didn't sound too happy with that idea.

"Like on television," Makeda explained.

Both girls went quiet and glanced at Terry with big, questioning eyes.

"Are you going to kiss Mark?" Makeda asked suspiciously.

Terry wanted to cry. It was such a touching scene and it was ruined for her. She evaded their questions. "We'll see," Terry promised them.

They lost interest quickly and went on to more of their little-girl talk.

"I'm going to be a chef when I grow up," Yvette informed them. "I'm going to wear a big floppy white hat. I'll be world-famous, too."

"I'm going to be a supermodel and I'll wear makeup all the time."

Terry listened and tried to get into the moment. "What," she said, "no doctors or lawyers?"

"Well, maybe I'll be a big businesswoman," Yvette amended, her head tilted as if in deep thought.

"Yeah," Makeda jumped in. "And we could make big million-dollar deals."

Terry watched with a pained heart as Makeda clapped her hands and rubbed her palms together. After that, she let the conversation drop. It hurt too much to see Makeda imitate Mark.

Mark and Terry waited in silence for the sitter to come.

Later, she could barely keep her mind on the show. It was a Broadway production that she had been wanting to see for months, but her attention wandered. Mark seemed equally distracted, and she caught him glancing her way from time to time. It was an unusual evening, not much of a date, actually, as they barely spoke a word to each other.

Afterward, they went to the Ethiopian restaurant. Despite the delicious spicy authentic East African cuisine, Terry was pushing the food around on her plate.

"You don't seem very interested in that." Mark indicated her plate with the tip of his fork. "Is there something wrong?"

Her fork slipped from her nerveless fingers to clatter on her plate. She shuddered and jerked her gaze to his. "No," she lied, and quickly tried to compose herself. "I've had a headache all afternoon."

Terry picked up the fork and ate a small mouthful of food. It didn't seem fair to spoil Mark's evening just because her nerves were a strained mess.

"Yes, the girls told me about your headache." Mark took a sip of his wine. "Well, have you had time to think about my offer?"

Despite her anguish, she couldn't help but notice that he'd called it an offer, like it was an auction and he had made a bid. She had been thinking of it as a proposal, but to Mark it was a business deal. Marrying her was nothing more than a minor merger.

She loved him but believed that if he ever found out about her marriage with Ronald he would come to despise her. People always looked down on women who had lived as she had.

Suddenly, she couldn't meet his gaze. She couldn't help wondering what he would say if he knew the full truth about her. Last night he had looked at her with admiration and complimented her on the work she'd done. *I'm not the woman he thinks. He thinks I can handle things.*

There was no way she could marry this man, who was so good that he would never imagine what she had been through. He didn't know what a coward she was. And without further thought, she knew what she had to do. Terry gave up trying to eat and placed the fork at the side of her plate.

"Mark, I can't marry you." There: she had said it, as she had known that eventually she would have to do. "I'm flattered, but I simply can't go into a loveless marriage."

There was a long silence. Her nerves were so taut, she felt as if her skin was stretched over a drum. She feared if anything touched her, it would vibrate and be repelled from her.

"I saw your ex-husband leaving this afternoon when I dropped the girls off." Shocked, her gaze flew to his face to find him regarding her with an intense appraisal. "Is that why you won't marry me? Because there's still something between you and him?"

She wanted to tell him the real reason, and also, that she feared and despised Ronald, but something told her this way was best. If she said she was still in love with Ronald, then she wouldn't have to explain any further. She wouldn't have to expose her painful past to this man whose regard she needed more than she'd ever imagined.

When she didn't answer, Mark asked, "Do you still love him?"

Mark thinks I still love Ronald. God, if he only knew. In that instant, she knew what she had to do. If she said yes, then she never had to tell the truth. She never had to lose his respect. She would at least be left with his having thought enough of her to ask her to be his wife. While the proposal hadn't meant he loved her, it had meant he regarded her with some respect.

Somehow, though, she couldn't bring herself to say the one word that would convince Mark. She couldn't say that she still loved Ronald—not for anything. But as she looked into Mark's face, she knew that by her saying nothing, he believed her answer was yes.

"Does he feel the same about you?" Mark asked. His voice sounded cool and neutral.

She felt her heart break as she realized only too well what she'd done. She had thrown away all her chances with Mark. A man's pride was fragile, and while he might not think he had to be madly in love with her, he wouldn't want a wife who loved another man.

"I don't want to talk about this," she said, and lowered her eyes to keep him from seeing she was on the verge of tears.

Terry knew that it was too late for that. She knew Mark had seen the tears already and suspected he believed she cried for Ronald.

Mark reached across the table and put his hand over hers. "Maybe it's none of my business, but I don't think he's good enough for you."

When she looked up, she saw nothing but pity in his expression. It was the death knell of any hope for them.

She felt as if a monstrous chasm had just opened under her feet and she was falling further and further from any happiness she'd hoped for.

After the failure of their so-called date, Mark and Terry had very little to say to each other. Though things at the office were running smoothly, Terry hadn't seen much of Mark because he spent a great deal of time at the Underwood site.

The girls would be starting back to school soon, and Terry had taken off some time to take them clothes shopping. It was late afternoon before they returned. Mark, Terry knew, would be late coming home, something that happened frequently ever since their night out.

Within an hour, Terry had the house full of the delicious smells of dinner cooking. Both girls were upstairs reading and playing with their crayons and coloring books. It was supposed to be homework, part of the academic part of the day camp. But from the frequent giggles, Terry wondered how much work was really being done.

When the doorbell rang, Terry went to answer it, not particularly expecting anything. She wasn't even afraid of Ronald turning up anymore, as he'd already done the real damage last time.

She opened the door to find a woman who could have stepped off a haute couture magazine cover, so absolutely perfect was she. Terry didn't need anyone to tell her the woman was Marlene.

A tall woman with beautiful tan skin, Marlene was flawlessly made up. Long auburn hair that looked mussed, but which Terry knew had been formed into charming disarray by a meticulous hairdresser, caught the evening breeze. There was a huge solitaire on the third finger of the woman's left hand.

Marlene sauntered in and gazed around the softly lit blue room with a sharp, observant glance.

Terry said, "Mark's not in yet. I don't expect him until late, but you can contact him on his mobile phone."

"You don't have to tell me that," the woman said haughtily. She glided toward one of the upholstered chairs. Once she was seated with her long legs crossed, she gave Terry a thorough once-over. When she seemed to have satisfied her curiosity, she said, "Bring me a cup of coffee."

Though annoyed by the woman's presumption, Terry served a cup of the coffee she'd made for dinner, then left to call Yvette. When she returned, Marlene wasn't as calm as she wanted to appear, as she jiggled one foot while watching Terry through narrowed, hostile eyes.

"So, things have progressed to 'Mark,' I see." Her face tightened into harsh lines, and suddenly she was no longer as beautiful a woman as Terry had originally thought, but rather a cold, spiteful facsimile.

Before either of them could say another word, Yvette and Makeda came into the room. They had come down the stairs with loud yelps and giggling, as was their wont.

"Mommy!" Yvette ran to hug Marlene.

Marlene actually moved away and held up her hand to stop the girl from hugging her. "Yvette, please. Don't muss me. What's happened to your manners?"

The child looked crushed. "I'm sorry . . . Marlene," she said, sounding suddenly subdued.

It was as if with just a few words, Marlene had turned Yvette back into the sad, suppressed child Terry had met that first day. Terry's heart constricted.

Then Marlene carefully leaned forward and presented Yvette with one perfectly madeup cheek to be kissed.

Terry had never disliked Marlene more than she did at that moment. Previously, she'd had so little contact with Mark's ex-wife that she'd considered the woman more pest than any-

thing else. Mark always seemed in a foul mood after one of
Marlene's calls, or Yvette would look a little listless. But she
had never actually seen the woman in action before. Now she
saw her as a self-centered, destructive woman who would
always disappoint those who loved her. Yvette moved back to
stand by Terry, as did Makeda. The two girls stayed near, as
if drawing strength to withstand Marlene's negative presence.

Marlene noticed the small girl's defection and her face once
again became tight with annoyance. "Yvette, come here." She
glared at Terry when the small child approached slowly. "Why
are you yelling and screaming like that? You've turned into a
little savage."

Terry was annoyed at Marlene's reaction to Yvette's being
more playful than before. Had she expected Yvette always to
remain a little mouse?

Yvette looked beseechingly at Terry. Terry wanted to hug
her back into good humor but knew that any such action would
only further antagonize Marlene.

"And these absolutely ghastly clothes. Where are your nice
dresses?

Terry tried to soften Marlene's anger. Both girls were wearing
two-piece short sets. She was the one who had bought Yvette's
clothing and she didn't want the child to suffer for that.

"I'm sorry about the shorts," Terry said, "but I thought it
was all right while she's in the house." There was no way she
was going to say they had gone shopping in those same shorts.

"It's not all right. Yvette's *my* daughter, and I know what's
best for her."

Terry wanted to let this pompous woman really have it, but
she bit her tongue, knowing anything she said could cause
Marlene to extract her revenge on helpless Yvette.

"Yes, I understand," Terry answered.

"I doubt you can," Marlene said with contempt. "My daughter's being groomed to fit into a world that you and yours,"

she cast a sharp glance at Makeda before going on, "would never understand."

Makeda looked shocked and turned bewildered, questioning eyes on Terry. Terry was furious that the woman had upset both girls. She couldn't remember the last time she'd been this angry or felt this helpless. She sat down in a chair and both girls leaned upon the chair arms as if needing protection and seeking it from her.

"Yvette, why don't you and . . . your little friend go back to your room and play while I have a talk with the housekeeper."

Once the children left, Marlene continued, "You seem to have taken over here, including alienating my daughter."

"That isn't true," Terry said, fists balled in her lap.

At last Marlene had taken off the kid gloves, such as they were, and Terry was glad. She welcomed the challenge and wanted to have it out with Marlene for both of the girls and for Mark, too.

"It's obvious you have some pretty big ideas about my husband, too."

"Mark's not your husband."

"And you think that he might someday be yours? Forget it. You're not his type." Marlene laughed with contempt and tossed her hair.

The laughter lacerated Terry's pride. From the minute Marlene had stepped through the door she had been battling the sudden female jealousy that had erupted. With shocking self-knowledge, Terry felt an unbelievably powerful urge to take after the beautiful woman. Her nails bit into her palms.

"Well," Marlene said, "you should thank your lucky stars that I'm not here at the moment. When I come back, there will certainly be some changes." She glanced pointedly at Terry's shorts. "Sure as hell your presence here will be one of the changes, too."

"Mark hasn't had anything to complain about," Terry

snapped, and realized that statement sounded more serious than she'd meant.

"I'll bet." There was something coiled and malignant about the way Marlene sat. She leaned forward to say, "I've heard this foolishness about him proposing marriage as a business deal. But if I were you, I'd forget it."

"That was all a mistake," Terry said. "There isn't going to be any marriage . . . "

"I didn't think there would be. It was too preposterous that Mark would be satisfied with you after having been with me. Mark is a big man in his community. He needs a wife who will be a credit to him."

It was too much. With her own feelings of loss after having refused Mark, she couldn't remain quiet in the presence of this woman. She couldn't seem to stop herself from answering the woman's jibes.

"Maybe what Mark needs is a wife who wouldn't desert him and who could be faithful."

"How dare you?" Marlene jumped to her feet, and Terry followed her. They were like two boxers ready to fight.

"The truth comes easily," Terry answered.

"You've allowed yourself to have dreams of grandeur. He's just using you because you're handy and you're obviously very willing."

"At least we're both single and not hurting anyone else." It was a deliberate reminder that Marlene had been unfaithful to Mark. Marlene's eyes narrowed viciously.

"You're hurting my daughter, to allow her to see this in her home."

"More than you were hurting her living in Weston Barkley's house?"

"Weston and I have a true relationship and we're engaged to be married, while you're a servant in this house."

There was no answer to that, Terry realized, except the truth, which was to admit that there was nothing going on in the house that would damage the children. Terry knew she had to take back her jealous words.

She swallowed her pride and took a deep breath. "Marlene, there's nothing between Mark and me. We're not doing anything here that would be bad for your daughter."

Marlene appeared mollified at this. The woman walked around the room, looking at various objects. Terry turned to watch her. "That may be so," Marlene went on in a calmer voice, "but it gives people ideas, doesn't it? I'll bet people already think you're lovers. Am I right?" Terry didn't answer, but Marlene took her silence as agreement. "Don't you think these stories would hurt my daughter if she heard them?"

"The stories aren't true."

Suddenly, Marlene stopped and turned to Terry. "Sometimes the truth doesn't matter." She walked into the foyer and called Yvette, who had gone upstairs. Terry had followed, concerned by the smug enmity that she saw in Marlene's face. When Yvette looked down at the two women, Marlene said, "Get your sweater. You're coming with me."

Chapter Seventeen

"No! Don't . . ." Terry said, putting out her hands in an attempt to deter Marlene.

Yvette's face looked sad as she slowly came down the stairs. Makeda came down with Yvette, one hand around the girl's shoulders.

"Yvette's my daughter," Marlene reminded them nastily, "and she's here only on my consent." Marlene took Yvette's hand and walked toward the front door, pulling the reluctant child behind her. "Mark promised to provide her with the correct environment, which he has failed to do."

Terry followed the pair, wringing her hands. "Marlene, please don't do this. I'm sorry if I've offended you. I'll do anything . . ."

"I think you've done far too much already."

"Then wait for Mark. He'll explain everything." Terry was rattling on, trying to delay the determined Marlene. She was actually on the verge of promising she'd move out. She would have done anything to keep the woman from taking Yvette.

Marlene pulled Yvette all the way to her car. When she drove off, both Terry and Makeda watched hopelessly as the car receded into the distance. Then Terry rushed in and grabbed the phone, hastily dialing Mark's number.

"Mark," Terry said, tears welled up when she heard his voice, "she took Yvette!"

"Who took Yvette?" he asked, but she could tell by his voice that he already knew. "I'll get back to you," he said after she explained, and then disconnected.

Terry hung up and looked at Makeda, who was crying.

"Why did she have to take her, Mommy?" her small daughter wailed, and buried her face into Terry's stomach.

It was so rare to see Makeda cry that it almost made Terry bawl along with her, but she knew she had to be strong for them both.

The thing Terry couldn't seem to do anything about was her own feelings of being responsible for the whole mess. She had allowed her emotions to get the better of her. Why hadn't she kept her mouth shut?

In a way, Marlene was perfectly right: people did assume that she and Mark were lovers. It had been true from the moment she moved in. To the world they appeared like a family group. The girls thought of themselves almost as sisters and it had happened instantaneously.

There had even been that one night when she'd made love with Mark. Though it had never happened again, she still wanted him.

And now she had cost Mark the most important thing in his life. Mark had been willing to marry her in order to save Yvette. Because she had not been able to hold her tongue, he had lost his daughter. She knew he would grow to hate her, if he hadn't already.

She sat in the green room and waited in dread for Mark to come home. Makeda tried to wait for Mark, too, but soon fell asleep with tearstained cheeks, leaving Terry alone in torment with her thoughts.

Several hours later, Mark came. It was raining and he'd gotten wet. The first thing Terry noticed was his slowed tread, which reflected how down he was.

It was one of the few times Terry had ever seen the normally energetic Mark look tired. She hated Marlene at that moment and felt that the woman had messed up her family. She also realized that by "family," she meant Mark and Yvette, too.

Mark sat in a chair, staring at the floor. He heard her and looked up. She was shocked at his bleak expression. Her heart felt as if it would break.

"Tell me exactly what happened," he said.

She wanted to cry. It had been excruciating when she'd realized that she couldn't possibly marry him. But now, knowing that once he understood what had happened he would despise her, was more than she could bear. Yet she knew he had to hear the whole story from her.

"We had an argument."

"About what?"

How could she explain that she had allowed jealousy to cloud her judgment? "Marlene heard we were thinking of getting married."

"How did she know that?"

"James, maybe," she said. "Or Beverly."

"How would they know?"

"James heard you on the phone the day you first proposed. Beverly told me," Terry admitted.

"But you didn't tell me?" When she shook her head no, he asked, "Why not? Didn't you think I should have known?"

"No, because I thought you had forgotten all about the marriage proposal."

"What happened then?"

"She made the girls cry and I saw red," Terry said, feeling full of self-contempt. How could she explain to him that Marlene's confidence that she could win him back had set her on edge?

"None of this makes any sense. I can't believe you antago-
nized her, knowing that she can be a very vicious woman."

She blinked back tears. She would have done anything to
turn back the clock to the moment when Marlene had first
walked into the house. She wanted to beg for his forgiveness.

"I'm sorry. I'll move out tomorrow."

He sighed and stood up. She couldn't even see him through
her tears.

"You can't," he said. "The least you can do is stay until I
can prove that I have adequate arrangements to take care of
Yvette when I petition the courts."

He walked out, leaving her alone. His door closed with a
quiet click. She felt lower than she had ever felt in her life.

She wanted to scream. She wanted to throw things. Maybe
all she really wanted to do was cry. Most certainly she would
have gladly packed and left Mark's home. But he was right,
she owed him more than she could ever repay. And even if she
hadn't owed him anything, she loved him. Because of that, she
would do anything she could to help him.

When Terry went to bed, she lay there a long time, tossing
and turning. Every time she thought of the small, sweet Yvette,
she wanted to cry. The house was going to be a bleak place
without her. Her heart ached for Mark.

A sound at the door caught her attention. It was Makeda still
in her nightgown.

"Mommy, can I sleep with you? I don't want to stay in my
room."

"Sure, you can, honey." Terry held up the bedcover so
Makeda could climb in next to her.

Makeda fell immediately asleep in Terry's arms, but it took
a while before Terry could doze off.

The sound of someone moving about woke her. One glance
at the bedside clock told her it was two in the morning. She
realized she had slept for a while despite her early restlessness.

Makeda was asleep next to her. Terry hastily threw a housecoat over her lightweight cotton gown and padded barefoot into the living room, where she found Mark wearing a black terry robe. His eyes were closed, and at first she thought he was asleep. But he heard her and sat up.

Risking a rebuff, she took a deep breath and said gently, "I'll make some coffee."

Mark followed her to the kitchen, where he sat in the breakfast nook. Terry took up the coffeepot and suddenly remembered that she had served Marlene a cup from it. Without hesitation she dashed the coffee into the sink and cleaned the drain with a vengeance, wishing she could wipe Marlene out of their lives in the same manner.

She perked fresh coffee, then poured two cups, setting them on the table. When Mark didn't take his, she placed a hand on his shoulder.

"Mark, I'm so sorry. I'd do anything if I thought it would help."

He took her hand and guided her closer. She was standing only inches from him and he put his arms around her. He put his head on her stomach, and it reminded her of when Makeda had done the same thing earlier, but with this man there was an awareness that was absent with Makeda.

He slipped his hands under her robe and drew her close to him. "Just let me hold you," he said, "All right? Nothing else."

After a while, it started to go further, and though she was willing, she went still. He misunderstood, seeming to think that she was withdrawing.

"Okay, okay," he said. "Don't get on your high horse." He rubbed his jaw where his beard had grown in overnight.

This made her want to laugh, for it sounded more like the Mark she was familiar with and less like the too-quiet man of last night. But she was also disappointed. She needed the comfort of being close to him tonight, too.

He stood up. "Anyway, you need to put your slippers on."

He picked her up and looked down a long time before turning and walking out.

His concern for her despite what she had done made her want to cry all over again. He had trusted her and she had let him down. He had done so much for her and she had failed him. He was paying for her pride.

He was carrying her to her room when she remembered that Makeda was there. She didn't want to leave him. She wanted to lie close and touch him—to comfort him and to be comforted.

"Mark." She spoke softly, not wanting to wake her daughter as they reached her room. "Makeda's in there. Let's go to your room."

Awareness flickered in his eyes, then desire, hot and raw. Mark carried her to his room, where he released her by letting her slide slowly down his body. The action caught her nightgown, dragging it up as high as her hips. She stood gazing at him and ran her hands up his muscular arms and over his shoulders and wound them around his neck. He watched her through glittering eyes. She went up on her toes and placed her mouth against his. He gasped and drew her closer. His mouth molded to hers and his tongue came into her. He crushed her to his long, hard body and groaned into her mouth. She felt his powerful manhood grow hard and expand to throb against her stomach.

She untied the belt of his robe and he shrugged out of it. His face was tight with passion. She took his hand and stepped back toward his bed. Mark followed easily.

When the bed touched the back of her knees, she sat. Mark pressed her to lie on her back. She gazed up as he came to join her. He embraced her. His hair-roughened body grazed over her flesh and her anticipation rose. She kissed him on the side of the neck.

Suddenly, he was all over her, rolling her nightgown and robe off while he rained kisses all over her body. When she was nude, he burned a trail of hot kisses down her throat and over her shoulder to her breast. There he generously lathed her nipples with his tongue, first one, then the other, generously before slipping one taut bud into his mouth. Pleasure streaked like lightning from her female core.

When he drew upon her breast, a persistent pulse created a desperate need deep within her. Liquid heat spread through her, forcing an eager moan from her lips. Her pleasure and hunger built. When she placed a trembling hand upon his rigid organ, he growled and rolled partially over her. His knee pushed between her legs and she opened to him.

He pressed one hand on the aching delta between her legs before slipping a finger inside. He stroked the sensitive flesh there while he caressed her breasts. It drove her insane. She thrashed about, arching up to him, wanting that final complete melding of their bodies. He lifted and pulled her to sheath himself within her. He stopped there and she clutched him tightly. Even in her desire-clouded mind she realized that she was going to lose him, and pain laced through her pleasure.

He thrust deep within her, creating an unbelievable red-hot joy, and covered her mouth with ardent kisses. Each breath came quicker than the last. The pleasure grew more and more unbearable, until finally she exploded. His powerful release followed immediately afterward.

Mark buried his head in the curve of her shoulder and his breathing became deep and regular. She held him as he slept, but all too soon he withdrew and rolled over. She lay there feeling bereft, listening to his slow breathing, which lulled her into sleep.

When she woke, she had no idea how long she'd slept. Mark breathed evenly at her side. Although it was still early, she knew she couldn't stay there, for it would soon be daybreak and she didn't want Makeda to wake alone. The child had had enough shocks in the last twenty-four hours.

Terry started to creep out of bed, but he caught her hand as she was about to sneak away.

"What was this all about?"

"What do you mean?"

"Were you throwing a bone to the dog? What about your precious ex-husband?"

She cringed and tugged at the sheet to cover herself. She tried to pull away, but he had a bruising grip on her wrist. His attack came unexpectedly. There was something about being nude and trying quietly to leave his bed that made her overly vulnerable. Besides, she was feeling unbalanced as she always did whenever Mark touched her. He made her go up in flames, and she never knew what it meant. How could she go on without him was always the first question she wanted to ask herself.

To have him confront her was more than she could deal with. She wanted to crawl away.

"Let me go," she said finally, after a few seconds of futilely trying to free herself. She sounded weak and frightened.

He pushed her hand away and rolled out of bed on the other side. He stalked around to stand over her like an avenging god. Not for him to cringe or grab for covering, as she had done. He was proud of his nakedness. He took her roughly by the shoulders and jerked her to her feet.

"Mark, we could get married," Terry blurted out, speaking the thought that had been in her head all night.

His face turned cold. "Why now? Because you feel sorry for me? Forget it. I was never one to accept a woman's pity!" He put her away from him. She left quickly after that—before she started crying.

The next morning, he was on his way out when he walked into the kitchen. She sent Makeda for her bookbag. Mark watched the child go, then he stared down at the floor for a while.

"About last night . . . " he started.

She was too humiliated to listen to whatever he had to say

and couldn't have borne an apology. "Forget it," she said hastily, to forestall him.

Somehow, life went on. School came for Makeda, but Terry didn't transfer her to the new school, as she had originally planned back in May. Without Yvette, Makeda was no longer the bright-eyed little girl who giggled at everything and thought up devilish antics to put everyone through. The fun had dampened for Makeda. Even the child's health seemed less stable. One day Terry got stuck in traffic and arrived to pick up Makeda only to find the girl waiting outside in the rain. She was soaked through. Despite Terry rushing the child home and putting her to bed, the next day she had a cold. It seemed to linger longer than usual.

James McNeil called one afternoon, sounding kinder and more sensitive than Terry ever expected.

"Don't blame yourself," James said. "It's Marlene. She's getting desperate. Weston Barkley is getting cold feet about marrying her. Marlene's never been able to live without a man. If she can't have Barkley, she wants Mark back, and she knows that Mark is fond of Yvette."

James's convoluted explanation only gave Terry a headache. "None of it makes sense," Terry said.

"That's Marlene. She's a real manipulative bitch, and she knows how to get to Mark. He'll negotiate, and she knows it."

That hurt. Terry put her hand over her eyes. She felt no better, despite James's attempts to reassure her. She still felt responsible for Marlene's taking Yvette, no matter what else was going on.

"Thanks, James. I appreciate your efforts to make me feel better."

Fall came and the weather cooled considerably. Terry packed away most of their summer clothes. She couldn't shake the belief that soon she would be moving.

Mark had started working out of the Underwood site and no

longer called every day for her input as he had previously done. Although Terry went out to work every day without Mark, she found the office depressing. As for their last night of lovemaking, it was as if it had never happened.

The first time Makeda went to the office without Yvette, Mrs. Dougan questioned the girl. Terry had known it would come out, but there was nothing she could do about it. Mrs. Dougan soon discovered that Yvette had returned to Marlene. The older woman looked stricken.

"Oh, I'm so sorry," Mrs. Dougan said.

Later, Terry knew the sweet, gray-haired woman had also spoken to Mark when he came to her office tight-mouthed one afternoon.

The news traveled quickly through the office. They watched her, but little was said. It must have been obvious to everyone that she and Mark barely spoke to each other.

On the nights that Mark came in early, he ate silently, never complaining. She knew that Mark's lawyer was busy trying to build a case to fight Marlene. Terry knew that Mark had never wanted to drag Yvette through a court custody case, and now, because of her, he was doing just that.

Of course, she made a lot of steak and potatoes, as she didn't want to cause any more arguments between them. He was so distracted and withdrawn that she seriously doubted he paid any attention to the food.

One cool evening, Terry came home from the office with Makeda, who had somehow picked up another cough, in tow. She didn't expect Mark to be home. She walked into the foyer, where light spilled down from the brass-and-crystal chandelier. At one time, it had been one of her favorite areas and had seemed warm and welcoming. Now she felt accused as she looked up at the prisms of illumination.

Then Terry realized that Makeda was still poking along outside and hadn't come up the three short front steps. She glanced back to see Makeda listlessly dragging her backpack.

Terry frowned and thought that her daughter looked slightly tired and had something odd about her coloring.

"Makeda, come here a minute, honey."

Makeda's eyes rose to Terry and she let the strap of the backpack slip from her fingers. The girl came toward Terry, but just as she would have taken the child into a brighter light, the phone rang.

Terry was shocked to hear Marlene say, "We need to talk again. Let's meet for lunch tomorrow. You can help both Mark and Yvette."

Terry almost hadn't recognized the voice because Marlene had sounded almost charming. She had never heard Marlene sounding anything but snide and condescending.

What's she up to now? Terry thought. *Hasn't she done enough damage to my life?*

Terry glanced at Makeda, who stood waiting. She didn't want her daughter to know that she was speaking to Marlene. Makeda had been taking Yvette's loss quite hard.

"Hold on a minute," Terry said to Marlene. Then she covered the phone and said to Makeda, "It's okay, honey, you go on to your room."

"What do you want to talk about?" Terry asked, once Makeda was out of hearing.

In truth, she never wanted to see or hear from Marlene again, so strong had her dislike of the woman grown. But she wondered what Marlene had to say.

"Yes, it's long past time for us to put our cards on the table."

In the end, Terry agreed. She couldn't see any way that her talking to Marlene would help the situation for Mark, but she was willing to do anything. She rarely ever saw Mark now, and when they did meet, he looked through her as if she didn't exist. It was more painful now, as it came after they had shared so much. She remembered the night the Underwood takeover had come through and how happy they had been.

She made dinner for Makeda, and as the two of them sat down to eat, the house seemed huge. The light didn't seem able to fill the corners. She had chosen to eat in the breakfast nook because it was only the two of them and she hoped the smaller space would appear more cheery. But it still looked bleak.

Her glance went to the window, and even through the bright yellow-and-white curtains the night loomed dark and menacing. It made her uncomfortable and she rose to draw the blinds.

Coming back to the table, she looked at Makeda and in the fluorescent lighting, the child's coloring seemed gray and drab.

Fearfully, Terry, with fingers under her daughter's chin, turned the girl's face to the light. Makeda still looked as if there was a slight gray undertone to her coloring.

"Are you feeling all right?" Terry asked.

"Yes," the child responded, without enthusiasm.

Terry's heart seemed to jump into her throat. She didn't like the way the child looked and made an immediate decision to take Makeda to the doctor as soon as possible.

They went to bed that night before Mark came. Terry was so tired that she went to sleep despite being worried. It seemed too much was coming to a head.

That next morning, Mark was gone before Terry got up. She called Dr. Silvester, Makeda's cardiologist, and he told her to come over—that he would try to fit them in. She then notified the office that she wouldn't be in that day.

Terry sat a long time, considering dialing the number to Mark's cellular phone, but didn't. Mrs. Dougan would give him the message. The truth was that she dreaded talking with Mark, who had become increasingly curt and distant. She missed their old closeness.

She sighed and rubbed her eyes. Finally, she reached for the phone and dialed Marlene's number.

"I have to cancel. Something's come up."

"Are you sure you're not afraid to meet with me?"

"I have to take my daughter to the doctor."

"Where is your doctor?" When Terry told her, Marlene said, "That's quite near. I can come and meet you in the lunchroom, say, at about noon. This will only take a minute. If you really want to help Mark and Yvette, you'll come."

Terry agreed, though she'd really wanted to postpone any meeting with Marlene. Her attention was focused on Makeda, and she didn't have the energy to worry about Marlene.

Usually, an appointment with Makeda's cardiologist would have meant an all-day wait. As it turned out, the doctor did manage to see them due to a last minute cancelation. He listened long and hard to Makeda's chest and appeared somewhat concerned. Terry's heart tightened, as if in a vise. Her palms started sweating. She worked to appear calm because she didn't want to frighten her daughter.

While Makeda was dressing, the doctor motioned for Terry to follow him out of the small cubicle where he had done the examination.

"I don't like the way her chest sounds," Dr. Silvester said. "I want her to have an X-ray."

Suddenly, Terry felt chilled. "What is it?" she demanded.

"Now, don't get yourself all upset. It's probably nothing. Has she been a little short of breath lately? Tiring easily?"

"Yes, but only for the last few days."

"Good. It's always best to catch things early."

He started writing on his prescription pad.

"What is it?" Terry demanded. She meant for him to be totally honest. She wanted to know what was wrong with her child.

"Could be a touch of pneumonia," he answered, after a pause,

"which is never good. With her cardiac condition, I don't want
to take any chances."

Makeda came out at that time, and he didn't say anything
further. Terry was a mass of nerves. Makeda smiled worriedly
at her mother.

It took the better part of the morning to have the X-rays
and other tests done. Makeda was having an MRI when Terry
glanced at her watch, realizing it was time to meet Marlene.
"Do I have time to run downstairs for a while?" Terry asked
the technician.

"Sure, your daughter won't be out for at least thirty minutes."

Terry rushed down to the lunchroom to meet with Marlene.
The woman was as gorgeous as ever, wearing a huge picture
hat, which despite being totally out of place, looked great on
her. They sat in a corner table with coffee.

"So," Marlene said with a snide twist to her mouth, "you
made it after all."

"Make it quick. I have to get back to my daughter."

"I'll get right to the point. I want you to move."

"Why are you doing this?"

"I'm fighting to win back my husband."

It was the best answer the woman could have given, and it
caught Terry off balance. If she'd been in Marlene's position,
she'd have been fighting with everything she had to get Mark
back.

"What happened to your engagement to Weston Barkley?"

"That's over." Marlene waved it away as if it were a pesky
gnat. "I've decided to give Mark another chance. You're the
only thing that's keeping him and Yvette from being happy
again. You can't possibly think he's still going to marry you
after all this." Terry realized that Marlene didn't know that the
marriage idea had been canceled. Marlene said the next in a
soft voice. "You can give Yvette back to Mark."

Terry knew it was only pride that kept her from falling apart
as she sat there. She felt as if she'd lost Mark twice. Marlene

was asking her to help. And to help Marlene win Mark back was a cruel blow at a time when too many blows seemed to be falling.

Marlene continued to push her advantage. "What do you think Yvette will think when she realizes how you've destroyed her chances of having her family together again? That you've selfishly taken her father away from her?"

"That isn't true!"

"That's what she'll believe."

Terry knew that Marlene was playing upon her feelings of guilt, but the other woman held one card that couldn't be beaten. She had the key to Mark's happiness. Marlene could give him back what Terry had caused to be taken away.

Marlene continued, "It's important for a child to grow up with both parents."

Terry knew only too well the wisdom of this. She had grown up without a father and with a mother who barely functioned. "Why are you just realizing that now? You were the one who left Mark, from what I hear."

"I didn't want to, but he was such a workaholic back then. Money and success meant *everything* to him. And then, just as I get him to slow down, *you* come along. Mark's a family man. Do you think you can make him happy if he loses Yvette?"

Terry turned to stare unseeing through the window. She blinked away the pending tears, not wanting Marlene to see how demoralized she was at that moment. "I'll look for an apartment," Terry said, and stood up to leave.

"Good. I knew you'd see the truth of what I'm saying." Terry stood there, watching as Marlene opened her bag, took out her makeup, and calmly powdered her face. She glanced casually at Terry around the mirror, saying, "And we can't tell Mark that we've had this little talk, can we?"

Terry walked away, feeling as if she'd been cut open and all her insides were exposed. She rang the bell and waited for the elevator to take her back upstairs.

She saw Dr. Silvester as she rushed off the elevator. He carried several large X-rays under one arm and looked tired when his glance met hers.

"It's pneumonia," he said simply. "I'll have to admit her."

Chapter Eighteen

Sometime later, Makeda had been admitted into the pediatric ward. Terry helped her daughter change into her pajamas. Makeda said, "I'm sorry, Mommy. I knew I was getting sick last week."

"Last week? Why didn't you tell me?"

"I didn't want you to worry."

"Oh, honey." She hugged the slim child close. "You must always tell me when something's wrong."

"I didn't want you to worry. I know you have a lot of things on your mind and I know Daddy worries you, too." Her little arms were around Terry and she pressed her face into her mother's stomach.

"Your father?" Terry said, going down on her heels to look at the child.

"We saw him the day you and Mark went on your date. Mark saw him, too. And everyone seemed so sad after your date, and then when, Yvette had to go back to her mother's house, I didn't want to cause you any more trouble."

"Not you, honey. You're never any trouble. You're my little sunshine."

It seemed as if Makeda's condition began to deteriorate as soon as she was admitted. By that evening, her temperature had gone up.

The nurse was sponging the child while Terry held her hand, trying to comfort her. The procedure seemed uncomfortable, and when Makeda started shivering, it had to be stopped. Mark came in and found her sitting in a chair, holding a sleeping Makeda. She had never been more glad to see him. He looked strong and capable. Terry had the urge to put her head on his shoulder and weep.

"Have you had anything to eat?" he asked, and when she said no, he went and returned with a bowl of vegetable soup and a cheese sandwich. While she ate, he held Makeda.

When she was finished, he said, "I've arranged for a private room so you can stay overnight."

She put her hand to her head. More than anything she wanted to stay with her daughter, but she was afraid about the expense of a private room. True, she'd been able to save a little, but she feared it wouldn't be enough. "How much will it cost?"

"Don't worry about that," he said coolly.

"Mark, I can't afford to go into any more debt."

"You want to stay with her?"

"Yes," she whispered.

"Then leave it alone."

A short while later, an orderly and several nurses came in to move Makeda's bed and other belongings into the private room. Terry pulled the chair up close to her daughter and sat with her head resting on the bed. Mark sat on the other side. Makeda slept through the whole thing.

Mark stayed there until late that night. When he left, he said, "Don't even think of coming into the office. I'll be back tomorrow and talk with the doctor." She nodded and put her head back on Makeda's bed.

A nurse entered, lugging a folding cot, which she made up

with fresh linen. "Your husband said you were going to stay overnight."

For the next few days, Terry left Makeda's bedside only when she absolutely had to. Makeda looked forward to Mark's visits. He often seemed able to cheer the child up when all else failed.

One dark, rainy fall afternoon Terry woke when the doctor tapped her on the shoulder. She had been talking with Makeda, and when her daughter fell asleep, Terry had dozed off also.

"Come outside," Dr. Silvester whispered, gesturing for her to follow him.

Terry's heart jumped. It felt as if it had lodged in her throat as she clumsily got up to follow the doctor into the outside corridor.

"She's not bouncing back as I thought she would."

Terry wrung her hands. "Do you think it's something really bad?" she asked.

He took a deep breath and said, "I think it's her emotional state. She seems more down than I ever remember. That could be the reason she hasn't rallied as I had hoped. Her emotional state isn't as good as it was. I suspect that's why she came down with this infection. She misses her sister, Yvette."

"Yvette isn't her sister," Terry said.

"But they had built a good rapport, and now they're not together anymore."

Terry nodded, feeling tears sting the back of her eyes.

"Isn't there any way that Yvette can come? Even for a short visit? I think it would do Makeda a world of good just to see the other little girl. Usually, children under fourteen aren't allowed unless they're family, but I'll give permission in this case. I think it's just that important."

Terry's eyes felt hot and dry. She wondered if she could convince Marlene to let Yvette visit. "I'll try," she said. Only God knew how she could manage to convince Marlene to let Yvette visit.

"Good," the doctor said, and left after giving her a paternal pat on the arm.

That night, she was sleeping when Mark arrived.

Mark said, "You need to go home and get a decent night's sleep."

"I don't want to leave her alone."

"I'll stay. Terry, she can see you're worried and she follows behind you. I'll call you if anything happens. You go and sleep in a bed. You won't be any good to her if you get sick, too."

Terry hesitated before speaking. "Mark, the doctor thinks a visit from Yvette would be helpful for Makeda's recovery."

He glanced at her with a frown. "Okay, I'll talk to Marlene."

"Thanks," she answered.

Terry decided to take his advice and left. The house looked strange and foreign, as she hadn't been there. It was lonely with both girls gone, and too quiet. She felt as if every sound echoed off the walls.

In the kitchen, she found that Mark had piled unwashed dishes in the sink for Mrs. Young to put in the dishwasher. It was a sad reminder that he'd been eating lonely meals. She stacked them in the washer. It was hard to break old habits. She looked around, remembering all the breakfasts they had eaten here with Mark reading his paper and the girls giggling at everything. Now that was all over.

As soon as she could, she would find an apartment and move. Except for grabbing her clothes in the few times that she had left the hospital, she hadn't even been in the house that much since Makeda had been hospitalized. She only hoped Marlene realized that her still being there wasn't deliberate.

Nothing had been mentioned to Mark about that last visit of his ex-wife. She hadn't bothered to tell him she would soon be moving. Although he had insisted she remain as housekeeper, she knew it was impossible. She simply couldn't do it. It wasn't only Marlene's demanding that she move, it was her own feelings that she had to think of. She couldn't live with this man she loved so much and be able to endure his contempt. She was too much of a coward to watch him grow to hate her as he would with each passing day of Yvette's loss.

Besides, with only Mark in the house, Mrs. Young was more than adequate. The last thing he needed was a full-time house-keeper. There wasn't much Terry could do right now. But the minute Makeda was out of danger, she would be gone. Now she needed a stable base more than anything. It only pained her more to see how great he had been during these awful days after she had damaged his life so much. It grieved her more than anything that she would never have him as a lover and that she was also losing a friend.

But she put those thoughts away. Experience had taught her the sooner she accepted the reality of her situation, the better it would be. Living with Mark Holden had been the most wonderful experience of her life, but it was all over now. Best to get on with the rest of her life. She was resigned. That night, she felt all cried out. Hopeless exhaustion made her fall asleep almost instantly.

The next morning, Terry was rushing to get back to Makeda when she ran into Ronald. He was waiting in the hospital lobby.

"What are you doing here?"

"Waiting for you. You slipped out of here last night before I could catch you."

Suddenly, without any warning, Ronald grabbed her purse, giving her a shove that sent her banging against the wall. It left her frozen for a few seconds.

In terror, she looked around, wanting Mark to appear at that moment. There were no security guards visible, and the few people who passed walked hurriedly by with averted faces when they heard her say, "Ronald, give me my pocketbook." No one wanted to get involved in something that appeared to be a family argument.

Ronald rummaged through the purse, searching for her wallet. He was so determined that he couldn't have cared less when other things fell out onto the floor as he rummaged.

Terry was on the verge of tears but refused because she knew they would only enrage him more. She kept glancing around for Mark.

Once Ronald had the wallet, he tore into it and the plastic packet of photos came loose, falling to the floor. The packet landed with a photo of Mark with Makeda and Yvette. It was one she had taken at Sebago. The three of them were smiling into the camera. Terry found herself staring stupidly at the photograph. For a few seconds, it was almost as if the three in the picture were witnessing the whole sorry scene with Ronald.

It was when Ronald stepped on the photo in his haste that everything changed for her. It seemed like the last straw.

Suddenly a feeling of unbearable shame flooded through her. Was this what she wanted to show Makeda, who had been so brave through all her challenges? Would she want Yvette, who had stolen her heart, to see this? Did she want Mark to see her as a sniveling coward as well as the woman who ruined his life?

Suddenly, Terry's rage seemed to boil over and she swung out and punched Ronald. He stood there holding his jaw and looking as if the world had turned upside down. That only made her angrier.

Of course, he was shocked. She had never stood up for herself when they were married, so he'd always considered her a total pushover. Unfortunately, hitting Ronald had hurt her hand.

Suddenly, she remembered the moves that she had been practicing from the self-defense group. It was like a light going on in her head. Here she had been, practicing all this time, and it hadn't really gotten through to her that those moves were something she was supposed to use. Everything the teacher had said suddenly made sense. She aimed a foot at his groin, and when his hands flew to protect himself, she brought back her hand, and aiming it like a knife, chopped him across the Adam's apple. He looked even more shocked, if that was possible. He dropped the purse and grabbed his throat. His eyes became round with shock as he stood there incapacitated.

Her first response was to think that he was going to die. She looked at her hand in total shock. Suddenly, she felt ten feet tall. She was too high to feel the pain. When she realized that he was recovering, fear galvanized her. She was terrified that if he recovered, he would retaliate.

The elevator door opened and Mark stepped out. Despite her concentration on Ronald, she saw Mark's sudden realization of what was happening. Before she could blink, he was on them. He jumped in front of her, confronting Ronald. Mark gave Ronald an almost gentle shove, and finally her ex-husband fell. It infuriated her that Mark had accomplished so easily what she'd been trying to do for the last few moments. Then Mark released her and went for Ronald.

"No more! No more!" Ronald was on the floor, holding his throat.

Mark stepped back and looked at Terry. "Are you all right?" he asked.

"Yes." She answered because as soon as she thought about it, she realized that she had fought Ronald back and done a good job of it, too. The adrenaline was pumping, and she had half a mind to give Ronald a few more swipes with her purse. The whole thing hadn't taken more than a few moments.

Mark put his hand on her almost as if he had read her mind and was trying to restrain her. "Why don't you go up to Makeda?" he said. "I'll take care of this."

Without another word, she turned and rushed to see her daughter.

Makeda was awake and looked a little better. "Mommy," she said, holding out her arms. "Mark went to put quarters into the parking meter."

"I saw him," Terry said, wondering what Mark had done with Ronald.

She needn't have worried, for she looked up to find Ronald at the door, looking rather sheepish, with Mark right behind him. It was a shock. Ronald looked neater, as if he'd made some effort to straighten himself up in the few minutes since she'd seen him down in the lobby. She looked at Mark and her heart nearly burst. She knew he had done this.

"Daddy?" Makeda said, when she saw her father. Her head was tilted to the side.

"Yeah," Ronald said, walking to the bed. He leaned over and kissed his daughter.

Makeda was obviously surprised, but she smiled. She looked behind him to Mark, and Terry wondered if the child guessed that it was Mark who'd brought her father in to see her.

Mark motioned Terry to leave Ronald with Makeda and they stood outside the door.

"What was that scene down in the lobby all about?"

"I don't want to talk about it."

"Don't you think your not talking about things has gone on long enough? Is fighting the way you two usually solve your problems?"

"No, it isn't. Except . . . he did hit me once."

"Once? When was that?"

"It happened the last night of our marriage."

"I'll kill the bastard," Mark said, and balled his fists as if ready to fight.

"No," she put a hand on his arm. "It's all over now."

"Why didn't you tell me before? You let me believe you were still in love with him."

"I was afraid of him and my fear humiliated me. I never wanted anyone to know I'd been abused."

"It wasn't your fault that he took his frustrations out on you."

"Somehow, I thought it was. But I don't think he'll ever do it again," she said.

Mark smiled and seemed to relax. "After what you did to him in the lobby, I seriously doubt it."

She had to smile. She felt pretty satisfied, now that she'd confronted her ex-husband.

Ronald didn't stay long, but still Makeda had been glad to see him. Later, when both men were gone, Makeda smiled at Terry. "I know Mark made Daddy come, but I'm still glad to see him."

"Honey, your father has so many problems that he doesn't know how to be a real daddy to you." She took a deep breath, wondering where to begin. "You see, people love in different ways. I believe your father loves you but is afraid that he'll let you down ... " It was curious, but in a way, Terry realized that she did believe what she was saying.

"I know, Mommy. Yvette and I were thinking that if her mother was going to marry Mr. Barkley, maybe you could marry Mark and then he'd be my daddy."

Suddenly, Terry, who had been feeling triumphant since the scuffle down in the lobby, wanted to cry again. She feared Makeda was asking for the moon.

Makeda rallied, and within ten days she was back home again. Home was still Mark's house, as Terry hadn't had time to find an apartment. Terry had called Marlene several days ago in an attempt to explain why she hadn't moved. Marlene, however, didn't display much interest in Terry's promises. The other woman listened, but offered nothing. It was almost as if she'd never demanded that Terry leave.

Makeda had recovered so well that Dr. Silvester predicted the child would grow out of the heart murmur. It was the best news he could have given her, Terry thought.

Terry had been totally involved with caring for Makeda since the child's discharge. Earlier that day, she had taken her daughter outside to sit in a chair in the garden. The warm indian summer days made it seem like summer again. It was a Saturday, and Mark joined the girl for a chat. Terry had heard them outside, laughing about something. It did her heart good to hear her daughter sounding like her old self. The only thing missing was Yvette.

The next time Terry looked outside, Mark was swimming, steadily traveling smoothly from one end of the pool to the other, back and forth. His relentless, never-pausing stroking was a sure sign that he was working off energy, which she now understood was mostly why he exercised so much.

He'd been swimming nonstop for about thirty minutes when Terry heard someone say, "Daddy!"

It was Yvette, and Terry rushed to the window to see the small child run around the back of the house and fling herself into Mark's arms. Terry almost dropped the dish she had been holding. Just as she was about to run outside, Terry saw Marlene and a handsome older man come into view and she stopped, remaining in the kitchen.

The older man, Terry thought, had to be Weston Barkley, Marlene's on-again-off-again fiancé, and the two of them were dressed as if going to a garden party. Yvette wore a frilly dress with patent leather pumps and white lace socks. The little girl looked charming, but it seemed as if she was dressed for a Sunday outing.

Mark came out of the pool, and both men shook hands. Mark donned his white terry robe and the three adults stood talking as Yvette and Makeda hugged each other and laughed.

Terry anxiously gazed at the scene, wanting more than anything to run outside and hear what they were saying. It was like watching a pantomime. She could see Yvette chatting away to Makeda and pointing back at her mother and Barkley.

Terry also saw Mark and the other adults walking toward the back door. She hastily put the dishes down and opened the door.

Mark came in followed by Marlene and Barkley. Marlene

hung on to the older man's arm as if he were some sort of prize she had just won. Terry wondered if Marlene thought this was the way to win back Mark. She doubted it would work. The two girls were the last to come in.

Mark introduced her to Barkley simply, neglecting to say she was his housekeeper. Marlene barely nodded.

"We'll be in my office," Mark said, and led the way from the kitchen. Marlene cast a bored glance around the kitchen. Aside from that first nod, the beautiful woman gave no more interest to Terry than she had given to the kitchen. She seemed detached and disinterested. It was as if the last two meetings between them had never occurred, but were just a figment of Terry's imagination.

The three of them then went into Mark's office.

When the other three adults left Makeda, Yvette, and Terry in the kitchen, Yvette turned to Terry, saying, excitedly, "Marlene's letting me come back to live with you and Daddy."

"Isn't it great, Mommy?" Makeda said. "It'll be just like I said."

Terry hugged both girls. She didn't mention that this wasn't going to work out as they'd thought. True, Mark would be glad to have Yvette back, but that didn't mean things were the same as before. She didn't feel he would ever forgive her for jeopardizing Yvette. Besides, the only reason he'd proposed was to get Yvette, and now he already had her. There had been so many things that had changed.

"I'm so glad," Terry said, feeling the tears well up.

"If you're glad, why are you crying?" asked a puzzled Yvette.

"I guess it's because I'm really *very* glad," Terry said, grabbing a dishtowel to wipe her eyes.

Yvette grinned. "Weston told Marlene that I should live with Daddy because he doesn't want me around all the time."

"Oh, honey, that's not true," Terry said, her heart constricting at the careless cruelty of the adults.

"That's a mean thing to say." Makeda was back in her role as protective big sister.

"I don't care," Yvette said with real sincerity. "I'd rather be with Daddy and you, Terry."

"Me, too," Makeda seconded the opinion, and the girls smiled at each other. When they turned to look at Terry, she thought they seemed rather calculating for two such small girls.

After Marlene and Barkley left, she asked Mark what had happened.

"Marlene and Barkley suggested that I be Yvette's caretaker parent while Marlene gets reasonable visitation rights. Marlene has agreed to do it through the courts."

"I thought you didn't want to do it in the courts."

"It's to ensure that Marlene won't pull this sort of thing again."

"I'm glad it's worked out, but why did she change her mind so suddenly?"

"It was just as I suspected all along. Marlene and Barkley were having some sort of scrap and she was scared that she'd come out losing everything."

"That's all it was? And you knew it?" It was bewildering. It didn't seem possible that Marlene would wreak that much havoc in people's lives just because of a few minutes of feeling insecure. Terry must have spoken her thoughts, because Mark spoke again.

"Marlene is very insecure. But I think Barkley may be good for her."

A sound at the door, and both Terry and Mark saw the girls standing there with arms folded across their chest. Terry thought that the position reminded her of something, while Mark laughed out loud upon seeing them. He glanced sideways at her.

"Daddy, we'd like to see you privately to discuss an important matter." They sounded incredibly serious.

"Well, certainly," Mark said.

Mark seemed a bit taken aback, Terry thought. She was, too, she realized. He left with the girls and she followed the three of them only to have Makeda turn to face her right outside the library.

"Not you, Mommy," her daughter said, as the three of them went into Mark's office and closed the door. Terry was a bit chagrined, standing out there, staring at the closed door.

Back in the kitchen, she wondered what the girls wanted to say to Mark. Absently pulling out one of her old cookbooks, she flicked through the pages. She took a deep breath and looked out the window. Suppose I don't have to move, she thought. Mark at least was talking to her again, and the girls behaved as if nothing had happened these last few weeks. Could it all come together just like that? So, okay, the marriage was off, now that Mark had solved the child custody issue, but maybe he could forgive her and they could be friends again.

Suddenly, Makeda and Yvette came through the door and she noticed that Mark hung back, shifting from one foot to the other. Yvette was hugging a pillow to her chest.

Makeda came right to her and taking her hand, led her to sit at the breakfast nook. "Mommy, Mark has something to say."

Terry's glance flew to Mark where he hovered in the background, deliberately not looking at her. Yvette came and placed the pillow on the floor in front of Terry's feet. They both went back to Mark and each taking a hand pulled him to stand in front of her.

Mark slapped his hands and rubbed his palms together. But then he stopped to say plaintively, "What about my easel and my graphs?"

"Come on, Daddy," Yvette said.

Yvette stood arms akimbo, saying, "You said you'd do it right this time!"

They pulled Mark down until he was kneeling with one knee on the pillow in front of Terry.

"Not even a little mood music?" Mark's glance snapped to Makeda.

"No music," Makeda insisted.

"This isn't a sales presentation, Daddy," Yvette said, sounding peevish.

He seemed barely able to contain his mirth until he looked in Terry's face. Once he gazed into her eyes, he became very serious. But though he tried to clear his throat, his voice still came out low and rumbling.

"Redding," Mark said, "I think you should know that I love the ground you walk on and . . . would you do me the honor of becoming my wife?"

Epilogue

Several hours later, Mark and Terry were in the kitchen, chopping vegetables for Moroccan vegetable soup. The girls were out with children from the neighborhood.

Suddenly Terry turned to Mark and said, "You should have been glad to get down on your knees and propose. You should have groveled," Terry said.

"I did grovel," Mark answered.

"Not enough! You owed it to me. You know how long I'd been waiting for you to wake up and really propose?"

"Ever since the morning of the oranges?"

"Tsk." She sucked her teeth at him. "I don't want to talk about that."

He laughed. "You didn't wait as long as I did. I'll bet I've been in love with you longer than you've been with me."

"Hah. When did you realize you loved me?"

"My heart knew from day one."

"No way am I going to believe that." She threw up her arms and stalked off. "Don't bother with that salesman sweet-talk. I'm not falling for any of it, so just forget it."

"My heart was lost when I stepped out of my office and saw your skirt rise over those great legs that you had stuck in those old-fashioned shoes. Before I even dreamed that you had red toenails."

"That's not called love." After a pause, "Why didn't you do something?"

"I did. I bullied you into letting me feed you and take you home. I even fed your child. What woman can resist a man who feeds her and her child? That's when I knew you were mine forever."

"You said I was overqualified."

"I meant that you were too good for me."

"Holden, you are such a con man. You'll tell me anything. You couldn't stand me. I wasn't even your type. Everyone said it."

"You were my *only* type. Maybe my brain didn't know, but my heart did. What man will follow his brain, once his heart has decided? However, when you tried to castrate me . . . "

"I never tried to do that. I only made a few gestures that you mistook for . . . "

"Redding, you're turning into quite a con woman yourself. I do have a question, though—why did you bait Marlene that day?"

"I was so jealous that I wanted to scratch her eyes out."

"You? Jealous?"

"She seemed to have everything, including your love."

"Marlene could never had held a candle to you. All she ever had was an ability to play on people. There was never much love between us. I let her father convince me that she would be able to create the type of home that I wanted, and she thought she would be the wife of an incredibly wealthy man who would do nothing but keep her company every day. I couldn't do that; she'd have bored me to tears."

"Would you give up your business for me?"

"Would you want me to?" he asked.

Terry paused before answering. "Yes," she said. "Maybe," she corrected. "Maybe I'd just want you to be home more."

"Okay," he responded simply.

"Okay? Just like that? You'd give up the business and making your deals?"

"Yes, if it made you happy."

She thought about it for a while. "No, it wouldn't make me happy to take you away from something you loved. I didn't even mean that. I don't know why I said it."

"I do." Mark cut her off. "You want me to prove my love, and I'm willing. I'd do anything to show how deeply and completely I love you. Of course, you know what that would mean, I hope."

"What?"

"If I give up the business, all my plans to make it Holden and Holden Home Health Care Providers would go down the tubes. Can't you see that name written in lights?"

"Don't you think Yvette's a little young for that?"

"I wasn't thinking of Yvette. I was thinking of you."

"Me?"

"Why not? Once we're married, you'll be Holden, too. That is, unless you go into your great queen-and-liberated-woman mode and make me call you 'Ms. Redding' for the rest of our lives. Of course, you'll have to buy your partnership, and I don't come cheap."

"You think I can afford it?"

"We'll work it out. Maybe with a little trade." He leered at her as his eyebrows went up and down.

She leaned close and said in as sexy a voice as she could manage, "That's a lot of trade. What do you suggest I use to deal with?"

"I'm sure we can work something out. And I do know something that you're very good at."

"Holden, it's like I've said before. You're a beast. How could you suggest such a thing? Is it legal?"

"It's better than having you accuse me of stealing."

"When did I say that?"

He stepped away and put one hand on his hip while he pointed with a limp wrist at her. "You stole my virtue," he lisped in a mimicry of her voice.

She roared. He waited until she stopped laughing to say, "Partners in everything, right? While, I'll probably find that you're overqualified in this, too. Still, we do make a great team. Wouldn't you agree?"

She didn't answer right away, and he elbowed her in the ribs. "Mark, we may have a really serious problem."

"I know, but we'll talk about it, and I figured that I could always handcuff you to the bed," he said, but after the elbow in the ribs, he was trying to peek down the neck of her t-shirt.

"Handcuff me to the bed? What are you talking about?" she shrieked.

"Your problem with post-coital depression."

She sucked her teeth at him, but she had to laugh, too. "I have no such problem, but what about this crazy addiction to exercising and your overdose of energy?"

He smiled smugly, saying, "Don't worry, we'll have you shaped up in no time."

This annoyed her, as it implied that there was something wrong with *her,* when she wanted him to see that the problem was with him. However, by now, he'd decided to look under her t-shirt, and she forgot what she was going to say.

Several hours later, Terry glanced through the kitchen window at Mark, who was sitting in a lounge by the pool. He had been sitting there thirty minutes without a push-up—without even a twitch.

Terry suspected that she now knew the secret to keeping Mark a happy, delightfully calm man. She finally remembered the one time she'd seen him calm and relaxed. It was immediately after they'd first made love. Of course, sex always made her feel energetic.

Maybe she'd run a couple of miles herself before she checked out that new Ethiopian recipe for spiced green beans and carrots.

ABOUT THE AUTHOR

Layle Giusto danced professionally in Modern and African folk dance before she left the theater to marry and raise a family. She then got a degree in nursing and now works in a drug/alcohol rehabilitation center. She enjoys writing, sailing, swimming, and travel.

ROMANCES THAT SIZZLE
FROM ARABESQUE

AFTER DARK, by Bette Ford   (0-7860-0442-8, $4.99/$6.50)
Taylor Hendricks' brother is the top NBA draft choice. She wants to protect him from the lure of fame and wealth, but meets basketball superstar Donald Williams in an exclusive Detroit restaurant. Donald is determined to prove that she is wrong about him. In this game all is at stake . . . including Taylor's heart.

BEGUILED, by Eboni Snoe   (0-7860-0046-5, $4.99/$6.50)
When Raquel Mason agrees to impersonate a missing heiress for just one night and plans go awry, a daring abduction makes her the captive of seductive Nate Bowman. Together on a journey across exotic Caribbean seas to the perilous wilds of Central America, desire looms in their hearts. But when the masquerade is over, will their love end?

CONSPIRACY, by Margie Walker   (0-7860-0385-5, $4.99/$6.50)
Pauline Sinclair and Marcellus Cavanaugh had the love of a lifetime. Until Pauline had to leave everything behind. Now she's back and their love is as strong as ever. But when the President of Marcellus's company turns up dead and Pauline is the prime suspect, they must risk all to their love.

FIRE AND ICE, by Carla Fredd   (0-7860-0190-9, $4.99/$6.50)
Years of being in the spotlight and a recent scandal regarding her ex-fianceé and a supermodel, the daughter of a Georgia politician, Holly Aimes has turned cold. But when work takes her to the home of late-night talk show host Michael Williams, his relentless determination melts her cool.

HIDDEN AGENDA, by Rochelle Alers   (0-7860-0384-7, $4.99/$6.50)
To regain her son from a vengeful father, Eve Blackwell places her trust in dangerous and irresistible Matt Sterling to rescue her abducted son. He accepts this last job before he turns a new leaf and becomes an honest rancher. As they journey from Virginia to Mexico they must enter a charade of marriage. But temptation is too strong for this to remain a sham.

INTIMATE BETRAYAL, by Donna Hill   (0-7860-0396-0, $4.99/$6.50)
Investigative reporter, Reese Delaware, and millionaire computer wizard, Maxwell Knight are both running from their pasts. When Reese is assigned to profile Maxwell, they enter a steamy love affair. But when Reese begins to piece her memory, she stumbles upon secrets that link her and Maxwell, and threaten to destroy their newfound love.

Available wherever paperbacks are sold, or order direct from the Publisher. Send cover price plus 50¢ per copy for mailing and handling to Kensington Publishing Corp., Consumer Orders, or call (toll free) 888-345-BOOK, to place your order using Mastercard or Visa. Residents of New York and Tennessee must include sales tax. DO NOT SEND CASH.